REBORN

BOOK TWO OF THE DARK HEART CHRONICLES

REBORN

Published by Drezhn Publishing LLC
PO BOX 67458
Albuquerque, NM 87193-7458

Print Edition - July 2018
Version 1.8 – June 2023

Cover design by Drezhn Publishing LLC
Cover illustration by Jonathan Myers

HARDBACK (DUST JACKET) ISBN: 978-1-947328-08-2
HARDBACK (CASE LAMINATE) ISBN: 978-1-947328-76-1
PAPERBACK ISBN: 978-1-947328-02-0

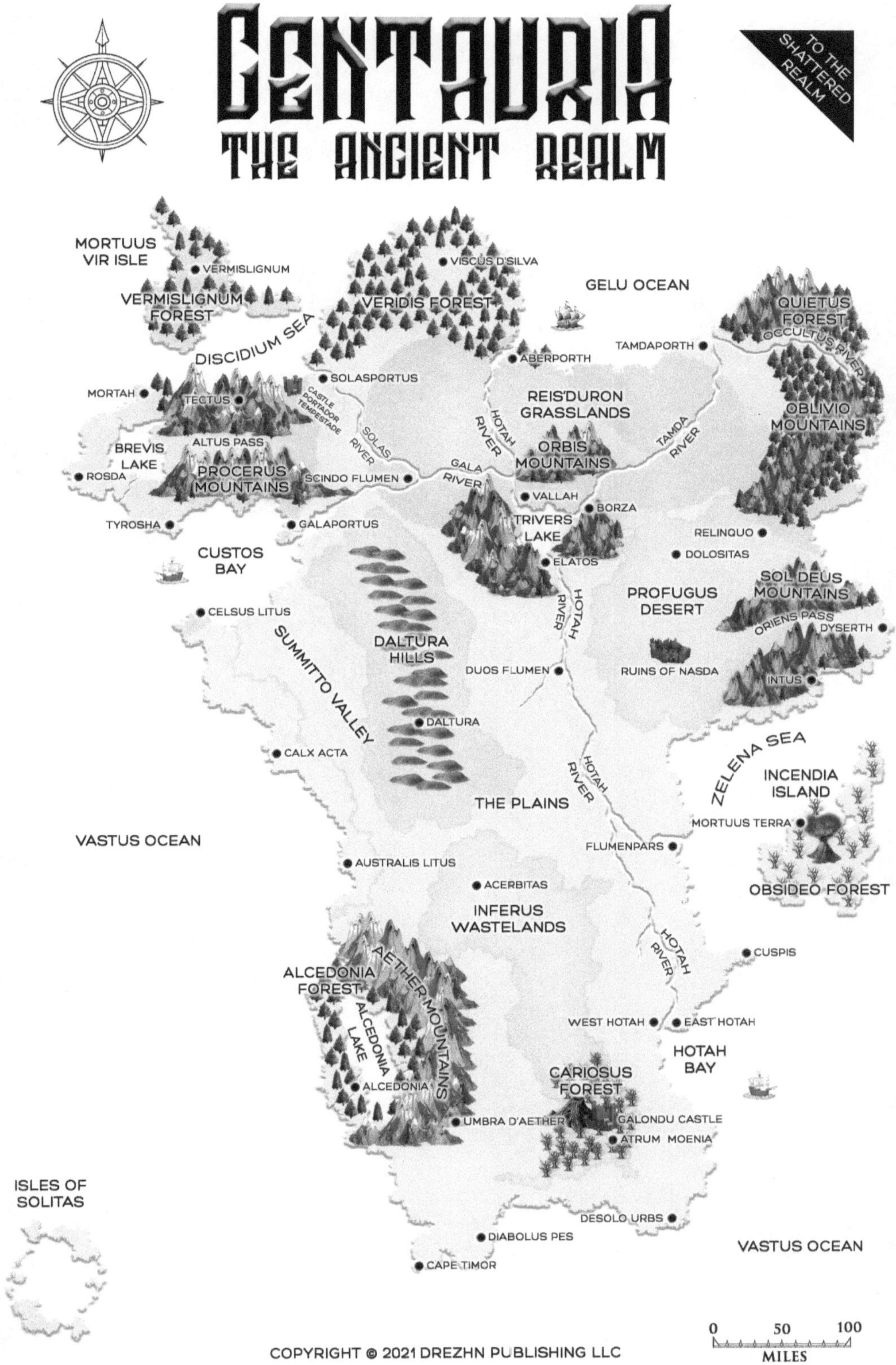

COPYRIGHT © 2021 DREZHN PUBLISHING LLC

READ *SCOURGE* FOR FREE

Do Eshtak's tattoos hold the key to the between?

danielkuhnley.com/become-a-conqueror

Sign up and read *Scourge*, A World Of Centauria Novella. Be the **FIRST** to get sneak peeks at my upcoming novels and the chance to win **FREE** stuff, like signed books.

Never use persuasion magic on a powerful wizard.

That was Emorith's hardest lesson to learn. Right from that fateful moment, Magus forced her to use her manipulative sorcery to further his evil purposes. She regretted everything he put her through with one exception: their son Illian. Him, she loved with all her heart.

Magus demanded she cast an apocalyptic curse and destroy an unsuspecting city. She steeled herself to refuse him… but then he threatened the life of her beloved child.

With Illian's life on the line, what choice did she have? She wanted to protect the city and its citizens, but her son would always come first. No, there must be another way. Will she be able to thwart Magus and save them all in time? Or is their fate already sealed?

Scourge is a prequel novella to *The Dragon's Stone*, the first book in The Dark Heart Chronicles epic dragon fantasy series. If you like thrilling adventures and terrifying magic, then you'll love Daniel Kuhnley's enthralling tale.

BOOKS BY DANIEL KUHNLEY

EPIC DRAGON FANTASY

<u>The Dark Heart Chronicles</u>
*†The Dragon's Stone
*Reborn
*Rended Souls
True Heir

Scourge (novella)

SUPERNATURAL SERIAL KILLER

<u>Alice Bergman Novels</u>
*Birth Of A Killer (novella)
*The Braille Killer
*The Night Mauler
*The Chrono Slasher

CHRISTIAN YA SCI-FI/FANTASY

(as Daniel Luke Kuhnley)

<u>VR Academy</u>
Kiara Kole And The Key Of Truth

* - Also available as an audiobook
† - Previously released as Dark Lament

Visit Daniel's website to find these books and more!
danielkuhnley.com

To Marsha and Phylls, my first and biggest fans.
Never stop reading, and I'll never stop writing.

THE DARK HEART CHRONICLES

REBORN

•2•

DANIEL KUHNLEY

CHAPTER ONE

With her right hand, Theyn clung to the side of the lava crag, several thousand feet above the blackened earth of Mortuus Terra. Her heart raced, and every muscle tensed as the wind tousled her hair and rocked her to and fro. She lived for these moments.

A nest of twigs, bramble, and feathers nestled the back wall of a small, flat, rock shelf thirty feet to her right. Three baby birds peered over the nest's edge and squawked at Theyn with a deafening frenzy. She knew little about most birds, but these were rare. Their bald faces and red plumage gave them away.

Theyn smiled. *Little red rooks.*

Despite the wind at her back, the smell of sweaty fur wrinkled her nose. A blue dingo—not named after its dingy brown fur but by its long blue tongue—peered over the crag's top edge, head low and ears pinned back, splitting its attention between the rooks and Theyn.

Theyn growled deep in her throat. "You even think of making a meal of those birds, and I'll gut you like a troller, you mangy mutt."

The dingo glared at her for several moments, snorted with a twist of its head, and shrank away from the edge.

"Theyn!" Berggren bellowed.

Theyn rolled her eyes. *Guess I didn't climb high enough to escape his loud mouth.*

Still holding on with one hand, she swung around backward and leaned against the cliff wall. She dug her boot heels into the half-inch grooves she'd carved out on her first ascent many months before and gazed down at the two men far below.

Berggren stood atop a rounded berm of lava rock, his arms crossed over his barreled chest and his forehead rutted by his brooding scowl. Beads of sweat glistened on the top of his bald head.

"Stop gallivanting, and tell me what you see," barked Berggren.

Shaul stood next to Berggren, just as tall but not as muscular. He held one hand in the air and waved in a wide arc, but he held his other hand just below his nose—one finger buried inside of it.

Theyn shook her head. *Disgusting.*

"Yes, boss," she yelled.

Theyn glanced back up at the crag's edge but didn't spot the dingo. However, she still smelled it. She wrinkled her nose. *I'll deal with you in a few.*

She reached down, freed the bronze spyglass that hung from the leather loop on her belt, and held it up to her left eye. Its powerful lens took her right into the middle of the rolling fields of bubbled and sharpened lava. Greyish-white corpses of once-mighty trees speckled the blackened landscape like leprosy and stretched miles into the distance.

She swept the eyeglass back and forth, searching for any changes. The daily routine wore on her mind and eroded any sense of time she'd once possessed; the weeks blurred into months—or perhaps years.

Incendia Island had little to offer outside of its complete seclusion from the civilized world, and she hated living there. She didn't understand why Berggren chose to move them out into the middle of nowhere, but she owed him everything and so she kept her mouth shut.

Three miles out, Theyn spotted a human man lying on the ground. Her breath caught in her throat, and she froze. *Zhedäz 2ʊn… The man with the scars.*

Several moments passed before she realized she'd let go of the spyglass. It plummeted toward the ground, and its glass lens shattered when it collided with a cluster of rocks that jutted up from a small ledge far below, but she kept her gaze trained on the man.

He's here. He's here!

"Theyn!" yelled Berggren, his voice tunneled and distant. "You can't fly!"

Fly? How absurd. But what had Berggren meant by it?

Theyn looked down, and the ledge far below raced toward her. She gasped, cried out, and twisted in the air. She reached out and dug her nails into the crag's rocky wall as she slid down its steep face, but the effort didn't slow her descent.

Each heartbeat jolted her entire body like seizures. She tensed up, closed her eyes for a moment, and braced for impact. She hit the ledge hard and gasped as shards of pain ripped through her soles, streaked up her legs, and into her chest.

Her mind sharp, Theyn used the force of the impact to springboard herself sideways, toward a small ledge. She met the wall again with a grunt but managed to grab the ledge with her fingertips before she plummeted again.

She exhaled, then laughed.

"Gonna beat you when you get down here," bellowed Berggren. "Never scare me like that again."

Theyn laughed harder.

"He's here," she said. "He's here!"

† † †

Nardus lay on his back in the middle of the lava fields of Incendia Island, just outside the ruins of Mortuus Terra, where his journey to find Ƨʈōn Dhef Dädh had begun. The red sky hung over him like a pall, suffocating him.

The air around him crackled with energy as lightning sliced through the air, tearing the red fabric sky like claws through flesh. In its wake, the ground trembled beneath him. Or was it he who trembled?

"Black lightning—" The hairs on his arms stood on end. "—what have I brought into this world?"

He swallowed hard. *Or whom?*

Flashes of a hideous horned beast—what he imagined Diꙅäfär to look like—riddled his mind. Words of warning from both Tharos and Gnaud whispered in his ears like spectres from the past. Had he brought damnation upon the world?

If I have, for what?

He clenched his fists. *Ƨʈōn Dhef Dädh.*

Pravus assured him that the small, reddish-black stone held the power to resurrect the dead. He'd placed his faith in Pravus and the stone—he'd had no choice. Nothing mattered more to him than family, and his desire to be with them again drove him through Zhäíțfäí Fäíțƨ and helped him prevail through the seven trials.

He'd accomplished the impossible, yet hope, love, guilt, and fear warred in his mind and heart. As usual, he'd only heard the words that he'd wanted to hear. Ƨțōn Dhef Dädh may indeed bring the dead back to life, but at what cost? Did he really want to bring his family back into the world only to condemn them to a waking nightmare with everyone else?

How would it help? I've let them down so many times already. And they're in a better place now. I've been such a fool, blinded and driven by the pain of their loss.

Then again, why endure all the pain and suffering if not to bring his family back? His fractured mind seemed incapable of piecing it all together and making a rational decision.

Aren't they better off with me than with Ƨäțūr? Haven't they suffered enough by His hand?

Nardus sat up, pulled himself to his feet, and brushed the dust from his tattered trousers. His boots needed more than just a shine—the worn leather had ripped clean through in spots.

Where's a good cobbler when you need one? He smiled.

He reached inside his coat's left inner pocket, but his fingers pushed against its bottom.

Empty? His pulse rose.

He turned the rest of his pockets out, but none of them contained the stone. "This isn't happening."

He threw his pack to the ground and sifted through its contents.

"No stone," he growled.

Unsatisfied, he emptied the contents of his pack on the ground and shuffled through them.

No stone.

He unlatched the straps that held Brinzhär Dädh and its scabbard to his back and let it drop to the ground. He grabbed the sword's hilt and slid it free. The golden blade rang, but its sweet song gave him no comfort. He laid the blade on the ground and turned the scabbard upside-down and shook it violently, but nothing fell out of it.

No stone.

He tossed the scabbard to the ground, stripped off his clothes, and rifled through them.

No stone.

He thrust his hands in the air and screamed at the sky, "Just strike me dead, Ɂäʈūr! Send a bolt of lightning through my heart. I'm begging You!"

Nardus dropped to his knees, weary from his sufferings and spent of energy. He'd lost everything. Nothing mattered.

He glared at the red sky. *Damn this world and everything in it.*

He traced the scars on either side of his left bicep with his fingers.

The arrow that'd started it all. To what end?

A single moment in time—a lapse in judgment—had cost him everything. The scars tortured his soul, filled his mind with sorrow and rage, and drove him toward redemption—not for himself, but for his family.

Vitara, my love. Shardan. Shanara. Savannah. Don't give up on me.

Nardus looked down at his arm. Under the dim light of the red sky his skin looked pale and grey—*dead.*

Dead within and without. So be it.

His mouth and throat were a wasteland of lava and sand, and the act of swallowing a task unto itself. He needed water *soon.*

Despite his dire predicament, he couldn't hold back his laughter.

Madness.

How had he fallen so far so fast? Not so long ago, he'd had everything he'd ever dreamed of—the perfect life. Now, despite his best efforts, he had nothing left to show for it but a severely fractured mind.

No stone.

What had he done with it? How could he have lost it? Had Tharos stolen it from him?

It didn't matter. He was a dead man either way.

I'm naked and alone in this godforsaken wilderness. Where are you, my love?

Vitara's violet eyes—full of scorn—filled his head. Guilt twisted around him and squeezed the air from his lungs like a constrictor. Tears filled his eyes and spilled down his cheeks like rivers of ice, stinging his skin as they streaked down his chin.

I'm so sorry, my love.

Nardus roared at the sky like an animal.

"End me now, Ɂäṭūr. I demand it of You!"

He wiped the tears from his chin with the backs of his hands. The flesh on his hands sizzled from his tears. He rubbed the back of his left hand with his right, and layers of skin sloughed away.

What's wrong with me now?

Frantic, he rubbed his arms and legs, and a pile of dead skin gathered on the ground. Underneath the layers of grey skin his flesh glowed like red-hot coals. Was it the tint of the red sky playing tricks on his mind?

If only it were true. But he *knew* better. He *felt* it. He *was* different—*changed*. His acceptance of it furthered his panic.

Pain stabbed his heart like daggers of fire, burrowing deep inside and ripping him apart. He grabbed at his chest, dug his dirty, broken fingernails into his skin, and ripped at his flesh like a rabid animal. Madness raged within him, and he dug his fingers deeper—striking what felt like bone.

A wave of unprecedented pain swept across his body and Nardus screamed. His vision blurred, and the pain dissipated. But a few moments later the world snapped back into focus, and the pain rained down on him like thousands of needles. He drew a deep breath, flexed every muscle in his body, and fought through it until the pain dropped to a level he could bear.

He looked down at his mangled chest. Had he just done that? His stomach soured, and he thought he might vomit.

This is madness!

But the need to know what lay hidden within him grew. He didn't have a choice, did he? He *needed* to know. He *had* to know. The need consumed him again.

Nardus cringed as he peeled back the flesh around the hole in his chest. Beneath the layers of skin and lodged underneath his ribcage—where his heart should've been—sat a familiar reddish-black stone.

Ɂṭōn Dhef Dädh.

Fear swelled within him.

I've gotta get it out!

Nardus pushed his fingers deep inside the hole in his chest and tried to wrap his fingers around the stone, but he couldn't grasp it. Nauseating pain twisted his stomach, and his vision dimmed as he teetered on the edge of passing out.

Despite the pain and dry heaving, he pressed on. Black sludge oozed around his fingers and seeped from the open wound. The stench of death rose into his nostrils and gagged him. He coughed and spat up ash.

Spent of energy and unable to dig at his flesh any further, his hand slid out of the hole in his chest and drooped to his side. He fell back against the sharp lava rocks. They bit into his back and head like spearheads, but he did nothing to stop them.

Just let me die. Set me free.

Rip my soul from this body, Ʒäṭūr. Damn me no more.

Nardus closed his eyes and withdrew into his mind—his self-made prison. Gruesome images of his slain family bombarded him and tormented him further. The pain within and without united, and from them he had no escape.

I am the stone. I am death. I am dead, yet I live.

Madness.

The great dragon Tharos had said the stone could raise the dead. But had he ever made the price known to him? Nardus couldn't recall.

If it's my life for theirs, I'll gladly pay it, Ʒäṭūr. I'll endure any such nightmare for my family. Just bring them back.

Pravus, the man who'd sent him down this path of madness, had mentioned no such price. Perhaps Pravus had been unaware of it? Or maybe Pravus knew and kept it to himself, believing Nardus wouldn't go through with it knowing the price of doing so.

Am I the key? Is there still hope?

Yes!

But how do I get my family back?

Knowledge.

He needed a better understanding of the stone and how it worked. Eventually, he'd seek out Pravus, but first he needed answers—ones he could find in only one place: Nasduron.

Gnaud.

Excited by the prospect of seeing the little gordak again, Nardus sprang to his feet with a burst of renewed energy. Despite the gaping hole in his chest, the pain faded—at least the physical part. But was that really a good thing?

What does it mean?

Am I really dying? He shuddered the thought away.

Nardus gathered up the clothes he'd strewn across the lava field and pulled them back on. He returned all the items to his pack and strapped his scabbard onto his back. He picked up Brinzhär Dädh, felt its surge of mezhik course through his veins, and reluctantly slid it back into its scabbard.

Damned mezhik. He spat at the ground but produced no saliva.

Nardus lifted his foot to step out of the lava field and into the Great Library, but a voice from behind called his name. He stopped, turned, and watched an ox-of-a-man approach him from within the ruins of Mortuus Terra.

The man—a walking mountain—carried no weapons, but his size set Nardus on edge. The man's rounded head perched atop mounds of muscle, and the green shirt he wore stretched across his massive chest—seemingly to its limit. Strange ridges wrapped the man's torso and marred his chest. They reminded Nardus of a network of tree roots.

Nardus reached up and put his hand on the hilt of Brinzhär Dädh. The tingle of its mezhik seeped into his palm and calmed his nerves. "That's close enough."

The man halted and crossed his arms over his massive chest. "As you wish." His deep voice vibrated the air.

Nardus, his brow furrowed, stared the man down. "How do you know my name?"

A broad smile parted the man's lips. "Mutual friend sent me to await your return. I'd all but given up on you."

Pravus? It must be. But how does he know I'm back? He looked up at the red sky. *Right.*

Nardus relaxed further as the sword's mezhik continued flowing into him, but he kept his hand on its hilt as he eyed the man. "And you are?"

"Berggren, but my friends call me *Iceberg*." He took a step forward.

Brinzhär Dädh slid from its sheath with a *ring*.

Nardus growled, "I said you're close enough. Take another step, and I'll make a mound of you."

Nardus twirled the sword between his hands then raised it above his head, at the ready. He felt alive inside as the mezhik from the sword flowed through his entire body.

I still hate you, mezhik.

Berggren raised one of his meaty hands in the air, still smiling. "Easy, friend. I'm not here to hurt you."

Nardus spat on the ground again. "Then you won't mind stepping back."

Berggren chuckled. "Like your enthusiasm, friend, but it's not that simple. We both know I can't do that."

"Then prepare for your death." Nardus took a half-step back, resolved to take the "Iceberg" down by any means necessary.

Berggren stuck his smallest fingers in the corners of his mouth and whistled. Nardus glimpsed movement out of the corner of his eye but had no time to react before the large rock struck the side of his head. The blow knocked him off his feet and sent Brinzhär Dädh flying from his hands. His head slammed into the lava rocks, and a high-pitched noise filled his ears.

Pain swept through his head like a tidal wave, and his vision blurred. He screamed, but the third blow to his head cut it short and sent him spiraling into darkness.

CHAPTER TWO

Darkness surrounded Alderan, and the damp, musty dungeon air saturated his mouth and throat. He swallowed the air like foul medicine, and its taste gagged him and curdled the contents of his stomach.

Forget about the air. Forget everything.

Alderan faced the steel cell door, his palms pressed firmly against its cold surface. He exhaled and closed his eyes. *How hard can this be?*

Rayah stood behind Alderan with one hand on his shoulder and whispered words of encouragement in his ear. "You can do this, Alderan. I believe in you. The door's no different than those metal cuffs."

"What are you waiting for?" growled Rakzar.

"Back off, and let the boy concentrate," said Amicus.

"Ignore him," whispered Rayah. She kissed the top ridge of Alderan's ear.

Gooseflesh rippled down Alderan's nape and tensed his shoulders. *Does she understand how torturous that is? She must.* One day, he'd return the favor.

Alderan closed his eyes, cleared his thoughts, and focused his mind on the steel—its makeup. Several moments passed—more than he could count—with no change. He pressed harder against the door and willed the steel to give in.

The sounds within the cell—dripping water, heavy breathing, Rakzar's claws clicking on the rock floor as he paced impatiently, Rayah's fluttering wings—diminished until none remained except the beat of his heart.

Alderan concentrated his thoughts on the connection between his hands and the steel door. His breathing shallowed, his heart slowed, and his fingers and palms tingled with mezhik. Every arc, indentation, and flaw in the steel revealed itself to him. He understood it in a way he'd never thought possible.

The cell door vibrated, softly at first, then tremored violently. His hands became red, fiery magma, and he pushed them through the door's surface. The tingling in his hands intensified, and a soft glow penetrated his closed eyelids.

The tingling subsided, the light faded, and he opened his eyes. His palms still rested against cold steel. *I don't understand. What did I do wrong?* He balled his right hand and punched the door. Shards of pain ripped through his hand and up his arm, and he grunted.

Alderan shook his head.

He leaned forward and lowered his head until his forehead rested against the door. His hands fell to his sides. "It's no use. I can't do it."

Rakzar growled, "You're a pathetic excuse for a wizard." He shoved Alderan and Rayah to the side.

Alderan met the wall hard with his left shoulder. "Hey!"

"I'll get us out of here," said Rakzar.

"Got mezhik of your own?" asked Rayah.

Alderan reached out and grabbed Rayah by the waist—err… perhaps by the breast, but it was dark—and pulled her to him. She struggled for a moment, then relaxed and leaned into him. He gripped her tighter, and the handful of flesh he held squished like a sponge. *Definitely a breast!* He swallowed hard and adjusted his hand as his cheeks burned with fire.

Rayah turned in Alderan's arms and hugged him. "Another time, perhaps."

She giggled, and his cheeks burned further. *Does she know how I feel about her?*

Rakzar pounded on the door, and Amicus called out to Eshtak. After several minutes, Rakzar grew still, and Amicus fell silent.

Rakzar breathed heavily. "Any of you opens your mouth about this, I'll bite out your tongue."

Alderan released Rayah and slid to the floor. She settled next to him.

How will I save the world when I can't even get through a door?

What would Aria do?

✝ ✝ ✝

Alderan sat on the floor next to Rayah and leaned against the mossy cell wall. Complete darkness—save Rakzar's glowing yellow eyes—engulfed the four of them, and only Amicus's heavy breathing kept the silence from rendering them deaf.

Despite being trapped inside a dank, underground dungeon, Alderan sat on top of the world. He turned the bracelet—*Aria's* bracelet—between his fingers, engrossed in the images he'd seen through it as they repeatedly played in his mind.

She's happy. She's smiling. She's alive.

At that moment, nothing else mattered. So many questions swirled in the back of his mind, begged to be answered, but the knowledge of Aria still living and breathing consumed him and kept them at bay.

Where are you Aria? Why can't I feel you? Is it because of the distance between us? Can you feel me? Or do you think I'm dead too?

I pray that you're still safe, sister. No matter where you are, know that I'm coming for you, and nothing will stop me.

Alderan pushed the bracelet over his right hand and let it hang on his wrist. He probed the darkness with his left hand and found Rayah's hands woven together in her lap. He glided his hand across the tops of hers. *As smooth as porcelain.* He wedged his hand between hers and interlocked his fingers with hers.

Rayah lifted his hand in hers, and the touch of her moist lips on the back of it curled his toes and sent waves of gooseflesh across his skin.

I love you, Rayah.

Alderan's world revolved around Rayah and Aria, and he refused to live without them both by his side. He and Rayah must find Aria. *They'll be inseparable once they finally meet.*

He pondered the cloak of darkness surrounding Aria. *Who captured you, Aria? Where were you off to when you gave the bracelet to Amicus?*

Alderan needed some light shed on the events that led to Rakzar hunting him and to Aria's capture. *Rakzar must have answers.*

Alderan asked, "So, why haven't you killed me, Rakzar? You've had plenty of opportunities now."

Two dim, yellow lanterns appeared in the air a few feet in front of Alderan. Rakzar snorted and they disappeared, but they returned a moment later.

"Despite what you think, I'm not a mindless killer. When I failed to kill you in the woods the night we met, I questioned why I'd been ordered to kill you in the first place. However, you scarred my reputation by escaping, and so I continued my pursuit. Even now, I fight the urge to end your life so that I can bring honor back to my name."

Rayah's hand stiffened in Alderan's. "*Honor*? You call that honor? You don't even understand the meaning of honor, you wicked beast!"

Alderan interjected, "What she means is that the kind of honor your race exemplifies isn't the same as what our races do."

Rayah sat up, jerking Alderan's arm. "No, Alderan. That's *not* what I meant. There's no *honor* in slaughtering the innocent. Rakzar and his kind destroyed your village and killed everyone in it, including your father."

Amicus spoke up. "She's right, Alderan. There's no honor in such heinous acts. They slaughtered everyone in Solasportus as well, including my family. My sweet little Vonah had only seen four name days. She didn't deserve such a short life or the death she faced."

"Hold on a minute," growled Rakzar. "There are lots of accusations flying my way. To be clear, I wasn't involved in either of those events."

Heat rose in Alderan's cheeks. "You told me you *ate* my father."

Rakzar scoffed. "A farce to scare a young boy, nothing more. At the time they attacked your village, I hunted you, White Knight." The light from his eyes shifted out of view. "And, when *your* town was attacked... whoever you are—"

"Amicus. My name is Amicus."

"Right, Shadowman. Amicus. Whatever. At that time, I stalked the White Knight and his fearless *girlfriend* outside a small cottage in Viscus D'Silva. Besides, *orcs* attacked your town, not gnolls."

Alderan tried running his fingers through his matted hair, but they caught in tangles and clumps of blood and soot. "Fine. We concede you had nothing to do with either attack, but that doesn't matter right now. I need to know if I must continue watching my back around you. If so, we need to finish this. Now."

"You'll always have to watch your back, and not only from me. As you've seen, I'm just one of many that have been sent to kill you. And, so I'm perfectly clear, I make no guarantee that I won't try to kill you again in the future. If I change my mind, you'll be the second one to know."

Well at least he's being honest.

Rayah squeezed Alderan's hand hard. "You'll have to go through me to get to Alderan."

"And me," Amicus added. "Even though Alderan *did* try to kill me."

Rakzar snorted. "Since we're playing a game of blame, how about you find a way out of here, White Knight? You're the one who put us in this situation to begin with."

"Me? Seriously?" The accusation boiled Alderan's blood.

Everything they'd endured over the last several months stemmed from Rakzar's blind faith in his orders.

If I knew how to use my mezhik, we wouldn't be having this conversation.

† † †

Males.

Locked in a cell with three of them wasn't Rayah's idea of an enjoyable time. She'd spent the last hour listening to them bicker like children. It sickened her, and she couldn't take it any longer.

"Shut up! All of you. We each share in the blame, okay? Arguing about it won't get us out of this cell."

Even without a hint of light, Rakzar's yellow eyes glowed like tiny lanterns. "And what do you suggest, *dryte*?"

Dryte wasn't a derogatory term—it's what she was, after all—but from Rakzar's mouth it made her feel small, even dirty. Hateful words formed on the edge of her teeth, so she clenched her jaw and pursed her lips to keep from voicing them.

Alderan had no such constraint. "Watch your tongue when you speak to her, or I'll cut it from your mouth."

Rakzar growled, "I'd like to see you—"

Rayah screamed as loud as she could. She continued screaming until she'd depleted every bit of air from her lungs. No one spoke a word after she'd finished.

She huffed. *Finally, some silence.*

She leaned back against the cell wall, exhausted. She scarcely remembered her life prior to the events over the last year. Had she not met Alderan, she would've begged Ɂäʈūr to reverse time so that she could find a more peaceful path in life. She hadn't asked for the life dealt her, but she'd never want to forget Alderan, either.

The stench of the cell had never been pleasant, but its foulness intensified with each passing moment. They needed a plan of escape. She seemed to be the only one capable of thinking constructively, so she put her mind to it.

How can we get out of here?

Solid rock, top to bottom, made up the cell, so she had no chance of finding a way through it. She'd also left her things in the room beneath Alderan's house, including the book through which she communicated with Savric. What else could they do?

I wish Alderan knew how to use his mezhik. We would've been gone long ago if he did.

She smiled. *And Rakzar would be dead too.*

Alderan's voice shattered the silence. *"I'm sorry, Rayah. This is all my fault. I'm incapable of keeping you safe."*

Rayah's eyes watered, and she blinked back tears. "This isn't your fault, Alderan. And it's not *your* job to keep *me* safe. It's *my* job to keep *you* safe."

Alderan's hand went rigid in Rayah's. "Did I say that out loud?"

"I think your *girlfriend's* hearing things," said Rakzar.

Rayah realized what had happened, and her heart leapt in her chest. *Our bond is strengthening!*

She focused her mind on Alderan and imagined throwing a rope around him and pulling him to her. She forced her thoughts toward him. *"Can you hear me, Alderan?"*

"Yes," Alderan said aloud. He squirmed and cringed. "I'm certain the dead heard you as well. My ears are still ringing."

"What's going on with you two?"

The sound of Amicus's voice startled Rayah. She'd forgotten that he shared the cell with them.

Rakzar growled, "They're speaking to each other through their thoughts, but they're both too foolish to realize it."

"I might be, but Rayah certainly isn't," said Alderan. "I didn't even know such an ability existed."

Amicus cleared his throat. "Finally, some good news. Can one of you use your mind to call Eshtak?"

Rayah shifted and leaned into the wall. "The only reason I can send my thoughts to Alderan is because we share a bond. Outside of a common bond between those who wield mezhik, only a wizard possesses the power to enter another's mind, and that's only if that person's mind is weak or left unguarded."

"Then Alderan could do it?" asked Amicus.

Rayah shook her head. "It's a bit more complicated than that."

Alderan sighed. "What she's trying to say is that I'm still learning how to control my mezhik. Technically, I could."

Amicus jeered, "You had a pretty good grasp of your mezhik when you tried to kill me with that fireball."

"I'm sorry about that, Amicus. My mezhik seems to be triggered by deep emotions, like rage and sorrow. The first few times it happened I didn't even know it was me doing it. I assumed the mezhik came from Rayah."

"Alderan!" Rayah shoved him.

"What? It's true," said Alderan.

Rayah sighed and shook her head. *Why does he freely share his weaknesses with our enemies?*

"An *emotional* wizard," mocked Rakzar. "Just what we need. I have a great idea. How about we rough up your girlfriend and get your emotions flowing?"

Rayah snapped at them. "Can we stop with the threats? *Both* of you?"

"I'm thinking creatively," snarled Rakzar. "What've you come up with, *dryte*?"

"Her name's Rayah," yelled Alderan. "Use it."

"As you wish, White Knight. What have you come up with, *Rayah*?" Rakzar laughed.

Rayah pursed her lips and wrinkled her nose. "I have the perfect idea. How about we all pray? We can ask Ɛätūr to free us from this dungeon cell."

Rakzar roared with laughter. "Are you serious? You've had all this time to think, and that's your single *great* idea? 'Let's all pray to an imaginary deity?' Well, let's just test that out right now, shall we?"

Rayah cringed. *Dear Ɛäṭūr, what have I done?*

Rakzar cleared his throat. "Please, oh great Ɛäṭūr, Master of the world and Controller of the universe, open the cell door for us. Oh, and while You're at it, let there be light too. We can never ask too much of You, right?"

Click.

The cell door's locking mechanism disengaged, and the loud squeak as the door swung on its hinges couldn't be mistaken.

Yes!

Rayah couldn't help but giggle. "You were saying, Rakzar?"

Rakzar scoffed again. "Even if Ɛäṭūr does exist, that wasn't His doing. Unless He's a pale, short man wearing nothing but a scarf around His neck."

"Eshtak?" cried Amicus.

"Eshtak was scared. Eshtak ran away from fire but came back for friends."

Amicus sighed. "You did well, Eshtak. You did really well."

"What's in your hands?" growled Rakzar.

"Eshtak brought fire stones." He clicked them together, and sparks fluttered in the air.

Rayah grinned. *Thank You, Ɛäṭūr! You even answer the prayers of the faithless.*

"A mere coincidence," snarled Rakzar. "Hand them over."

"Eshtak doesn't like bad thing."

Rakzar growled, but Amicus interceded, "It's okay, Eshtak. You can hand him the stones. He won't harm you."

Eshtak complied, and with a few clicks and a spark, the torch ignited to life in Rakzar's paw-like hand and filled the cell with light. Eshtak clapped and danced in circles in front of the cell door.

Rayah closed her eyes. *Thank You, Ɛäṭūr.*

CHAPTER THREE

Savric held a large book in front of his face, and the pages nearly touched his nose. "I do believe the writing in this book continues to shrink."

Savric lowered the book just enough to see Qotan, who sat in a chair on the other side of the table, over the top of it.

"Pardon?" Qotan's bright, green eyes twinkled in the candlelight as he peered over the top of the book he held.

Savric eyed Qotan and lowered his book farther. "The writing. This book. Smaller. Harder to read. Do you follow, or shall I draw you a picture?"

A mischievous, crooked smile curled Savric's lips.

Qotan lowered his book and scratched his bald chin for a few moments, feigning deep thought.

"Perhaps—and correct me if I am wrong—it is your eyesight that is worsening and not the size of the writing that is shrinking." Qotan smiled wide and chuckled. "I daresay, though, a picture would be delectable."

Savric set his book on the table and leaned back in his chair. He had no idea what he'd do without Qotan around. The man could light a dark room with his mere presence and give reprieve to the foulest of moods with the simplest of looks.

My dearest, guardian angel.

Savric beamed. "My dear brother why is it that I keep you around again?"

"I would love to think it is for my wit. Alas, I do believe it is my looks you are truly fond of." Qotan ran his fingers through his wiry, grey hair and batted his long black lashes.

Savric chuckled and raised his finger in the air. "True enough. You are indeed a striking fellow."

"As are you, brother." They both chuckled and returned to their reading.

Qotan broke the silence. "I believe I have a solution to your problem, dear brother. That is, of course, if you are still soliciting for a solution."

Savric kept his head buried in his book. "Pray tell, brother. What does your solution entail?"

"I think a simple enlargement spell would suffice. And, before you say anything apropos, I speak of the enlargement of the writing and not of your eyes." They both laughed.

Savric leaned back in his chair and stretched his bony old legs. "Brother, age has left a sweet taste upon my tongue. I dare not ask Ɂätūr for anything more. I will live with my visual inadequacy and be thankful for the things I have yet to lose."

"If it is your faculty that you next lose, perhaps then you will have lost everything."

"Even if an existence such as that were bestowed upon me, I would still have you with me, brother. Always."

"Always, indeed."

Silence settled between them and held for several minutes, but then a deep groan far below the small cottage rose. Savric and Qotan laid their books down on the table and looked at each other. Savric cocked his head to the left. The lines in Qotan's brow deepened, and his smile faded.

A low rumble vibrated the table as its intensity grew. A moment later, the little cottage shook violently; dishes rattled in the cupboards, and books fell from the shelves. Savric and Qotan latched onto the edges of the table with their hands and gave their full attention to the phenomenon.

Savric surveyed the room. "Quake?"

Qotan's brow wrinkled further. "I believe it may be something more devious than a quake... the *zheballin*, perhaps?"

Savric released the table's edge with his right hand and pulled at his beard. "Ah, the *zheballin*. Could be, yes. It seems the demons who creep in the night have emboldened as of late. I fear we are heading into dark times."

Qotan stroked his chin. "Dark times, indeed."

The shaking ended abruptly and left a cloud of dust in its wake.

Savric coughed. "Remind me to reprimand the maid, brother. This place is a monument erected in honor of the very nature of filth."

Qotan pulled himself to the edge of his chair. "Perhaps—"

Calen burst through the door like a cannonball. "Master Savric!" His chest heaved as he labored to catch his breath.

Savric turned his focus on Calen. "My dear boy, you are prone to take the door from its hinges with an entrance like that."

Calen took a deep breath. Beads of sweat poured from his forehead in droves. "Sorry for the intrusion, but I came as fast as I could."

"Am I to surmise that this intrusion has something to do with the recent quake?" asked Savric.

"Quake?" Calen wiped his forehead with his shirtsleeve. "I'm not sure what you're referring to."

Savric looked at Qotan. "An isolated event then?"

Qotan stroked his chin, lines of concern drawn across his brow. "Indeed, I believe it was."

Savric pulled at his beard. "This will need to be looked into."

"Consider it done, brother." Qotan pulled himself up from his chair and disappeared into one of the back rooms of the cottage.

Savric turned back to Calen. "Well, if it is not the quake that has you flustered, what has?"

Calen wiped his palms on his trousers. "Remember when you asked me to be your eyes and to keep watch for anything out of the ordinary?"

"I do."

"Well, I wasn't sure what you'd meant by that until earlier today. I was outside the northern town gates minding my own business when a tall and very well-dressed man appeared out of nowhere."

Calen thrust his hands in the air. "I mean he wasn't there one second, and the next he was! Then he made four copper coins appear in his hand and offered them to me to keep quiet about seeing him. I told him I couldn't take them, but he insisted. He pushed them into my hand. I really didn't wanna take the money. I swear it."

Savric thought of Calen as the grandson he'd never had. He loved the boy dearly, especially his brutal honesty. "Do you know if this man is still in town?"

Calen shrugged. "I'm not sure, but it seemed as though he was waiting for someone."

"Do you think you could show me where you saw him?"

Calen's eyes brightened. "Yes, sir!"

"Good. Now before we go, I would like to cast a spell over you."

Calen's eyes widened. "Like *mezhik*?"

Savric rubbed his hands together. "Yes, my boy, *mezhik*. I believe I may know who this man is, or at least why he is here, and I would like to keep him from knowing that I am here, if possible."

Calen squinted. "What will the spell do?"

"It will allow me to see and hear things through your eyes and ears as though I were there myself."

Calen walked over to the table and plopped down in Qotan's chair. "Really? Will it hurt?"

Savric chuckled. "You will only feel a small tingle, I promise."

"I trust you, Master Savric... but will you be able to read my thoughts?"

Savric let out a whistle. "Heavens no, my boy. I am certain I would go mad were I to traipse around in that head of yours."

Calen twirled his finger in his ear. "Would you still be able to see and hear if I were to close my eyes and cover my ears?"

Savric smiled at the boy. "You are certainly full of curiosity today, Calen."

"I'm sorry, Master Savric." Calen pulled his finger from his ear and rolled the earwax he'd retrieved into a ball. "Well... I guess you can go ahead and do it then."

Savric waved his hand at Calen. "*Fzíū frʊm fidhin.*" Mezhik flowed from his fingertips, filled the air with its clean and fresh scent, and warmed his cold hands.

Calen sprang from the chair and shook his whole body like a dog after a bath. "You said it would be a small tingle! It felt like someone stripped me naked in the middle of winter, sprayed me with water, and blew cold air across my whole body."

Savric chuckled. "Perhaps I am a bit rusty and used more *mezhik* than necessary."

Calen scrunched his face. "I've never known you to be rusty with anything, Master Savric. You're always in control of everything. Are you sure you didn't do that on purpose?"

Savric winked at Calen. "Now, let us see if it worked."

"What do I need to do?" asked Calen.

"You need not do anything but be patient, my boy."

"Yes, sir." Calen cocked his head. "How does it work, and where does it come from?"

Savric squinted his eyes and looked past Calen. *Mezhik…*

Savric explained, "*Mezhik*—formed from energy created by Ɂätūr, molded by the nature of the spell itself, and infused with the essence of its caster. Every spell, no matter its base, traces back to a specific wizard—a signature of sorts. Of course, one must know what to look for, the wizard whose essence is contained in the spell, and the skills to do so.

"Any wizard can trace their own spells, whereas a good wizard can learn to trace the spells of other wizards if they know the caster's essence. However, the greatest of wizards can trace a spell back to its caster regardless of knowing the caster's essence or not.

"I fall right in the middle of those. I can trace my own spells with little effort, but tracing spells cast by those whose essences I know still proves daunting at times. I have accomplished it but a single time and doing so quickly drained me of energy."

Savric's mind eased into the past.

He'd been so young when he'd done it—just sixteen name days. He'd only had mezhik a few months and little time to study it when his dog, Corla, came home bloodied and near death. Savric searched through books and cast every spell he could think of to heal Corla, but none of them worked.

Corla died two days later.

Savric, Qotan, and Zerenity buried Corla in the woods where she loved playing. A few days later, Corla came running up to the cottage, covered in dirt and dried blood. Her matted fur fell out in chunks. She wagged her tail when Savric pet her, but her nose remained as dry as a summer desert.

Corla had died. He'd buried her. Yet she stood there.

Conflict tore him up inside. Despite his love for her, he knew she'd become an abomination—no longer a creature created and breathing by the gift of Ɂätūr but by mezhik.

Mezhik derk.

Corla needed to be buried again, but Savric couldn't just take her back into the woods and throw her into a hole. She'd dig herself back up and be at his doorstep before the morning light. Only the caster could undo what had been done to her. He had a good idea of who had cast the reanimation spell, but he needed proof.

He spent days poring through the few books on mezhik he had but found no reference to how one might trace a spell. Qotan offered no help either.

Reluctantly, he decided to confront Zerenity about it. She was the only other person who knew where they'd buried Corla and the only other person he knew capable of casting such a spell.

Zerenity denied it, but Savric recognized the deceit in her face. She couldn't even look him in the eye for more than a few seconds without averting her eyes. A few days later, she finally confessed.

A few name days older than him, Zerenity had a better grasp on mezhik than he did. She showed him how to trace his own spells and how to recognize the essence of a caster when they'd cast a spell. Every spell left a distinct aura of color and smell—sometimes even taste—in the shape of the caster's primary mezhik ability that could be matched to them, but detecting it took great concentration, energy, and skill.

After several hours of deep concentration, Savric finally glimpsed the aura surrounding Corla for a moment. Weakened by the effort, he blacked out and then woke up hours later in bed. It took him several days to recover from the experience.

You were always the stronger one, Zerenity.

Hands grabbed Savric's shoulders and jolted him. His vision came into focus as the past faded from his thoughts.

"Master Savric. Are you okay?" Calen's ashen face contrasted the dimly lit room.

Savric patted Calen on the arm with his hand. "Yes, my boy, quite so. Just reminiscing on some fond memories, nothing more."

Calen moved around the table and plopped down in Qotan's chair again. "You had me worried. Your eyes turned white, and you stopped moving. I called to you several times, but you didn't respond. I thought you might be dying."

Savric smiled at Calen. "My dearest boy. I believe my time has yet to come and may still be some time down the road."

"I sure hope so. I'm not sure what I'd do without you."

"And I you, my boy. Now, let us see if my spell is working."

Savric closed his eyes, connected with the spell he'd cast on Calen, and then saw himself through Calen's eyes. "Good. Very good. This will do nicely."

"What do you see?" asked Calen.

Savric sighed. "An old man. Much older looking than I had anticipated. Where have the years gone?"

Calen snickered. "To the past. Like your mind, I guess." They both laughed.

Strange seeing and hearing myself laugh. I had no idea how funny I truly sounded.

Savric opened his eyes and rose from his chair. Calen jumped up from his chair too.

Savric rubbed his hands together. "I believe it is time we go find ourselves a wizard."

Calen's eyes brightened, and the corners of his mouth curved into a big smile. "My very first quest!"

"Yes, my boy. And certainly not your last."

Savric's twisted old staff leaned against the wall, next to the door. He stuck his hand out. The staff vibrated in its place for a moment, and then it flew across the room and into his outstretched hand.

Calen gasped with wonder—as he always did.

Savric chuckled softly and swept his hand toward the door. "Lead the way, my boy."

The door swung open without assistance, and Savric and Calen made their way out of it and into the cold afternoon. The door closed behind them and locked itself.

Savric stroked his beard. *And just who are we to find?*

✝ ✝ ✝

Don't muck this up, Calen. Master Savric's counting on you.

Calen rubbed his arms with his hands as he walked along the side of the muddy road. The slight breeze chilled him all the way down to his bones.

I should've worn a coat.

He knew more factors played into his shivering than just a lack of proper clothing. Could he really do what needed to be done? He didn't believe that the wizard would take too kindly to him snooping around.

What if he catches me? Calen's heart pounded.

"Master Savric, can you hear me?" whispered Calen.

"Yes, my boy."

Calen glanced to his left even though he knew Savric stood a block away and had spoken directly into his mind.

"I'm not sure I can do this. What if he tries to hurt me or comes after me?"

"I doubt the man will want to draw attention to himself. However, if he does go after you, I suggest you run faster than you ever have before."

"But what about you? What if he sees you?"

"Do not anguish over me, my boy. I will be nothing more than a shadow among shadows."

Calen sighed. *Why can't I have just a little mezhik, Ƨäţūr?*

Calen stopped at the corner of the main road—next to Dougett's Leather Shop—and peered around the corner of the wooden structure. Someone ruffled his hair, and he spun around and nearly fell into the road.

Mrs. Dougett gasped and stepped back. "Oh, Calen, I'm so sorry! I didn't mean to frighten you."

Calen put his hand to his chest and wheezed. "N-no, ma'am. I-I'm okay."

Mrs. Dougett crossed her arms and tilted her head slightly. "What are you doing skulking around my husband's shop, anyway?"

Savric's voice echoed in his head. *"Calm down, my boy. Tell Mrs. Dougett that you are playing a game and that you are trying to keep from getting caught."*

Calen took a deep breath and then let the air escape slowly. "It's just a game, ma'am. I'm on a secret quest, and I'm at risk of getting caught just by talking to you." He glanced left and then right. "My adversaries are everywhere," he whispered.

Mrs. Dougett's eyebrows lifted. "Oh. Well then, I guess I'd better move on. Wouldn't want you getting caught on my account." She winked at him.

Calen smiled. "No, ma'am."

"Well, good luck with your quest, Calen. I hope you find what you're looking for." Mrs. Dougett continued around the corner, and the ring of a bell sounded as she entered the shop.

"Good job, my boy. Now, let us find that wizard of yours before I starve myself out of existence."

Calen poked his head around the corner and looked from shop to shop. Several people walked about, but the couple sitting at a table in front of Orna's Café just down and on the other side of the road caught his attention. He tried to get a better look at them by squinting his eyes, but it did him no good.

Why can't I see better? I hope I won't need to wear spectacles soon.

The man at the table faced Calen's direction, but the man had his eyes trained on the woman across from him.

Calen sighed. *She must be beautiful.*

"The man's wearing different clothes," said Calen. "But I'm pretty sure he's the one I saw outside the northern gates."

Savric's voice entered Calen's mind again. *"Thank you for doing this, Calen. You are a brave young man. I do not know the man, but it would take few guesses as to who he is and what he represents. Ordinary people do not dress as he does. I must see the woman who sits with him. I am certain I know who she is."*

"Do I know her too?" asked Calen.

"There is no way you could. Now, please do not be afraid of what I am about to ask you to do. I would not ask if it were not of grave importance."

Calen swallowed hard and closed his eyes. *Ʒắṭūr, make me brave.* "I trust you, Master Savric. What do you want me to do?"

"Stay right there. Everything will happen as it should."

"Yes, sir." Calen opened his eyes, and his stomach gurgled.

Be brave, Calen.

CHAPTER FOUR

A fine line separated elation and despair. Aria found herself perpetually swinging across it like a pendulum.

In one moment, she stood on top of the world, betrothed to a great man and destined to be the future queen. But in the next, she remembered who she was and where she came from. Her arrival in Daltura placed her firmly in the latter.

Ɂät̪ūr, what am I doing here? I feel like a puzzle piece that goes to another puzzle, but I'm being forced into the one being put together right now. I just don't belong. How am I supposed to deal with all this pressure? She looked down at her hands. *And having this mezhik on top of everything else?*

Her pulse accelerated, and her toes curled as the carnal touch of Pravus's mezhik flowed into her. His hand rested on hers, but for how long?

"Aria are you in there?" Pravus's voice sounded muffled and faint, as though it'd traveled a great distance to reach her ears.

She looked up at him, startled. "I'm sorry."

Pravus squeezed her hand. "You haven't even touched your food. Do you feel unwell?"

A wooden bowl filled with soup sat in front of her. Bits of spinach, carrot, and potato floated on the soup's surface, but no steam rose from it despite the frigid air. She had no recollection of ordering food.

The wooden chair's edge cut into the backs of her legs and left them numb. *How long have I been sitting here?*

She looked up at Pravus and gave him a half smile. "I'm okay, really."

The frown he wore confirmed his disbelief in her words. "I may not be able to read your thoughts, but I'm certain you're *not* okay. You can tell me anything, Aria. You know that, right?"

Aria withdrew her hand from Pravus's and placed it in her lap next to her other hand. The carnal touch of his *mezhik* faded. She looked down at her lap, unable to look him in the eye any longer. Her lower lip quivered, and she bit down on it to keep from crying.

Aria sighed. "There are so many things changing in my life all at once. It's hard for me to adjust to it all. I've never been away from home for so long, and now I don't even have a home or a family to return to."

She took a deep breath. "I'm afraid of becoming a queen. I'm afraid of being a mother. I'm afraid of being in love. I'm afraid of being with you. I'm afraid of *not* being with you. How will I ever adjust to it all?

"And, on top of it all, I have this *mezhik* I can't control. *Mezhik* I didn't even know I had until a week ago. What if I hurt someone with it? Or kill someone? How would I live with myself?"

"Aria, look at me."

Reluctantly, Aria lifted her head and met Pravus's gaze.

"*What?*" The word spewed from her mouth like venom. She sighed. "I'm sorry. I didn't mean for it to come out like that. I'm just so frustrated."

"As am I. I wish I'd come for you quicker than I did." Pravus placed his hands on the table, palms up. He wiggled his fingers. "Give me your hands, my queen."

"Must I?" She wrinkled her nose at him and then complied.

"You're frozen—" Pravus's gaze moved beyond her.

Aria turned to see what had captured his attention so abruptly, but nothing seemed amiss. Plenty of people went about their business, some selling their goods and wares and others just walking about.

She turned back to Pravus. His gaze still focused beyond her. "Do you see something?"

Pravus, his jaw set, spoke through clenched teeth, "We're being watched."

Aria stiffened. "By whom? Or what? Did the *zheballin* follow us? Are we in danger again?"

"I'm uncertain by who, but I don't believe we're in danger." Pravus stood. "Stay here. I'll return in a few moments."

Aria rose from her chair. "I'll come with you."

Pravus looked at her and, for a moment, the lines in his face hardened.

"Please, my queen, sit back down. I won't be gone long."

She sank back down in her chair and pushed the cup of cold soup to the other side of the table. The soup sloshed around, and some of it spilled on the thin, yellowed fabric spread across the table. She stared at the tablecloth. *You're stained and worthless. Like me.*

She turned in her seat and watched Pravus cross the road and disappear behind a tall, wood-and-brick building. An iron sign with big bold letters that read Derst Forge stretched across the building's face.

Thwack.

Aria gasped and spun around so fast that she nearly fell off her chair.

An old man dressed in light-brown robes and a dark-brown cloak stood next to the table. He clutched the table with one liver-spotted hand and held a twisted staff in his other. Strands of wiry white hair stuck out from underneath his hood on both sides of his wrinkled face and joined with his scraggly beard underneath his chin. The culmination resembled a rat's nest.

"Dearest me. I am so sorry, my dear girl," said the old man. "I can be ever so clumsy at times. Please forgive me."

The old man's bright blue eyes shone underneath his hood. *He has the kindest eyes.*

A familiarity Aria couldn't place surrounded the old man. She eased back into the middle of her seat and relaxed her shoulders. "Have we met before?"

The old man beamed at Aria. "Heavens, my dear girl. Despite my ailing mind, I am quite certain I would remember meeting a beautiful young lady such as yourself. Your face is one I will never misplace."

Heat flared in Aria's cheeks as she absorbed his kind words. She peered over her shoulder—the direction Pravus had gone—to hide her embarrassment. Pravus was still out of sight. When she turned back around, she sat alone. She looked about, but the old man had vanished.

How did he manage to leave so quickly? Was it mezhik?

The brief encounter struck her as odd. She sat back in her chair and placed her hands in her lap. The tablecloth's edge felt rough against her fingers. She moved her hands to the side and peered down at her lap. The tablecloth didn't rest in her lap. However, a piece of paper neatly folded into a seven-pointed star did.

She stared at the paper star, bewildered by it. Had she ever seen something like it before? She couldn't recall. When Pravus returned, she'd tell him about the paper and of the old man she *knew* had left it in her lap.

She touched the paper, and her pulse quickened as mezhik flowed into her fingertips. Its mezhik didn't contain the same intoxicating potency as Pravus's did, but she still enjoyed its touch.

Each passing moment left her more possessive of the paper star. The old man had left it for her, had he not? *Keep it to yourself, Aria. At least until you know what it is.*

Aria covered the paper with her hands and casually looked around to see if anyone watched her. The late afternoon drove most people about their business and away from the outdoor café where she sat.

I am alone.

She peered down at the paper. Her heart galloped in her chest. She drew in a deep breath and held it. She felt like a little girl again, about to unwrap a marvelous gift.

It's probably nothing. So why give it to me? And in such a manner? He must give them to all the young girls.

But they knew each other, didn't they? She'd seen the recognition in his eyes and felt it in her heart as well. *But why give it to me and then leave without another word?*

It doesn't matter. Just open it.

Her fingers trembled, and her throat tightened. She lifted the paper star, carefully unfolded it, and made sure she kept it hidden under the table's edge. She looked about again.

I'm still alone.

She bent over and rested her forehead on the table's edge. She exhaled and held the paper up where she could see it. The paper contained just two words.

Two words.

Powerful words.

Those two words drove the breath from her lungs like a punch to the stomach. She stared at the paper in disbelief, her mind unwilling to register their meaning even though there was no question as to what they said.

Can it be?

Tears slid from the corners of her eyes, and she let them flow freely. Her head spun with emotion, leaving her dizzy. Her body trembled, and perspiration dampened her palms as the two words sank in. They filled her mind and pushed out everything else.

Never had words lifted her spirits like the two scrawled on that piece of paper did. The words themselves were insignificant—two very common words. But the delivery of those two words and the emotional weight they bore made them special. She had little doubt as to their meaning.

They were only two words.

Life-altering words.

Her heart sang as tears of joy streamed down her cheeks.

He lives!

† † †

Pravus stomped through the muddy roads of Daltura, chasing after a portly young boy. He recognized him from earlier in the day. *Calen.* Had the coins not been enough to silence him? He cursed under his breath.

To Calen's credit, he moved fast for his size. Pravus would've just teleported in front of him and ended the chase were there not so many people walking about. He had half a mind to do it anyway.

In their first encounter, Calen exhibited little desire or skill for spying or stealthiness. Even simple conversation stuttered his speech. In truth, Calen spied on him for someone else. Pravus eyed those around him suspiciously as he narrowed the distance between himself and Calen.

But who? Who knows me here? And how would they have known I was here?

He glared at the back of Calen's skull. *Unless the boy talked.*

But Calen didn't seem like the spying type. Maybe he hadn't been spying at all.

Then why did he run when our eyes met?

Being chased through town by a wizard might've been cause enough for Calen to run. Had he been in a similar situation, he might've done the same.

Aria. Is it her they're after?

Pravus stopped in the middle of the road, and a lump formed in his throat. What if Calen had been a decoy to draw him away from Aria? His stomach rumbled with discourse, and it wasn't from the café food.

Abandoning all caution, Pravus summoned his mezhik and stepped from the muddy, rutted road to the side of the café in one motion. His stomach settled as he rounded the corner and saw Aria still seated at the table, alone. He scanned the area as he approached her from behind, but no one lingered about.

Pravus stopped short of the table and watched Aria for a long moment. She sat with her arms drawn in and her head down, huddled over the edge of the table and unmoving. If she knew of his presence, she didn't make it known.

He quickly assessed the scene, homing in on the subtle differences from when he'd left. Aria's soup bowl had moved across the table, and some of its contents had spilled on the tablecloth. The table stood askew from how it had been when he'd left a few minutes prior.

Why's she sitting like that? What are you up to, my queen?

Pravus loathed secrets—at least the ones not of his own making. He rounded the side of the table and sat down in the chair opposite Aria. She gave no indication that she'd heard him.

He cleared his throat, "Aria?"

Aria sat straight up in her chair, eyes wide. "Pravus. When did you return?"

"Just now."

The distinct *crinkle* of paper folding registered in his ears. Had he not been paying attention, he would've missed the subtle flex of Aria's upper arm muscles.

She's hiding something.

"What's in your lap, my queen?" Plumes of vapor hung in the air from his hot breath.

Aria placed a folded piece of paper on the table. Pravus leaned across the table and picked it up. He turned the paper over in his hands.

A seven-pointed star.

His pulse quickened.

Ūrdär Dhef 2äfn Dhä. How is this possible?

Pravus peered into Aria's eyes—his future queen. Her piercing green eyes didn't waver from his gaze.

He held the star-shaped paper between his thumb and finger. "Where did you get this?"

She smiled at him with her eyes. "I'm unsure where it came from."

Pravus cocked his head. "Then how did it come into your possession?"

"As I said, I'm unsure. When you left, I turned and watched until you were out of sight. When I turned back around, the paper was lying in my lap."

"You saw no one leave it, and no one walked away from here?"

Aria shook her head. "It appeared out of nowhere, like *mezhik*."

Pravus stared at her for a long moment.

Why can't I ever read you, Aria? How will I ever know what you're thinking?

He spun the paper star on two of its points between his thumb and finger. "If I were to unfold this paper, what would I find written on it?"

"Nothing of use, I'm sure. See for yourself."

Pravus eyed the paper star. He didn't believe in coincidence. He'd been drawn away from the café for a reason, but for a simple piece of paper? Something didn't add.

She's lying to me. But why?

Pravus carefully unfolded the piece of paper and turned it over in his hands.

Blank?

Pravus frowned at Aria. "There's nothing on this paper, Aria."

Aria beamed at him. "I know. Just a pretty star."

For an instant, Pravus swore something else had flashed in her eyes.

What are you hiding? Had there been words on the paper before?

Pravus set the piece of paper on the table. "And you're certain it contained nothing when you opened it the first time?"

Aria raised her eyebrows. "If it had, wouldn't it still be there?"

Aria controlled herself well, but Pravus knew she'd just lied to him again—not because of a telltale sign, but intuition. He'd lied enough times in his life to know when someone else lied to him. It stung.

Rage rose in his throat and tightened the muscles in his face. "You're lying to me, Aria."

Aria gasped. "Lying to you? Why would I lie about a blank piece of paper?"

Pravus gritted his teeth and poked the piece of paper with his finger, "You and I both know this wasn't blank. Tell me what it said. *Now.*"

Aria jumped to her feet. Her chair fell back with a *clunk* as it hit the wood-planked floor. "How can you just sit there, seething and ready to explode, and accuse me of lying to you? Why would I lie? If there were words on that paper, then why aren't they there now? How does that make any sense?"

"*Mezhik*," he sneered.

Aria folded her arms in front of her. "*Mezhik*? I can't even use my *mezhik* with this stupid collar on. Besides, I don't even know *how* to use *mezhik*."

Pravus slammed his fist into the table. "Why would someone leave you a piece of paper folded into a seven-pointed star if it didn't contain a message of some sort?"

Aria thrust her hands in the air. "How would I know? Maybe some kind person just thought I'd appreciate the shape. Or maybe the message *was* the shape of the paper. Did you think of that? Maybe a seven-pointed star is supposed to mean something to me. Maybe they thought it might trigger a memory or something like that. How would I know the intention of it?"

"Well, *did* it trigger a memory?"

Aria lowered her arms. "No. Should it have? Does a seven-pointed star mean something to you? Maybe I was supposed to give it to you."

She's lying.

Pravus grabbed the piece of paper off the table and crumpled it into a ball. "Tell me the truth, *my queen.*"

Aria's face flushed red. She turned her back to him and walked away.

Pravus grabbed the edge of the table and threw it sideways, sending it and the cup of cold soup into the middle of the muddy road. He kicked Aria's chair aside and stormed after her. "Don't you walk away from me."

Aria quickened her pace. In a blink, he appeared behind her, grabbed her arm, twisted her around, and nearly pulled her off her feet.

Aria struggled against his iron grip. "Get your hand off me!"

Pravus glared at her. "We're not doing this here. We'll talk about this in the carriage."

"No!" Aria drove the heel of her boot into the top of his shoe.

Enraged, Pravus snarled, "*ʕəlläb.*"

Aria fell into his arms like dead weight, fast asleep.

Across the road, a man stood in front of his shop and watched the scene. Pravus glared daggers at him until the man finally returned to his own business.

Be glad I don't end your life.

Pravus stood at the corner of the road with Aria in his arms, fuming and frustrated with himself. Seldom did he ever allow his anger to get the best of him.

This day has turned into a disaster.

The notion that he'd damaged his relationship with Aria brought with it a sorrow he'd never experienced before. In such a short time, she'd become everything to him, and the fact that she'd so easily angered him scared him.

I can't allow myself to be this way with her. I need her to trust me and love me, not fear me.

But why would she lie to me? What was on that piece of paper that would make her betray my trust? She loves me, doesn't she?

Because of his harsh upbringing, he had no grasp of trust and kept everyone in his life at arm's length. He had no friends for a reason. In his experience, trust only brought about deceit. Trust had ultimately killed his father.

Am I reading this all wrong? Maybe I'm forcing myself to distrust her. Could she be telling the truth?

I must learn to trust her.

With his mind, he sent word to his driver to pick them up. It was high time they made an exit from Daltura before making any further scenes.

While he waited for the carriage, he further mulled over the day's events.

He believed in predestination through prophecy, and, in that belief, little room for coincidence existed. An important detail dangled in front of him, but he couldn't put his finger on it. Calen had distracted him for a reason, hadn't he? If so, what was that reason?

He looked down at Aria. She lay in his arms like a corpse.

My beautiful queen, was it to get to you?

His muscles tensed, and he scowled. *No... you must be hiding something from me.*

What happened while I was away?

Pravus pushed his thoughts aside as the carriage rounded the corner and stopped directly in front of him. The driver hopped down from his seat and opened the carriage door. Pravus handed Aria to the driver, and the driver carefully carried her up the two steps and laid her on the rear seat.

Knowing the discretion of him being a wizard surpassed repair, Pravus swept his hand across the road in front of the horses.

The table pulled itself from the muddy road, righted itself, and settled on the wood-planked floor of the café where it'd previously sat.

The two chairs flew back into position on either side of the table, and the yellowed tablecloth slithered back in place. Lastly, the soup cup returned to its prior position. With the flick of his wrist, the soup cup filled with copper coins. His coin purse lightened. *If only I could conjure money from nothing.*

The crumpled piece of paper lay under the table. Pravus reached out, and the paper flew into his hand. He looked around and made sure he'd returned everything to place.

Pravus turned toward the café. The owner stared through the open window with wide eyes. Pravus gave the woman a curt nod, turned back to the carriage, and stepped into it. The driver closed the carriage door and returned to his position atop the carriage.

Pravus knocked on the roof. With a jolt, the carriage pulled away from the corner and bumped along the muddy, rutted road through Daltura and eventually out its southern gates.

Pravus slumped against the rear-facing seat, depleted of energy. The scene he'd made with Aria replayed in his mind. The way he'd handled himself sickened him, but he couldn't shake the notion that she'd concealed something from him.

He hadn't been honest with Aria on a few occasions, or at least he hadn't disclosed the fine details of many things, but he'd had good reason for it. Given time, she'd know everything in his heart, every dark deed and thought.

That time isn't now.

He didn't view their relationship as a two-way road. She had no right to hold anything back from him, did she? After all, he'd saved her life.

He stared at her still form on the opposite seat. Her chest slowly rose and fell.

You owe me everything, my queen. Especially the truth. I'll have it from you one way or another.

A tinge of guilt in using a sleeping spell without her consent seeped into his mind, but the alternative would've been far worse. When she woke up, he'd face the fullness of her wrath regardless.

We'll have it out, my queen. I look forward to it.

He stretched himself across the seat and stared at the carriage ceiling. The day still lingered, but he fought for it to be over and forgotten. A day best left in the past.

He opened his hand, let the crumpled paper fall to the floor, and smiled to himself.

We'll see if she can resist taking it.

His head ached, and he desperately needed some sleep, uninterrupted.

Ɂəlläb.

His thoughts faded as the spell took hold of him and pulled him into the darkness.

CHAPTER FIVE

Nardus woke to a world of darkness, a splitting headache, and a loss of memory. His entire body ached, especially his arms and shoulders. His arms were wedged underneath him, and when he tried moving them something bit into his wrists.

Am I in constraints?

His throat felt raw, as though he'd swallowed shards of glass, and something filled his mouth. He swallowed through the pain, and the taste of dead fish lingered in the back of his throat.

Bound and gagged?

Small pinholes of light began forming as his eyes adjusted to the darkness. He turned his head to the side, and a rough surface scratched his face. He inhaled through his nose, and a familiar, earthy smell filled his nostrils. *Burlap.*

What's happening to me?

Images of the catacombs below Ṱämbəll Dhef Däd Dhä filled his head. His pulse quickened, and he labored for every breath. Thousands of tiny, imaginary spiders crawled across his body and nipped at his skin. He shuddered and squirmed like a fish out of water.

Nardus struggled against his constraints, but it only tightened them and deepened the pain in his arms and shoulders. He cried out, but the rag in his mouth muffled the sound. He tried spitting the rag out but doing so only gagged him.

Fear rose in his throat—manifested as bile—and choked him further. *I cannot die. Not now.*

I have the stone, Ɂäṯūr. I will resurrect them. You cannot keep them from me!

Nardus closed his eyes and swallowed the acrid substance that bubbled up in his throat like magma in a caldera. *Calm down and think this through.*

He breathed deep through his nostrils and caught a whiff of another scent buried beneath that of the burlap sack. *The sea. I smell the sea.*

Nardus relaxed and allowed his body to melt into the surface he lay on. Lapping water sounded in his ears, and a rocking motion roiled his stomach.

A boat. Why am I on a boat?

He concentrated his mind on the last event he remembered: trying to rip ʒţōn Dhef Dädh from his chest cavity. He hadn't succeeded in removing it, but what'd happened after?

Gnaud.

He was about to step into the Great Library when—

Berggren!

Nardus had drawn his sword to defend himself against the ox-of-a-man, but he hadn't realized Berggren wasn't alone until it was too late. Berggren had distracted him just long enough for someone else to sneak up and hit him in the head with a rock. *Twice.*

But why did they knock me out? And why have they bound and gagged me? He couldn't make any sense of it.

Berggren had said that a mutual friend had sent him. Nardus had no friends—not after Bradwr. Only one person knew where he'd gone besides Gnaud.

The wizard Pravus.

But why send Berggren? Why hadn't Pravus come himself? Wasn't the stone the most important thing to him?

It made little difference. Nardus intended to find Pravus, but first he had to see Gnaud. He needed answers, and the little gordak might be the only person who could help him.

Gnaud. Nardus smiled. *I guess I do have one friend.*

In his mind's eye, Nardus pictured the Great Library. He willed himself to smell the wondrous aroma of the dorus pine shelves that lined the Great Library's walls from floor to ceiling. He strained his ears to hear the click of his boot heels on the white marble floors but heard nothing beyond the lapping water.

Gnaud's voice echoed in his mind: *"...there are a few rules to coming here."*

His memories—and his head for that matter—were hazy, but he hadn't lost the general idea of the rules Gnaud had laid out on accessing Nasduron and the Great Library. With Ꝗṭōn Dhef Dädh buried in his chest, he was confident that he satisfied the rule of having great purpose to seek out Gnaud and the Great Library.

He recalled another rule—not being in a place conjured by mezhik. He felt certain that he wasn't in some conjured world. Just the idea of mezhik brought with it a brief streak of anger and a slew of profanity to his restrained tongue.

A third rule crawled into his mind: *cannot be escaping death.*

I'm not dead yet, and don't seem to be in imminent danger. That makes three satisfied rules. And the last?

The fourth and final rule popped into his head via Gnaud's voice again: *"...you must be moving to come here."* He knew for certain he violated it.

Damn! I've gotta get up. I must get to Gnaud. Otherwise all is lost.

Nardus sat up but doing so tightened something around his neck and sent pain spider-webbing in every direction. He convulsed for what felt like an eternity, fell back against the hard surface, and then his body went numb from the neck down.

His thoughts retreated to the dark corners of his mind, scattering like night bugs in the light. *What in Ꝗäṭūr's name just happened?*

"Like that, don't you?" said a deep, rumbling voice.

Berggren. Nardus nearly sat up again.

"Remove the gag," said Berggren. "See what he's gotta say for himself."

"But if I touch him, I'll die."

The young girl's voice startled Nardus, and her words confused him. *Die? Why would she say that? No one's ever died by touching me.*

Berggren grumbled, "Then I suppose you'd best be careful. No sense in two deaths today."

Two deaths? What's going on?

Nardus felt a presence next to him.

"I have a knife and will slit your throat if you try anything, understood?"

The girl's soft voice sounded as though her mouth were right next to his ear. Had he not had a sack over his head, he might've felt her warm breath on his skin.

Nardus nodded.

"Don't move," she said.

As though I have a choice.

The burlap sack slid up the front of his neck and pulled on his beard. The sack snagged on his chin for a moment and then caught on the underside of his nose. She left it there and removed the rag from his mouth.

Nardus jostled his jaw and tried to speak, but the words hung in the back of his dry throat. He turned his head and coughed, and the act of doing so felt like it ripped holes in his throat.

Nardus groaned, "Water."

"He wants water," said the girl.

"Then fetch him some, Theyn. Didn't go to all this trouble just to let him die of thirst." Berggren's voice came from farther away.

Trouble? They've gone to trouble over me? I'm the one bound and gagged!

"Yes, boss," she replied.

Theyn's presence faded before the sound of her retreating footsteps reached Nardus's ears. She treaded lightly.

A small girl, perhaps?

A few moments later, he heard the soft brush of her feet against what had to be a wooden floor as she returned to his side. "I'm going to kneel beside you again. If you try anything other than swallowing the water I give you, I won't hesitate to slit your throat. Understood?"

Her threat sounded forced, but Nardus nodded anyway.

Water slowly poured over Nardus's lips and ran down his cheeks and chin. The water wasn't cold, but that didn't diminish the glorious feel of it on his face. He groaned when the flowing water ceased.

"You need to open your mouth," she said. Then, her voice strained, "We don't have water to waste."

Nardus forced his tongue between his lips, tearing layers of skin as they parted. The taste of fresh blood lingered on his tongue as he pulled it back inside his mouth.

"Here it comes again," she said, softer.

The water tasted a bit stale, but the feel of it sitting in his mouth and then trickling down the back of his throat gratified him. He swallowed the last of her pour and groaned for more.

Theyn obliged him and said, "This is the last I can give you for now. We still have a long distance to travel and limited supplies."

Nardus swallowed most of the water down hard, hoping to wash the feeling of gravel and sand from his throat. He gargled a bit with the rest of the water and then swallowed it as well. The taste of fish and sulfur lingered on the back of his tongue, but he tolerated it easier.

"Thank you." His rough voice sounded much deeper than he remembered.

Nardus cleared his throat. "Is the sack over my head necessary?"

"You killed my cousin, Shaul." Theyn said it matter-of-fact and without emotion. "How can I be certain you won't try and kill me too?"

The accusation slapped Nardus in the face. "Me? Killed your cousin? When did I have time to do that?"

Theyn exhaled deeply. "About four hours ago. After he knocked you out with the rocks."

Nardus coughed shards of glass. "Wait a minute. *After* he knocked me out? If I was unconscious, how exactly did *I* kill him?"

"With your *mezhik*," she replied, matter-of-fact again.

Me? Mezhik? He would've spat on the floor if he could've.

He scoffed. "That's impossible. I don't have *mezhik*."

"Tell that to Shaul."

The left side of his chest burned within, and he gritted his teeth. "How did it happen?"

"When he reached down and grabbed your hands to pick you up and carry you to the boat he went rigid—like a statue. I reached for his arm to pull him away from you, but my hand went right through it. His entire body collapsed into a pile of ash. The wind finished the job."

Disbelief forced its way to Nardus's lips. "There's no way—"

Pain sliced through the center of his forehead like a bolt of lightning, and images of dead skin—piles of it—flashed in his mind's eye. Glowing red skin covered his naked body.

The stone! It must be. What has it done to me?

The left side of his chest burned. *Am I some kind of monster?*

The images in his mind morphed into his family: Vitara, Shardan, Shanara, and Savannah. One by one, he embraced them, and they turned to ash. Bile rose in his throat.

I thought the stone brought the dead to life, not the other way around. How will I ever make physical contact with anyone again? How can I bring my family back when I'm like this? I'd never be able to embrace them.

Damn You, Ƶäʈūr! Why must You torture me at every passing? Why can't You just let me be?

"All this *mezhik* be damned," growled Nardus. "Kill me, Theyn. Or have Berggren do it. I can't live this way. It's not worth it."

Theyn spoke softly, this time her voice full of emotion. "Even if I wanted to, I couldn't. If you die, we all do."

Her words spun Nardus's head. "What are you talking about?"

Theyn sniffed. "I've glimpsed the future, and there's no doubt. Death will consume us all."

Nardus swallowed hard, but the lump in his throat remained. "You mean the three of us, right? The three of us would die. You, me, and Berggren."

"No, Nardus. All of us—" Theyn sniffed again. "—the entire world. I've seen it."

Theyn's words punched Nardus in the gut and left him breathless. *She can't be right, can she?* In his heart, or where his heart had once been, he believed her words, but he just couldn't coil his mind around them.

Nardus's entire body tingled as the numbness began wearing off, and the blood-red sky and the spreading ring of fire flashed in his mind. *Could it be the damned stone?* The thought soured his stomach. He turned his head to retch, but nothing came forth but guilt.

He grimaced. *The entire world. This can't be true, can it?*

Droplets of sweat formed on his brow, trickled across his temples, and ran into his hair. "How can you be sure? How are you able to see the future?"

"I'm one of *Drämärz Dhä*. You know of my kind, do you not?"

Nardus searched his mind but came up empty. "No, I don't think so."

"The Dreamers. Our visions often come to fruition."

"Prophecy? I've heard of that, but I didn't realize one race produced all of it."

"I'm not speaking of prophecy, and *Drämärz Dhä* is not a race, but an *ability*. I can often see the possibility of things—potential futures. I've seen your face several times in my dreams over the last week, Nardus."

Nardus frowned. "I still don't understand."

"Each time I've dreamt of you, you die—and the entire world perishes with you."

Gnaud has all those books of prophecy and he never told me this? Why would he keep it from me? To protect me? Or to keep me from giving up?

He sighed. *Maybe he doesn't know. No, he mustn't. He would've told me.*

"Have you seen when or where this happens?" His arms ached, and he struggled against his restraints.

"It's not that simple. Every day that passes and every choice made affects future events like ripples in the water. The only thing constant in my dreams is how it ends. When you die, the dead rise and consume the world. It's like an unstoppable plague. Every time I have this dream, I can't sleep for days."

Berggren's voice cut through the weight of the moment. "Enough of this pointless talk, Theyn. Remove the sack. We have business to discuss."

"Yes, boss."

Nardus's nose popped as Theyn yanked the sack off his head. The light stung his eyes, and he blinked back tears. As his eyes adjusted to the light, the face of the girl leaning over him came into focus. Only she wasn't a girl, and her beauty surprised him.

Theyn's caramel skin stretched smooth and taut against her thin face, high cheekbones, and sloped forehead. Her yellow eyes, frayed on the outer edges and lined in black, pierced into him. White strands of hair tucked behind her pointed ears and hung at her shoulders. A yellow orchid pushed through her hair over her left ear, and its coloring further accentuated her eyes.

Apart from his wife, Vitara, Nardus had never laid eyes upon a woman more beautiful. Theyn left him speechless and breathless. His chest burned with fire, and a deep need to be with her birthed inside his reddish-black, stone heart.

Panic grabbed his stomach with its claws and dug deep. He squeezed his eyes tight and shook his head, desperate to rid himself of his lustful thoughts.

This isn't me, Vitara. I'd never betray you, my love! Don't be jealous. Her beauty's no match for yours. You're my rock and my anchor, forever.

"Is something wrong?" asked Theyn.

Nardus forced his eyes open. Theyn leaned over him, her brow furrowed. "No—I mean—it's just the light. By the sound of your voice I'd imagined you to be a young girl."

Her light pink lips parted as she smiled, revealing pearly teeth including fangs on both upper and lower sets like a saber-toothed cat but not nearly as pronounced. "I hear that a lot."

Nardus stared at her, completely embarrassed by his boldness, but unable to look away. Her beauty demanded his attention.

Be still, heart. She's only a woman and not one for me.

Theyn's gaze never left his, and the dimple in her left cheek when she smiled highlighted her beauty further. How could any man resist such a regal creature? He forced his mind and his eyes elsewhere.

To his surprise, the vessel that carried them across the rough sea stretched beyond his limited vision. To his left, a second deck rose above the one he lay on, and far to his right a stairway led down into the vessel's bowels.

Several men and a few women scurried about their business, most of whom paid him no attention. However, a handful of them scowled at him with each passing, and fewer still gestured toward him with two extended fingers—the crude meaning not lost on him. He assessed their anger toward him stemmed from Shaul's death.

But it wasn't my fault.

He looked back up at Theyn. Her eyes had never left him, and he swore desire filled them. Did she find him attractive? Most women had his entire life, but none had roused him the way Theyn did. None, but Vitara.

She wants me.

He shuddered the visive thought and changed the subject. "Was your cousin like you?"

Theyn laughed—a glorious melody in Nardus's ears. "Oh, I doubt you'll find another quite like me. Shaul was a warrior, just like his uncle, Berggren. But it was Berggren's second wife, Dhaldra, who took me in when I was a young girl."

Berggren pushed Theyn aside. "Shaul was a good lad, and he served his purpose well. As for you, I'd just as soon kill you right here if I didn't believe in Theyn's visions."

Nardus stared up at Berggren. "I'm sorry about your nephew, but he's the one who attacked me."

Berggren crossed his arms. "Our mutual friend warned us that you'd be dangerous, and we did what we felt necessary to detain you. He never said anything about your *mezhik* though."

Their accusations of wielding mezhik infuriated Nardus. "I don't have *mezhik*. But there's something wrong with me. No one's ever died by touching me before. I need to go see a friend. I think he might be able to help me."

Berggren's stare hardened. "You're not going anywhere. We're on a boat in the middle of the Incendia Sea, and we still have many days before reaching West Hotah."

West Hotah? Nardus had heard of the great port cities of East and West Hotah, but he'd never traveled so far east on land before. When he'd started the quest for the stone, he'd sailed out of the small fishing town of Desolo Urbs and didn't make landfall between it and Incendia Island.

Nardus slowly sat up. "Then you should have no issue with unbinding me. I've nowhere to go, as you say."

Berggren flexed his biceps. "We've got lots of things to discuss before there's even a chance of me freeing you. Besides, Shaul's dead by your hand. I set you free, and the whole crew might be dead by nightfall."

"Release me, and I swear I'll touch no one." Nardus looked over at Theyn. *Except maybe her.*

Theyn smiled at Nardus. Had she winked at him too? She slid the tip of her long index finger between her parted lips and stared at him intently.

Heat rose in Nardus's cheeks, and he felt like an adolescent. *What has this stone done to me?*

I swear I'm not attracted to her, my love. His pulse raced, and his body said otherwise.

Theyn lowered her hand and turned her attention to Berggren. "There's something I must do, boss."

The veins in Berggren's arms and neck bulged, and his bushy black eyebrows met just above the bridge of his nose, forming what looked like a single eyebrow. "I know exactly what you're thinking, Theyn. I won't allow it. You'll most certainly die."

Theyn set her jaw, and her face flushed red. "This isn't your decision, boss. It's mine. I must know."

Nardus's interest piqued. "What do you mean? Must know—"

"Keep quiet," growled Berggren. He didn't even look down at Nardus.

Theyn rolled her eyes at Berggren. "I'll be careful. I promise."

Berggren grabbed Theyn by her shoulders. "No, Theyn. I'm your father. You *will* listen to me."

Nardus moved to stop Berggren, but his restraints held him down. He shook his head. *What am I doing? I don't care about her.*

Theyn pushed Berggren's hands off her shoulders and placed her hands on her hips. "I'm no longer a little girl, *father*. I'm not asking for your permission."

Nardus caressed Theyn's female form with his eyes. *Every curve, perfection. Her skin, flawless. Her scent, seductive. Her eyes, begging.*

Nardus forced himself to look away. *No, no, no! Quit twisting my mind. My eyes are only for you, my love. My anchor.*

Nardus looked up at Berggren, whose veins still bulged in his neck.

Berggren pointed his meaty finger at Theyn. "If this kills you, I swear I'll bring you back to life just to kill you again. Do you hear me?"

Berggren glared daggers at Nardus. "And then I'll kill you."

Theyn nodded at Berggren. "Leave us."

"You'll answer my questions soon enough." Berggren turned and stormed away, his weight quaking the wooden planks Nardus sat on.

Theyn looked down at Nardus and smiled faintly, but in her eyes, she seemed a thousand miles away.

Nardus's heart pumped hard. He cleared his throat and searched for his lost voice. Would he tell her anything she wanted to know? Did it even matter?

No. I'll answer any question she gives me truthfully.

Unless she asks me what I think of her.

Nothing, Nardus. Vitara's your wife. Theyn's no one. She'll always be no one.

"What must you know, Theyn?"

I'm a taken man.

Theyn's gaze focused on him, and he felt drawn to her. Had he not been restrained, he might've taken her in his arms and pressed his lips against hers. He sensed a deep connection with her—emotionally, spiritually, sexually. In that moment, no one else in the world existed but the two of them.

But she really isn't no one, I am. She's the only one.

"Whether or not you're going to kill me." Tears glistened in the corners of her eyes, but they didn't fall.

Kill you? Only if I can't have you. Nardus's chest burned, and his head spun. *No! What is this madness? I love you, Vitara.*

Nardus looked to the heavens. *Ƨäṭūr, if You exist and You care about my lost soul, rip this stone from my chest. It's twisting my thoughts and corrupting my mind. I cannot take it.*

The suffocating red sky hung low over them, and dark clouds circled like vultures. Fear rose in his throat, and he choked it down. He gave Theyn his best smile. "I give you my word, Theyn. I won't harm you." *At least not on purpose.*

But what good is my word when I have no control of this madness?

Theyn walked over and knelt beside him. "You and I both know you can't promise that. I trust that you had no intention of killing Shaul, but it still happened."

"But I—"

Theyn put her finger to her lips—the same finger she'd had in her mouth previously. The urge to take it and place it in his own mouth nearly overwhelmed him.

Sweet as nectar. The forbidden fruit. One taste of her wouldn't kill me, would it?

No! Nardus screamed in his mind. Had Theyn noticed?

I cannot be near her. This stone's driving me mad.

Or is it her? Her scent—summer orchids in full bloom—tortures me. If she were only a little closer and my constraints removed.

No! My love, I need you more than ever to fight this madness. Be my anchor. Keep me grounded. Sever this lustful bond! Protect me from myself.

Theyn's yellow eyes cast an alluring glow and spoke to him on a deep level. Did she want him too? *How could she not?*

"What I'm about to do will feel strange to you—*foreign*. I'll place my thumbs on your temples, and our minds will connect, allowing me to see the end of our paths—one potential future for us."

Nardus squirmed in his mind. *I can't let her touch me! But why would I stop her?* Wasn't it what he wanted? Needed?

Nardus's heart pounded. "Don't—"

"As I told Berggren, I must do this." The steel of Theyn's gaze dissolved his will to resist. "If it kills me, then it's always been my fate."

Nardus sighed. "Can you at least untie me first? I mean you no harm and promise to keep my hands to myself."

But can I? Yes, I must!

He quickly added, "And, like Berggren said, there's nowhere for me to go anyway."

Theyn laughed. "Patience. If this works—and I live—I'll consider doing so."

Theyn placed her palm on his chest and pushed him back down. Only a thin piece of fabric separated his skin from hers. Sweat moistened his entire body like a light spring rain. Did he feel the familiar tingle of mezhik under her hand? He couldn't be sure, but he thought not.

Vitara. Shardan. Shanara. Savannah. Be my strength. Keep me sane.

Nardus exhaled forcefully. "Just do it, then, but don't blame me if you die."

Theyn swung her leg over Nardus's chest and straddled him. "If I die, it won't be me that you'll need to worry about."

Be gentle.

Theyn pushed the pads of her thumbs against her sharp upper fangs until she drew blood. Droplets of crimson ran the length of her thumbs and onto her palms.

Until that moment, blood had never looked so delectable to Nardus. He heard himself whimper like a puppy waiting for its food.

I am truly mad.

Theyn reached down and, just before contacting his skin, closed her eyes. Nardus braced himself, but for what, he had no idea.

Just don't kill her, Nardus.

Theyn pressed her bloody thumbs against his temples. Her skin felt warm against his, and her touch tingled with mezhik. He'd hoped he would revolt the sensation, but he found himself relishing it instead. Could sharing anything else with her be more sensual?

His skin burned with fire. His heart knocked in his chest.

Theyn's mind joined with his, and he stiffened. The feeling reminded Nardus of the times Tharos had entered his mind, but Theyn's presence felt different—*welcomed.*

"Prepare yourself," she said in his mind. *"Every sight, noise, and feeling will be shared between us."*

Nardus swallowed hard. *Will she know that I want her even as I pretend to back away and cower in the darkness?*

No, I won't give into this lust. Vitara. My anchor. My heart is yours. I swear it.

But for how long?

Nardus closed his eyes. "I think I'm ready. You can proceed, my love." His words registered in his mind just as he slipped into what felt like a dream.

† † †

Through multiple layers of clothing, the frigid air penetrated Nardus's bones as he fought through the deep snow of the high mountain pass. Thick layers of rolling fog limited his visibility to less than ten feet.

Theyn walked just a few paces ahead of him, leading the way. "Hurry, Nardus. Time's running out. We cannot win this war without their help. We must find them, or all is lost."

Nardus sensed another presence, and his skin crawled. He looked over his shoulder, but only flurries of snow chased them. When he turned back, Theyn was gone. Crimson droplets dotted the white canvas.

"Theyn!" he bellowed.

Nardus drew his sword, Brinzhär Dädh, from its scabbard and trudged forward. The droplets of blood became spatters, and the spatters grew larger.

He halted. "Theyn! Where are you?"

He waited several moments, but she didn't answer. He continued forward.

Ahead, the mountain pass turned to the right. Nardus rounded the corner and stopped short. His stomach twisted with woe, and his heart burst with pain.

Theyn hung in the air, limp, with a large black claw thrust through her middle. A giant dragon, black as obsidian and with eyes red as fire, clutched her motionless form in the rest of its talons.

Anguish swept through Nardus in waves, and his body convulsed. He dropped to his knees. Theyn symbolized everything he'd lost, and the memories of his family's deaths raged in his mind like the surrounding storm. Vitara screamed, Savannah cried out, and the twins writhed as their delicate limbs were ripped from their torsos.

Rage strengthened Nardus, and he rose. He lifted his sword over his head, roared like a mighty lion, and lunged forward. "You'll die for this, you scaly bastard!"

Nardus swung at the dragon's wrist. Metal struck bone, but the force of the blow reverberated back down the length of the sword and ripped the sword from his grasp. The sword sank into the deep snow and disappeared.

The dragon lowered his head to Nardus's level and bared his sharp teeth as his thin lips curled into a smile. "Am I the enemy? Perhaps, but you've far worse things to contend with."

Defeated, Nardus sank to his knees again. His rage steamed, cooled, and then fell away. He reached out and hugged Theyn's stiffened legs—slabs of crimson ice.

"What does this mean? Can she not be saved? Is the war lost?"

"No war is greater than the one that rages within you," bellowed the dragon. "Lose that war, and all will be lost. You must fight the sickness within. If you do, Theyn will not die."

Nardus released Theyn's legs and grabbed his burning chest. "It's the stone…"

"Yes, the stone. Allow her to purge it from you. It is the only way you'll ever right the world."

"Theyn must do this? Take the stone?"

The dragon laughed. "No. Your daughter."

† † †

Nardus and Theyn gasped in unison as Theyn withdrew her thumbs from his temples. Theyn sat back, stunned.

Nardus's pulse raced. "What in ʕäṭūr's name did we just see?"

Theyn rubbed her stomach where the dragon's claw had protruded. Her lower lip quivered. "I don't understand. That wasn't normal."

Theyn buried her face in her hands and trembled. The need to embrace her overwhelmed Nardus, but his constraints only tightened as he fought against them.

He relaxed. "I'm so sorry, Theyn. If you felt half of what I did, I can only imagine your pain."

"I've never seen my own death before." Theyn wiped the tears from her face. "I felt the claw thrust into my back and rip through my stomach. All my limbs went numb. Never have I experienced a pain so intense before." She lifted her shirt and poked at her flat, muscular stomach. "Some of it lingers still."

Nardus forced his gaze upward. "I know nothing of the future, Theyn, but, based on that vision, our lives must be intertwined somehow. Seeing you impaled like that—dying before my eyes—brought back memories of my family and the pain I experienced from their loss. I felt as though I'd lost you too."

Theyn shivered, a lost look in her eyes. "That presence… that dragon. He probed my thoughts. How is that possible? How could he be inside my head."

Nardus frowned. "I didn't feel him in my mind like that. I thought you said we'd share everything in the vision. Why didn't I feel what you did?"

Theyn shook her head. "I don't know. There's something different about you, Nardus. I've joined with many people over the years, but never have I had an experience like that."

"Is it possible that the dragon actually entered the vision and altered it?"

Theyn stared at Nardus for several moments before answering. "That's not possible. Dragons are extinct."

Nardus groaned. "That's not true. I've met one. Can't say we're friends though."

Theyn sat up straight, and her eyes widened. "You've met a dragon and lived to tell of it?"

Nardus chuckled. "I have. His name's Tharos the Cunning, and cunning he is."

Theyn cocked her head to the left. "You'll have to tell me more about this dragon friend of yours. I hope he's not the one in the vision."

Reflected in Theyn's eyes, Nardus noticed that his eyes glowed red, but she didn't seem to notice. Then, shards of pain ripped into Nardus's chest, and he jerked against his restraints. Above them, black lightning tore through the red sky like the dragon's claw through Theyn's stomach.

I must reach Gnaud before this thing kills me.

Concern flashed across Theyn's face, and she stroked Nardus's cheek. "Are you okay?"

She wants you.

"It's just the vision—" He lied. "—I'll be fine. It's like aftershocks of pain. Unbind me, and I'll answer any questions you have about dragons."

Theyn lightly smacked his cheek. "You're not in a position to make demands."

Nardus grinned through the pain. "Maybe not, but I know you want answers."

Theyn stood up, exhaled forcefully, then pulled a small blade from between her supple breasts. Nardus swallowed hard, and his cheeks warmed. Theyn winked at him, and his embarrassment grew.

Control the madness, Nardus. She's a beautiful creature, but Vitara's far superior.

Is she? —in what way?

Theyn pushed against his side with her foot. "Roll over before I change my mind."

Nardus complied, and Theyn cut the twine that bound his ankles and wrists. He rolled on his back again, and Theyn stepped back. He sat up and worked his shoulders back and forth, trying to loosen them up after so many hours of restraint. He turned his wrists and winced as they crunched and popped.

His knees cracked as he pushed himself to his feet, but he welcomed the newfound freedom. "Thank you, Theyn."

"You're welcome. Just don't do anything stupid." Theyn returned the blade to its hiding place between her breasts.

Nardus quickly looked away and dipped his head. "You have my word."

He raised his hands and stretched his back. Then he placed the back of his hand to the side of his jaw and cracked his neck multiple times. He repeated the process on the other side of his jaw with his other hand, but his neck still felt stiff. He reached behind his neck to massage it, and his fingers touched a thin ring of cold steel.

Nardus ran his fingers around the ring. It encircled his neck.

What is this? There's no seam. No clasp.

He wrapped his fingers around the ring and tried pulling it apart, but nothing happened. He growled loudly.

Nardus turned to Theyn, who just stood there and watched him. Somehow, he felt she'd betrayed him, but sorrow filled her eyes. Berggren came down from the upper deck and stood next to her.

Nardus fumed and glared at Berggren. "Why is this ring around my neck?"

Berggren folded his arms across his chest and smiled. "That collar is assurance."

Theyn turned and walked away.

Nardus thrust his hands in the air. "Assurance? Of what?"

Berggren chuckled. "Assurance that there'll be no further incidents. It blocks the wearer from using mezhik."

Nardus stomped the deck with his boot. "You can't do this to me! I don't have *mezhik!*"

Berggren sneered at Nardus. "We already have, and Shaul's death is proof of your mezhik."

With immeasurable resolve, Nardus closed his eyes and took his first steps into the Great Library. "Gnaud!"

"Who's Gnaud?" Berggren's deep voice startled Nardus.

Nardus opened his eyes—he still stood on the lower deck of the boat with Berggren. His hands balled into fists at his sides. He stepped forward again, saw the interior of the library phase into view for an instant, but then the deck of the boat snapped back into place again.

Damn!

Nardus advanced toward Berggren. His fists shook at his sides. "What have you done to me?"

Berggren unfolded his arms and let them hang at his sides. He held something in his left hand, but Nardus couldn't get a glimpse of it. "Step back my friend, or you'll regret it."

Nardus spat on the deck. He stepped forward and swore he saw fear flash in the big man's eyes. "What's in your hand, Berggren?"

Berggren set his jaw. "Take another step and you'll find out."

Madness swirled in Nardus's mind. Berggren obviously held something Nardus needed. He'd pry it from Berggren's dead hand if necessary.

Big man or not, you can't stop me.

Nardus stepped forward, and Berggren clenched his left fist with a snarl. The collar around Nardus's neck constricted and cut off his air supply. Nardus grabbed at the collar, staggered forward two steps, and dropped to his knees.

He looked up at Theyn who leaned against the upper deck railing. *Help me, Theyn!* Theyn's head lowered as she turned away.

Nardus's hands fell to his sides, and the world around him melted like wax candles. Fingers of darkness reached down and snuffed out the light.

CHAPTER SIX

Alderan breathed in the fresh sea air, happy to be alive and out of the dank, musty dungeons. He stood on the edge of the cliff, staring across the Discidium Sea at Mortuus Vir Isle. Behind him—to the east—the sun began its descent.

Far below, dozens of grey-billed gulls glided just above the water's surface in search of food. *How simple their lives must be. Hunt, eat, sleep. Free.*

Rayah stood next to Alderan, her arm wrapped around the back of his waist. Rakzar and the others still lingered in the dungeon below, gathering their things together.

Alderan sighed. "You know I won't rest until I find Aria, right?"

Rayah leaned into him. "I know. I wouldn't if I were you either. You won't be alone though. I'll never leave your side again. *Ever.*"

He squeezed her shoulder. "I'm not sure I'd let you."

"Before we run off in search of Aria again, we need to go back to your house. I need my things."

He looked down at her, into her hazel eyes, and knew she loved him. She deserved better than him. He would deny her nothing, if it didn't interfere with finding Aria. "We'll retrieve your things first, and then we'll find Aria. Just knowing she's alive will get me through a few more weeks before we renew our search."

Rayah smiled up at him. "Thank you."

He kissed the top of her head. Despite the smoke, the fire, and her time in the dungeons, she still smelled marvelous. He had no doubts as to how he smelled. He needed a bath and a fresh change of clothes.

"I've been thinking about everything that's happened with us…" He ran his fingers through his hair. The soot and sweat from the fire, along with the dried blood, had turned his hair into a matted mess.

Rayah nudged Alderan with her head. "And?"

"I don't trust Rakzar being with us." Alderan wiped his hand on his trousers.

"I don't either. Sounds like there's a *but* in that statement though."

"I trust him even less *not* being with us. At least if he's with us we can keep an eye on him."

"He's tried to kill you numerous times already. Both of us."

Alderan raised his arms. "I know. Part of me wants to kill him too. I'd love to be done with this business. When I killed his two friends on that hill I felt anguished—like it had bruised my soul somehow. It was necessary, I know, and I'd do it again, given the same choice. I'd kill anyone that threatened your life. But that's just the thing, Rayah. He's not currently a threat, and I can't just kill him in cold blood."

Rayah's arm dropped to her side and her face reddened. "He *will* try to kill you again. Of that I have no doubt. He even said so himself. You need to kill him before he gets that chance."

Alderan ran his fingers through his hair, frustrated. "I'm sorry, Rayah, but it can't be that way. I'll fight him to the death if it comes to that, but I will *not* be the instigator. You saw what happened in the dungeon down there. I can't control myself. I nearly killed an innocent man because I refused to listen to him."

Rayah grabbed hold of his arm. "But you didn't, Alderan."

"If Rakzar hadn't intervened, I would've. I could've killed us all." He peeled Rayah's hand off his arm, turned, and walked a few paces away.

"You weren't in your right mind at that moment, Alderan. Given all the stress you've been under, it's completely understandable. Normal, even."

Alderan turned and faced Rayah again. "But that's the point, Rayah. I'm not in control of my body. I didn't ask the fire to leap into my palm. The only thought I had was that the man who stood in front of me had killed my sister and deserved to die. Everything else just *happened*."

Alderan pushed his hair behind his ears. "If I really am to be the *savior* of this world—whatever that even means—I need to understand my mezhik and learn how to use it. I can't rely on triggering it solely by my emotions.

I'm a danger to us all right now—even to you."

Rayah floated over to Alderan. "I completely agree. That's *exactly* why we need to go back for my things. I need my book. Master Savric sent me to protect you, Alderan, but that was only part of my assignment."

Alderan sighed. "And what was the rest of it?"

"He also told me to deliver you to someone. I resisted taking you there because I didn't know why I was supposed to deliver you. I care so much for you, and I didn't want you to hate me."

Alderan ran his fingers through his hair. "I thought we agreed to have no more secrets. You keep telling me that you have none left, yet I keep finding out that you do. How can I trust you?"

Rayah said nothing.

Alderan glared at her. "What *else* are you keeping from me?"

Rayah's eyes glistened with moisture. "Nothing else, Alderan." Her voice trembled. "I swear it. I need to get my book so that I can contact Master Savric. He'll know exactly what to do."

"I don't know anything about this Master Savric fellow. How do you know we can trust him?"

Rayah grabbed Alderan's hand. "I trust him with my life, just as I trust you. Besides, he's the reason we ended up together. Without him, I wouldn't even know you. And you might've been dead now if it weren't for him."

Alderan raked his head with his fingers. "But if this Master Savric knew about Aria and me then why didn't he come for us? Why did he allow everything to happen the way it did? You said he knew of the prophecies. The destruction and slaughtering of all those innocent people—my father included—did Master Savric know what was going to happen? Was that part of his plan? Be an observer and not lift a finger?"

"Alderan, you're being unfair." Rayah let go of his hand and retreated to the cliff's edge. "From what I understand of it, prophecy's never quite that specific, and there are always many potential branches. Sometimes the only way to bring about the desired outcome is for terrible things to happen. The path to any given prophecy never lacks casualties of some sort. Life just doesn't work that way.

"Choices must be made. Sometimes the paths that fork from a prophecy are all terrible. On one side, you may have to sacrifice saving your sister to save another, like me. Or maybe the choice is even more desperate than that. Maybe the choice is to save the life of one you love and condemn the whole world in the process or allow the one you love to die to save the world.

"Assuming that you're aware of a given prophecy, you can never take any of its paths lightly. You must know and study the paths before making decisions. Using pure emotion as a guide usually leads to destruction.

"So, don't judge the choices that Master Savric has made before you're aware of the full details of what the alternative would've meant. And, as I said, he was most likely unaware as to the details of what his decision would bring about. After all, he's a wizard, not a prophet."

Guilt rose into Alderan's throat and tightened his muscles. Every breath became harder than the last, and he pulled at the front of his shirt to relieve the tension. Every word Rayah spoke settled in his mind and rang with truth. In an odd way, she reminded him of his mother. Tears moistened his eyes, but he refused to relinquish them.

I love her, mother. Would she have approved of Rayah? He smiled. *I know you would've. Father would've too.*

Alderan walked up behind Rayah and laid his hands on her shoulders. She trembled, and his heart ached. *Why do I always find a way to hurt her?*

Alderan bent his head forward and rested his chin on the top of Rayah's head. "You're right. I'm sorry. This is exactly why I need you—to keep me in check. I'm not smart enough about these things to understand how they work. I'll try to keep an open mind going forward, but I'll make no guarantee. Just promise me there are no more secrets. We can't afford to keep circling like this."

Rayah turned and faced him. "I swear on my life. I'll never keep anything from you ever again. And I'll do my best to help you see the other side of things—the bigger picture."

Alderan cupped Rayah's face in his hands and kissed the top of her forehead. "Deal."

She completed him like no one else ever had in his life. With her at his side, he felt whole. He yearned to vocalize his love for her, but the timing didn't seem right. *Will it ever?*

From where they stood, he could just make out the shape to the west that gave Mortuus Vir Isle its name—a dead man floating face-down in the water. Did it foreshadow his fate as well?

Prophecy. How could he ever understand it? The thought of choosing between Rayah and Aria twisted his stomach in knots. *I hope it never comes to that. I'm not sure I could ever choose between you two. I love you both.*

But would failing to choose between them spark an even worse fate, like losing them both? He cringed at the notion.

I'd find a way to save you both, no matter what the prophecies might say.

I'll make my own path.

† † †

Balance. Prior to yesterday's tragic events, Amicus had found balance through his wife, Vorene. Life without her rendered him lopsided—heavy on despair and light on hope. However, having been on the receiving end of Alderan's anger and enduring that moment right before certain death had altered his mindset.

He was but one man and couldn't face an army of innumerable orcs and gnolls alone. He'd certainly be able to take out a few of them, but it wouldn't take long for them to overwhelm and kill him. Dying in that manner wouldn't bring honor to his family, and it certainly wouldn't protect other towns and cities lying in their destructive path.

I need an ally.

As tempting as it sounded, Amicus knew vengeance would not suffice. Instead, he'd seek justice for his family and the others lost in Solasportus, Castle Portador Tempestade, and Viscus D'Silva, but through proper channels.

He set his mind on traveling to the heart of the Ancient Realm—the city of Vallah—to seek an audience with King Zaridus. He'd personally bring the atrocities carried out by the orcs and gnolls into the light. Anything less he'd deem a failure on his part.

I will not fail you again, Vorene.

The beast named Rakzar brushed past Amicus without as much as a glance. He growled, "Little man, where are my axes and armor?"

Eshtak emerged from his hidden room in the lower section of the dungeons, his eyes bulging under Rakzar's glare. Eshtak looked to Amicus for help, but Amicus just shrugged.

Eshtak scrunched up his face and boldly puffed out his chest. "Eshtak found axes and armor. Eshtak keeps them."

Rakzar snarled, "You shouldn't take what isn't yours, little man."

Amicus smiled at Eshtak, surprised by the amount of courage he displayed. "Eshtak, give Rakzar his property back so we can leave. I'm tired of being in this wretched dungeon."

"Axes are Eshtak's now." His thin, black, lower lip quivered.

Rakzar puffed up his chest and roared at Eshtak. The sound echoed through the passageway. Eshtak screamed and ran into his hidden room.

Amicus shook his head. "Was that really necessary?"

Rakzar turned around and stepped in front of Amicus, towering over him like a tree. He poked Amicus in the chest with one of his clawed fingers. "I saved your life, Shadowman. You'd best remember that."

Amicus cleared his throat and craned his neck to look Rakzar in the eye. "For an eternity. I owe you my life."

"You do, and, until you repay your debt to me, I'll hold it over your head."

"What's your price, beast?"

Rakzar smiled, baring his sharp, yellowed teeth. "A life for a life. I saved yours, and now you'll take one for me."

Amicus's throat tensed. "I won't kill the boy for you, so you might as well kill me now."

Rakzar laughed. "I'm not asking you to kill the White Knight. The one I'd have you kill will serve both of our interests."

Amicus relaxed a little. "Then who?"

Rakzar's jaw tightened and the hate in his eyes burned bright. "Murtag."

Amicus shrugged. "And who's this Murtag? Why would I want him dead?"

"He's the one who ripped away your happy life and stole your hope from you. He's the one responsible for killing your family. He's the leader of those filthy orcs."

Amicus closed his eyes and bowed his head.

Is this a sign, Ɂäţūr? Is this the ally I've requested? Are You granting me this revenge? Or is it for the greater good that You've provided me this knowledge? Or is this not of You at all, but the work of Diʑäfär?

Amicus sighed, opened his eyes, and looked back up at Rakzar. "And how does this play into your hand? Why do you want him dead, *beast?*"

Rakzar barked, "He's a thorn in my side and a stain on my honor."

Rakzar's spittle peppered Amicus's face. He wiped it away with disgust. "Then why don't you kill him yourself?"

Rakzar slammed his fist into the wall next to Amicus's head. "He would've been dead years ago if I'd had a choice."

Amicus stood his ground. "And what's holding you back? It's not like you haven't killed before. Recently, even."

Rakzar growled and walked away. "There's a blood pact between Murtag and I, bound by blood and mezhik. Orcs and gnolls don't mix, so we were forced into an alliance. If I try to kill him, I'll die instead. The same goes for him trying to kill me."

"To what end? What is this alliance for?"

Rakzar charged Amicus but pulled up just short of ramming him. His rancid breath spoiled the stale air. "Do I look like I know? I've been a mercenary since I was a pup. I don't ask questions—I just do the job. Keeps things simple. You need someone roughed up or killed, I'm the one you come to. End of story."

Amicus pushed Rakzar back, hoping to gain some breathing room. "Killing Alderan is just a job for you? A payday?"

"What else would it be?" Rakzar picked his teeth with one of his claws. "The first night, he escaped and left me stunned. I'd never failed a job, and he's just a boy."

Amicus scratched his head. "What's keeping you from killing him now?"

"Move on, Shadowman. I've already answered that question."

"Perhaps you did, but I want the full story. Otherwise our deal is off."

Rakzar grabbed Amicus by the throat and pinned him against the wall. Fire burned in his eyes. "You don't get it, do you? There's no negotiation to be had. Kill Murtag, or I'll kill you right now."

Amicus gritted his teeth. "Then do it. Get it over with. You'd be doing me a favor."

Rakzar leaned in, and his wet nose pressed against Amicus's nose. The stench of his breath permeated the air with each word. "You think I'm a mindless animal, don't you?"

Amicus gasped, and quickly regretted it as the putrid air soiled his lungs and stung his nostrils. "No, but you don't have the upper hand here, beast. I'm ready to die. I look forward to seeing my family again. If you kill me, who's going to kill Murtag for you?"

Rakzar released Amicus and slammed his other fist into the wall next to Amicus's head. "I'm fighting my very nature right now. A week ago, you'd be dead already."

Amicus side-stepped Rakzar and rubbed his throat. "As I said, give me the full story or we have no deal."

Rakzar turned and glared at Amicus, but the fire had left his eyes. "Time. Time left me with a rare opportunity to think about the job. I began wondering why grown men would hire someone like me to kill a boy. What kind of threat could one as weak as him possibly pose to them? Why were they so insistent on ending his life?

"The more I thought about it, the harder it became for me to finish the job. Just like you, I needed answers. Who is this boy? Who is the White Knight? What do they stand to lose by him living?"

Amicus nodded. "I see. Time and curiosity can be a deadly combination. Well, I'm sure Alderan will be glad to know that you're no longer bent on killing him."

Rakzar got in Amicus's face again. "Let me make one thing clear, *friend*. You breathe any of this to him or his *girlfriend* and I may find keeping you alive less useful than I do right now."

Amicus raised his hands. "My lips are sealed. I won't breathe a word of it."

"Eshtak keeps secret too if bad thing protects Eshtak from other bad things. And from people."

Rakzar whirled around and faced Eshtak. Rakzar's armor and axes lay at Eshtak's feet.

Rakzar pointed a clawed finger at Eshtak. "You've made a wise choice, little man." He bent down, scooped up his property in his massive arms. "Breathe a word, and you die. Both of you." He turned and walked toward the dungeon stairs.

Eshtak smiled at Amicus and twirled around in a circle. "Eshtak has cloak now." The mouse-brown fabric swished around him and dragged the floor.

Amicus chuckled. "Indeed, you do, my little friend." *And finally, a moment without someone's manhood showing.* He laughed heartily, and Eshtak grinned.

Eshtak bounced from foot to foot, full of energy. "Eshtak take from lizard man who was not lizard, but man."

Amicus frowned. "What do you mean by that, Eshtak?"

Eshtak held his left hand out. A silver ring circled his second finger.

Amicus reached down, palm up. "Can I see the ring, Eshtak? I promise I'll give it back to you."

Eshtak nodded with a wide grin, yanked the ring off his finger, plopped it in Amicus's hand, and danced in circles.

The ring warmed Amicus's hand. He held it up in the torchlight to get a better look at it. Its silver band started thick on one side and wrapped around the other side into a point, like a lizard's tail. A round emerald sat atop the ring, sculpted to appear as though it had scales.

Inset in the emerald, an egg-shaped stone made of golden amber with strands of red veins. A sliver of obsidian sat inside the amber stone, placed vertically at its center. The gem-and-stone setting resembled a lizard's eye.

Magnificent.

Amicus handed the ring back to Eshtak. "Where did you get that?"

Eshtak shoved the ring back on his finger and smiled. "Eshtak took ring from lizard man. When Eshtak took ring, lizard man became man."

Amicus scratched his chin. *Mezhik...* He hadn't known such powerful mezhik existed. Then again, he knew little of mezhik at all.

What would it feel like to wear it? Would it hurt to be transformed? Can it be reversed once donned? Does it slowly kill its wearer, feeding off their life force? Should Eshtak be wearing it? Who better than him?

The mystery and implications of such mezhik allured and scared Amicus, but a single question stood out in his mind: *What makes Eshtak immune to mezhik?* He mulled it over for several moments but couldn't come up with a single answer.

Amicus shook his head and the question from his mind. He clapped his hands together. "Let's get out of here before we can no longer wash the stench of this place from our skin."

Eshtak stopped dancing and pointed to his hidden room. "Eshtak bring things too."

Amicus bent down on one knee and looked Eshtak straight in the eye. "I'm sorry my friend, but where we're going is a long journey from here. We can't possibly take it all with us. Perhaps you can find a favorite thing or two and bring them. But nothing more."

Eshtak's head slumped, and he shuffled his feet as he walked over to his hidden room and disappeared. The sounds of Eshtak rummaging through his things filled the passageway.

Amicus sat on the stone floor, leaned against the wall, and closed his eyes, weary and anxious to leave this constant reminder of what he'd lost. So many of his memories encompassed the dungeons, both joyous and tragic. The visits from Vorene and Vonah, though rare, eclipsed the rest of them.

Hold on to them. Never forget.

In a strange way, Eshtak reminded Amicus of Vonah. Like him, she'd been a collector of things too. She'd kept a box under her bed that contained all sorts of things she'd found while fishing along the Solas River and exploring the roads and alleys of Solasportus.

An image of Vonah and Vorene embracing each other as they passed into death filled his mind again. Amicus wept.

My precious little girl. How will I go on without you? You brought such light into my life and a smile to every face that laid eyes on you. Now you share your light with our Creator, Ʒäṭūr. I miss you so much. And your mother too. Take care of them, Ʒäṭūr, until I find my way home to them and to You.

Two arms wrapped around Amicus's chest from behind him and embraced him. Despite knowing the impossibility of it, for an instant he thought it to be Vonah. He opened his eyes and stared down at the four-fingered hands. He placed his hands over Eshtak's and gave them a squeeze.

"Thank you, Eshtak." Amicus wiped the tears from his eyes. "I needed that more than you could know."

"Eshtak friend of Amicus. Eshtak not like friend hurt." Eshtak walked around Amicus and put his hand out to help Amicus up. Tears wet his cheeks, but he didn't try to wipe them away.

Amicus grabbed Eshtak's hand, and Eshtak pulled him to his feet. Amicus wiped the last remnants of his tears on his sleeves. "Are you ready to go, my little friend?"

Eshtak smiled and patted the limp, brown, cloth sack he'd slung over his shoulder. "Eshtak ready." His lime-green eyes glowed even brighter in the torchlight.

Amicus couldn't help but laugh. "Of all the things you've collected, that's your favorite? An empty, brown bag?"

Eshtak shook his head and giggled with a snort. "Eshtak bring everything."

Amicus scratched his head and frowned. "Everything? You've lost me, little man."

Eshtak grabbed Amicus's hand and dragged him toward the hidden room. Amicus reached back and snatched the torch from the sconce on the wall. The two of them squeezed through the narrow opening and into the small room.

Amicus gasped and stepped back. When he'd seen the room before, it'd been full, from front to back and top to bottom. This time, only two things occupied the room: him and Eshtak.

He looked down at Eshtak. "You've stolen my breath and confounded me, Eshtak. What did you do with it all? Can you use mezhik?"

Eshtak shook his head vigorously, beamed up at Amicus, and patted his cloth sack again. "Eshtak bring everything."

Amicus's eyes widened, and his eyebrows lifted. "You're telling me that you managed to shove everything from this room into that empty bag?"

Eshtak nodded vigorously. "Eshtak did. Bag not empty."

Amicus eyed the limp bag. *Impossible.*

Mezhik.

"Eshtak show friend?" He hopped from one foot to the other.

A sense of youthfulness fluttered in Amicus's stomach. "Yes, yes. How could I resist?"

Eshtak dropped to his knees, slung the bag on the floor, loosened its drawstrings, and spread its top wide. A dim light emanated from the open bag. He looked up at Amicus and grinned wide.

Amicus handed the torch to Eshtak and knelt next to the bag. His palms dampened, and his heart raced. A tinge of fear rose in his throat like a lump of half-swallowed food. He stared at the open bag.

What are you waiting for? Something to leap out of it?

"Look, look, look," squealed Eshtak. He jumped up and twirled in circles with the torch. The tiny room spun with shadows and light.

Amicus rubbed his palms on his trousers then grabbed the sides of the bag's top. He drew a deep breath and held it as he plunged his head inside the bag. His eyes adjusted to the dim light, and he stared down at an expansive cave that stretched beyond his vision.

Dear Ɂäṭūr!

Amicus exhaled and drew another breath. The rank scent of dead fish and mildew burned his nostrils and soured his mouth, but he couldn't pull his head from the bag—not because he physically couldn't, but because his mind refused to comprehend what his eyes showed him: piles and piles of shiny things everywhere.

A dragon's treasure. Had Eshtak gathered it all, or had someone else?

From deep within the cave, beyond his sight, the sound of crashing waves emanated, battering his ears and rocking his head to and fro. Bile rose in Amicus's throat. He pulled his head from the bag and gasped, but the dungeon air only enhanced his nausea. He sat back on his heels and closed his eyes until the feeling subsided.

Eshtak grabbed the bag's drawstrings, yanked them tight, and flung the bag over his shoulder. "Eshtak keep everything."

Amicus stood. His vision darkened, and his legs quivered, but he remained upright. *Steady me, Ɂäṭūr.*

Eshtak took Amicus's hand and peered up at him.

Amicus forced a smile. "You never cease to amaze me, my little friend." He rubbed Eshtak's bald head with his free hand. "Let's get out of here before the dungeons become our tombs."

Together, hand-in-hand, they walked out of the dungeons, up the stairs, and into the courtyard above. The crisp air, still teeming with smoke, smelled like a dream. The setting sun fell behind the eastern wall of the castle—the only wall left standing—and enshrouded the five of them under its foreboding shadow.

Amicus shook with a chill. "I don't know where we're staying tonight, but I don't want it to be here."

"Neither do I," said Rayah. "This place is a graveyard now."

"Then let's move," growled Rakzar. "We can find some shelter and warmth north of the valley, in the Veridis Forest. We'll be safe there."

Alderan reached over his shoulder, grabbed at the air, and sighed. "We'd be safer if we had more weapons than just your battle-axes."

Rakzar scoffed. "So that you can shoot your girlfriend again? Sounds like a perfect plan."

"Enough," said Amicus. "None of us will survive if we don't find a way to work together. Like it or not, we need each other right now."

Rakzar turned and glared at Amicus. "Speak for yourself, Shadowman. I've survived my entire life on my own. What makes you think I need any of you now?"

Amicus glared back at Rakzar. "One word: *Murtag.*"

Rakzar tensed and slashed the air with his claws. "That filthy, overgrown boar will be dead soon enough."

Rayah levitated and fluttered over to Amicus's side. "Who's Murtag?"

Rakzar clenched his jaw. "Stay out of it, dryte. He's no concern of yours." He turned and walked several paces.

"Clearly hit a sore spot," said Rayah.

"Everything that's happened has been at the hand of Murtag," said Amicus. "He's only taking orders, as Rakzar did, but that doesn't lessen his responsibility in what's happened. My family's dead because of him. My friends. He's taken nearly everything from me."

Rayah smacked her open palm with a fist. "Then let's do something about it."

Amicus smiled, appreciative of Rayah's fire. He looked over at Alderan. The boy stared at the valley below, but Amicus guessed his thoughts lingered well beyond the focus of his eyes.

We've all lost so much. How much more will we lose before we meet our ends?

Several paces ahead, Eshtak danced and skipped around in circles. His new brown cloak billowed behind him like a flag in the wind, and his brown cloth sack twirled around his arm by its drawstrings.

Amicus shook his head. *So much for the reprieve of exposed manhood.*

Repeatedly, Eshtak sang his song:

> *Swords and knives and bows with strings,*
> *These are all my favorite things.*
> *Slash and stab and shoot to kill,*
> *All these things are such a thrill!*

Amicus walked over to Eshtak, bent down on one knee, grabbed ahold of Eshtak's arm as he twirled by, and brought Eshtak to a halt. "Do you have weapons in that bag of yours, Eshtak? Is that what you're singing about?"

"Are you blind?" said Rakzar. "The sack's clearly empty."

Eshtak bounced on his heels, and his thin, black lips curled into a smile. "Eshtak has weapons. Lots of weapons."

Amicus released Eshtak's arm and stood. "Would you mind sharing a few of them with the rest of us?"

Eshtak's face brightened. "Eshtak likes sharing! Eshtak share with friends."

Eshtak dropped the sack on the ground and spread it open as wide as the drawstrings would allow. He shed his brown cloak, lifted the opening of the sack, and stuck his head inside.

"Looks like the sack's eating the naked little man," said Rakzar.

Alderan laughed. "Or giving birth to him."

Rayah giggled. "The full moon's early. Tides will be really high."

Amicus looked to the heavens and smiled. *Thank You for showing us humor in such a dark time, Ɂäṯūr. You always know just what we need and provide accordingly.*

With a few grunts and several shakes of his rump, Eshtak shimmied himself all the way into the sack. The sack slackened and fell flat against the ground.

Alderan bent down next to the sack and patted it. "How in the—"

The sack moved, and Alderan pulled his hand back. A long, wide, dark-brown leather scabbard slid from the sack's opening. Amicus reached down, picked up the scabbard, pulled the iron-forged broadsword from it, and examined it. A nick, just beyond the cross-hilt, marred the otherwise perfect blade.

Amicus's hands trembled, and moisture formed in the corner of his eye. He used his shirtsleeve to wipe his eye. "I believe this was Brently's sword."

"Brently?" asked Rayah.

Amicus turned and stared at the carcass of Castle Portador Tempestade. "One of my fellow guardsmen. Lost to the fire, I'm sure. He was a good man. Peace be on his soul."

Amicus sighed. *And on all of ours.*

He turned back to Alderan. "He's the one who helped me save Aria. Without his help, she'd probably be dead."

Alderan rose, moved around the bag, and stood next to Amicus. "By wielding his sword, you'll bring honor to his name." He squeezed Amicus's forearm.

"And justice," said Amicus, his voice quavering.

Amicus slid the sword back into its scabbard, pulled the belt straps around his waist, and tied them in a knot. The sword hung at his left side, the hilt just above his waist and the tip of the scabbard about ten inches from the ground—a perfect fit.

Amicus pointed down at the brown cloth sack. "I believe that weapon may suit your needs, Alderan."

A recurve bow and quiver full of arrows lay on the ground just beyond the sack's opening. Alderan reached down and picked up the quiver. He placed his left arm through the strap, lifted the quiver over his head, and let the strap rest on his right shoulder. He reached over his right shoulder with his right hand and pulled an arrow from the quiver.

Alderan examined the bare-shafted arrow. "This arrow's like nothing I've ever seen before." He ran his fingers down its length. "There's no fletching, and the shaft's made of a metal I can't place. It's so light. And the arrowhead—" Alderan passed the arrow to Amicus. "—have you ever seen anything like it?"

Amicus turned the silver shaft between his thumb and fingers and examined the three-inch-long, tri-bladed metal arrowhead. Its black, hinged blades protruded slightly from the diameter of the shaft, a design he'd never encountered before. He surmised the blades would expand after the arrow met its target, inflicting greater damage and increasing difficulty in its removal.

Amicus handed the arrow back to Alderan. "Those are definitely unique and dangerous. Be careful with them."

Alderan nodded, returned the arrow to his quiver, and picked up the roughly five-foot-long recurve bow. "Whoa... This is as light as the arrow. Maybe lighter."

The bow, a melding of bronzed metal and stag wood, gleamed in the fading sunlight. Alderan strung the bow, drew the string from its nocking point, and loosed an imaginary arrow.

Alderan shook his head and smiled. "I don't think I could've made a better-fitting bow myself." He handed the bow to Amicus.

Amicus examined the bow. A thread of gold, intricately woven in knotted patterns, stretched the length of its lower and upper limbs. He placed his right hand around its obsidian grip—it fit perfectly inside his large hand. Just above the arrow rest, on the inner curve of the upper limb, two words were inscribed in white gold: *Birzär Drezhn*.

Amicus handed the bow back to Alderan. "There are two words inscribed on it, but I don't know their meaning."

Alderan scrunched up his face as he studied the words. "They're lost on me as well."

Rayah fluttered over to Alderan's side and leaned close to the bow. "I've never seen the first word, but the second one is familiar. *Drezhn*—I believe it means *'Dragon.'*"

Alderan narrowed his eyes. "*Drezhn...*"

Amicus glanced over his shoulder and took in the towering Procerus Mountains just to the southwest of them. He shook his head. *Orcs, gnolls, and now dragons. What else lurks around the bend?* From the moment he'd discovered Vonah and Vorene huddled together in a statue of ash, his wonder of the world diminished, and the place he'd called home his entire life morphed into one unrecognizable.

The brown cloth sack lying on the ground hemorrhaged, and Amicus, Rayah, and Alderan stepped clear of it. Its mouth opened wide, and Eshtak crawled out of it and stood.

Eshtak clenched a six-inch silver dagger between his teeth and clutched a pair of tan leather gloves and a tan leather belt with five throwing knives in his right hand. A newly-acquired brown leather belt hung loosely from his bare waist. He took the dagger from between his teeth and slipped it into the leather frog attached to his belt. Oddly, the frog looked amphibious with its dark-green sheen.

Eshtak skipped over to Rayah, handed her the gloves and belt with the throwing knives, and smiled wide. "Eshtak gives best weapons to girl."

Rayah strapped on the belt. "You're too kind, Eshtak." She kissed the top of Eshtak's bald head.

Eshtak's cheeks reddened—a stark contrast from his pasty white complexion. "Eshtak likes girl."

Amicus and Alderan laughed.

Rayah slid the gloves on and balled her hands several times. "So soft and comfortable. Warm too."

She reached toward the belt, and one of the knives slid from its sheath and into her open hand. She squealed and fluttered backward.

Alderan grabbed Rayah's arm. "Are you okay? Did the knife cut you?"

She stared at her gloved hands. "No, but these gloves must have some sort of mezhik. The nominal shock caught me off guard."

"Mezhik shocks you?" asked Amicus.

Rayah shrugged a shoulder. "Sort of, but more like the feeling of a wool blanket when you pick it up—the static energy it produces."

Alderan pushed his hair behind his ears. "For me, mezhik tingles like your arm does when it has fallen asleep and is waking back up."

Rakzar returned to the group. "Blah, blah, blah. Now that we've all got weapons, can we break up this gossip circle and get moving before the sun is rising again in the west?"

Amicus frowned. *He sure knows how to spoil a moment—and the air.*

Amicus bowed his head. *Ɂäṭūr, forgive me. That wasn't a nice thing to think.*

Alderan swept his arm toward the valley. "Well then, lead the way Rakzar."

Amicus stood there as the others followed Rakzar through the maze of rubble and toward the valley. *Can I do this, Ɂäṭūr? Can I walk through the valley of the shadow of death?*

No, it's not a shadow anymore. This valley is death.

Amicus drew in a deep breath. Filled with angst, he exhaled and followed the others.

Give me strength, Ɂäṭūr.

Dusk settled over the valley's expanse and blended in with the dark smoke that lingered. Amicus drew his coat over his mouth and nose, and the thought of his family suffering through it gave him pause once more.

A lone, mournful cry rose from the valley below. Amicus stopped mid-stride and listened intently. Moments—perhaps minutes—ticked by in silence.

Amicus swallowed hard and choked on his own saliva. *A survivor?* His heart thundered in his ears and his pulse raced. Beads of sweat formed on his brow and his nape. Wracked by grief over the loss of Vorene and Vonah, had he forgotten to search for survivors? A dense fog clouded his memories.

Amicus squeezed his head between his hands. How many lives were lost because he'd failed to act? The question crushed him and forced him to his knees. Both smoke and guilt stung his eyes, and he trembled.

Dear Ɂäṭūr. "I... I can't remember." Amicus leaned over and dry-heaved.

Alderan halted and turned back toward Amicus. "Remember what?"

Amicus shivered and rubbed his shoulders. "Survivors. I don't think I looked for any."

Another cry rose from the valley.

"There!" Amicus sprang to his feet, raced past Alderan, caught up with the others, pushed past them, and rushed down the steep slope with abandon. "I'm coming!"

CHAPTER SEVEN

Calen stood outside the front door of Savric's house, pushing leaves around with the tip of his boot while he waited for the old wizard to return. He hummed a song about drinking, fighting, and women—three things he knew very little about. The catchy tune had been stuck in his head for weeks, one of his Aunt Tahmara's favorites.

Nothing interesting ever happened in Daltura, but today had proven exceptional. He'd met a new person, witnessed some mezhik he'd never seen before, and taken part in a secret quest. He didn't know what role he'd played in the quest, but just being part of it felt spectacular.

A perfect day.

Every day he spent time with Savric was an exceptional one. To Calen, Savric was the kind of man he wished his own father would've been, and the grandfather he'd never known.

Calen heard the *tap* of Savric's staff against the foot stones well before Savric turned the corner and strolled up the front walk. Calen kicked the leaves away and stepped to the side, allowing Savric room to get to the door.

Calen sniffed and wiped his nose on his shirtsleeve. "Master Savric, I was starting to wonder if you were ever coming back."

Savric beamed at Calen, his blue eyes gleaming behind wire-framed spectacles, and his wrinkled skin drawn tight over bony, rosy cheeks. It warmed Calen's heart like a cup of hot cocoa on a cold day. "You did well, my boy."

Calen wiped at his nose again. "Thank you, sir."

Savric's front door swung open on its own, and Calen grinned. He never tired of the simple use of mezhik. Savric walked through the open door and into the house, and Calen followed him. Calen turned and watched the door close itself.

Calen stared at the door. He set his jaw and furrowed his brow and willed it to open again, but the door made no attempt to move. Not even a wiggle. He pointed his finger at the door. "One day, you'll listen to me."

Calen turned around and faced the room. "When you gonna teach me mezhik, Master Savric?"

Savric chuckled as he settled into his favorite rocking chair next to the fireplace. "If it were a possibility, my boy, I would have started teaching you long ago."

Calen walked over to the hearth and plopped down on the floor, facing Savric.

Savric waved his hand at the fireplace. *"Ɂäƫ äbəlläíz."*

Calen turned and watched as the parchment stuffed between the cracks and crevasses of the wood began smoking and then burst into flames. A minute later, the fire blazed and pumped out much-needed heat.

The burkwood timber's sweet maple aroma bloomed in the room. Calen breathed deep through his nostrils, savoring the scent. *Like smelling winter.*

Calen stared into the flames. "I feel like I wasn't made complete. Maybe I was taken from my mother's womb too soon. You know, before I was given the ability to use mezhik."

Savric chuckled. "My boy, there are far greater things in life than wielding mezhik. Ɂäƫūr handcrafted each one of us individually, down to the last hair on our heads, to be unique. No two of us are alike, and that means we are all special in our own way.

"Just because you cannot open a door with your mind or start a fire with a flick of your wrist only means that you have a different talent. You are a kind young boy, and that is saying something considering the tepid and demoralized state of our society. You may not know what your talent is yet, but it will certainly manifest, given time.

"You might wind up being an advisor to the king or a world-renowned chef. Perhaps you will become a great husband and father. Maybe you will grow into a mighty warrior and save the world, or you will lead others when all seems lost. You are still young, my boy. There is plenty of time for you to grow into whatever you are meant to be."

Leading others? Maybe I could, but how?

"I suppose anything is possible." Calen twirled his finger in his ear and continued staring into the flames. "Who was that man today, Master Savric? Is he someone important?"

"Important…" The *squeak* of Savric's chair rubbing against the wooden floor filled the silence as he rocked back and forth.

Calen looked up at Savric, whose eyes focused somewhere beyond the room. "Master Savric?"

Savric's eyes came back to life, and he looked down at Calen. "I cannot be certain as to the identity of the tall man, but I can be of his intentions. Aria, the girl who was with him, is my goddaughter. I fear what he might do to her and what she might become under his influence.

"Many prophecies surround her and her brother, and the paths between them are troubling. Fulfilling one path in one prophecy—for the greater good—brings another path of prophecy to fruition that could potentially be far worse. Reverse them, and the paths still point toward a horrific future for us all."

Calen's pulse raced, and he sat up straight. "Are there prophecies about me?"

Sitting in his chair, Savric seemed to have aged many years over the last few minutes. He slumped against the arm rests, his shoulders raised to his ears, and the lines in his face had deepened like ruts in the road. Great sorrow filled his blue eyes and extinguished the twinkle they normally possessed.

Savric pulled at his beard. "Only in some cases are names mentioned in prophecy, my boy. Most of them only provide a vague reference to a place and time, rarely with people involved."

Calen sighed, lay back on the floor, and stared up at the pitched ceiling. "I thought so. I'm just a fat kid. There's nothing special about me, is there?"

The *squeak* of Savric's chair ceased, and Calen cringed, knowing what would come next.

"Look at me." The tone in Savric's voice demanded Calen's attention.

Guilt rose in Calen's chest. He reluctantly looked up at Savric. "I'm sorry, Master Savric."

Savric leaned forward in his chair, his brow furrowed. Fire replaced the sorrow he'd held in his eyes moments before. "I do not associate with people who are not *special*."

"No, sir." Calen wanted to look away but thought better of it.

Savric shook his finger at Calen. "You are *not* in that category. There are things in your life yet to come that will set you apart from those around you. You *are* special, my boy. Mark my words."

Calen squinted his left eye and wrinkled his forehead as he sat back up. "How so? What do you know about me? My father always told me that I was worthless. I figured he knew me as good as anyone. He said I'm the reason my mother died and the reason he drank and beat me. If I hadn't killed her, he wouldn't have been a drunk."

The makings of tears glistened in Savric's eyes. He put his hand on Calen's shoulder and squeezed. "My boy, your father was a drunk and beat your mother well before you were ever born."

Calen trembled and stared at the floor. "Then why do I always feel so guilty about it? I feel responsible for her death."

Savric sat back in his chair again and started rocking. "The night you were born, while your mother was in labor with you, he nearly beat her to death because she made too much noise. When you were only four, he finished the job. That is why he sits in a cell, rotting away. You have no blame in the matter. None."

Calen shook his head. "If I hadn't been born then maybe she'd still be alive."

"The past should only be used as a learning tool, not to dwell on what happened or what could have happened. You must understand that none of it was your fault, my boy. You are a wonderful young man, and you bring me joy with every visit."

Savric wiped his eyes. "Look at what you did today. You helped me get a message to someone I have not seen in years. Had you not informed me that a wizard had arrived in town, I would have missed the opportunity. Furthermore, if you had not been born, none of it would have been possible."

Calen fingered the head of a nail protruding from the floor. "I guess I can see that."

"Calen, think of all the things you have done in your life. Every choice you have made since you were born has altered the world in some way. You *are* significant. Never doubt that.

"Ʒäʈūr does not make anyone insignificant. People choose to be so. You will find your purpose. You will continue to be great, just as you already have been. I promise you that, my boy."

Am I really not worthless? Will I truly be great one day? The thought of being great seemed as likely as him waking up with mezhik.

Calen sighed. "I suppose I'll just have to wait and see."

Savric chuckled. "As do we all, my boy. Now, run home to your aunt before she comes looking for you."

Calen slowly pulled himself up from the floor, reluctant to leave the warmth of the fire and Savric's company. "Yes, sir." He put his hand on Savric's shoulder. "Have a good evening, Master Savric."

Savric reached up and squeezed the top of Calen's hand. "You too, my boy. Make sure you tell Tahmara I said hello."

Calen pulled his hand from Savric's, walked over to the front door, and turned around. "Will I see you tomorrow?"

Savric looked back at him. "Of course. A day without you around is like a day wasted. I expect you will stop by after school?"

Calen sighed again. "I'd rather just come here straightaway in the morning."

Savric frowned. "You may one day need some of the skills they teach you in school. Now be a good boy and run along. And shut the door on your way out. It will not shut itself, you know." He winked at Calen.

Calen smiled and showed himself out the door. He didn't shut it, though. Instead, he stood there and waited to see it shut itself. A moment later, the door obliged, slamming itself with a bang. The lock engaged with a *click*.

He chuckled, walked out to the road, and started making his way home. His stomach growled like an angry dog. *I wonder what we're having for dinner. I hope it's biscuits and gravy.*

† † †

Savric sat back in his chair at the table and contemplated the events that had unfolded. Seeing Aria after so many years brought tears to his eyes.

She'd transformed into such a beautiful young woman.

Gretchen would have been proud of her.

Savric wished he could've sat with Aria and made sure everything was okay, but he knew the wizard would return at any moment, and the risk of getting caught was too great.

At least he'd left Aria a note. He was certain she'd know its meaning. Yet even doing that much had been risky. He'd placed a spell on the paper that would make the words disappear a few seconds after she opened it. He hoped she'd read the note before the wizard had returned.

Ɂäbräᴈär—the archaic, barbaric silver collar locked around her neck—drove his blood pressure higher. He'd give just about anything to wrap one of them around that wizard's neck.

I wonder what that wretched man told her of it.

Every day that'd passed over the last decade pained him like a thorn in his side. He bore the pain in knowing the events and trials Aria and Alderan would face, but his pain paled in comparison to the agony those events and trials would cause the two of them.

Every waking moment, he wrestled with the temptation of rescuing them from their fate, but he knew the consequence of doing so outweighed his desire. Everything they'd suffered through pretzeled his stomach.

Savric was their godfather and sworn protector, yet he felt helpless to defend them from their fate. Neither knew of his existence, but it had to be that way for their safety. What he would've given to be in their lives, though—to have watched them grow into the young adults they'd become.

Savric wiped a tear from his eye.

Why did it need to be this way, Ɂäṭūr? Why must the fate of the entire world hinge on two children? I fear it is too much for them to bear.

Savric sighed. "All I can do is pray and hope for the best for them both."

"Both of whom?"

Savric looked over his shoulder. Qotan stood in the doorway to the kitchen. His hair looked disheveled—more so than normal—and dirt and mud caked his forest-green robes. "Never mind that, brother. What kind of mischief have you been up to?"

Qotan's green eyes sparkled in the firelight. "The usual kind. The incident earlier led me down to the root cellar. Were you aware that far more items are growing down there than just roots?"

Savric smiled sheepishly. "Oh?"

"Seems as though someone has found it a fitting place to plant a garden." Qotan rubbed his chin and pulled at a rogue hair. "And, although the cellar receives no sunlight, it has grown into a jungle."

Savric chuckled. "I am at a loss as to how that garden may have come into existence. And just below our noses. That is curious, brother."

Qotan raised his hands. "Curious, indeed. I daresay I found myself lost for nearly two hours down there."

"As riveting a tale as that is, were you able to discern the cause of the quake?"

Qotan smiled wide. "Indeed. Our friend Speckles was more than happy to be of service. With his help, I gained access deep within the ground."

"Amazing, those moles are," Savric quipped. "Nary a lick of sight, yet they see everything."

"Colors may be indistinguishable to them, but they are far from being blind. Less so than you, perhaps?"

"As of late, I am inclined to agree with your jab at my ocular deterioration."

Qotan's smile faded. "The infestation is severe. Less than 300 meters below the surface the ground has begun rotting. The stench and filth exceeded anything I have experienced before. Soon, I fear, it will surround us as the decay begins to surface."

In his mind, Savric saw some of the words from the prophecy of *Ꜣʈōn Dhef Dädh*:

"In the beginning of the last days, when Ꜣʈōn Dhef Dädh has been removed from its place within Ṭämball Dhef Däd Dhä and brought into the light, the core of the world will begin rotting. From that point in time there are two paths, each devastating and with little hope."

Savric leaned back in his chair and closed his eyes. "I feared what you would find today, brother. Seems as though I had good reason."

"Indeed. We can no longer sit aside and watch the events as they unfold. We must rise and prepare for what is coming. We must find the boy and train him."

The book. Rayah.

Savric opened his eyes and sat up in his chair. "There is no need to find Alderan, brother. I know right where he is. I must contact Rayah and have her take him to Zerenity."

Qotan stepped into the room and sat in the chair on the opposite side of the table. Lines of concern marked his forehead. "Zerenity? The sorceress? Can *we* not train the boy?"

Savric rose to his feet. His old bones cracked with protest. "You know as well as I that we lack the proper knowledge to train him. Our mezhik abilities are limited compared to the power he will possess."

Qotan rubbed his chin. "If he is the one you claim him to be then I concede to that, but surely there is someone other than *her* who can train him."

"Despite any differences the two of you may have had in the past, you know she is the only one who can. It is her specialty."

Qotan raised an eyebrow. "'*Differences?*' That is what you are labeling it now? Indeed. Those *differences* nearly cost me everything."

Savric moved over to the fireplace and warmed his hands. "You and your flair for the dramatic, brother. Perhaps you should have studied theater."

"Indeed. Now, I would like to meet the boy. I want to know whose shoulders the fate of this world rests upon."

Savric leaned from side to side, trying to loosen up his stiff back. "Rest assured, brother, we will meet the young boy there."

"And where is this '*there?*'"

"Zerenity's. It is time to see an old friend."

Qotan grimaced. "An old friend, *indeed*. You know, I have felt a touch of frailty as of late. Perhaps I will accompany you to meet this boy another time. Tyrosha is a long way for an old man to travel with a condition such as mine."

Savric turned around and smiled mischievously. "By ordinary means, yes. But we have the *other* way, brother."

Qotan stood to meet Savric's gaze. "Indeed, we do. Even so, I believe I will bow out of this adventure."

Savric scowled at Qotan. "How odd it is that you suffer from an insurmountable number of *conditions* at the most opportunistic of times?"

Qotan frowned, grumbled incoherently, sighed loudly, and finally waved his hand around. "Oh, very well. I shall accompany you, but I will not enjoy it."

"I suspect not." Savric smiled and then walked over to the built-in bookcase to the left of the fireplace. He pulled out a leather-bound book and returned to the table with it. His bones cracked again as he settled down in his chair.

Qotan sat down in a chair on the other side of the table. "That book has *ʕäəll Dhef ʕäfn Dhä*. Where did you get that?"

Savric shrugged. "This book, along with its twin, was given to me so long ago I hardly remember the circumstance." He waved his hand over the book. "*In əllíṭ Hiz.*" He opened it.

"The Great War…" Qotan scratched his chin.

Savric nodded. "Precisely, brother. This very book was used to send secret messages to the allies of *Ūrdär Dhef ʕäfn Dhä.*" Savric pulled out a fountain pen from within an inner pocket of his robes.

Qotan leaned on the edge of the table and stroked his chin. "Until this very day I thought I knew my brother as I do my own heart. Now I feel as though a stranger sits across the table from me, wearing my brother's clothes and his baggy old skin. Who are you, and what has become of my brother?"

Savric chuckled. "I am no different today than I was yesterday or the day before, only older. Perhaps you have become complacent and less observant with age. I have been communicating through this book for many years now."

Qotan tapped the table with his finger. "What other things have you been keeping from me?"

"I keep no secrets from you, brother. You need only be more observant." Savric tapped the page with the tip of his pen, and words began forming on the page. He looked up at Qotan, who stared at the page as though he'd never seen mezhik before.

Qotan sat back in his chair and yawned. "I can only fathom the complexity of the mezhik that went into creating those books. To have lived in a time such as those would have been exhilarating."

Savric chuckled. "Very true, brother, and deadly."

"Indeed. Could you imagine trying to outrun a dragon?"

"Not even in the peak of my youth."

Qotan pulled a long pipe from within his robes and set it on the table.

Savric's jaw slackened, and he sat back in his chair.

Qotan's face brightened with glee, and he winked at Savric. "I have secrets of my own."

Savric scowled and waved a hand at Qotan. "Take that contraption outside if you plan on smoking it. No sense in permeating the house with the smell of tobacco."

Qotan scoffed. "Tobacco is for the masses. What I have here would make your head spin. And the aroma is truly wondrous."

Savric glared at Qotan. "I need no remedy to get my head spinning, brother. It spins just fine on its own. Now take that contraption outside before you light it up and burn the whole place down."

Qotan yawned again and closed his eyes. "I believe this day has worn me down too far to find my feet again. I will save the smoking for the morning."

"Glad to hear." Savric looked down at the words on the page. He blinked several times to clear his vision, hoping he'd misread them, but they held fast.

He read them again: *'I cannot do what you've asked of me. My heart won't let me betray him again. I love him too much. You must find another way. -Rayah'*

Savric's stomach lurched. "Feathers! My dear brother—" His voice trembled, and he choked on the rest of his words.

"Have you seen a spectre, brother? Or have you become one? The color in your face has abandoned you."

Savric stared at the page before him, distraught and unable to respond.

How can her words be true? Especially at a time like this. The fate of the world rests in her hands. She knows this.

Qotan rose to his feet. "Brother?"

Savric closed his eyes and squeezed the bridge of his nose between his thumb and finger. *She knows the plan. She knows the cost of its failure. How can this be true? How could she do this?*

A hand squeezed Savric's shoulder. The touch pulled him from his thoughts. He looked up and into the steady green eyes of Qotan. Any other time, the man's smile would've warmed him, but those words had chilled him deep into his bones.

Qotan lifted the book from the table, and his eyes scanned the page. The color drained from his face, and he snapped the book shut. "Dear Ƨäṭūr."

Savric rubbed his eyes. "We are in deep trouble, brother. The entire world is."

"Why would she do this? Does she not know the whole truth? How can she be so blinded? Love is no excuse!" Qotan slammed the book down on the table and returned to his chair. He grabbed the pipe from the table, shoved the end of it in his mouth, and gnawed it between his teeth.

Savric exhaled deeply. "I believe this is all my fault, brother. I limited Rayah's knowledge to information I thought pertinent. I did not foresee this outcome."

Qotan pulled the pipe from his mouth and held it between his thumb and forefinger. "The information she *needed*? Please explain what that means, dear brother. You did convey the utmost of importance in her delivery of him at the appropriate time, did you not? And the reason for it?"

"I never thought it pertinent. I told her to keep her distance from him. I had no idea the two of them would become confluent. How would I have guessed that?"

Qotan banged the bowl of the pipe against the table. "Oh, you are right. A young girl falling in love with a young boy. Absolutely preposterous. The world has never seen such an event."

Savric looked at Qotan and shook his head. "I concede. Romantic relationships are not my strong point."

Qotan pulled himself up from his chair. "We must remedy this situation before it ventures beyond our control. If the girl will not deliver the boy, then we must. Without proper training, he is a danger to everyone around him."

Savric rose to his feet, and the fountain pen on his lap fell to the floor. "Yes, yes, I know. I was trying to protect her from the truth. I never told her to whom or for what reason the boy was to be delivered."

Qotan straightened his robes. "I pray your decision has not condemned us all, brother."

Savric took the book with Ɂäəll Dhef Ɂäfn Dhä from the table and placed it inside a pocket within his robes. "As do I." He bent down, grabbed the pen off the floor, and placed it back in his inner pocket.

He eyed Qotan and pulled at his beard. "We must return to where this all began. From there, we will find the boy."

Savric and Qotan each held out a hand, and their staffs flew into them.

"To the beginning!" Qotan smacked his staff's butt-end against the floor and disappeared in a whirlwind of dust.

Qotan had a certain, undeniably charming flair about him. Savric chuckled and then coughed from the stirred dust.

To the beginning, brother.

Savric smacked his staff against the floor and spun into the night.

CHAPTER EIGHT

Aria sat in the corner of the carriage seat with her knees drawn to her chest, consumed in darkness. Pravus's earlier behavior infuriated her. The fact that he'd used mezhik on her without her consent fanned the flames of her anger.

However, despite all the anger swirling through her mind, her thoughts kept circling back to the old man at the café.

Who was he? How did he know where to find me? How did he know about Alderan?

Why am I keeping this from Pravus? What difference would it make to him? He's never even met Alderan. Perhaps I should've told him everything.

But Pravus's anxiety put her on edge. She wasn't even sure what had set him off. Just before he'd run off to who knew where, everything had been normal.

Nothing's normal now. Where did he go? And why? Did he confront the person spying on us? Did he kill them? If he did, what did he do with the body? What do you do with a body? I suppose getting rid of a body is much easier for a wizard than a normal person.

Why am I even thinking about this?

Until the day she'd been taken captive, she didn't know she had the capacity to kill. But the moment those beasts took her father's life, she wanted nothing more. Revenge suited her, but it wasn't Ɂäțūr's way, was it? The satisfaction she'd garnered from it scared her.

We all wear disguises, some better than others, but underneath it all we are little more than savage beasts.

She loved the man sleeping on the seat across from her. He'd saved her life.

Or had it been Ɂäțūr? The more she contemplated the events in her life the more distant she felt to her Savior, ʕäṭūr.

Are You really out there watching over me? If You are, why have I felt so alone? Why don't You talk to me? Am I unworthy of You? Or do You not exist? If You do exist and You care about me then why did You let me suffer for so long? Why didn't You rescue me? Was it never part of Your plan? Do I mean nothing to You?

She no longer needed rescuing. She'd proven she could take care of herself. The zhebəllin that had attacked her in the Daltura Hills stood no chance against her. Once she learned how to wield her mezhik, nothing would ever stand in her way again. *Even Pravus will bend to my will. Even now, without mezhik, he's clay in my hands.*

She drew her arms in as a chill washed over her.

What am I thinking? I know You exist, ʕäṭūr. You must. Otherwise, I'd be dead by now.

She pushed all the thoughts from her mind and focused on the piece of paper the old man had left in her lap at the café. In her mind's eye, the two words shone as clear as day: *He lives!*

She couldn't deny the meaning of those two words, could she? How could they not be about Alderan? Then again, maybe they weren't about him at all. But if not him, then who?

Amicus? Absurd.

She had no reason to believe that he'd been in danger to begin with. Besides, Pravus had ensured her that Amicus and his family lived.

My father?

A tear slid from her eye as she watched him die again. It certainly wasn't him.

Another thought struck her: *Sandcastles.*

Who was that man?

Her memories of him lingered at the fringe of recollection. In each of them, he'd felt like a father to her.

An uncle perhaps? Or a close friend of the family?

His identity eluded her.

Another tear slid down her cheek. The probability of Alderan being alive was slim. In fact, in her heart she knew he'd died. Before the night of the attack, his presence had always been with her, but she hadn't felt it since.

You're a fool, Aria. You know he's dead. He's been dead for a long time now. Bury him with the rest of your family and move on.

Her lower lip quivered. Could she? She must.

I'm sorry, Alderan. I'll always love you and will never forget you.

A sob escaped from her mouth, and she clamped her hand over it to keep silent, but she knew it was too late. She didn't need the ability to see in the dark to know that Pravus awoke and stared at her. She *felt* his eyes on her.

Pravus's voice filled the carriage. "I'm sorry, Aria. I'm not sure what came over me earlier. I didn't mean to scare you or press you. And I'm sorry I used mezhik on you without your consent. It's no excuse, but I didn't want to lose you, and I panicked. This kind of relationship is new to me. At times, I don't know what I'm doing. Truthfully, most of the time. Can you please forgive me?"

Should she? She must, but maybe stringing it out a bit would do him some good. "You hurt my feelings, Pravus. I don't deserve to be accused of lying or pressed for answers like a common thief. I'm your future queen and deserve to be treated as such."

Pravus cracked his knuckles. "You're right, my queen. I was out of line. I swear I saw something in your eyes, though. You're certain I was mistaken?"

Aria's pulse quickened, and her palms moistened with sweat. She didn't want to keep secrets from him, but, for a reason she couldn't identify, telling him the truth felt wrong. If they'd sat in the light, she would've told him everything, but the darkness that filled the space between them comforted her.

A quote her mother Gretchen instilled upon her and Alderan rose from the depths of her memories: *"In the darkness, seeds of evil are sewn, but in the light, no evil shall escape detection. —The Book of Truths"*

"I'm certain. Why would I keep anything from you?" The lie lingered on her tongue like soured milk, and she swallowed it down.

"I believe you," he said. "We'll speak of it no more."

Despite the sincerity in his voice, Aria *knew* Pravus didn't believe her. She couldn't explain *how* she knew, but she did. Then again, maybe it was her guilty conscience trying to justify her own deceit.

It's just one lie, Ɂäṭūr. I'll tell him no more.

"Good." She slid down in the seat, stretched her legs out, and closed her eyes. "I think I'll rest my eyes a bit longer."

"As you wish."

✝ ✝ ✝

Despite his company, Pravus felt trapped inside the dark carriage. With every passing minute, the walls moved closer, and the ceiling lowered. He hadn't traveled such a distance by carriage since he'd been a small boy. He never would again.

He'd used the ancient mirrors to get to Castle Portador Tempestade, but the risk of traveling back through them with Aria outweighed the convenience. Were they to travel through them, Aria's collar would have to be removed. He would take no such risk with his own life. She'd wear the collar until they wed and their souls joined, not a moment before.

Her petite frame belied the raw strength she possessed. In the dungeons, she'd killed several of Dragnus's men without the use of a weapon. How much stronger would she be wielding mezhik? Never could he have groomed such a perfect match for himself.

Pravus shook his head and smiled. *We will be unstoppable.*

Pravus reached down, retrieved the diary from his leather satchel, and set it on his lap. He drew a deep breath and pushed the air through his nostrils. The events of the past week wore on him, and he needed some good news.

He opened the diary to the first page and withdrew a fountain pen from within one of the hidden pockets of his robes. Across from him, Aria seemed nothing more than a deeper shadow sprawled out on the seat. He needed more light to penetrate the deep darkness of the night.

Pravus set the pen on the open book and held out his arms, hands cupped together and palms up. *"Ɂllíṭ ʊb."* A small orb of reddish-white light—about six centimeters in diameter—formed just above his palms.

He lifted the orb just above and in front of his head, and its light illuminated the inside of the entire carriage with a red tint. He lowered his hands, and the orb held its position in the air. Across from him, Aria groaned, pulled a blanket over herself, and rolled onto her side, facing the back of her seat and away from Pravus.

My beautiful queen. What are you keeping from me?

Pravus thought of a spell that would allow him to enter Aria's mind and reach down into her memories. He'd used it just once before, but the spell had proven extremely dangerous. The woman he'd used it on went mad and threw herself from a cliff.

Mother. He chuckled quietly.

Aria's importance far outweighed any information he might gain from using such a spell on her. Besides, he wasn't completely certain she'd lied to him. Given her truthful nature, if she *had* lied, she wouldn't be able to keep it from him for long.

I'll wait you out, my queen.

Pravus moved his foot and kicked the crumpled piece of paper on the floor. He reached out, and the wadded paper flew into his hand.

Mezhik.

There had to be a way to reverse the spell that hid the message, right? It made perfect sense. He'd have to look through his spell books when they arrived at Atrum Moenia. He smoothed out the paper, folded it twice, and slid it into his satchel.

Pravus picked up the pen and tapped its tip against the first page of the diary—a blank one. Nothing happened, and Pravus scowled. He flipped to the second page and repeated the process, but that page stayed blank as well.

No news.

He sighed and closed the diary. He set the pen on the seat, leaned his head back, and stared at the orb of light suspended in the air. He scarcely remembered life before mezhik. The thought of living without it—being one of the *onzhiftäd*—left a bitter taste in his mouth.

The ungifted. Nothing but sheep. Mezhik is power.

All Pravus's knowledge of mezhik came from books, and, because of it, he had little grasp of the intricacies of the craft. Given a spell, he could cast it. But the skill required to invent mezhik surpassed his.

Pravus looked down at the diary sitting in his lap. The edges of its leather cover and binding were worn with centuries of use. How many hands had touched it over the years? He couldn't even begin to guess.

Unlike most items of mezhik, the diary contained no trace of it. The familiar signature of mezhik had been suppressed in it somehow. But how? A true wizard would have the knowledge to accomplish such a feat, but he was less than that.

Pravus clenched his jaw and gritted his teeth. *But not for long.*

Soul bound with Aria, he'd be unstoppable. Her power, his cunning. The perfect match. Foretold by prophecy. Fulfilled by destiny.

However, not everything in his plan had aligned.

Pravus grabbed the diary and twisted it in his hands. He wanted to rend it. Break its spine. He closed his eyes, frustrated. Many pieces of his plan had fallen into place, but the most significant one—the part that would allow him to resurrect his father's kingdom—lay beyond his reach. Without *Ɛṭōn Dhef Dädh*, nothing mattered.

Had he been foolish in placing his fate in the hands of a man like Nardus? *No. He's the only one capable of retrieving the stone.*

Pravus opened his eyes and stared at the diary. Premonition compelled him to open it again but not to the first or second page. No, he flipped over to the middle of the book—to the dog-eared page. He grabbed the pen from the seat and held its tip just above the blank page.

The dog-eared page—*the page*—had been blank for so many years. A message on it would change the world.

Could it be? Have we finally reached a major fork in prophecy?

The pen trembled in Pravus's hand.

Touch the page. Change the world. It's in your hands.

But what if I'm wrong?

I'll have lost nothing. But if I'm right...

Pravus stared at the page intently, held his breath, and let the tip of the pen caress the blank page. The sound of the contact—a small, nearly undetectable *tap*—thundered in his ears. His pulse raced, and anticipation beaded his skin with sweat.

He refused to blink—afraid to miss the world-changing event—, and his eyes burned. An eternity passed, and nothing happened. His small thread of hope dwindled with each heartbeat until nothing remained.

He blinked once. Twice.

He let the pen slip from his fingers and watched it bounce against the pure-white surface. Disappointment settled into his bones, and he blinked again, this time with an elongated pause.

His eyelids slid open, and his gaze penetrated the pure-white page, down to the individual fibers of its makeup. The page held less light than a moment before, didn't it? Every moment aged the page, and its color yellowed. Pravus held the book up to the orb of light he'd created. Never had the pages aged before.

Have I done something wrong?

Pravus gasped as a small pool of blood surfaced on the page. Slowly, the blood spread over the page, covering it completely, but it didn't spill over the edges. His hands trembled, and he dropped the book on his lap.

Blood seeped back into the yellowed parchment in large areas, leaving behind tendrils, squiggles, lines, and shapes. Then, the tendrils, squiggles, lines, and shapes began forming letters and words. A sentence. Two. Three.

Pravus's heart thundered as the entire message became clear: *'After all this time, it's finally happened. He's returned, and we have him. We have Nardus. -Iceberg'*

CHAPTER NINE

Being out at sea felt like home to Theyn, especially at night. She enjoyed gazing up at the sea of stars that filled the night sky and wondering what might be out there just waiting to be found. Did life exist beyond their world? She imagined so.

Tonight, though, the stars held no inspiration. After seeing herself die—feeling that dragon's claw skewer her like a fish—she couldn't shake the notion that her life held little significance. A deep hollowness filled her.

Her visions had never haunted her before, but none were like this one. Her pain in dying so vivid. Her essence—her *soul*—had detached from her body, and darkness had enveloped her. She'd never felt so alone or such complete despair. She didn't understand where death took her, but she never wanted to return there.

Where were you, Zhedäe ʒon?

The frigid sea air caressed Theyn's bare shoulders and sent gooseflesh crawling down her arms. She rubbed her shoulders with her hands, but the chill ran much deeper than her skin. She needed more than her own hands. She needed a partner. She needed the touch of a male—someone to curl up with.

She knew little of Nardus, and the shroud of mystery surrounding him intrigued and excited her. She knew men, though, their sexual nature and how to manipulate them to do her bidding. She needed to get *close* to him. To *understand* him. To *be* with him. He'd fill the emptiness inside her. She'd see to it.

Theyn grabbed the boat's railing with both hands and kneaded it with her long, sharp nails. She closed her eyes and purred like a cat.

Soon you'll be mine, Nardus.

Small whitecaps rocked the boat, sending her mind drifting back to her vision and the war they'd spoke of. Fear gripped her again. She'd experienced more than fear, though—deep-seeded emotions had driven her. Love and hope, but something more profound. Something she couldn't quite grasp. Perhaps something greater than her?

Nardus is right. Our futures are intertwined. For what purpose, though? More than the physical pleasure she sought?

In her vision, the obsidian dragon spoke of a daughter, but to whom and of whom had he spoken? She had no children. Even so, did the dragon allude to a child of hers? Both hers and Nardus's? She dismissed the idea, but it planted seeds of intrigue in the back of her mind.

Nardus.

Theyn knew nothing of Nardus's past, but the details held no relevance to her. She had no part in his past, but she'd make certain they would share a future together. Even if Nardus already had a wife or a lover, she didn't care. She would supplant them if necessary. Besides, she didn't need a life partner, and she'd be content sharing him, wouldn't she?

I will have you. Soon.

"What do you think you're doing, Theyn?"

Theyn sighed and opened her eyes. Berggren stood to her right. She turned and looked up at him. "Enjoying the night air, *father*."

Seldom did she call him that. She knew it made him uncomfortable when she did. He preferred her calling him "boss," but at times he needed a reminder of who he was to her.

Berggren set his right hand on the railing, next to hers. "I *saw* you, Theyn. I know what you're thinking, and I won't allow it. I know your *condition* and what it does to you, and I've always looked the other way, but this is different."

Theyn rolled her eyes and shook her head. "You know nothing of me, *father*. You've never understood me or accepted me as your daughter. If it hadn't been for Dhaldra, you would've left me to die when my father passed."

Berggren placed his left hand on Theyn's shoulder and squeezed lightly. "You know that's not true, Theyn. I love you more than *Zhedäz Zon*. You're the closest thing I've ever had to a daughter of my own. And you're only saying these things to distract me from the subject at-hand."

Theyn rolled her eyes again and turned toward the sea. "You don't know me as well as you think you do."

Berggren leaned against the railing. "I see everything concerning you, Theyn. You're my daughter. Nardus is a dangerous man, and we don't know what he's capable of. Lord Rosai warned us of him."

Theyn shrugged Berggren's hand off her shoulder. "You know I'm just as dangerous as he is. More so, perhaps."

"He *killed* Shaul. Is your memory so short you've already forgotten? Did Shaul mean so little to you?"

Theyn stared at the calm sea, but a violent storm brewed inside her and neared the point of breaking containment. "What do you want me to say, father? Shaul's death broke my heart? How could I possibly go on living without him? No. I will miss him, but I never loved him. How could I?"

Berggren sighed. "Maybe not, but he certainly loved you. You're the only reason he came with us to begin with."

Theyn turned to Berggren with steel in her eyes. "And now he's dead. Because of me. Is that what you're trying to say? His death's my fault?"

Berggren grabbed Theyn by the shoulders and pulled her into his massive chest. She tried to pull away from him, but her strength couldn't match his.

Theyn beat her fists against his sides. "Let me go!"

He wrapped one arm around her and stroked her head with his free hand. "Calm down, Theyn. I know you're a strong young woman, but you're not heartless. I *know* you cared for Shaul whether you'll admit it or not. It's okay to be upset. Angry even. But please don't get involved with Nardus. I'm begging you, father to daughter. Don't pursue him. If you do, I know he'll be the death of you. I fear he'll be the death of us all."

Theyn squirmed in Berggren's embrace. "You know nothing, father. I've seen my own death, and it isn't by Nardus's hand."

Berggren released her, staggered backward, and dropped to one knee. A deep sorrow filled his eyes. Guilt rose in Theyn's chest and quelled the angry storm within her.

Berggren's head slumped, and his eyes closed. "Please, Theyn. Tell me it's not by my hand. I know sometimes my temper gets the better of me. Rather die now and never have a chance to lay a hand on you."

Theyn moved toward Berggren and cupped his squared jaw in her hands. Tears slid down her cheeks. "Not you, father. Never you. You've never lifted a finger against me."

Berggren opened his eyes and smiled at her. In the moonlight, his grey eyes glistened with moisture. "Never forgive myself if I did something like that. You're the only thing that keeps me going."

Theyn wrapped her arms around his neck. "I love you, father."

He lifted her up as he stood and squeezed her tight. "And I, you."

"Then trust me." She kissed his cheek. "I've seen the future again. My life is intertwined with Nardus's. I don't know exactly what that means, but I must pursue it."

Berggren opened his mouth, but Theyn put her finger over it.

"As you said earlier, you know my *condition*. And, in understanding that, you know I can't be alone for much longer. He's here now, and there are no other men on this boat that could lie with me. You made sure of that when you only hired eunuchs. Besides, I can't back down from Nardus. I need him. I need to be with him. Please understand that, father. You know the alternative." Theyn leaned back in Berggren's arms and looked at him.

Berggren shook his head and sighed. "Don't like this one bit. Saw Shaul turn into a pile of ash by touching the man. Might not be the death of you, but that doesn't make Nardus less dangerous. Don't know what he's capable of. Like I said before, Lord Rosai warned us of his great power. Now you're telling me you want to be with him. How can I allow it?"

Berggren set Theyn back down on the wooden deck.

She turned and walked a few steps away. She eyed her long nails. "You know my condition, father. I didn't ask to be born this way—*cursed* like this. I've no choice."

"Keep your voice down, Theyn. Some on this boat wouldn't understand your condition."

Like you? Why doesn't anyone understand me? Nardus must.

Theyn turned and faced Berggren again. Heat rose in her cheeks, her hands curled into fists, and she thrust them down at her sides.

"Damn all these people! Let them think me a wanton seductress. I don't care. I'm what *Zhedäɜ ɔʊn* made me to be. I'm *her* daughter, the daughter of the great sun goddess." Theyn swept her arm wide. "May she burn all these *ʊnbäəlläfärz* with her wrath."

Berggren glanced around the boat. "*Ʊnbäəlläfärz*? Not all are unbelievers, Theyn. Some believe in *Zhedäɜ ɔʊn*, as we do, but that holds no relevance where your condition is concerned. The two are unrelated."

Theyn crossed her arms. "How can you be so sure? Perhaps *Zhedäɜ ɔʊn* made me this way for a reason. Did you ever think of that? Maybe, just maybe, my condition isn't a condition at all. Maybe I was born for a higher purpose. To serve her."

"No doubt you're special, Theyn. You're a smart and beautiful woman."

Theyn rolled her eyes and walked away from Berggren. "I'm going to bed. Alone. In case you were wondering. I won't spread my legs for any man tonight."

She crossed the lower deck, toward the stern of the boat. She looked up at Nardus who sat on the floor of the upper deck, leaning against the railing. She smiled when he looked down at her, but he didn't return her smile. Instead, he turned his head the other direction.

Pretend all you want, Nardus. You know you want me. I saw it in your eyes. You will be mine.

Theyn entered the captain's quarters located directly under the upper deck and slammed the door behind her. She walked over to the starboard-side room—her room—and collapsed face-first on the bed.

Tears moistened the blanket under her face, but she didn't care. Fighting with Berggren had rent her heart. He'd always been a good father to her, but she couldn't say she'd always been a good daughter to him.

I'm sorry, father. You know I have no choice, though.

It'd been six days since she'd lain with Shaul, a gentle giant like Berggren. They were so much alike. She *did* miss Shaul, just a little, but not as a lover.

By tomorrow, I'll think of you no more.

Theyn rolled over and stared up at the cedar-planked ceiling. Nardus sat directly above her. His proximity comforted her. No matter how much Berggren pleaded with her to the contrary, she knew she had to be with him.

There are no others. Besides, I want to be with him. And I will be. Soon.

As Theyn lay there, a plan formulated. She knew Berggren well. Eventually, he'd bring Nardus into the captain's quarters and have a drink with him. He always did, no matter how much he claimed to dislike a person. Nardus wouldn't be an exception.

Berggren kept a stash of ground níɛzhäíd bəllū in his quarters beneath one of the floor planks. She knew he kept it there for her—in case of an emergency. Just a pinch of the powerful substance could knock someone out cold for hours.

Fortunately, Berggren didn't know that she knew where he kept it, or that he kept it at all. After what she'd done to him so long ago, she didn't blame him for keeping some of it around. She would've too if the tables had been turned.

I'll take matters into my own hands.

Theyn rolled off the bed and onto her feet. She walked from her sleeping quarters over to Berggren's and stood at the open door. Her heart knocked in her chest. Could she really cross the line?

Do I have a choice?

She turned around but couldn't walk away. What alternative did she have? She thought of none. She closed her eyes and resolved herself to move forward with her plan.

If I don't, they'll all die, including Nardus, and the world will burn...

She opened her eyes, turned back around, entered the room, and walked over to the port-side wall. She bent down next to the wall, dug a fingernail between the last two wooden floor planks that paralleled the wall, and pulled the board up.

A fist-sized, brown leather bag sat at the bottom of the hollowed-out space. She reached down and lifted the bag from the hole. She stared at it.

It must be done.

She carried the bag from Berggren's sleeping quarters into the main room of the captain's quarters. To the left—the port-side—of the main entrance into the room sat a wooden desk made from honeyed birchwood. A dark, redwood cabinet hung above the desk.

Theyn set the bag of níɛzhäíd bəllū on the desk and opened the cabinet's two wood-framed, glass doors. She pulled down several bottles and jugs and set them on the desk. She untied the knot in the leather drawstring that held the bag closed, loosened it, and pulled the bag open. Bluish-grey powder filled the sack.

She pulled the stoppers and corks from the bottles and jugs and then stood back. She wiped her sweaty palms on her trousers. Could she really go through with it? Berggren would be drugged too.

Is that a bad thing? At least he wouldn't be able to interfere.

She forced air through her nose and stepped back up to the desk. She took a pinch of the powder between her trembling fingers and released it over the opening of the first bottle. She shoved the cork back into the bottle's opening and placed it back in the cabinet.

What if Berggren doesn't choose that one? Guess I'd better put it in all of them to be certain.

She quickly sprinkled the powder in each of the bottles and jugs before she could change her mind. She replaced the plugs and corks and put the bottles all back in the cabinet, then she re-tied the leather wrap around the bag and put it back where she'd found it.

She sprinted from Berggren's quarters, back into her own, and plopped down on her bed. Excitement and guilt rose in her chest. She'd never done anything so sinister and deceitful before, but she had no choice.

Zhedäz Ƨʋn, I leave it in your hands now. I beg you, bring him to me.

She reached down, pulled her boots off, and tossed them on the floor. She grabbed the edge of a green wool blanket from the foot of the bed, drew the blanket up to her neck as she lay back, closed her eyes, and dreamed of Nardus.

And of dragons.

† † †

Nardus leaned against the starboard-side railing on the upper deck, chained to a post by the silver collar around his neck. Theyn had retreated to her room hours before, and now a light snow fell from the sky like ash, blanketing both decks of the boat with its greyish-white powder.

A bitter-cold wind rose from the sea, but its bite failed to penetrate Nardus's fevered skin. Heat radiated from the stone lodged inside his chest, or so he assumed. What else could it be? He didn't feel sick.

However, his neck itched something fierce. He lifted the collar and rubbed where it had dug into his skin and drawn blood. The faded tenderness surprised him. Earlier, the slightest touch made him wince.

He didn't understand how the collar worked, but he knew it had to be made by mezhik. *Why did it only tingle when Berggren squeezed whatever he'd held in his hand? A trigger of some sort...*

Nardus spat on the deck. *Mezhik be damned.*

In a way, he felt trapped like he'd been with Akuji—the soul-sucking, skin-stealing guardian of Zhäíțfäí Fäíțə—yet this time he had no means of escape. He punched the deck with his fist.

Damn this collar. What've you done to me, Pravus?

Nardus tried several more times to get to the Great Library, but each time he phased in and out of it as though he were nothing but a spectre. He needed answers. He needed to know more about the stone. He needed to reach Gnaud. But how?

Can I get there by dreaming again? Or just thinking about it?

He'd done it before, despite breaking all the rules Gnaud had laid out about getting to Nasduron and the Great Library. Besides, he had nothing to lose by trying. He closed his eyes and focused on every detail he could remember of the Great Library.

He pictured the rows of dorus pine shelves chock full of books—thousands upon thousands of them, and Gnaud had read them all. He breathed deep, hoping to get a whiff of pine, but only the sea filled his nostrils.

This is pointless. I need to get this damned collar off.

He stared out at the rough sea, and his thoughts drifted back to Theyn.

The pain in her beautiful yellow eyes as she hung in the air—skewered by a large black claw and bleeding out—haunted him. She still lived, but the guilt of her future death lingered in his mind.

His heartbeat filled his ears—a symphony of drums pounding ever faster. He closed his eyes, and Theyn stood before him, wearing nothing but a smile.

This is madness! I don't even know the woman. Why can't I purge her from my thoughts?

Vitara, my love, give me strength. I swear I haven't forgotten you! Everything I've done has been for you and the children. Every breath I've taken since your deaths will not be in vain. I swear I'll bring you back or die trying.

Theyn…

Why did she call herself a wanton seductress? She'd said it earlier when she'd fought with Berggren, but he didn't believe it.

Theyn…

Her voice echoed in his mind like a distant memory. *"Come to me, Nardus. Lie with me. Love me. Don't let me die like the others."*

Her voice hadn't been real, and he knew it. Nevertheless, her words stabbed him right through the heart.

Theyn…

Nardus squeezed his head between his hands. "Stay out of my head!"

"Who's in your head?"

Nardus's eyes shot open. Berggren stood two paces in front of him, his arms folded across his chest. Nardus spat on the deck, and the phlegm skidded through the snow.

In the frigid air, Nardus's words came out in plumes of steam. "No one. What do you want, Berggren?"

Berggren glared down at him. "Answers."

Nardus spat again. "Why would I tell you anything?"

Berggren uncrossed his arms and tossed a small silver orb in the air with his left hand. "I think you know *exactly* why." He snatched the orb from the air and chuckled. His laughter rumbled like thunder.

"First, you attack me and take me against my will. Then you bind my hands and feet, gag me with a dirty cloth, put a sack over my head, and place some mezhik collar around my neck. After that, you nearly strangle me to death with this damned collar.

"Now, you've chained me to a post. On a boat. In the middle of the sea. During a snowstorm. Without a blanket. And you expect me to answer your questions? You're killing me slowly. I've got *nothing* to say to you."

"You're right. I did all of that, and I'd do it again. You *killed* my nephew, and I *still* saved your life. You would've died on that wretched island if not for me. You owe me answers."

Nardus's bones ached and his knees popped as he pushed himself to his feet. "Saved my life? I've been through *Ef Demd Dhä*. The only thing you've done is kept me from completing my quest. I owe you *nothing*. Free me, and maybe I won't kill you."

Berggren laughed. "No one needs to die, *Unbäalläfär*. Just tell me why you were sent into the ruins of Mortuus Terra. What were you after?"

Nardus scoffed. "Our mutual *friend* didn't explain that to you? You know what that means, don't you? You're expendable. In times of war, you never reveal your battle plans to the grunts. Their only job is to fight and die. You mean nothing to him."

Berggren sneered. "Lord Rosai may not have told me of your purpose, but he made mine very clear. You're expendable too, *Unbäalläfär*."

Nardus cocked his head and raised an eyebrow. "Lord Rosai? Is that name supposed to mean something to me?"

Berggren shook his head. "Lord Rosai didn't even trust you enough to tell you his name. Who's the grunt now, *Unbäalläfär*?"

Nardus shrugged. "The man who sent me on my quest called himself Pravus."

Berggren stepped back, eyes wide. "No one calls him by that name. If he heard you call him that, you'd be dead."

Nardus scoffed. "And yet here I stand. And why do you keep calling me that? '*Unbäalläfär*.'"

Berggren rubbed his hands together and blew air into them. "Don't you know of *Zhedäz Zun*?"

Nardus leaned back against the railing of the boat and curled his hands around its top edge. "Should I? Is it a place? Or a person?"

"You're a fool, *Unbäalläfär*. *Zhedäz Zun* is a goddess. My goddess and Theyn's. *Zhedäz Zun* is the sun goddess. Those that don't worship her are *unbäalläfärz*—unbelievers. Ones obviously like yourself."

Nardus chuckled. "You can keep your sun goddess. I've done away with my God, and I'm not looking for another."

Berggren crossed his arms again. "And to whom did you worship?"

"*Zäṭūr*." Nardus spat on the deck.

The veins bulged in Berggren's neck, and he gritted his teeth. "Ȝäṭūr. The *true* God, as you call Him. To us, He is called *Fäíȝṭ Ṭū Dhä*—the two-faced. He saves you while wearing one face and then turns around and damns you with His other. You're better off without a god than with Him."

"We agree on something after all."

"Suppose we do." Berggren stroked his square jaw. "I think it's time we get to the truth of why we're both here. We don't trust each other, and I don't see that changing. However, we're in this together, so let's make an agreement."

Nardus ran his fingers through his snow-moistened hair. "And what exactly are you proposing?"

Berggren stepped closer and pointed his right index finger at Nardus's chest. "You answer my questions and agree to the terms that I lay out, and I'll remove your constraints again."

Nardus eyed Berggren's balled left hand. "You'll also give me that orb."

Berggren guffawed. "You know I can't do that."

Nardus shook the moisture from his hands. "Then we have no deal."

Berggren squeezed the orb in his left fist, and the collar tightened around Nardus's neck. Nardus wheezed and tugged at the ring. Berggren smirked and then let his fist slacken. Nardus released his grip on the ring, drew in a deep breath, and coughed.

Berggren opened his left palm and stared at the silver orb. "I don't need this little thing to crush the life out of you. I could do it with my bare hands."

Nardus gazed at the orb. All that power in such a tiny ball. Were there no limits to the power of mezhik?

I hate mezhik.

"I don't doubt you could, Berggren. But Theyn said that if I die, we all do. If that's true, why do you keep threatening my life? Do you not value yours?"

Berggren looked from the orb to Nardus and then back. "This life is only the beginning for me. When I pass into the next life, I will become a god myself. I welcome death."

"Then why do you keep hiding behind that orb?" Nardus stretched his hand toward Berggren. "If you have no fear of death, then give it to me."

Berggren closed his hand. "Fine. Answer my questions and agree to my terms, and it's yours."

Nardus let his arm drop to his side. "So be it. What are your terms?"

Berggren crossed his arms over his chest. "There are only a few. The most important one is that you keep your distance from Theyn. Like her, you're different. That intrigues her."

Berggren rubbed his forehead with the palm of his hand. "She may ask you to do certain things for her. No matter what those things may be, you must refuse her request. As I said, this is the most important term of our agreement. Fail to comply, and I *will* kill you."

"I have—"

"Let me finish," growled Berggren. "Once we reach West Hotah, I'll allow you to walk about freely if you don't try to run. If you do run, I'll be forced to chain you and drag you around the streets like a dog. Am I understood?"

Nardus nodded, but he'd be gone the first chance he got. He had an appointment to keep at the bottom of the ocean. *I'll see you soon, my furry little friend. It's been too long, and I have so many questions.*

"Good." Berggren placed the orb in his trouser pocket and rubbed his hands together. "Now to get some answers."

Nardus rubbed his left bicep. "I'll answer anything I can."

Berggren took the end of the chain and slipped it off the steel ring attached to the post. Nardus's jaw dropped. He'd worked at getting the chain off the post for nearly an hour before giving up, and Berggren slipped it out of the ring as though it hadn't been attached at all.

"You have mezhik too?"

Berggren glowered at him. "Not an ounce of it. It's the collar." Berggren pulled on the chain and walked toward the stairs leading down to the lower deck. "Let's go inside where it's warm."

Nardus looked around. "Who's steering the boat?"

Berggren chuckled. "We're in the middle of the sea, *Unbäalläfär. Ɛäzhed*, the sea god, watches over us now. Besides, it's Felix's job to keep us on course."

From the lower deck, a man black as night ascended the stairs. At the top of the stairs, the man tipped his broad-brimmed hat toward Nardus. A torch hung atop the post, and the swaying shadows cast by its light distorted his view of the man, but Nardus could see the man had no ears. The man walked past without a word and took his place behind the wheel of the boat.

"No need to talk to him," said Berggren. "He cannot hear, and he has no tongue to speak. He's the perfect man to have around."

Nardus shrugged. "Hadn't planned on it."

Berggren pulled on the chain attached to Nardus's collar. "Come on."

They descended the stairs to the lower deck and made their way into the captain's quarters.

Just inside the door, on either side, sat a desk made of honeyed birchwood. A lit candle sat atop each desk. A dark, redwood cabinet hung on the wall above each desk, and wood-framed glass doors of the same color covered the cabinets.

The cabinet above the desk on the starboard side contained trinkets and other feminine items. The cabinet above the desk on the port side contained numerous bottles of all shapes and sizes, each full of liquid.

Booze? I could certainly use a drink about now. And some food.

Cabinets full of books and maps lined the port side of the room. These cabinets matched the ones above the desks, including their wood-framed glass doors.

A rectangular table and four chairs sat in the center of the room, each bolted to the floor. Two lit candles sat on the table, one at each end. Berggren slipped the tail-end of the chain attached to Nardus's collar into an eye-bolt at the center of the table.

A door at the back of the room—the stern side—led into the captain's sleeping quarters. Deep shadows filled the room. Berggren walked over and closed the door.

The starboard side of the room was barren, save a lone door leading into a second sleeping quarter. The door hung open, and Theyn lay on the bed within. Her chest rose and fell slowly. *Asleep amidst all the ruckus.* Even at a distance and cloaked in shadows Theyn's beauty shone.

Nardus's chest ached on the left side.

You want her.

No!

Nardus swallowed hard. He pushed Theyn from his mind and set his focus elsewhere. Berggren glared at him, walked over to Theyn's door, and quietly closed it.

Vitara. Shardan. Shanara. Savannah. Why do I need a reminder of my family? Everything I've done has been for them. Be strong, Nardus. For them.

Nardus looked away. *Theyn isn't mine to want.*

Nardus sat in the chair on the table's port side and stared at the eye-bolt. Berggren joined him at the table, sitting in the chair opposite him. They stared each other down in silence, each content to wait for the other to break.

Nardus gave in. "Can I have a drink? I've had nothing to drink since earlier this morning. And maybe some bread?"

Berggren growled, but said nothing. He rose from the table and walked over to the port-side desk. He opened one of the cabinet's doors and grabbed a large clay jug. He retrieved two wooden cups from the other side of the cabinet. He returned to the table, cups and jug in hand, and settled back down in his chair.

Berggren pulled the cork stopper out of the top of the jug and set it on the table. He filled one of the cups to the brim then set the jug down. He took the cup, emptied its contents into his mouth, and swallowed it down in one big gulp. He slammed the cup down on the table and whipped his head around to Theyn's door.

Berggren's gaze returned to Nardus, his brow furrowed, and his bushy black eyebrows hunched over his grey, deep-set eyes. "Keep it down."

Nardus stared at the empty cups and then the bottle. Just thinking about a drink dried his mouth further.

What are you waiting for? Give me a drink already.

Berggren filled both cups and slid the second toward Nardus. "No food. Just drink."

Nardus nodded, reached over and grabbed the cup, and pulled it over to the table's edge. He stared into the cup and at its murky contents. *Water from a muddy stream.* It pulled his thoughts into the past, back to the Ferzh's Head Inn.

Another life. It felt that way. Nardus remembered that first touch of mezhik when Pravus had touched his hand. That touch had turned him into a stone statue from the neck down. His simplistic, worthless, drunken life had changed that day. Looking back, he wondered if he'd made the right choice.

Will it have been worthwhile in the end? Will I get my family back?

Nardus clenched his jaw. *I'd better, or Pravus will pay with his life.*

The *snap* of fingers brought Nardus back into the present.

Berggren scowled. "Plan on drinking it or staring it to death?"

Nardus picked up the cup and held it to his lips. The smell of fermented grains rose from the cup and filtered through his nostrils. Just the thought of how it used to make him feel—numb to the core—watered his mouth. He desperately wanted that feeling again. He needed it, if for no other reason than to drown his thoughts of Theyn sleeping in the room just ten feet away.

She must be a seductress.

He knew she had little to do with his thoughts. The stone buried in his chest poisoned his mind. Could he keep resisting its power, or would it eventually take control of him?

Damn mezhik.

He tipped the cup forward, and its liquid contents poured into his mouth, slid down his throat, and filled his belly. It burned his throat, and he wanted more.

He set the cup on the table and slid it back over to Berggren. "Keep it coming."

Berggren growled, "Every drink requires answers. The more you answer, the more we drink."

Nardus leaned over the table. "Then you're in luck. I'm quite parched."

Berggren sat back in his chair. "Good. Why did Lord Rosai send you into the ruins of Mortuus Terra?"

Nardus rubbed the scars on either side of his left bicep. "To bring my family back."

Berggren raised his chin and furrowed his brow. "What do you mean? Back from where?"

"My entire family was brutally murdered, and I'd given up on everything when he found me. He offered to resurrect my family. How could I say no? It's all I wanted."

Berggren guffawed. "Lord Rosai is anything but charitable. Why would he help you? What's in it for him? Why did he send you there?"

Nardus pointed at the cup on the table. "Drink."

Berggren scowled, but filled the cups again. He pushed Nardus's cup across the table.

Nardus stared at the cup, but continued, "Deep in the ruins, there's a doorway that leads straight into *Ef Demd Dhä*. Terrors straight from nightmares exist in that world."

Berggren scoffed. "Liar. No one goes to that place and lives to tell about it."

Nardus drained the liquid death from his cup and wiped his mouth with the back of his hand. "Well, it's not really *Ef Demd Dhä*, but it might as well have been. A world crafted by mezhik lies through that doorway."

Berggren twisted the cup in his hand but didn't drink. "You still haven't answered the question. What's in it for him?"

Nardus pushed his cup across the table again. "He had me retrieve a stone from *Ţämbəll Dhef Däd Dhä*."

Berggren sipped from his cup. "You didn't have a stone on you when we found you. Did you not find it, or did you lose it somewhere?"

"Oh, it's not lost." Nardus pulled his shirt open and pointed at his chest's left side. "Right here under the skin, where my heart should be."

The red glow captured Berggren's attention.

"I tried to dig it out with my fingers."

Berggren tilted his head back and downed the rest of his cup's contents. He filled both cups again, and they both drank.

Several cups later, the room spun around Nardus. Or was it his head that spun? Either way, numbness sank into his bones, and he felt *good*. He couldn't focus his eyes, and his head refused to stay straight on his shoulders.

Nardus smiled. "Why did I ever stop drinking?" The words sputtered and hung on his tongue.

Across the table, Berggren slouched in his chair. His head twisted to the side, and a string of drool hung from his open mouth and pooled on top of his shoulder. Nardus laughed and then vomited all over the floor. Nothing came up but liquid.

His stomach rumbled. He needed something to eat. He stood up from the table, staggered sideways as he tried to clear the chair, twisted around backward, and fell forward. He couldn't get his arms in front of himself to break the fall, but his head stopped just inches from the floor.

The collar around his neck bit into his flesh as the chain went taut, and then it whipped him backward several inches before slackening again. He coughed and spit up more liquid as he hung by his neck just inches from the floor. He wheezed as he struggled to get air into his lungs. His arms flailed at his sides like fish out of water, uncooperative.

Every breath became more and more of a struggle with the force of the collar against his neck. His vision swam and then turned black.

Is this the end? Is this the way it all ends for me? If Theyn's right, the world dies too. What do I care?

Nardus stopped struggling against his weight and exhaled for the last time. His heart knocked in his chest. His head nearly floated from his neck, his body burned with fire, and then every ache and pain faded until nothing remained but numbness.

Are my eyes open? I see no light.

Despite all the trials he'd endured and his sole purpose of saving his family, his last thought was of Theyn.

CHAPTER TEN

Savric and Qotan stood in the middle of the forest a few miles south of Daltura's southern gates. Twenty paces west, tucked between two hills and concealed amongst the thick yellow oaks, sat a small cave carved out of the dense quartz rock.

Savric pushed through the last few trees, Qotan right on his heels. They halted just within the small clearing, still enveloped in darkness underneath the thick canopy and rising hills.

Savric cocked his head. "Did you just snicker?"

"Snicker? I think not." Qotan brushed past Savric. "Perhaps your hearing has degraded further. You are most certainly unraveling, brother. Soon, you will be little more than a pile of old yarn and twisted threads."

"I fear I am well beyond yarn and threads." Savric squinted, but nothing came into view. "The darkness is far deeper than I remember."

"In more ways than we can fathom. Its presence haunts my bones and gnaws on my flesh like carrion beetles."

Savric shuttered the vivid image from his mind, but his bones ached with empathy. *We must get through this, Ɂäţūr. The darkness cannot prevail.*

Savric held out his hand, palm up. "*Əllíţ ʊb.*" A small orb of light formed above his palm, moved forward, and rose. He squinted again, this time through the dim light, and gasped. They didn't face the cave's opening as they should have. Instead, they stood in a small circular clearing amongst the thick oak trees.

He scanned the area, perplexed. *This is the right place… is it not?* He turned and faced Qotan. "Honestly, brother, I left the cave right here."

Qotan scowled, exhaled loudly, and shook his head. He tapped his staff's butt-end against the ground, and its top end—twisted and curled in the shape of a ball—lit the surrounding area. Savric's small orb of light shrank to a pinpoint and then fizzled out with a hiss.

Qotan's green eyes gleamed in the pure-white light, and the lines in his scrunched-up brow deepened. "Explain to me exactly how one goes about losing a *cave*?"

Savric gazed intently at Qotan and chuckled. Every moment he spent with Qotan was an adventure waiting to happen, and he cherished every one of them. "It has taken me eighty-five name days to perfect, brother. Plenty of practice, plenty of items lost, but never an entire cave. This is a first for me."

Qotan's features softened, and the ends of his mouth curled up slightly. "Are you implying that you have lost part of a cave before? If so, which part did you lose? The opening? The back? Perhaps the bottom? If you lost the top, then I would speculate that the cave was never a cave to begin with. Are you certain we are looking for a cave now?"

"Your quick wit astounds me, brother. Perhaps, if you were to use your wit to locate the cave, we would not still be standing here."

Qotan wagged a finger. "Ah, but I am not the one who has misplaced it. Besides, I take pleasure in your struggles, as infrequent as they are. It reminds me that you are indeed human and not some sort of automated perfection entity."

Savric raised an eyebrow. "'Automated perfection entity.'" He nodded slowly. "Intriguing. However, if you ever find yourself requiring a reminder as to the authenticity of my humanity, you simply need query and I shall produce evidence of it."

Qotan tilted his head back and laughed. "Which of us is expelling his wit now?"

Savric dipped his head toward Qotan. "Touché, brother. Shall we proceed with our quest?"

Qotan smiled. "I believe I have exceeded my quota of laughter for the evening. Let us move on."

Qotan raised his staff and thrust its butt-end into the ground. The light from its curled top fizzled out, the earth shook below their feet, and the trees parted. The hills beyond the trees slid forward, and a cave opening formed between them as they continued to slide forward. The cave's mouth swallowed Savric and Qotan as it passed beyond them.

"You certainly have a flair for the dramatic." Savric's voice echoed off the cave walls.

Qotan grinned. "Would you prefer I do things another way?"

Savric gasped. "Never. I could travel the world and have my fill of ordinary. Your antics are exceptionally exceptional and would be world-renowned if you were to get out more."

Qotan stroked his bare chin. "I concede to the truth of that. Now, shall I open the portal?"

Savric stepped back. "Please do. I will wait right here with great anticipation."

"*Fūr fōírk Hiz,*" said Qotan.

Savric dipped his head. *For His work, brother.*

A six-foot circle of golden sand materialized in the middle of the rocky cave floor.

Qotan drew a large heptagram in the sand with his staff. Within the heptagram he drew a circle, about two feet in diameter. Then he drew a bolt of lightning at the center of the inner circle.

Qotan stepped back and eyed the drawing. "Yes, I believe that will suffice."

Savric put the tips of his thumbs together with his forefingers up and framed the heptagram like a picture. "A portrait of perfection, brother. Proceed."

Qotan shouted, "*In ǝllít Hiz,*" and thrust his staff's butt-end into the center of the lightning bolt.

Always in Your light, Ƨäṭūr.

Qotan withdrew his staff and stepped backward, next to Savric.

The golden sands shifted, and the center circle turned black as obsidian. Striations fissured out from the black circle of sand to the outer edges of the circle of golden sand. Gooseflesh crawled across Savric's arms and left the hairs standing in their wake.

Í Dhef Ƨäṭūr.

The lines of the heptagram liquefied like molten steel and then solidified into a vibrant-blue glass. The lightning bolt, drawn in the sand at the center of the inner circle, turned from black to bright-yellow and then flashed several times in succession. Thunder rumbled through the small cave and reverberated in Savric's chest.

Savric moved his hand over his heart. Its rapid beat reminded him of his youth and the mis-adventures they'd embarked upon so often. *Zerenity...* His palms moistened, and his heart raced faster.

Beyond the outer circle, a portion of the innermost wall of the cave collapsed, revealing a hidden chamber. Savric and Qotan stepped around the circle of sand and over to the chamber's entrance. Stale, musty air poured forth from the dark chamber.

Savric looked at Qotan with raised eyebrows and shrugged. "Perhaps we should visit more often."

Qotan sneezed three times and wiped his nose with the sleeve of his robes.

Savric smiled. "*Bəlläʑ zíū*, brother."

"Indeed. Thank you." Qotan sniffed and cleared his throat. "Would you do the honor of lighting this place up?"

Savric stared into the darkness for a moment, then he snapped his fingers together. From the corners of the room, four torches ignited, and their light chased away the darkness.

Savric turned to Qotan and chuckled. "Like mezhik."

Qotan closed his eyes, shook his head, and blew air from his nostrils. "Moments like these give me pause and cause me to contemplate the true nature of our Creator, Ɂäʈūr. Did He intentionally create us with the desire to never grow up, or have we made that determination of our own accord?"

"Ɂäʈūr delights in His children, regardless of their age or maturity. Let us embrace it with thanksgiving."

Qotan stroked his chin. "Childlike, indeed. But never childish."

"Oh, yes, of course. And moving the entrance to a cave would never fall under that kind of categorization, would it?"

"Could you imagine a child hiding a cave? Preposterous. It could only be categorized as true wit."

The smell of burning pitch and dust wafted through the chamber's opening, made its way into Savric's lungs, and made him cough. Qotan sneezed three times again.

Savric put his hand on Qotan's shoulder. *"Bəlläƹ zíū*, brother."

"Blessed, indeed." Qotan wiped his nose. "Perhaps we should carry on with our quest before there is no more questing to be had. Time is of the essence, is it not?"

Savric squeezed Qotan's shoulder and moved past him, through the chamber's entrance, and into the small, sparse space. Besides the four sconces, the chamber sat empty, save a large, rectangular mirror propped against its far wall.

Qotan stopped next to Savric, and they both turned and faced the chamber's entrance. Qotan held out his left hand. *"Bí hend Hiz."*

The ground trembled, and the chamber's entrance backfilled with rock, sealing them inside.

Savric sighed and walked over to the mirror. Qotan followed him. Savric grabbed the sleeve of his robes in his right palm and began wiping the dust from the mirror's surface.

Qotan raised his left arm and covered his nose and mouth. "Does the thick coating of dust affect the mirror adversely? Does it not work unless cleansed? Or perhaps the layer of dust is a safeguard, warding off those who suffer from allergies such as myself."

Savric frowned at Qotan's reflection in the mirror. "The only thing I have ever known you to be allergic to is work."

In the mirror's reflection, Qotan lowered his left arm and grinned deviously.

Savric's eyes widened. "What are you—"

Qotan buried his head in the folds of his robes, pointed at the mirror, and shouted, *"Bəllō äfäí."*

Savric's wiry white hair flew over his shoulders and into his face as a strong gust of air blew past him. The gust blasted the mirror and sent a cloud of dust into the air. A dust storm showered Savric before he had a chance to cover his head.

Savric wheeled around on his heels and faced Qotan. "Amused yourself, have you?"

Qotan kept his head buried in his robes and chuckled. "Indeed. I can imagine the look of indignation on your face right now, and it is beyond value."

Savric wiped dust from his eyes. "Just you wait, brother. When you least expect it, I will return the favor in kind."

Qotan lifted his head from under his robes and smiled wide. "I would accept nothing less."

"As you say." Savric shook out his robes. "Have you prepared yourself for what comes next?"

Qotan cocked his head to the side and frowned. "What *is* coming next?"

Savric smiled smugly. "Zerenity."

Qotan clung to his staff with both hands and leaned into it. "I believe our quest together must come to an end. There are urgent matters I must attend to."

Savric set his jaw. "Yes, brother, and this is it. This matter is not up for discussion. You will accompany me to Zerenity's, and you will be on your best behavior."

Qotan lowered his head. "Do not make me face her again, brother. I beg of you. You know how she treats me. She pretends as though I am not there. To her, I am nothing more than a spectre."

Oh, my strong brother. May Ӡäţūr lift your spirit.

Savric put his hand on Qotan's shoulder and squeezed it. "Never be discouraged by her, brother. I need you by my side. You are my hands when I have none to spare, my eyes when I am blind, and my ears when I have grown deaf. Zerenity can never understand you the way I do, but do not let that be a hindrance."

Qotan looked up, his face ashen. "Have you forgotten the way she wove her spell around you? She charmed you, seduced you, and nearly made you forget me altogether."

Savric closed his eyes as his mind drifted back in time.

He and Qotan were twelve name days old again. Early that summer, they'd climbed more than a hundred feet high in a giant, sacred-heart tree, chasing after a blue-eyed girl they'd just met named Zerenity.

From that point on, the three of them played together daily, but Qotan always complained of being an outsider. As the years faded, so did Qotan's involvement with them. Eventually, Savric and Zerenity stopped inviting Qotan on their adventures altogether.

Savric wiped a tear from the corner of his eye with the back of his hand. "I remember, and regret still anguishes me, but that was so many years ago. A lifetime has passed since. We are all vastly different people now."

Qotan straightened. "I will go with you, but do not expect me to engage with her. I will keep to the shadows."

Savric smiled. "Do what you must to endure, but you must come."

Savric turned back toward the mirror and placed his right hand against the glass. It warmed with mezhik, and his reflection faded into darkness. The mirror's surface vibrated against his palm and fingers and became warm and wet.

Tyrosha. He stepped through the mirror and into the darkness.

"*Əllı̨ṭ ʊb.*" An orb of yellow light formed above Savric's open palm and lit the small coat closet.

A moment later, Qotan bumped into him from behind. "Does this conclude the extent of our quest? Are we to stay in this coat closet and ponder the logic behind each decision made in the purchase of these ghastly outfits, or does your plan include exiting this cramped space?"

Savric chuckled. "Childlike, brother, not childish."

Savric reached for the door handle, grasped it, and thousands of bursts of energy raced up his arm and into his chest and knocked him backward. He cried out and stumbled over Qotan. Clothes fell all around them and entangled them in their snare.

The smell of burnt flesh and singed hair permeated the closet.

Qotan sneezed three times. "Remind me to make my own travel plans the next time you wish to go on an adventure, and I will meet you there."

"Do not start—"

Creak.

The sound came from just beyond the closet door. Savric closed his palm, extinguishing the orb of light and casting them into darkness.

Click.

The latch on the door disengaged.

Creak.

The door slowly swung outward until it could open no further.

Savric's pulse raced as his eyes adjusted to the light. He thought he saw movement through the open door, but it could've just been his eyes playing tricks.

A warm breath caressed his left ear and cheek.

Savric flicked his left ear with his finger. "What are you doing, brother? Get away from my ear."

Qotan's voice came from the right. "Whatever you are referring to, it is not I."

A soft voice whispered in Savric's left ear, "What are we waiting for, darling?"

Savric stumbled out of the closet and fell to the floor, taking half the clothes from the closet with him. He rolled onto his back and stared up at the silver-haired woman who emerged from the closet. Her radiant blue eyes were unforgettable.

Zerenity. Older, but still a beauty.

Zerenity beamed at him. "Savric, darling. So nice of you to drop in. You certainly know how to make an entrance."

Savric could barely move amongst the sea of clothing. "Grand entrances are a specialty of ours."

Zerenity cocked her head to the side. "Ours?"

Savric glared at her. "Qotan is here as well."

Qotan stepped out of the closet and moved to the other side of the room, but Zerenity paid him no attention.

"Oh, I see," she said. "Things certainly haven't changed, have they?"

Savric tilted his head back and caught a glimpse of the top of Qotan's head. "Perhaps you might offer a little help here, brother?"

Zerenity stepped to the side. "Where are my manners? Allow me." She swept her hand over Savric and toward the closet. *"Ūrzhäníz."*

One by one, the articles of clothing spread across the floor and on top of Savric came to life and sprang into action, righting themselves and finding their proper place in the closet. Savric sat up and watched the last of the clothes situate themselves.

Savric looked up at Zerenity. "What need could one person possibly have for so many clothes? There are enough items in that closet to dress an entire village."

Zerenity scoffed. "Half a village at most. No more than that. Besides, you never know when you'll need a change of clothing. And with the different seasons and changes in fashion, you never want to get caught without the proper outfit."

Savric pulled himself to his feet and held out his hand. His staff jumped from the floor and into his open hand. "I doubt you have ever been caught without proper clothing."

Zerenity spread her arms wide. "Come over here and give an old friend a hug, darling."

An old flame lit within Savric's heart, and he struggled to snuff it out.

For Qotan's sake, I cannot involve myself with her again.

Savric scowled at her. "I am certain that would be unwise, given our history."

Zerenity smirked. "Our history? What're you remembering about our history that I'm not? Is it something juicy?"

"You are a seductress, Zerenity. And I am no longer available to play your games."

"Seductress? Don't you mean sorceress?"

Savric folded his hands across the top of his staff. "I always say what I mean, woman. I nearly lost my brother because of your twisted mind games."

Zerenity's eyes flickered like little blue flames. "'Twisted mind games?' You're still blaming me for that? I did nothing but love you, Savric. You're the one who chose *him* over me."

Savric flicked his hand. "Contort the words any way you like. I know the real story."

You crushed my heart, woman. And for what?

Zerenity glided over to him, wedged her way between him and his staff, and put her arms around his waist. "I've missed you, Savvy."

He breathed deep, relishing the tantalizing scent of fresh roses in her hair. *Just as I remembered.*

She kissed his right cheek and then his left. Her hands slipped below his waist and curled around his buttocks, and she gave him a good squeeze.

He clenched his muscles and groaned. *And again, as I remembered.*

Savric dropped his staff and reached behind himself. He tried prying her fingers off, but she had an iron grip. "Get your hands off me, woman. We hardly know each other."

Zerenity laughed. "I believe we know each other better than most. I've not spent more time with anyone else in this world than I did with you, darling. And this rump of yours has become nothing but a sack of bones."

"Well, it is *my* sack of bones, and I would appreciate it if you would remove your talons from it."

Zerenity let go of his buttocks, gave it a slap with her left hand, and laughed as she spun into nothing.

Savric turned around and saw that he was alone in the room. *You have left me too, brother?*

Zerenity's voice echoed from another room. "Would you like something to eat, Savvy? I've got a nice rabbit stew on the fire and some biscuits warming."

Savric's stomach rumbled. He hadn't eaten in some time, and the sound of rabbit stew watered his mouth. He grabbed his staff, and his nose led him to the food.

To Savric's left, a fire blazed in the fireplace and warmed the large living area. A doorway at the far end of the room led to a second bedroom, and to his right, two large windows flanked the front door.

Outside the nearest window, Savric spied Qotan sitting in a rocking chair on the porch, smoking his pipe. He sighed, and the tension in his jaw faded. *Curious.* Had he expected something else? He shook his head. *She is already in my mind.*

The thought faded as the succulent smell of stew filled his nostrils and melted away all the aches and pains brought on by the long day. Zerenity stood next to the fire and stirred the stew. She held out her hand, and a wooden bowl appeared in her palm. She scooped some of the stew into the bowl, grabbed a biscuit from the hearth, and set it atop the thick stew.

She motioned him over. "Come sit by the fire, Savvy."

Savvy.

Only Zerenity had ever called him that. After more than sixty years of not hearing the name, it felt good. So long ago, he'd called her Reni.

Savvy and Reni.

He remembered the tree they'd carved their names into that very first summer. It'd hurt Qotan when they hadn't included his name in the carving, but sometimes there was little room for three.

Savric walked over to the fireplace, and Zerenity handed him the bowl she'd just filled. He smiled at her. "Thank you, Reni."

She smiled back. "You haven't forgotten. I was worried that you had."

Two rocking chairs sat next to the fire, and Savric settled into the one closest to him. For a long while, he sat and watched the steam rise from the bowl in his lap. Until he'd seen Zerenity's face again today, he hadn't realized how much he'd given up when he'd left her. She'd been the only woman he'd ever loved. Everyone else he'd ever met paled in comparison.

I still love you, Reni.

But the way she'd treated Qotan puzzled him. Initially, she bent over backward to please everyone around her, including Qotan, but, after several years, she started pretending he didn't exist. At first, Qotan and Savric thought it was an elaborate hoax, but the ruse never let up. Animosity grew between the two of them, and Savric finally had to make a choice.

I made the right choice, did I not?

Had he found a way to make it work on both sides, he would've jumped at the chance. Instead, he gained a loyal brother and a broken heart. He rubbed the part of his chest over his heart, but it still hadn't healed.

Savric let go of his staff. It shot across the room and settled in the corner to the right of the front door and large window.

Savric held the bowl of stew up to his mouth with both hands and blew on it. He tipped the bowl just enough to get a sampling of the broth and sighed with pleasure as the salty liquid slid down the back of his throat. He tipped the bowl farther, slurped more of the broth, and pulled a purple carrot into his mouth with his tongue. The mushy carrot dissolved in his mouth.

He set the bowl on his lap, broke off a corner of the biscuit, and plopped it in his mouth. The biscuit burst with the savory, garlic-butter flavor he'd spent decades trying to reproduce. *How does she do it?*

Savric turned his head to the right. Zerenity had settled in the rocking chair next to him and gazed at him as though nothing else in the world existed but the two of them. His cheeks warmed, and he turned back to his bowl of stew.

"I cannot remember the last time I had a meal that tasted this good. Thank you again, Reni."

She placed her hand on his forearm. "Wait until you've tried the rabbit."

Savric chuckled. "You might want to leave the room before I do. As you may recall, food and I have an intimate relationship."

Zerenity rose from her chair and walked toward the hallway. "I'll be back in a few, Savvy."

Savric looked up from his bowl of stew. "I only jest, Reni. My intention was not to drive you away."

Zerenity turned her head and winked at him. "Enjoy the stew."

She disappeared down the hall, and Savric turned his attention back to the bowl and devoured the rest of the stew and the biscuit. Satisfied, he leaned back in the chair, rubbed his belly, and belched.

He mused, "Now, that was a meal! And the rabbit..." He licked and smacked his lips.

A cold draft filled the room, and the front door slammed shut. Savric's torso tensed, and his shoulders shook as the frigid air raced down the back of his neck and into his robes. A moment later, Qotan sat down in the chair next to him.

Qotan cleared his throat. "I am unsure as to the purpose of this particular part of our quest. Now that you have had your fill of food, can we move forward?"

"No, brother. I must speak with Reni. We need to find the boy, and she may be the only one who can help us."

Qotan rose from the chair and stood by the fire. "Reni again, is it? We have been down this road, and it ends at the bottom of a cliff."

"It is not like that, brother. You know I never stopped loving her, but this is not about her and me. This is about saving the world. And, for the record, saving the world on an empty stomach is never preferable or advisable. Have some of the stew. It will make you feel better. We will both need our strength before this is all over."

"Call me when you are ready to leave. I will not be far, but I will not stay in this house another moment." Qotan thrust his staff into the floor and disappeared in a whirlwind.

Savric sighed. *What are we doing here? Is Reni really the only one who can help us, or am I simply trying to justify coming here? How else would I find the boy?*

Savric relaxed in the chair and let the last hour's events sink in. He rocked himself in the chair a bit and quickly found his eyelids too heavy to keep open.

I only need a few minutes.

He smiled as Zerenity's blue eyes drew him into the past and into a world where they were much younger.

† † †

Zerenity stood in front of the full-length mirror wondering when her youth had faded. One day she'd been young and attractive, then the next she woke up and found herself an old woman. She couldn't remember a transition period between the two. It'd just happened.

Every inch of her sagged. Her eyes still burned, vivid blue and full of life, but creeling's feet had entrenched from the outer edges of her eyelids to her temples. Clothing went a long way to hide some of her unsightly features, but nothing could restore her lost beauty—except mezhik.

How could Savvy still find me attractive when I can't convince myself of it?

If a beauty spell existed to tighten things up, she'd be all over it. But deceptive mezhik, *mezhik derk*, she'd never stoop to using, especially not for vanity. She cherished her soul more than her beauty. In her youth, she'd used some questionable mezhik, but eventually she'd found Ɂäțūr's light and hadn't looked back since.

Over the years, she'd tried many salves and creams, tea leaves, and every other remedy she could find, but nothing made a lick of difference. Her best would have to suffice. However, her clothes were a different matter.

What does Savvy like?

She spun out of her drab clothes and into an ankle-length green dress lined with lace. Its low-cut, V-shaped neck did little for her sagging breasts. In fact, it made her look as though she had a pooch and no breasts at all.

"Definitely not. I've moved well beyond the help of this dress." She pointed at the dress in the mirror. "Your future lies within the fire."

Zerenity spun out of the green dress and into several more outfits before settling on a simple pair of grey trousers, a white, long-sleeved shirt, and a red shawl. She tied the ends of the shawl in a knot and let it hang over her shoulders and down to her midriff.

With a snap of her fingers, strands of her silver hair wove into braids at her temples and wrapped around the back of her head. A strand of red ribbon wrapped around their ends and wove into them. She pushed the rest of her hair behind her ears while a brush ran itself through her hair.

She picked up a small mirror with a brass handle and turned around so that she could see the back of her head. Satisfied with her work, she set the mirror down on the nightstand next to her bed and closed the closet door. She went over to the nightstand on the far side of the bed, dipped her smallest finger into a jar of beeswax, and spread the beeswax on her lips.

She pressed her lips together as she walked out of her room and snapped her fingers. The myriad of candles spread throughout her room extinguished. A dim light traveled less than half the length of the hallway, but she knew her home well.

Zerenity entered the living area. All the candles had blown out or fizzled down to nothing, and the fireplace had grown cold and dark. Had she been in her bedroom that long?

Savric still sat in the rocking chair, snoring lightly. His head hung over the back of the chair in what seemed an uncomfortable position. She grabbed a blanket from one of her closets and draped it over him. She bent down and kissed his cheek.

Sweet dreams, Savvy.

She turned to walk away, but Savric grabbed her wrist. "We need to talk, Reni. Qotan and I did not travel all this way just to eat some food and nap."

She put her hand over his. "I'm sure you didn't, but it's late. I shouldn't've woken you."

"I was merely resting my eyes. You were gone quite some time."

She patted the back of Savric's hand. "You worked up quite a snore for eye resting. Let me tend the fire, and then we can talk."

Savric released her wrist and sat up in the chair. "Please do. The air up here feels much cooler than it does at home."

She lifted the pot of stew off the hook, carried it around the side of the fireplace, and took it into the kitchen. She set the pot on one of the wooden counters then returned to the living area.

A wooden box filled with chopped wood and tinder sat on the other side of the fireplace. She took a few of the logs and placed them over the black coals. She bent down in front of the hearth and held her hands just below her lips.

"*Ɂäṭ äbəlläíz.*" Green flames formed in her hands and lapped at the air. A faint, rosiny scent tinged the air.

Zerenity blew into her hands, and the flames leapt onto the logs. The logs erupted with orange and blue flames, and, within moments, the sap oozed from them and popped loudly. The smells of pine and cedar filled the room.

Savric put his hands together and clapped a few times. "Now that is how you tend a fire."

She smiled and moved over to the second rocking chair. She scooted the chair across the wood floor—butted it up next to Savric's—and sat down in it.

Miniature flames flickered in Savric's eyes. "You look beautiful, Reni. But you need not go to all the trouble on my account. You looked beautiful earlier as well."

Her cheeks warmed, but she didn't care. He'd noticed her. "I had a vision of this night, Savvy. I know why you've come, but you needn't worry."

Savric sat up in the chair, eyes wide. "Have you seen him already? You had a vision of him?"

"No, but I'll know where he is soon. Like Ɂäṭūr's done with you, I have faith that He will bring the boy back into my life very soon."

Savric sank back in the chair. "I have received word from Rayah, my emissary. She has fallen in love with the boy and will not deliver him to you."

Zerenity lay her hand on Savric's. "Have faith, Savvy. Our paths will meet again. Ɂäʈūr knows the end from the beginning and has already set events in motion to alter the course of the future and deliver the boy at the appointed time. You will see."

Savric breathed deeply. "In these matters, I trust you, Reni."

"Trust me with your heart, Savvy. Let yourself love me again. We have both grown old alone. Let us not die that way as well."

Savric closed his eyes and leaned his head back. "How can I allow that to happen? I cannot abandon my brother. He is the only family I have left."

She stood. "You're a foolish man, Savvy. I don't understand why you continually throw my love back in my face. How can I mean less to you than a figment of your imagination? I'm real, Savvy. I have flesh. I have a heart. And you've rent it again."

She stormed down the hall, slammed her bedroom door behind her, and sat down on her bed in the dark. She clenched her fists and every candlewick in the room burst alive with flames.

"I'm finished with you, Savvy. For good."

Forever.

CHAPTER ELEVEN

Earlier, purpose drove Amicus into the valley, but nothing remained of it. He sat on a large rock in the middle of Solasportus, defeated again. He, Alderan, Rayah, Rakzar, and Eshtak had searched through the rubble and debris for more than an hour but found no traces of anyone or anything living amongst them.

Only Amicus had heard the wails, and they still echoed in his mind. *Have I lost myself?* He looked to the sky, but no stars penetrated the haze. *Ɂätūr, what would You have me do? I've returned. Is this not what You wanted? Guide me.*

Alderan walked out of the dark haze and stood in front of Amicus. "You're a strong man, Amicus, much stronger than I am."

Amicus gazed up at Alderan. "There's no strength left in me."

Alderan swept his arm wide. "You've faced this place twice now in a single day, and it took me many months to return home for fear of what I'd find or that all the loss I'd suffered would solidify in my mind the moment I saw Viscus D'Silva. I deceived myself into thinking that if I stayed away everything would continue to exist as it did before I'd left. So, yes, you are stronger."

Amicus shrugged. "I may have some closure, but certainly not peace. Anger rages within my heart. Had I been here, my family might still be alive, and I'm not sure I'll ever forgive myself for that."

Alderan pushed his hair behind his ears. "I feel the same way you do. Everything's gone, and for what?"

Amicus shook his head. "I don't know. Ɂätūr always has a plan, but I'm at a loss as to what it is. Why did so many have to suffer and die?"

Alderan scratched his head. "There's very little in this world I understand. Understanding Ɂätūr's plans is something I'll probably never grasp.

"For what it's worth, I'm sorry for your loss, Amicus. I'm sorry about what happened back in the dungeon cell too. I hope you'll find a way to forgive me for that. I love my sister more than this world, and I'd do anything for her."

Amicus stood. "Family's everything, so I won't fault you for that. I hold nothing against you."

Alderan held his hand out. "Friends?"

Amicus clasped Alderan's hand. "Beyond death. For our families. For Aria."

Alderan squeezed hard. "For Aria."

Rayah floated toward them. Her wings swirled the smoke and mist as they fluttered. "We must get moving. I don't think I can handle much more of this smoky air. Rakzar and Eshtak have gone ahead to set up camp."

Amicus released Alderan's hand, closed his eyes for a moment, and shook his head slowly. "I reckon there's nothing more we can do here. I've wasted enough of our time already." He stretched his arm out toward the northern end of the valley. "Lead the way, Rayah."

And guide my heart, Ẑäṭūr.

† † †

In the third watch of the night, Rakzar woke to the sound of a snapping twig. He quietly rose to his feet and sniffed the air but detected no scents outside of those in his party. He twisted and turned his ears, listening for additional noises, but none came.

Rakzar accounted for everyone in the camp, save Eshtak.

Where did you go, little man? What're you up to?

Rakzar knelt, grabbed one of his double-edged battle-axes, and strapped it to his back. He dropped on all fours and sniffed around the perimeter of the camp. Eshtak's scent led north, farther into the Veridis Forest. Rakzar stepped into the trees and then halted.

I'd better wake the White Knight. He snorted, annoyed at how the White Knight had burrowed beneath his skin. *No need to wake him. They'll be fine.*

Rakzar tried to take another step, but his mind wouldn't let him. In that moment, he realized he'd lost his edge, but what could he do? He hung his head with disappointment and made his way over to where the White Knight slept.

I should slit his throat right now. Be done with this.

The thought of killing the White Knight—his adversary—left an uneasy feeling in the pit of his stomach. He'd never lay a finger on the boy again, but he could still pretend, right? The tension between them satisfied him on some primal level.

Rakzar reached across the White Knight and clamped his hand over the White Knight's mouth. The White Knight's eyes shot open and he tried to sit up, but Rakzar held him firmly against the ground. Rakzar put his finger to his own lips and the White Knight settled.

Rakzar removed his hand from the White Knight's mouth. "The naked little man's run off somewhere. I'm going to go find him and bring him back. Keep watch while I'm gone."

The White Knight nodded and sat up. "How long—"

"If I'm not back by first light, go on without us. I *will* find you." Rakzar turned and moved toward the northern edge of the camp.

"Don't hurt him," said the White Knight.

Rakzar looked back at the White Knight and flashed him a wicked grin. "No guarantees."

Rakzar followed Eshtak's trail north from the camp and into the thickening forest. The farther north he traveled, the denser the dorus pine trees grew, and he soon had to force his way between them like people in a crowded marketplace—not that he had experience navigating populous cities.

Sap leaked from the trees, stuck in his fur, and infuriated him. *You'd better have a good explanation for running off, little man.*

The fishy scent of ocean air overwhelmed the clean smell of the dorus pines long before Rakzar pushed through the last of them and stumbled onto the white-sand beach. 300 yards ahead of him, the waves of the Gelu Ocean crashed against the beach with ferocity.

Rakzar swallowed hard. *That's a lot of water.*

To Rakzar's left, twenty yards beyond the beach and in the middle of the ocean, a small, naked man stood atop a rock formation with his hands thrust in the air. *Eshtak.* He held something in his left hand, but Rakzar couldn't make out what it was.

What's he doing out there?

Cold, wet sand clung to the bottoms of his feet as Rakzar sprinted toward the edge of the water. He moved as close to the water as he could without getting wet.

"Eshtak! Get back here!" Rakzar barely heard himself over the crashing waves. There was no way Eshtak could've heard him.

Rakzar glared at the water. He and it were natural born enemies, and he didn't swim so well either. In moderation, he could handle wading through a small pond or brook, or fording a shallow river, but the ocean was a whole other level.

He scanned the beach but found no rocks or pebbles to chuck at Eshtak. *How am I supposed to get his attention?*

Rakzar huffed. "Guess I'll have to get wet." He unstrapped his battle-axe, removed his leather mail, skirt, and sandals, and placed them farther back on the beach where the water couldn't reach them.

He walked over to the water's edge. Another wave crashed against the beach and rolled up to his shins. Even through his thick fur, the liquid ice stung.

Maybe I should just wait here. He'll eventually come back.

The ocean roared as a massive wave careened toward the rock Eshtak stood atop. The wave rose higher as it approached, far above the rock's surface. Eshtak didn't retreat, and the wave engulfed him and the rock. The rock resurfaced as the water receded, but Eshtak no longer stood upon it.

A few weeks ago, Rakzar would've walked away and not thought twice of Eshtak's fate, but he'd changed. On this night, he scanned the dark waters with urgency. *Where are you, little man?*

About forty yards beyond the rock, Rakzar thought he spotted Eshtak's body bobbing around in the rough waters. Self-preservation abandoned, Rakzar drew in a deep breath and sprinted toward the incoming wave.

The icy water prickled his skin like thousands of needles all at once as the wave slammed into his legs and midsection. He stood his ground, then he pushed farther into the water as the ocean receded.

The force of the next wave slammed into his chest like a blow from a club. It knocked the breath from his lungs, took him from his feet, and pulled him under. The undertow grabbed and pulled him farther into the ocean's depths. Disoriented, Rakzar struggled to find the surface again.

He opened his eyes, but the salty water burned them like fire and forced him to close them again. His head broke through the water's surface and he gasped for air, but another wave pulverized him and pulled him back under in mid-breath.

Salty water rushed down his throat and into his lungs, choking him. He coughed, swallowed more of it, and knew he had no chance of survival.

Questions of the afterlife circled his mind like sharks. *Where will I go when I die? Is there another life after this? Or will I cease to exist?*

The idea of death had never bothered him before but being so near it filled him with fear.

I can't die. Not like this.

Rakzar struggled to reach the surface again, but something had wrapped around his ankles and held him under. He reached down and clawed at whatever held him, but he couldn't free himself.

Pain stabbed his chest and lungs like glass shards. His head throbbed. Every muscle in his body spasmed. A flash of warmth covered him like a blanket and fought off the biting cold.

What if there is a god out there?

He sank into oblivion.

† † †

Alderan circled the camp's perimeter with an arrow nocked and ready on his bow. He fought to keep his mind alert and focused, but his anxiety compounded with every passing minute. Rakzar had left long ago to go find Eshtak, and neither of them had returned. Instinct told him that something had gone wrong.

Maybe I should wake Amicus.

No, nothing's wrong. I'm just imagining things.

But what if I'm not?

From the north, deep in the forest, Alderan thought he heard a scream. His heart thumped in his chest and his fingers trembled against the bowstring. He took a deep breath and focused on the darkness. It reminded him of his first encounter with Rakzar.

He strained his eyes to see deeper into the darkness. The shadows moved, crouched, approached. Were there glowing yellow eyes staring at him?

A voice whispered, "Is something out there?"

Alderan jumped out of his skin, and, somehow, he'd managed to draw his bow and loose an arrow in the process. He whirled around and faced the shadow he knew to be Rayah. "Don't sneak up on me like that. I could've shot you by accident."

Rayah giggled. "I think you might've murdered a tree."

Alderan scowled. "It's *not* funny."

Another scream cut through the night, this time much closer. Alderan spun toward the north. Rayah moved next to him and grabbed his hand.

"That scream was Eshtak's." Amicus came up beside Alderan. "We need to go after him."

Alderan stuck his arm out and blocked Amicus from moving past him. "We're not going anywhere. He's headed straight for us."

Amicus pushed Alderan's arm down. "It sounded like he might be hurt."

"No. We need to be ready. We have no idea what's happening out there. Something might be chasing him."

Alderan let go of Rayah's hand, pulled another arrow from his quiver, and nocked it. Fifty yards away, tree branches cracked and popped, and the screaming morphed into understandable words.

"Bad thing! Bad thing!" cried Eshtak.

"To the air, Rayah!" yelled Alderan.

Alderan didn't have time to look back and make sure Rayah listened, but he prayed she had. He raised his bow and drew the string back. Next to him, Amicus pulled his broadsword from its scabbard with a *shing* and held it at the ready. Whatever followed Eshtak wouldn't stand a chance.

Eshtak burst through the trees and skidded to a halt. He grabbed Amicus's arm and pulled on it. "Must come! Must come! Bad thing hurt. Maybe dead. Hurry!"

Rakzar?

Alderan had imagined Rakzar dead on numerous occasions, even begged Ʒäțūr to kill him a few times, but now the thought of it filled him with sorrow.

Have I grown fond of the beast? He didn't have time to ponder it.

Without a word, the four of them stormed into the forest and toward the unknown.

† † †

Amicus had never run so fast in his life. The trek through the forest blurred in his mind. By the time they reached the beach, he struggled to breathe. He staggered a few steps in the deep sand and had to stop. He bent over to catch his breath.

Eshtak stood next to him, seemingly unaffected by their quick pace. Alderan and Rayah had fallen behind. *They'll find their way.*

Amicus straightened and Eshtak pointed to the west. "Bad thing!"

A couple hundred yards away, a large furry body lay on the beach—face-down, unmoving, and just beyond the reach of the waves.

Rakzar.

Amicus and Eshtak ran over to Rakzar and fell on their knees next to him. Amicus rolled Rakzar onto his back, searched for a pulse, but found none. Rakzar wasn't breathing either. Amicus turned Rakzar's head to the side and started pumping Rakzar's chest.

Don't you die on me. I still owe you my life.

Eshtak clasped his hands over his head and murmured "bad thing" repeatedly.

A few minutes later, Alderan and Rayah joined Amicus and Eshtak on the beach and knelt on the other side of Rakzar.

Amicus kept pumping Rakzar's chest, but he looked over at Alderan and Rayah. "Don't just sit there. *Do* something."

Rayah glowered at Amicus. "What would you have us do?"

Amicus wiped his brow with his shoulder and continued pumping Rakzar's chest. "I don't know, Rayah, but we can't sit back and let him die."

Rayah folded her arms. "After everything he's put us through, I'm okay with him dying. In fact, I hope he does."

"Don't say that, Rayah." Alderan groaned. "I don't want him to die."

Rayah turned her glare on Alderan. "How can you say that, Alderan?

How many times has this filthy beast tried taking *both* of our lives?"

Amicus slammed his fist into the sand next to Rakzar's head. "Arguing isn't helping!"

Alderan grabbed Amicus's other hand and stopped him from pumping Rakzar's chest. "It's not working, Amicus. You've been at it for quite some time now. He's not responding."

Amicus jerked his hand away from Alderan and sat back in the sand. "I can't handle all this death. Everyone around me keeps dying."

Alderan placed his hands on Rakzar's chest. "I brought Rayah back from the edge of death once before. I'll try to bring Rakzar back."

Alderan contorted his face for more than a minute, but nothing happened.

Amicus stood. "There's no point. He's hasn't breathed for a long time. He's dead."

Amicus felt a tug on his sleeve and looked down at Eshtak. "What is it, my little friend?"

Eshtak's thin black lips parted, showing his stained, yellowed teeth. "Eshtak's friend help."

Amicus frowned. As far as he knew, Eshtak had no other friends. "What are you talking about, Eshtak?"

"Lady in mirror. Eshtak likes lady. Lady likes Eshtak."

Amicus looked at Rayah and Alderan and they both shrugged. He looked back down at Eshtak. "Can you show me this mirror?"

Eshtak bounced from one foot to the other then trotted a hundred yards down the beach. He stopped, picked up his brown cloth sack, and trotted back over to them. He reached into the sack and pulled out a small mirror with a brass handle.

Amicus took the mirror from Eshtak and peered into it. A tired, black-skinned man stared back at him. The past few days had taken their toll on him, and the mirror reflected it.

Amicus turned the mirror over. "I don't understand, Eshtak. All I see is my reflection."

Eshtak snatched the mirror from Amicus's hand and held the mirror up to his own face. His lime-green eyes glowed bright in the reflection.

Eshtak grinned big at the mirror. "Hello?"

Amicus gasped as Eshtak's reflection morphed into that of an older woman's. The woman's tanned, wrinkled skin drooped on a face framed with wiry silver hair, but her bright blue eyes brimmed with life and a sense of compassion.

She would've been beautiful in her prime, like my Vorene.

The woman's voice sounded hollow as it burst forth from the mirror. "Eshtak! What can I do for you, my sweet darling?"

Eshtak bounced from foot to foot. "Bad thing needs help. Bad thing dead."

Amicus snatched the mirror from Eshtak and peered into it.

The woman in the mirror smiled. "You must be Amicus. Eshtak's told me so much about you. I'm sorry about your family. I know all too well what it's like to lose those you love."

An image of Vorene and Vonah surfaced in Amicus's mind—the two of them huddled together in the middle of their burned-out home. His wounded heart ripped into pieces all over again, and his chest tightened with grief. He took a moment to collect himself.

I'll bring your killers to justice, my beauties. But I need Rakzar alive to do that.

Amicus cleared his throat. "Thank you, but we have a pressing matter that Eshtak said you could help us with. One of our party members got pulled under the water and isn't breathing. Eshtak believes you can revive him."

The woman's eyebrows raised. "He does, does he? How long has it been since your friend's last breath? More than a few minutes?"

Amicus breathed deeply and then recognized the irony of it. He looked down at Rakzar.

If only I could breathe for you.

Amicus scratched his head. "We've no idea how long it's been since his last breath, but I'm certain it's been more than a few minutes."

The woman jabbed, "And you still think I can help?"

Eshtak chimed in. "Eshtak knows lady help."

"I cannot raise the dead, darling. Nor would I want to. A human cannot survive more than three or four minutes without breathing. It's an impossibility. I'm truly sorry."

Amicus smiled at the woman. "I understand, but he isn't human. He's a gnoll, his name's Rakzar, and he recently saved me. I owe him my life. I'd like to exhaust every possible way to revive him before we give up. Isn't there anything you could try?"

Amicus knew he sounded desperate. He was. He needed closure.

I need Rakzar alive.

The woman placed her folded hands on the bridge of her nose and shook her head. "I'm not sure why anyone would want to save the life of a gnoll, but I took an oath to share my light with the entire world. I'll see what I can do. Give me a moment."

"Thank you," said Amicus, but his own hollow reflection had already replaced the woman's image.

Please hurry.

† † †

Rakzar's fur matched the red hues of the early morning sky, and, despite the dire situation, it made Alderan smile. He stood over Rakzar's body. Not long ago, he would've relished this moment, but now, guilt feasted on his conscience like maggots. Had he tried to revive Rakzar, or had he just gone through the motions?

What kind of person am I? Do I really want him dead?

"What now?" asked Rayah.

The wind kicked up, and sand swirled in the air like a cyclone. A moment later, a woman stood on the beach next to them. Butterflies fluttered in Alderan's stomach.

I wanna know how to do that.

Amicus pointed at the woman. "There's your answer."

The woman wore a low-cut white top, red trousers tucked inside of knee-high white boots trimmed with white fur, and an assortment of necklaces, brooches, rings, and bracelets of all shapes, sizes, and materials. She wore more jewelry than Alderan had ever seen.

A red velvet cape hung over her shoulders and rested on the sand at her heels. Fluffy white fur lined the cape's outer edge, and a golden chain hung at the base of her wrinkled neck, tying together the left and right sides of the cape.

Based on the woman's appearance, Alderan assumed she held a position of importance. Her blue-eyed gaze left him without words. She peered into his soul like a person would peek through a window, and it piqued his inhibitions. However, her knowing smile resonated within his heart and mind.

Who are you? How do you know me?

Alderan ran his fingers through his hair and looked down at Rakzar, too embarrassed to keep eye contact with the woman any longer.

The woman waved her hands. "Step aside, my darlings. Let me see what I can do for your friend."

Alderan, Rayah, and Amicus stepped back and gave the woman room.

Eshtak giggled and took off down the beach, twirling and dancing along the way. Alderan chuckled to himself. He wished he were as carefree as Eshtak, who didn't seem to care what anyone thought of him. Had Alderan been more like Eshtak, he would've divulged his true feelings to Rayah long ago.

The woman stepped over to where Rakzar lay and knelt next to him. She placed her hands above his chest and closed her eyes.

Alderan took hold of Rayah's hand and squeezed it. He knew she'd rather Rakzar stay dead, but he didn't feel the same way anymore.

Please, 2äṭūr, let Rakzar live.

The woman locked her fingers together, muttered some words under her breath, and plunged her hands into Rakzar's chest. The air crackled like thunder and a ring of dust spread out from around them, but Rakzar didn't move. A rosiny scent flitted in the air.

The woman repeated her actions but to no avail.

Alderan let go of Rayah's hand and clutched his side. His stomach twisted with nausea.

He can't be dead. It's not possible.

The woman stood and turned toward Alderan. "I need your help, darling."

Alderan's nausea deepened. His voice squeaked, "Mine?"

The woman held her hand out toward Alderan. "Of course. I'm not quite strong enough to revive him on my own, but together I'm sure we can save him. He has a lot of fight in him, and his spirit hasn't left his body yet."

Can she sense my mezhik? Is such a thing even possible?

Alderan raked his scalp with his fingers. "Why would you think I could help?"

She stared into his soul again. "You and I are gifted, but in different ways. One of my gifts is the ability to see the aura of mezhik around a person. Your aura is one of the strongest I've ever seen. You are truly gifted, darling."

Alderan looked to Rayah.

Rayah shrugged. "Don't look at me, Alderan. This is *your* choice. You already know how I feel. That beast can stay dead for all I care. He deserves it."

Alderan shook his head. *We'd all be dead if we received what we deserved.*

Alderan stepped forward and took the woman's cold, bony hand in his. He looked back at Rayah, and she scowled at him. "No matter the past or the future, I can't let Rakzar die if there's a chance to save him. Everyone deserves a second chance, Rayah, including him."

The woman looked at Rayah. "You know he's right, young one. Search your heart. What would Ɂäţūr have you do?"

Rayah continued to scowl.

The woman positioned Alderan on the opposite side of Rakzar from her, and they both knelt next to him. She and Alderan wove their fingers together and closed their eyes.

"What do I need to do?" asked Alderan.

"Just relax, darling. There's no need to be nervous."

I have every reason to be. How can I help bring Rakzar back without knowing anything? Alderan said, "But I don't know how to use my mezhik."

"It's okay. Let my mezhik guide yours."

"I'll try."

"Very good, darling. Let's begin. Do you feel my mezhik flowing into you?"

Every inch of Alderan's body tingled with mezhik, and he trembled. "Yessss."

"Good. Now, concentrate your mind on my mezhik. Let it be a guide for yours."

Alderan panted, "Okay. I think I'm ready."

"Yes, I can feel it. Now, when I say push, you need to focus your mezhik into your hands and visualize it flowing out of you and into Rakzar. Can you do that?"

"I think so."

Please let this work, Ɂäţūr.

"Good. Ready now… push!"

Alderan's and the woman's hands plunged into Rakzar's chest. The ground quaked as a wave of energy spread in every direction, sizzling and thundering. The aroma of roses and pine bloomed in the air.

Alderan and the woman separated hands, fell backward onto their elbows, and opened their eyes. Rakzar jolted straight up and spewed water from his mouth and nose. He coughed, spat up more water, and took a deep breath.

Amicus stepped back. "Ɂäţūr's ghost!"

Rakzar tried to speak but coughed up more water instead.

Alderan sat back up and beat Rakzar's back with the palm of his hand. "Are you okay?"

"I died, so what do you think?" Rakzar growled. "I saw the end of the world, and there was nothing there. No hope. No life. Only darkness. I never wanna go there again."

Alderan gazed at the surrounding sand. *In the end, we all die. Dust unto dust.*

Amicus stepped forward, bent down, and put his hand on Rakzar's shoulder. "You may have *felt* dead, my friend, but I assure you that it was only in your mind."

Rakzar shoved Amicus's hand away, grabbed a fist full of sand, and thrust it at the ocean. "You weren't there. You didn't feel what I felt. I've never felt so alone before. My existence had no purpose."

Amicus shook his head. "If you'd died, you wouldn't be here now. There's no coming back from death."

"Well if that wasn't death, then I never want to know what death feels like," snarled Rakzar.

Amicus sank to his knees. "I don't know what it's like on the other side of death, but on this side, it feels like a living nightmare."

Rakzar looked to his left. "Who's the bag of bones?"

The woman frowned at Rakzar. "I'm the one who brought you back from the cusp of death. With Alderan's help, of course."

Amicus turned to the woman and cleared his throat. "Sweet Ɛäţūr. I'm sorry, but I didn't catch your name."

The woman looked up at Amicus. "Oh, yes, of course. Where are my manners? I'm Zerenity."

Amicus dipped his head. "Thank you for doing this, Zerenity."

Zerenity smiled softly.

Rakzar turned to Alderan. "Why would you choose to save me, White Knight?"

Alderan smirked. "All lives are worth saving—even yours. And, after all, I'm the savior of the world, am I not?"

"Savior of the world?" Rakzar snorted. "Then who's going to save you?"

Rakzar posed a valid question. Would saving the world be Alderan's death? Is that what the prophecies foretold? Was that the truth of the matter?

Could I lay down my life for this world? For Aria? For Rayah?

The idea of death shook him to his core.

I don't wanna die. I'm no hero.

CHAPTER TWELVE

The morning sun crept up from the west like a demon rising from the bowels of Ef Demd Dhä, determined to make its mark on the world. Pravus sat in the carriage. His diary still lay open in his lap, but his thoughts wandered thousands of miles—and many years—away.

The night he'd encountered Nardus at the Ferzh's Head Inn, they'd made a deal that could change the world. He'd sent Nardus on a quest—into certain death—to retrieve a stone. Had prophecy not been on his side, it would've proved fruitless.

So long ago. But Nardus has returned.

Pravus grinned. Decades of planning were finally coming to fruition. The world would soon bend to his will.

"Who's Nardus?"

Aria's voice ripped Pravus from the past, pulled him thousands of miles north, and thrust him against the back of his seat like a kick to the chest. He jerked his head back and smacked it against the carriage wall.

Aria sat next to him, not across from him. He never saw her move. How long had she been there?

Pravus snapped the diary shut and glared at her. "What do you think you're doing? The matters within this book are no concern of yours."

Aria furrowed her brow. "You agreed to keep no secrets from me, Pravus. As your future wife and queen, I have the right to know what this is about, don't I? Who's this Nardus?"

Pravus studied Aria's heart-shaped face.. Her narrow-set, green eyes sparkled in the morning light like precious emeralds. Her flawless, fair skin accentuated her narrow jaws and high cheekbones. Her full, pink lips puckered slightly, and her upper lip sat a bit higher on the right side.

Two loosely braided strands of blonde hair, starting just below her chin line, hung over her shoulders and just past the middle of her chest. Yellow ribbons tied in bows wrapped the ends of the braids.

Beauty like no other. How could I deny her anything?

Pravus sighed. "Very well. I'll tell you, but you must promise to keep this between us."

Aria smirked. "Who would I tell? You're one of the only people I know in this entire world. Besides, I know how to keep a secret. I didn't even talk for months, remember?"

Pravus cracked his knuckles. "I hired Nardus to do a job, and now that job has been completed."

Aria poked Pravus's leg with her finger. "And what job was that?"

Pravus stroked the leather-bound diary with his thumb. "I asked him to retrieve a stone for me."

Aria scoffed. "A *stone*? Why would you need someone to retrieve a stone for you? They're everywhere."

Pravus chuckled. "This is a *special* stone. From a *special* place. There's no other like it in the world."

"Do the place and stone have names?"

"They do—*Ţämbəll Dhef Däd Dhä* and *2ţōn Dhef Dädh*. Do you know what they mean?"

Aria shrugged. "Should I?"

"You will soon enough. Their names come from Ancient Centaurian—the language of our ancestors. Part of your training will include learning it. It's paramount for someone with mezhik to learn. *Ţämbəll Dhef Däd Dhä* means Temple of the Dead, and *2ţōn Dhef Dädh* means Stone of Death. The temple only exists in the lower world."

Aria folded her arms. "*Ef Demd Dhä?* You expect me to believe that you sent someone there to retrieve some stone of death from the temple of the dead and that they've returned? That's not possible. The dead cannot return from there."

Pravus eyed Aria intently before answering her. "Nardus isn't dead."

Aria's eyes widened. "How's that possible? How can someone travel to the lower world and back?"

A dull throb emanated from the back of Pravus's skull. He reached back and massaged the tender spot. "Not just anyone can. Many have tried over the last few centuries, but I believe Nardus is the first to ever return since its creation."

Aria scrunched up her face. "I don't understand. Ɛäțūr created *Ef Demd Dhä* before He created us."

Pravus shook his head. *Ɛäțūr, the mighty creator of all. Pathetic. Soon she'll see the absurdity of the existence of any god. Except me.*

"*Ef Demd Dhä* is a world conjured by mezhik, not one created by Ɛäțūr or any other god."

Aria shook her head. "No…" She looked up at him, her eyes misted. "How can that be?"

The first thread of doubt sewn. Pravus smiled inwardly. "Many beliefs people hold are simple misunderstandings of mezhik and how it alters the world they inhabit. Some go as far as to refute the existence of mezhik altogether, while others vilify it and seek its eradication."

Aria looked down at her lap. "I was one who didn't believe."

"But now you do, and that's all that matters."

Aria nodded. "I guess, but there are so many things I still don't understand."

Pravus grinned. "Perhaps, but I know you'll learn quickly."

Aria twirled her hair with her finger. "So… what is this stone? What do you need it for?"

"*Ɛțōn Dhef Dädh*. It has the power to raise the dead."

"Why would Nardus agree to retrieve it for you? What's in it for him?"

Pravus straightened in the seat and smoothed his robes. "Nardus believes the stone will enable me to resurrect his family, but I intend to use it to restore my father's kingdom." He tilted his head. "What Nardus seeks isn't possible."

"Aren't you afraid of what he might do when he finds out that you've lied to him? What if he doesn't give you the stone? What if he keeps it for himself?"

Pravus steepled his fingers. "He sealed his fate the moment he agreed to retrieve the stone. Once I possess the stone, I'll have no more use for him."

The blood drained from Aria's face. "Is that my fate too? Will you dispose of me after you've had your go with me? Will you tire of me and find another more beautiful or worthier of being your queen?"

Pravus took Aria's hand in his. "There is no beauty greater than yours, nor will there ever be one worthier of being my queen than you. You're the one person in this world I'd never betray. I give you my word, on my life."

Aria pulled her hand away. "I'm not sure your word is enough. You've already done things to me that you promised you never would, and my trust in you has shrank to a narrow stream—easily crossed."

Pravus balled his hand. *How can I give this woman what she wants? She asks the world of me, but I want the world for myself.*

His knuckles whitened, but a glance at her beautiful features eased his tension. *But I want her too. She's my destiny. Our lives are woven together by fate, foretold by the prophets.*

She is the one, but am I willing to risk everything I've worked for and bind my soul with hers?

I'm just not sure.

Can I trust the prophets? What if they're wrong? Everything would be ruined.

Maybe she's not the one... But my heart says she is. My soul yearns for her when we're apart. She haunts my dreams like a fallen angel. I knew her before we ever met.

No. She must be the one. My soul cries out for her, and my mezhik yearns to bond with hers. I'd give up everything for her, wouldn't I?

Yes!

But I won't need to because my dreams will become hers. She'll see the world as I do and understand the necessity of my plan.

The world must be purged.

Pravus took Aria's hand and held it firmly when she tried pulling it away again. Her hand trembled in his, and guilt rose in his throat. "Calm down, Aria. I'd never hurt you. I'll admit I've done things and said things to you that I regret, but not out of hate or disdain. I struggle with my own ambitions and the love I feel for you.

"I'd never loved anyone before I met you, and I don't always know how to handle myself around you because of it. I'm terrified of what our relationship means to me. You're the single light in my dark world, and I don't want to snuff you out like a candle. I want you to burn bright, Aria."

Pravus gazed into her eyes. "You've already changed me in ways I thought impossible. You're the beginning to my end just as I am yours. Together, we're a circle of light and dark—without end."

Aria squeezed his hand. "If we are as you say, then show me. Widen my narrow stream until it becomes an ocean. Make the distance so great that I can never cross it and fall into distrusting you again."

"When we are wed, I will bind my soul with yours."

"You mean our flesh, as Ɂäʈūr has said: *'And the flesh of him will join with the flesh of her, and they will become one.'* Right?"

Pravus chuckled. "No, my queen. Those words refer to the physical bond of a consummated marriage. When I've gone into you, we will become one flesh, but only during that time. What I'm speaking of is far greater than anything a god could do. I'll use mezhik to bind our souls in an unbreakable bond that will last for all eternity."

Aria's brow furrowed, and her eyes narrowed. "Are you saying that you're more powerful than Ɂäʈūr—the Creator of *everything*?"

Ɂäʈūr.

The idea of an all-knowing god sickened him. Of any god, for that matter. The proof that no god existed surrounded them: Chaos consumed their world. His own life proved it.

In time, you'll see that I'm the only god you'll need.

Pravus patted the top of her hand with his. "No, my queen. What I'm stating is that the bond I speak of isn't created by Ɂäʈūr. Nothing more."

Aria withdrew her hand from his and crossed her hands over her lap. "And what does this *soul binding* mean? How would it change my trust in you?"

Pravus turned sideways in the seat and faced Aria, one leg crossed over his knee. "Have you heard of a blood pact?"

"Are you talking about the bond shared between those of the same family? Like my brother and me?"

Pravus cracked his knuckles again. "Similar, but much stronger. A blood pact is formed between two parties and sealed with blood and mezhik. The individuals bound by it can never kill each other, no matter how strong their hate for each other is or becomes. As you know, blood relatives have no such qualms in killing each other to gain what wasn't theirs."

Aria pursed her lips and nodded slowly. "Okay, and what does this soul binding do?"

"Once enacted, you and I will be inseparable. Our bodies, lives, souls, and fates will be as one. We will share everything—pain, sorrow, hate, joy, love, secrets, wounds—even death. But the strength of our mezhik will combine, and we'll become an unstoppable force."

Tears welled in Aria's eyes. "You'd do that for me? You'd tie yourself to me for eternity? Why? I am nothing." Her gaze lowered to her lap.

Pravus leaned forward, wrapped his arms around Aria, and pulled her into his lap. "Without you, I am also nothing. Together, we shall rule the world."

Together we will fulfill the prophecies. Our fates are sealed.

Pravus kissed Aria's forehead. "Knowing more about our future together, do you trust me now?"

Aria leaned into him, took a deep breath through her nostrils, and sighed. "Just a reminder of how good you smell eases my mind."

Pravus laughed. "I'll take that as a yes."

He kissed her forehead again then pushed her off his lap. "Because of Nardus's return, I must go."

Aria sat up straight. "What do you mean you must go?"

Pravus took the fountain pen lying on the seat next to him and placed it into an inner pocket of his robes. He reached down and picked up his satchel from the floor of the carriage. "I must get home today. Preparations must be made for his arrival—and yours."

Aria smacked the seat with her fist. "You're saying we could've avoided this stupid carriage ride across the entire continent? I don't care about preparations." She glared at him. "I'm coming with you."

Pravus reached for Aria's hand, but she pulled it away from his reach. He sighed. "I cannot take you with me. It requires an absurd amount of mezhik just to teleport myself, and I'm not strong enough to take you with me. It would kill us both."

Aria's face reddened. "So that's it? You'll leave me out here in the middle of nowhere to fend for myself while you lounge at home?"

Pravus tented his fingers. "Please understand, my queen, I wouldn't do this to you unless it was absolutely necessary. I promise you'll be safe. In another week, you'll arrive at my castle. *Our* castle."

Aria's silver collar glowed red—it matched her cheeks. "A *week*? You expect me to be cooped up in this stupid carriage for another week? By myself?"

"The time will pass quickly, I swear it."

Aria got up from the seat, threw herself onto the forward-facing seat—her seat—, and drew her knees up to her chest. "You might as well return me to Dragnus and lock me back up."

Pravus leaned across the carriage and placed his hand on the small of her back. "Please don't be angry."

Aria swatted at his arm but missed. "Don't touch me."

Pravus withdrew his hand. "Please don't make me leave like this. I don't want our last words to be a fight."

Aria turned over in the seat. Loose strands of blonde hair fell across her face, but her piercing green eyes shone through. "Maybe you should've thought about that before you said you were abandoning me."

Pravus couldn't help but smile. Aria's youth and vigor allured him. Their wedding night would be unforgettable.

Pravus held his hands up in surrender. "You're right. Securing our future together is a pointless task. I'll just stay here with you. The world be damned."

Aria sat up and swept her hair out of her face. "Just go. I never liked you anyway. I only used you to get away from Dragnus."

Pravus laughed, but in the back of his mind he wondered if there was some truth to her words. She'd been in such a low place when he'd met her. Had he occupied her position, he would've done anything necessary to get away from it too.

I know she loves me, though. I can see it in her eyes.

Her beautiful, penetrating eyes burrowed deep into his soul. She already knew him like no other ever had. Her fierceness would command the world.

And she's mine.

✝ ✝ ✝

Aria knew that her strength as a woman, both mentally and physically, exceeded most. Sure, she cried sometimes, but that didn't make her weak—it showcased her compassion. She embodied the spirit of a warrior, and sometimes that warrior protected her even from those she cared about.

She'd spent so many months locked inside a cell in the dungeons below Castle Portador Tempestade that she'd nearly lost her true self behind all the walls she'd erected around herself. Amicus's kindness had weakened those walls, but the time she'd spent with Pravus tore them down completely.

She felt vulnerable again, but it didn't bother her. She needed Pravus. Not because she was a woman. Not because she had no one else. She loved him. *Everything* about him. She melted every time she peered into his golden-brown eyes, and his curly, raven locks were silk between her fingers.

I can't stay mad at him, Ʒäṭūr. Just look at him.

She had to let him go, but it would be hard. She'd have to find a way to entertain herself until she arrived at the castle.

Maybe I can remember more about the sandcastles. And daydream of being reunited with my family again in Kinzhdm ef Häfn.

She leaned forward in the seat, fully resolved. "Go and prepare for Nardus, my lord. I'll see you again soon."

"That's it?" asked Pravus. "No more fighting?"

"I cannot keep you from your destiny any more than I could hold the sun in the sky. Now go, before I change my mind."

Pravus smiled, took the diary on his lap, and placed it in his satchel. He lifted the strap of the satchel over his head and then leaned across the carriage and kissed Aria on her lips. "I will see you soon, my queen."

Aria reached out to hug Pravus, but her arms swept through him as though he were mist. The carriage pulled her through his lingering lavender-colored aura, and her whole body arched as his carnal mezhik caressed her. She quickly turned around in her seat and looked out the rear window.

Beyond the carriage, in the middle of the dirt road, Pravus solidified. He turned and waved at her and then—in the blink of an eye—disappeared.

Aria slid down on the seat and then lay on her back. In that moment, when his essence had passed through her and his mezhik touched her skin, she felt ravished.

I want him, Ɂäṭūr. Does that make me a bad person? Wanting him makes me feel a bit dirty, but then I want him even more. If just a simple touch from him does this to me, how will I survive our wedding night? I'll be driven mad with ecstasy.

Aria wrapped her arms around herself and giggled.

Hours later, yips and howls erupted from outside the carriage and Aria tensed up. She couldn't identify the yips, but she knew the howls intimately.

Gnolls.

The hairs on her arms stood on end and her heart ached. She sat up in the seat, but her head refused to turn sideways so she could look out the window. The yips and howls grew louder and turned into snarls and growls. The carriage bucked, and Aria fell off the seat and onto the floor.

The taste of blood filled her mouth, but she had no time to assess it. She pushed herself onto her hands and knees, and the carriage bucked again, harder. Her heart thumped in her chest and beat in her ears.

The carriage tilted to one side, and Aria knocked her head against the door. It swung open, and she slid forward. The bright world beyond the carriage blurred her vision. She grabbed a handful of seat cushion and pulled herself back inside the carriage, but then the whole carriage lurched in the opposite direction.

She flew against the other side of the carriage and the door slammed shut. Something popped in her upper back, and pain radiated from that spot all the way down her spine. But the ride wasn't over.

The carriage bounced, shook violently, and then crashed onto its side. Spurred on by Diʑäfär himself, the horses galloped down the road, dragging her and the carriage with them.

Aria lay against the side of the carriage, absorbing every bump in the road. She tried sitting up, but her body wouldn't respond. Every breath ended in painful stabs, and her arms and legs tingled with numbness.

The carriage slid to a stop, and every thought abandoned her. For a moment, the world quieted around her, but then the noise and chaos rushed back in and swarmed her like hornets. Repeatedly, the carriage shook and then something or someone yelped.

Tears slid down her cheeks and she prayed, "Ẑäṭūr, save me." No other words came to her, so she repeated the prayer.

She lay there for what felt like hours before the chaotic noises surrounding the carriage finally ceased. Her heart raced as the silence ensued. She felt alone and abandoned.

I'm going to die here. Ẑäṭūr, please—

A muffled voice cut through the silence, but Aria couldn't make out what they were saying. The carriage shook, and then the click of claws echoed from the side of the carriage above her.

Something's on top of the carriage!

Aria tried to move her head, but it was useless. She was paralyzed from the neck down. A shadow fell over the door above her, and her breath caught in her throat. Wood creaked and moaned, then the door exploded outward.

Light flooded the carriage and blinded her. A shadow flashed across the opening. A howl ceased mid-stream, followed by a grunt, and the carriage shook as something fell on top of it.

More claws ticked against the topside of the carriage.

Why did you leave me, Pravus?

Aria's eyes adjusted to the light, but then an elongated, fur-covered face sank into the opening where the door had been. The beast's orange, lantern-shaped eyes glowed in the shadows. Even from six feet away, Aria smelled its nidorous breath as it panted.

Saliva dripped from the beast's open mouth, hit Aria's cheek, and slid down the side of her face. Half an inch to the right and it would've landed in her mouth. The thought gagged her.

The beast growled at her, and she screamed as loud as she could, but it didn't retreat. Instead, it swiped at her face with a paw full of sharp claws, but she was just out of its range.

The beast pulled itself back up and circled the door above her. It whined and yipped, confused as to how to get to her—its prey. It leaned in and swiped at her several more times. Eventually, it would crawl inside and kill her.

Just come down here and finish the job.

Another shadow filled the opening. A fur-covered, paw-like hand reached down, grabbed the first beast by its neck, and tossed it away from the carriage. The second beast bent down and peered into the opening. She recognized the beast immediately.

She'd never forget his face. It filled her nightmares. He'd wielded the axe that chopped off her father's head. She knew his name and had cursed him to death every night since that day.

Karraar.

His hateful yellow eyes plunged daggers into her heart, and the sadistic grin on his face roiled her stomach.

Aria glared at him. "Come to finish me off?"

Karraar lowered himself into the carriage and straddled her. He reached down and grabbed a fistful of her yellow dress. When he lifted her up from the side of the carriage, something slid out from between her shoulder blades.

She gasped.

Her body convulsed with waves of pain, and then Karraar's twisted, scarred face faded into darkness.

Take me, Ɂäṭūr.

CHAPTER THIRTEEN

Theyn hung in the air, her arms flailing at her sides and her face ashen and contorted with anguish. Blood poured from her exposed abdomen like a river, streamed down her legs, and pooled in the snow beneath her.

The obsidian dragon laughed, raised his head, and spewed a column of fire skyward. The grey sky above the mountain peaks erupted in flames and turned blood-red.

Nardus sank to his knees, unable to move. It was happening all over again, and he couldn't do anything about it.

Nardus looked to Theyn and then back to the dragon. "Tell me what I'm supposed to do. How can I save her?"

The dragon bared his sharp teeth in what might've been a smile, but he said nothing.

Nardus sprang to his feet and shook his fist at the dragon. "Answer me! I can't lose her. I can't lose my family all over again."

The dragon whipped his long, spiked tail in the air and thrust it into the ground at Nardus's feet, narrowly missing him. The ground trembled, and snow slid down the sides of the mountain, closing off the narrow pass at both ends. "While you fail to act, the darkness spreads like a plague—infecting those around you."

Nardus turned toward Theyn. "How do I stop this? How can I save her?"

"She's already lost," said the dragon.

"No!" yelled Nardus. "I will not accept this!"

Nardus turned toward the dragon and unsheathed Brinzhär Dädh, but its familiar ring sounded dull, and its mezhik failed to flow into him.

He lowered the sword and looked at it, but he held a viper instead.

The viper struck at his face. He slung it by its tail and released it, and it flew into a snowbank and disappeared.

"As she dies—" The dragon laughed. "—you play with vipers. Will you never learn?"

Nardus turned back to Theyn.

Her oozing blood blackened, and her flailing arms stilled. He grabbed her slacken hand in his and pressed it to his cheek. "Don't leave me, Theyn. I need you. Our daughter needs you. I never thought I'd love another after Vitara, but then I met you. I can't lose you, Theyn. Not now. I love you."

Bloody, black tears oozed from Theyn's eyes and crawled down her cheeks. Her hand trembled in his. "Let our child help you, Nardus, no matter the cost. Let her save you from the sickness. I am not worth saving."

Theyn's hand stilled in his, her eyes grew dim, and her head slumped against her chest.

"No, Theyn! Don't leave me!"

† † †

Theyn lay in bed under the green wool blanket, next to Nardus. She ran her fingers through his stringy brown hair. A cold rag lay across his forehead, and his naked body raged with fire next to hers. She'd re-wet the rag several times during the night, but his fever lingered.

Hours earlier, she'd come out of her room and found Nardus unconscious and hanging by his collar, just inches from the floor. He'd still been breathing, but only enough to survive. She'd unhooked the chain from his collar and then pulled him into her room.

Undressing him and lifting him into her bed had proven quite the undertaking, but the revelations of his hard, manly body as she removed each article of his clothing lessened the burden.

After putting Nardus in her bed, Theyn had taken a bucket of water and a rag and had washed his entire body. Seeing his nakedness and touching every inch of him had made her feel salacious, but she'd liked it. She'd wanted more. She wanted him still.

The nízhäíd bəllū did its work, and Nardus still lay unconscious. Theyn purred as she cuddled up next to him. She put her mouth next to his ear and kissed his earlobe.

"I know what you want from me," she whispered. "I saw it in your eyes the moment we met. You want me just as much as I want you."

Theyn pulled the blanket off and stared at Nardus's naked body once more. Every inch of his sunbaked body glistened with sweat in the candlelight. The muscles in his arms, legs, and torso formed a picture of perfection. She couldn't find an ounce of fat on him.

Muscular, but not overbuilt. The perfect male specimen.

She started with his left cheek and then made her way down the length of his body, tracing each of his scars with her fingers and her tongue, and then kissing them and letting her lips linger against his smoldering skin each time.

Take him, Theyn. Zhedäz 2ʊn has delivered him to you. He's yours.

Nardus lay unconscious. He wouldn't resist her.

Fulfill your destiny, Theyn. You were made for this moment. Take him into you.

Even bound and threatened when they'd met, he'd undressed her with his eyes, hadn't he?

Is it wrong of me to use him?

No. He'll never even know.

The more Theyn contemplated it, the more she rationalized her need of him.

He killed Shaul, my lover, and now it's his duty to pleasure me, awake or otherwise.

"*Zhedäz 2ʊn*, my goddess, hear my words and accept this deed. Let this union satisfy the terms of our agreement and fulfill the requirements of my condition."

Theyn rose from the bed, latched the door to her sleeping quarters, and slid the lock into place. She didn't want any interference from Berggren. Besides, he *knew* about her condition and what it required of her.

I have no choice.

Theyn unbuckled her belt, unbuttoned her trousers, and let them fall to the floor in a bunch around her ankles. She loosened the ties on the front of her blouse and pulled it over her head. She tossed it to the floor, stepped out of her trousers, and pulled off her stockings. She wore no undergarments.

Naked before Nardus, she felt vulnerable and a bit naughty. Had he been conscious, would he appreciate her slender features?

He doesn't even see you, Theyn.

Could she go through with it? She'd never lain with an unconscious man before. In fact, she'd never lain with anyone other than Shaul, and she hadn't chosen him.

What if it doesn't work? What if he can't be aroused?

Her pulse quickened.

You can't go back to what you were. You have no other choice but to be with him.

The brisk air in the chamber coated her naked body with gooseflesh.

Take him, Theyn.

Resolved in what she must do, Theyn crawled into the bed next to Nardus and pulled the covers up to their waists. Intense heat radiated from him and warmed her frozen flesh. She rolled on top of him and sat up.

Give in to your need.

She placed her hands on Nardus's chest, and he moaned. She leaned forward, and the stench of stale alcohol filled her nostrils. *The only thing he shares with Shaul.* She kissed his lips, and the sour taste lingered on hers. He moaned again, but this time it sounded like words.

She turned her head and put her ear close to his lips. "Did you say something, my love?"

His hot breath caressed her ear and traveled down the side of her neck. A soft moan escaped from the back of her throat and through her parted lips.

Nardus whispered, "Don't leave me, Theyn."

He needs you, Theyn. Take him.

Theyn smiled, turned her head and kissed his lips, and then parted them with her tongue. Every nerve in her body jerked with pleasure as she slid down his torso and gave in to the beast within her.

You're mine.

✝ ✝ ✝

Berggren's cheek peeled away from his arm as he lifted his head from the table. Tendrils of drool hung from his chin like snot. His head throbbed, and it took him several minutes to get his bearings.

The eye-bolt in the center of the table held the end of a chain in its grasp, but the other end of the chain lay loose on the floor. He looked over at the door that led into Theyn's sleeping quarters—it was closed.

Had her door been closed earlier? Had he closed her door? His memories were a bit fuzzy.

Why's there a chain attached to the table? And why did I drink so much? What was I thinking?

The events of the night trickled back into his mind, and his face flushed with anger.

"Nardus," he growled and stood up.

His head spiraled and spun. His entire body flushed with warmth, and his vision went black. He grabbed the table's edge to steady himself and waited until his vision returned.

He stumbled over to Theyn's door and pressed his ear against it. At first, he heard nothing, but then a series of soft moans ensued. He turned the knob and pushed on the door—locked.

Zhedäʒ ʒʊn, what has she done?

He pounded the door with his fist. "Open up, Theyn!"

She didn't answer.

"Theyn, open this door, or I'll break it down!"

"Go away, *father*," she panted. "We've just finished. He's *mine* now."

Berggren sank to the floor, defeated.

This can't be happening. Why does she never listen?

Berggren yelled through the door, "How could you do this to me? To us? Lord Rosai warned us about this very thing! You've damned us all, Theyn!"

The door latch disengaged with a *click*. The door swung open, and Theyn stood there, naked and drenched in sweat and blood. Her caramel skin glowed in the candlelight. Her nakedness embarrassed him, but she was his daughter, and he couldn't bear to look away from her either.

Theyn bent down and put her hand on his cheek. "You've nothing to fear, father. I've seen the future. I'll eventually carry his child."

Bile rose in his throat, and his hands curled. *The bastard. We had a deal.* He breathed deep and bottled his anger. "Why would you want to carry his child?"

Theyn rubbed his cheek. "Don't you understand? I love him. He *will* love me too. I've felt it in my visions."

Berggren forced air through his nostrils. "Love? You know nothing of it. Satisfy your *condition* if you must, but don't pretend you love him."

Theyn withdrew her hand from his cheek. "Why? Because I didn't love Shaul? There was nothing of him to love. He served a purpose, nothing more."

Berggren sneered at her. "Don't you *ever* speak of Shaul like that. He had more to offer than you could ever imagine."

"You're talking about him as though he were your son and not your nephew. Besides, Nardus is different and attractive. I *want* to be with him."

Berggren looked past Theyn and into her room. Nardus lay in her bed, naked and still—his abdomen smeared with crimson.

Berggren looked back to Theyn, troubled. "What've you done to him, Theyn? Is he dead?"

Theyn burst into laughter. "Nardus isn't dead, *father*. He's only unconscious. I found him that way."

Berggren's eyes widened. "Theyn! You took him while he lay unconscious? Have you no self-respect?"

Theyn smirked. "*Zhedäz ℰʊn* delivered him to me. He would've been mine either way, but I *needed* him this morning. You know I couldn't have waited much longer. Shaul and I hadn't been together for almost a week. Besides, he doesn't need to know. It'll be our little secret, father. Like the ones we shared when I was younger. The ones we kept from mother."

If only that were true. I wish you were still my sweet little girl.

Berggren closed his eyes and squeezed his brow between his thumb and finger. "You've known this man less than a day and know nothing of him. And then you couple with him while he's unconscious?"

"I did what I had to."

Berggren looked at her. "What am I to do with you, Theyn? What kind of person does that? You're reckless."

Theyn reddened and glared at him. "I'm sorry you think I've done something wrong, *father*, but I haven't. This has always been my destiny. I just didn't realize it until last night. I'll eventually become pregnant with his child—a daughter. I'm sure of it. This baby will be *Zhedäᴢ Ƨʊn* in the flesh. She'll rule this world, and we'll worship her."

Berggren forced air through his nose and shook his head. "Baby? You talk as though you're already pregnant."

Theyn looked down at her blood-streaked legs. "I'm not pregnant yet, but it'll happen soon. As you can see, I'm with blood now. Sometime in the next two weeks, when I've lain with him again, I *will* carry his child. Nardus's seed will grow inside me."

Zhedäᴢ Ƨʊn, have mercy on my daughter. She isn't herself.

"This *will not* happen again. I won't allow it."

"You know it must. Our voyage is still long, and, if I don't, you'll all be dead."

Berggren knew the truth of it, but it didn't change how he felt about it. He pulled himself to his feet. "Get yourself cleaned up. And put some clothes on."

Theyn curtsied. "Yes, *father*."

Berggren pointed at Theyn's room but didn't look that way. "And then clean him up and get him dressed so we can put him back in here before he suspects anything."

Theyn grabbed Berggren's hand, pulled him down to her level, and kissed his cheek. "Yes, father."

Berggren shook his head and walked out of the captain's quarters. He headed up the stairs and to the upper deck. His stomach rumbled with a bout of nausea.

Felix smiled and offered him the wheel. He shook his head and walked over to the port-side railing.

What was Theyn thinking?

Berggren leaned over the railing and purged the contents of his stomach—twice.

How can I keep this from Lord Rosai? The man has a way of knowing everything.

Berggren slammed his fist against the top of the railing. "Damn you and your *condition*, Theyn."

Lord Rosai will surely kill us both.

CHAPTER FOURTEEN

Savric sat next to the fire, but it didn't warm him. The words he'd exchanged with Zerenity festered in his mind like boils and left him distraught. He loved her, he always would, and he needed to make things right with her.

But how can I do that when she refuses to acknowledge Qotan? He is my brother. A part of me that I cannot leave behind. How can she not understand that?

He rose from his chair and walked over to the window. Beams of light from the morning sun filtered through the tall trees and spotted the ground. A grey-tailed deer stood in the middle of the yard just ten feet away, chewing off the golden leaves of a holly bush.

Savric's stomach rumbled. He looked down at his stomach and gave it a pat. "Old faithful. Perhaps I should find myself a few of those biscuits from last night before I talk with Reni."

Savric reached out with his mind and located Qotan. *"Come have some breakfast with me, brother. I believe there are enough biscuits left over from last night for the both of us."*

The air within the room swirled and Qotan appeared a moment later. "When your stomach is involved, there is never enough food. If I relied on sharing food with you, I would have extinguished long ago. Besides, I may have slipped in earlier and eaten it all."

Wide-eyed, Savric covered his hand with his mouth and gasped. "You would never, brother."

Qotan shrugged, and his eyes twinkled.

Savric sliced through the room and toward the kitchen. "May Ɂäṭūr hold back my wrath if your words are true."

Qotan's hearty laughter filled the living area and then transitioned into the kitchen. Savric entered the small kitchen and Qotan stood in the middle of it, his left hand tucked behind his back and his face beaming. Crumbs littered the floor at his feet, and he brushed a few more from his chin as he swallowed.

Savric stewed. "You stand on very weak ground, brother. You should know better than to vex me when I have had nothing to eat for hours."

Qotan raised an eyebrow. "Hours, is it? You have outdone yourself this time. How is it that you still stand upright?"

"You cannot deceive my nose. I smell the biscuits." Savric stuck his hand out. "Hand them over."

Qotan grinned and produced a cloth from behind his back with three biscuits wrapped in it. "Your nose is much too clever for my wit. I believe your nose would give a bloodhound stiff competition. Only where food is involved, of course."

Savric snatched the cloth and biscuits from Qotan's open palm and stuffed one of the biscuits in his mouth, whole.

Qotan clasped his hands behind his back. "While you were enjoying the comforts of a fire last night, I took a walk up into the mountains."

Savric devoured the other two biscuits, but his stomach still rumbled. He sniffed the air.

Fish. Not my first choice for breakfast, but it will have to suffice.

Savric opened the second cupboard on the left side of the kitchen and retrieved a small, rectangular wooden box. He opened the box and breathed in the succulent, smoky smell. He pulled out three pieces of dried fish, placed the lid back on the box, and then opened it again and retrieved a fourth piece. He finally closed the box and returned it to the cupboard.

Qotan leaned against the small table in the middle of the room and shook his head.

Savric frowned at Qotan. "Would you rather I starve to death, brother?"

"I simply find it hard to imagine one's stomach actually being larger than their eyes, yet you stand before me with that exact ailment. You are a perplexing individual, indeed."

Savric swallowed the last bit of fish and then shook the crumbs of biscuits and fish from his beard. He patted his stomach, his appetite satiated.

Savric turned his attention to Qotan. "As you were saying, brother? You took a walk into the mountains."

Qotan wrinkled his nose and brow. "Indeed. Seeing you eat is like watching a natural disaster occur. Despite its grotesque and horrific nature, I cannot make myself look away."

"Shall I find more food so that you can continue watching me with abject disgust, or will you continue your tale? It is your choice, brother. I will be gratified with either decision."

Qotan waved his hand. "Oh, I have witnessed enough of your eating to last the rest of my life, as long or short as that may be. How about we retreat to the front porch and continue our discussion there? My old legs tire of standing."

Savric dipped his head. "As you wish, brother."

The two of them spun out of the kitchen and onto the front porch. They sat down on the long bench that lined the front of the house and groaned simultaneously. The grey-tailed deer continued its assault on the holly bush, paying them no attention.

Qotan scratched his left ankle, pulled a pipe from inside his robes, and chewed on the end of it. "Deep in the forest I found sickly vines growing up and choking out the smaller plants. Dark orange thorns covered their dark-grey tendrils, and a yellowed gelatinous substance spotted their leaves.

"They produced a pungent odor that permeated the surrounding forest. As I walked amongst them, they shied away and hissed like serpents. I have never witnessed vegetation like them before."

Savric leaned back against the side of the house and rubbed his temples. "Two signs. This cannot be a coincidence. Those vines must be related to the world's rotting core. We have an obligation to present our findings to King Zaridus. Someone has brought *Ɂʈōn Dhef Dädh* back into our world and into the light. War is coming, brother. Of this, I am certain."

Qotan took the pipe out of his mouth. "Indeed. But will King Zaridus believe us when we speak of the prophecies? I have heard that he deems them folly. If he does not believe, how will we convince him to the contrary?"

Savric stroked his beard. "We must go see him, and we must be convincing. The world as we know it will not survive if he stands by and does nothing. We must bring him proof."

"*Izhníṭ.*" The bowl of Qotan's pipe sparked and a small line of smoke drifted up from it. He stuck the end of it in his mouth, took several puffs, and let the smoke slowly filter out of his nose.

Savric sighed. *Where did I go wrong with him?*

Smoke wafted in the air and gathered around Savric's head. Despite its pleasant smell, Savric waved the smoke away with his hand. "Is that really necessary, brother?"

Qotan smiled. "Indeed. Care to give it a puff? I am certain you will find it quite relaxing."

Savric furrowed his brow. "Fire in my lungs and one foot sufficiently dangling in the grave? I think not."

Qotan shrugged and sank into the bench. "Suit yourself. I feel much better already."

Savric snapped his fingers together. "We will take a sample of the vines with us when we go see King Zaridus."

Qotan scratched his left ankle again, and then he pulled a small clay jar with a rubber stopper from within the folds of his robes. His eyes twinkled. "Ahead of you, as usual. Perhaps you have slowed with age after all."

"I am like a fine wine, brother. I have sweetened with age, not slowed."

Qotan scratched his left ankle. "Sweeter, is it? You must have started out more bitter than any wine that has touched my palate." He scratched his left ankle again.

Savric cocked his head. "Brother, have you found yourself a home for fleas? Or perhaps your rash decisions have manifested physically?"

Qotan lifted the hem of his robes, exposing his bony left ankle and the bluish-purple welts and pockmarks encircling it.

Savric gasped. "Dear Ɂäṭūr!"

Qotan scratched at it again. "Getting a sample of the vines proved a bit of a chore. Apparently, they were averse to me taking a knife to one of their own. I cornered one of the tendrils and hacked at it, and the others attacked me from behind. I believe I narrowly escaped with my life. And this sample, of course."

Guide me, Ɂäṭūr. What shall I do?

Savric rose to his feet. "Do not go anywhere, brother. I will fetch Reni."

Qotan frowned. "Oh, yes, please do. I am certain she will be more than willing to help out where I am concerned."

Savric pointed his finger at Qotan. "This is no time to be frivolous, brother. You will both set your differences aside. Reni is the only one who might be able to help you."

Qotan scratched his ankle again. "I will stay put, but I doubt you will get through to her. After all, I am merely a figment of your imagination, remember?"

Savric sighed. "If she truly loves me, she will do this."

Savric turned and walked into the house. Save the fire and faint sunlight through the windows, everything still lay in darkness.

Reni should be up by now. Did my words really hurt her that bad?

Guilt bubbled in his stomach as he walked down the hall and stood in front of Zerenity's bedroom door. He reached out with his hand fisted but stopped short of touching the door's surface.

Should I knock? Or call out to her? Why am I overthinking this?

Savric knocked on the door, and it cracked open. No light penetrated the crack.

He leaned toward the door. "Reni? Are you in there?"

He waited a few moments, but she didn't respond.

"Reni?" he called again, louder this time.

Still no response.

He pushed the door all the way open, but the veil of darkness didn't recede.

"*Əllíṭ ʊb.*" An orb of yellow light formed above Savric's open palm, flew into the middle of the room, and lit it up.

All the candles in the room had burned down to nothing. The bed looked slightly unkempt, but not slept in. A small, hand-held mirror lay on the bed.

Where have you gone, Reni? I need you.

Savric sat down on the edge of the bed and lifted the mirror up to his face. The bags under his eyes were darker and heavier than they'd been when he'd seen himself through Calen's eyes.

Time has most certainly not favored me. Instead, it has left me devoid of youth.

Savric laid the mirror back on the bed.

A picture frame lay face-down on the nightstand next to the bed. Savric held his hand out, and the frame zipped the length of the bed and into his open hand. He turned the frame over and stared at the hand-drawn picture of himself and Zerenity as youths.

You are radiant even in this form.

His eyes watered, and a lump caught in his throat. *How fast the time has slipped from us, Reni.*

The picture reminded him that Qotan had once been a part of Zerenity's life too. Qotan had drawn the picture, and she'd kept it. How could she explain its existence if Qotan didn't exist?

There is more to this quibble than she lets on.

Savric released the frame, and it flew across the length of the bed and landed atop the nightstand. Savric stared at the frame for a moment, flicked his wrist, and then the frame righted itself. He smiled and stood.

With a pinch of his fingers, the orb of light extinguished itself and cast him into darkness. He carefully made his way to the door, stepped through it, pulled it closed, and walked down the hall and into the living area.

Savric couldn't see Qotan through the front window. His heart raced. He spun out of the room and onto the porch. Qotan lay on the bench snoring, and Savric reprimanded himself for worrying.

Dear brother, if you only knew some of the foolish thoughts I have had. Committed, I would most certainly be.

Savric tapped the side of the bench with Qotan's staff.

Qotan snorted and blinked a few times as he emerged from his slumber, and then he sat up. "I thought you were off fetching Zerenity. I do not see her here. Or have I misplaced her as she has me?"

Savric sat down on the bench. "She is not inside, and I am uncertain as to her whereabouts. I spoke unkindly to her last night, and I have not seen her since."

Qotan's face brightened. "I am certain Zerenity will be back soon. In the meantime, I suggest we make the most of the day and head down the hill to Tyrosha. You can leave her a note as to where we have ventured."

Savric eyed Qotan. "I know that look, brother. What ostentatious scheme are you formulating in that devious head of yours?"

Qotan feigned surprise. "Me? Scheming? I would never. But if I were to, it might involve a tub, piping hot water, some minerals, and perhaps a few bubbles—naturally occurring, of course."

Savric's grin faded. "The world is on the brink of war, and you suggest we go take a bath?"

Qotan shrugged. "These old bones care nothing of the world around them. They only know of aches and pains and the soothing properties of a good bath." He rubbed his chin and then scratched his left ankle.

Savric eyed Qotan's ankle. Black veins surrounded the wound and crept up his leg. He pulled on his beard. "Perhaps the heat and minerals will slow the venom's progression."

Qotan nodded and winked. "We would not have had this conversation, had I believed otherwise."

Savric stood up and opened the front door. He reached out, and his staff flew from the corner of the room and into his hand. He turned around, and the bench sat empty. A few leaves stirred and then settled on the porch.

Concern for Qotan gripped Savric's stomach. "I pray the baths help." He could think of nothing else to do until Zerenity returned.

He left a note for Zerenity on the kitchen table, set his mind to Tyrosha, and spun out of the kitchen and into the day.

CHAPTER FIFTEEN

A white-sand beach, covered in a thick layer of morning dew, stretched in either direction for miles. The waves of Gelu crashed upon it relentlessly and slowly crept inland. The last remnants of a bonfire smoldered in the cool morning air as the sun crept up from the west. The beach sparkled in the sunlight as though covered in tiny shards of glass.

Alderan stood at the edge of the world, surrounded by friends, yet alone. A battle raged within his heart, and his mind found no solace. Born a thatcher's son, he knew little of the world around him, and it scared him.

Was I really made for this? Is this Your plan for me, Ƨäţūr? Alderan walked up the beach, alone. *Am I truly the chosen one?*

Fear laced his veins and left him ice-cold. He hugged himself and rubbed the backs of his arms. "I don't know what I'm supposed to do, father. How can I become something I'm not? You were such a great man, but I'm nothing."

The savior of the world. He hated the title. It wasn't him, and it never would be. How could anyone expect him to save the world when he could scarcely save himself?

He sank to his knees and sat down in the cold, wet sand. Moisture penetrated his trousers and compounded the coldness of his fear. He ran his hands through the sand, picked some up, and then let it drop into a pile. He pushed the sand together from all around and formed a mound in front of himself.

Sandcastles. He hadn't thought about them in years.

Alderan formed four walls with the sand, dug a moat around the perimeter, and sculpted massive spires and bridges. Growing up, he loved building sandcastles with Aria. He wished she was there with him now.

He and Aria were alike in so many ways, but her carefree attitude didn't match his more serious one. She enjoyed building sandcastles and then watching the waves pummel them until nothing stood.

He hated it. The waves were his enemies, and he'd often cried when his sandcastle crumbled in their wake.

Sandcastles.

Every time he thought of the word *sandcastles,* something in the back of his mind tickled with recollection. He strained to retrieve the memory, but something held it back and kept it in the shadows of his mind.

Sandcastles.

His life had become a sandcastle. He'd built such a glorious one around himself—a life filled with love and excitement—but the events of his recent past had swept away its walls and left him with nothing.

No home. No family. Only emptiness and sorrow.

But in its wake, he'd found Rayah. He longed to build a sandcastle with her far away from the destructive waves of life and forget about the rest of the world. Could he allow himself to do so? Would they be safe together? Or would the waves seek them out and destroy everything they'd build together?

The answers to his questions held no mystery, and he knew it.

As much as he wanted to share a life with Rayah, he'd never find peace until he fulfilled his destiny. Prophecies were written to be fulfilled, right? Despite his plethora of inadequacies, Ɔäṭūr had a plan for him. *He must.*

Without a savior, the world would be damned.

Without a world, he'd never be with Rayah.

Without Rayah, he would've been dead already.

He had to stop running.

He had to stop building sandcastles.

Sandcastles.

Alderan swept his arm through the sand and leveled the walls he'd built. He rose to his feet, took a deep breath, and slowly let it out. A calm settled over him and flushed away his doubt. As much as it pained him, he knew finding Aria would have to wait.

Take her in Your hands and protect her, Ɔäṭūr. She is Your daughter, as I am Your son.

Alderan walked back down the beach and joined the others, but he knew it wouldn't be for long.

Destiny calls.

† † †

The moment Alderan returned to camp, Rayah knew something had changed in him. He'd chosen to sit across from her, not next to her, and every time she looked at him he turned his attention elsewhere. She reached out to him with her mind, but he didn't respond.

What are you thinking, Alderan?

She flew over to him, grabbed his hand, pulled him to his feet, and then dragged him away from the others. He didn't resist, but he didn't look at her either.

Rayah squeezed his hand. "Talk to me, Alderan. Tell me what's going through your head. Have I done something wrong?"

Alderan's eyes glistened, but he looked through her—beyond her. The air around them felt heavier than normal—burdensome.

"This cannot continue." The tone of his voice held no emotion.

Rayah felt lost. Had she missed something? "What does that mean?"

Alderan turned and faced the Gelu Ocean. "Us."

That one word twisted in Rayah's heart like a dagger. She gasped and couldn't catch her breath again. Tears swelled in her eyes. She clenched her fists and dug her fingernails into her palms, but it didn't keep the tears at bay.

"You're my friend, Alderan. You're all I have." Tears streaked her face, and she sobbed. "How can you think of abandoning me now?"

Alderan ran his fingers through his hair. "I'm not abandoning you. I finally understand my purpose, Rayah. I know what I must do, but I can't do it and worry about you at the same time."

Rayah tugged on his arm. "But that's the thing, Alderan. You don't need to. I've sworn to protect you and keep you safe. That's *my* purpose."

Alderan crossed his arms. "And you've done just that, Rayah. But now it's time for me to move forward."

Rayah wiped her eyes and nose. "You can't just throw me aside."

Alderan tilted his head back, closed his eyes, and sighed. "You know it's not like that, Rayah."

Tell him the truth. A lump formed in Rayah's throat. *He needs to know.*

She trembled as fear gripped her heart, but she knew that she couldn't keep it from him any longer.

She blurted, "I love you, Alderan."

Alderan's eyes shot open, and he stared at her. "No, you don't. You only think you do because we've been through so much together. You can't love me. I won't let you."

Rayah stomped her foot in the sand and shook her finger at him. "You can't decide who loves you and who doesn't. My heart's chosen you, Alderan Somneri. I'll never love another."

Alderan's jaw tightened, and he clenched his fists. "But you must, Rayah. If I allow you to love me then I might make the wrong choice in the end. I refuse to allow myself to love you."

Rayah put her hand on his shoulder, the rock she depended on. "I'm not asking you to love me, Alderan, but you can't stop me from loving you. I'm a dryte, Alderan."

Alderan scoffed, "What does that matter? That's not why I can't love you. I don't care what you are."

Rayah sniveled. "I know that. But, as a dryte, I can only bond with one person my entire life. And I've done that. That person's you, whether you like it or not."

Alderan turned his head and squinted. "What do you mean *bond*?"

In her mind, Rayah returned to the Veridis Forest. "From the moment we first met, I've loved you. I just didn't realize it until the day you said that you saw things through me. Your seeing and feeling the things I described wouldn't have been possible unless I'd bonded with you. Now, I'm bound to you forever and cannot love another. It's impossible."

Alderan took a deep breath. "Bonded… and you've kept this from me all this time? Why?"

Rayah lowered her head and stared at the white sand. The sand shifted, and a silver crab emerged. She moved her foot into the crab's path, and it climbed aboard and settled. She smiled. *A sign from Ɂätūr?*

Her smile faded. She couldn't face Alderan and tell him the truth, so she watched the crab. "Because I didn't want you to feel obligated to love me back." She convulsed with sobs, but continued, "I'll be content without your love, but I cannot live without being near you. Don't toss me away like refuse."

Alderan put his hand under her chin and lifted her head back up. "I'd never toss you away, Rayah."

Her sobs grew louder, but she didn't care anymore. She let go of every inhibition and let herself be vulnerable to him. "Can't you see it? That's what you're trying to do right now. Allow me to be near you, Alderan. I'm begging you. If you can't, then take my life. Leaving me alive and alone would be far crueler. I'd be dead inside without you in my life."

Alderan raked his head with his fingers and pulled on his hair. "Why are you making this so hard for me? I'm trying to do the right thing, Rayah. I'm trying to be the savior this world needs."

The anguish in his eyes pulled at her heart and forced her to push harder. "I understand what you're trying to do, but you don't need to. We can save the world together, Alderan. You're not alone."

Alderan groaned. "You're my world, Rayah. That's why I'm fighting so hard to save you now."

Guilt rose in her throat, but she couldn't help herself. "By pushing me away?"

I won't live without you, Alderan.

Tears welled in Alderan's eyes. "I love you, Rayah. With all my heart. I'd do anything and sacrifice everything to save you. Can't you see that?"

Did he just say that he loves me?

Excitement rose in Rayah's voice. "Then do exactly that. Let me be by your side and fight next to you. The only way to save me is to be with me, Alderan. Breaking my heart does neither of us any good. You'd never forgive yourself, and that's what will keep you from fulfilling your destiny, not your love for me. Love conquers all, Alderan. Together, our love can save the world. Don't you see? You can't leave me."

Alderan ran his fingers through his hair again. "I just don't know. It doesn't feel right. How can I put you in harm's way and then live with myself if you were to die? How do I know this is the right thing to do?"

Rayah grabbed Alderan's hands and placed them on her waist. "You already know, Alderan. Search your heart. Does leaving me and breaking my heart feel right to you?"

Alderan looked skyward. "You know it doesn't, but I'm trying to be rational. I have to think with my head and not my heart."

She grabbed his cheeks and pulled his head back down. "But it's your heart that's led us to this moment, not your head. Ɂäṭūr brought us together, Alderan. Is His plan not good enough for you? Don't you think He knows what He's doing?"

Alderan sighed and plopped down in the sand.

Rayah shooed the silver crab away and settled next to Alderan.

Help me with this, Ɂäṭūr! Help me make him see that You made us for each other.

Alderan pushed the sand around with his feet and stared at the water.

Rayah reached up and smoothed his hair back. "I'm tired of pretending that I don't love you and that I'm not good enough for you. I'm the best thing that's ever happened to you, Alderan Somneri. You'd be a fool to push me away."

Alderan puffed up his cheeks and then let the air out. "I know, Rayah. You're right. You're always right. I've loved you since we first met too. Everything about you drives me crazy with love. The way you smell. The way you look. The way you feel when I hold you in my arms. I love you like I've never loved anyone before.

"And it scares me. What would I do if saving the world came down to sacrificing you? How could I ever be able to make that decision? Even worse, how would I ever be able to choose between you and Aria? To me, our three hearts are one."

Three hearts? No! I will not share your heart with another, not even if it's your sister. She fought the urge to say something derogatory about Aria. *I don't even know the girl, and I'm already starting to hate her. Who does she think she is?*

You're mine Alderan. No one else's.

Rayah crawled in front of Alderan and faced him. "I trust that Ɂäṭūr will give you the wisdom to make the right choice. If my death was the catalyst that saved the world, then I'd freely give my life."

Alderan mounded the sand between them. "I'm not sure I could live in a world where you didn't exist. That's why I wanted you far away from me, so that my love for you couldn't be used against me. I fear the choices I'd make otherwise. It haunts me."

Rayah pummeled the mounded sand with her fists. "Confide in me. Let me inside your head. Let me inside your heart. Promise to love me forever, no matter the cost."

Alderan built up walls in the sand. "I'll always love you, Rayah, but I have other concerns as well. My thoughts are always on you."

Rayah frowned. "You say that like it's a bad thing."

Alderan swept the walls away with the back of his hand. "How will I ever learn to use my mezhik while you're around?"

Rayah laughed. "You think driving me away will keep you from thinking about me? It'd drive you mad. You'd probably never learn a thing without me around."

Alderan scoffed. "You think so, do you? Then what's your plan? How can I do both?"

Rayah smiled. "That's simple, Alderan. Take me as your wife."

Alderan's hands froze in the sand, the blood drained from his face, and his eyes bulged. "T-take you as m-m-my wife?"

I've got you now, my love.

Rayah put her hands over his. "You fear losing me because I'm not yours."

Alderan swallowed hard. "I don't understand. What would that solve?"

Rayah stared at Alderan intently. "Once we're together—when you've *known* me—our bodies and souls will be as one. You cannot lose what's become part of you. I'd always be with you no matter the future."

Alderan's nose and forehead scrunched up, and his left eyebrow lifted. "But I already know you, Rayah. And I still have this fear. How will taking you as my wife change that?"

Rayah giggled and slapped his chest playfully. "Sometimes you can be so silly. I said when you've *known* me."

Alderan shrugged. "I heard you say that the first time, but I still don't understand."

Seriously, Ɂäṭūr? "*Physically*, Alderan."

He stared at her blankly.

Rayah thrust her hands in the air. "When we've lain together. When you've gone into me. I'm not sure how to be clearer."

Alderan's face turned bright red, and he looked away.

Rayah sprang forward and tackled Alderan. "I love you so much, and I feel so liberated now that I've finally told you."

Alderan looked toward the group in the distance, his face still flushed red. "So how would I go about making you my wife?"

Rayah trembled. *Is this really happening?*

She straddled Alderan's chest and smoothed back his hair. "All we need is a witness—" She pointed toward the others. "—and there are four of them right over there."

Alderan squirmed under her. "Not now. After my training. When I've come of age. We're too young to marry."

She bent over and kissed his forehead. "I'll wait as long as it takes, Alderan. I'll never stop loving you."

Alderan relaxed and smiled up at her. "Then it's settled. After we find Aria. I couldn't possibly get married without her being there."

Aria? Rayah wanted to scream.

She rolled off Alderan and lay in the sand next to him. *Will I never be free from her shadow?*

† † †

Alderan watched Zerenity stroll over to where he and Rayah lay in the sand. The light breeze blew her silver hair across her face. She swept it back with her hands.

Zerenity leaned over Alderan's head and stared down at his upside-down face. "Have you made up your mind, darling? Will you be accompanying me back to Tyrosha?"

Alderan sat up and turned around to face Zerenity. "I think I'm finally ready to face my destiny. Are you certain you can train me to use my mezhik?"

"You'll be an expert in no time, darling."

Alderan looked over at Rayah. She still lay in the sand.

"Rayah, can you hear me?" thought Alderan.

Rayah's voice entered his mind. *"Yes."* Her lips didn't move.

"Do you think I can trust her?"

"She said she knows Savric, but I'm not sure that means we can trust her."

"Who can we trust? It's not like I know any other wizards."

"I wish I had my book. I'd contact Savric and ask him about her if I did."

Another presence eased into Alderan's mind. *"Can I join the conversation, darling?"*

Zerenity.

Alderan rose to his feet. "I don't know. How can I trust what you say is true? I'd never even met you until a few hours ago?"

Zerenity's eyes softened. "Search your heart, darling. You know we've met before. I've known you most of your life. From the shadows, of course."

Do I know her?

A thought popped into his mind, and he snapped his fingers together. "Are those your books in the room under my house? And your mirror?"

Zerenity laughed. "Heavens, no, darling. Those old things are Savvy's—um—Savric's."

Rayah rose from the sand, fluttered over to Alderan, and took his hand. "Help us find a way to speak with Savric, and then we'll decide if we'll go with you or not."

Zerenity looked at Rayah with raised eyebrows. "We?"

Rayah tightened her grip on Alderan's hand. "Alderan's not going anywhere without me."

Zerenity tugged on her earlobe. "I see. Well, it's settled then. Savric's at my house as we speak. You can talk to him when we arrive."

Rayah glared at her. "Bring him here, and then we'll decide. Otherwise, the answer's no."

Alderan looked at Rayah with wide eyes. *"Calm down. Maybe there's another way."*

Rayah let go of Alderan's hand. *"And what's that?"*

"Zerenity, how about you go back home and let Savric speak to us through the mirror?"

Zerenity tapped her chin with her right forefinger. "I can do that, but I wouldn't be able to come back today. My energy isn't what it used to be."

Alderan put his hands in his trouser pockets. "That's okay. You won't need to. We won't be going to your house today even if we decide it's the right thing to do."

Zerenity smoothed out the wrinkles in the red velvet cape that hung from her shoulders. "Oh? And why is that?"

"We have to go back to my house first. There are some things there that we left behind. And some unfinished business."

"I see."

Rayah piped up, "Zerenity, if we decide to go to your house, could we use the mirror in the room under Alderan's house to get there? Or at least use it to get somewhere closer?"

Zerenity smiled. "You're a clever young woman, darling. How about Savric and I meet you at Alderan's house."

Rayah looked up at Alderan. "Then it's settled?"

Alderan looked over at Rakzar, Amicus, and Eshtak. "I suppose it is. I guess we'd better let the others know."

"I'll leave you to it, darlings. We'll see you soon." Zerenity spun up a whirlwind of sand and disappeared.

Alderan removed his hands from his pockets, took Rayah's hand in his, and they walked back over to where the others sat.

"...and that's the last thing I remember," said Rakzar.

"That's some tale." Amicus looked up at Alderan and Rayah. "Is everything okay?"

Alderan smiled at Rayah. "Never better."

Eshtak jumped up and twirled in circles. "Eshtak is ready."

Rayah laughed. "Well, Eshtak, I believe this is where we part ways."

Amicus frowned. "Part ways?"

Alderan scratched his head. "There's no need for the three of you to continue on with us. You and Rakzar have a score to settle, and I'm in need of training."

"Fine by me," growled Rakzar.

Amicus pulled himself up. "What about Aria?"

Alderan shook his head slowly. "I hate to say it but finding her must wait. I don't know when I'll be called upon to save the world, so I need to be prepared. Aria's always been strong. I have faith that she'll find a way to survive. Ɂäʈūr will see to it."

Amicus chuckled. "She's most certainly a fighter."

"She's always been more skilled with weapons and in combat than I've ever been." Alderan stuck his hand out toward Amicus. "Until we meet again?"

Amicus took Alderan's hand in his own and grabbed Alderan's elbow with his other. "We'll see each other soon, my friend."

Eshtak ran over and hugged Rayah and then Alderan. "Eshtak miss friends."

Alderan rubbed Eshtak's bald head. "We'll miss you too, Eshtak."

Rayah reached up and hugged Amicus. "Be careful, Amicus. Rakzar can't be trusted."

Amicus winked at Rayah. "I'm off to fulfill Ɂäʈūr's business. He'll protect us all."

Alderan looked over to where Rakzar sat, but Rakzar had already gotten up and started walking down the beach.

No need for goodbyes I guess. I'm certain we'll meet again, though.

Amicus turned and trotted after Rakzar. Eshtak smiled, twirled a few times, and then zigzagged down the beach after Amicus and Rakzar.

Alderan put his arms around Rayah and hugged her tight.

Alone again, at last.

But deep within, he had a feeling it wouldn't be for long.

Trouble always seems to find us.

CHAPTER SIXTEEN

It'd been a full week since Pravus arrived home, and he still hadn't recovered from the journey. The distance between Daltura and Atrum Moenia proved greater than he'd remembered, and it'd nearly cost him his life. The first two days back, he couldn't get out of bed without help. The timing couldn't have been worse.

He limped along one of the long, curved corridors of Galondu Castle with a weighty tome wedged under his left arm and a walking stick in his right hand. Golden sconces—staggered and spaced ten feet apart—hung from the corridor's tall, black, obsidian walls. Paintings hung in the space between the sconces and dated back many centuries. Each depicted a brutal, bloody scene from the Great War.

Pravus paused at the second intersection and admired the oversized painting of Magus Carac and his black dragon, Cinolth The Dark. Cinolth spewed fire across a vast battlefield as they flew over it.

True power. With Aria by my side, I'll achieve even greater power than you, Magus.

Pravus turned left and walked to the end of the corridor. Two inordinate steel doors, each measuring fifty feet high, fifteen feet wide, and three feet thick, stood open. He envisioned all the dragons that had passed through them so long ago.

He shook his head. *How did the dragons fall?*

Pravus stepped through the doors and into the massive, pentagonal-shaped atrium. Each side of the atrium housed steel doors of equal size at the center of their 300-foot-long walls. Thirty-foot-wide, charcoal-grey gravel paths led from each set of doors and met at the points of a central, pentagonal-shaped area.

Between the five sets of doors—the areas between the gravel paths—

stood handfuls of millennial firs, each stretching skyward at more than 300 feet tall. The bases of their trunks spanned more than thirty feet in diameter.

Pravus walked down the gravel path a short distance and settled on one of the many benches that lined both sides of the gravel path. Each bench, carved from a single block of black obsidian, featured a unique backrest chiseled out and backfilled with brilliant, amber-colored stones sculpted to look like flames.

Countless hedges of black-stemmed rosebushes wove between the benches. Their red thorns stood out like drops of blood running down from their red, tear-shaped petals.

He leaned his walking stick against the bench, reached over to one of the rosebushes, and plucked a rose from it. He held the rose to his nose and breathed deep. Its sweet fragrance reminded him of Aria. *I'll see you soon, my queen.*

He tossed the rose into the middle of the path. Its petals shriveled and turned black, and then the whole thing reduced to a pile of black dust and seeped into the gravel until no evidence of its existence remained.

As it will be for all who oppose us.

He pulled the tome from under his arm, set it on his lap, wiped the dust from its leather cover with the sleeve of his robe, and ran his finger across the embossed lettering of its title: *Räfəlläíezhnz Dhef Ilia.*

Pravus mused, "Little did she know her writings foretold of her own daughter."

He opened the book to a page marked with a strip of leather, and his fingers trembled as they rested on the yellowed page. The bold heading at the top of the page spoke to him, moved him to tears: *Fädinzh dhä Bəllek.*

The Black Wedding.

"Our wedding, my queen."

His fingers and eyes traced the ancient text:

> *If the man, born unto darkness, weds the woman, born unto light, a union will be formed that cannot be broken except by one who shares the same blood of either.*

Once united, the souls of the man and the woman will be bound together for eternity, either unto salvation or damnation, unless the one who shares the same blood breaks the union through self-sacrifice.

If, by this union, the man of darkness is drawn into the light then hope for the future will remain. However, if, by this union, the woman of light is drawn into the darkness then hope for the future will cease. A hopeless world has no chance of surviving the approaching darkness.

Brothers and sisters, I know not when this event may occur, so be steadfast and watchful for the signs, and be expedient in your pursuit of halting this union, even unto death. Our world depends on it.

—Ilia, Ef Ƨäfn Dhä

Pravus closed the book and set it on the bench. He stood, grabbed his walking stick, and walked to the pentagonal-shaped area at the center of the atrium. Five metal poles, sixty feet high and seven feet in diameter, stood at each of the angles of the inner pentagon. Massive chains hung from the tops of each pole.

The dragon posts.

Magus had used the posts to chain down and train his army of flying dragons. Pravus leaned against the closest pole, winded. Feeling so weak enraged him, but he had no one to blame but himself.

With Aria's strength, this will never happen again.

At the very center of the atrium, six six-foot-wide circles of white sand— one at the center and five surrounding it—adorned the ground. Translucent green stones outlined the inner circle, and translucent red stones outlined the outer five.

The sacrificial circles.

Pravus walked over to the center circle and stood in the middle of it.

More than a millennium ago, many great wizards—Magus, the most famous of them—used that very spot to perform rituals and spells invoking mezhik derk. He closed his eyes and imagined the energy rising from the ground and engulfing him.

This is where my father's kingdom will be reborn, and nothing will stop us as we usher in the darkness.

The crunch of gravel underfoot brought Pravus out of his thoughts. He opened his eyes. Credan approached.

Credan halted five feet from Pravus and knelt. "Lord Rosai."

Pravus extended his left hand toward Credan. "You may rise."

Credan stood and placed his arms behind his back. "My lord, we've finished the preparations for Mistress Aria."

"Excellent. And what of the lower dungeon? Have you prepared the space for our other guest?"

"Yes, my lord. Would you care to see the accommodations?"

Pravus waved his left hand. "That won't be necessary, Credan. I'll see to them myself."

Credan bowed his head. "Yes, my lord. Any further instructions?"

"Not at this moment. You may dismiss yourself."

Credan nodded then turned and walked back the way he'd come.

Pravus stepped out of the circle and walked back over to the bench. He bent down, picked up the book, and placed it back under his left arm. He made his way back to the central pentagon, continued across the atrium, and headed for the second set of steel doors to the right of those he'd originally come through.

The doors were closed, but, with a small burst of mezhik, he opened the one on the right wide enough to squeeze through. Once inside, he dropped to one knee and leaned on his walking stick. The book slipped from under his arm and landed on the hard floor with a *smack*.

The muscles in his arms and legs trembled. He couldn't recall the last meal he'd had. He desperately needed meat. *Bloody* meat. And he didn't care the source of it.

The sound of thudding boots and clinking mail echoed through the corridor. A moment later, a young man rounded the corner.

"My lord!" The young man bent down and held his hand out to Pravus. "Take my hand, my lord. I'll help you to your feet."

Pravus glared at him. "I don't need your hand. I need meat. Rare meat. The bloodier the better. Find me some before I take it from your neck."

The young man's eyes widened, and he pulled his hand back. He blinked a few times and swallowed hard. "My lord, I'll return as quickly as possible."

Pravus set his jaw. "See that you do."

The young man dipped his head, rose to his feet, and sprinted away.

Pravus thought of all the great men who had roamed the corridors of Galondu Castle over the centuries. He imagined none of them had ever been so weak that they couldn't even stand under their own power.

He breathed deep through his nose. "You're pathetic, Pravus. Unworthy of being the master of this great palace."

He reached down and slid the book across the floor. It stopped just short of the far wall.

Pravus gathered his strength and propped himself up with his walking stick. His legs trembled, and his head rocked on his shoulders. The corridor swam in front of him as though he were out at sea. He closed his eyes and breathed slowly.

You're stronger than this, Pravus. Don't let this overcome you. You're about to become the ruler of the world. Act like it.

He opened his eyes and the corridor steadied, but the far wall seemed immeasurably distant. He forced himself forward a few steps before the burden on his legs overwhelmed him again. His vision sparkled, and his body flushed with warmth. The marble floor raced toward his face, and he turned his head sideways in anticipation of the impact.

Pravus hit the floor, his lower jaw shifted, and then he heard a loud *crack*. The coppery taste of blood filled his mouth and slid down his throat. Pain radiated from his jaw, slithered around his head like a serpent, and pulled him into the darkness.

† † †

A throng of voices surrounded Pravus. He opened his eyes, but the world around him refused to relinquish the darkness. He reached out with his mind, but it made the pain unbearable, and he had to retreat.

I should've stayed with you, my queen. I'm just happy you're not here to see me this way.

I am pathetic.

Pravus recognized Credan's voice.

"Bring in Ilder. He will fix this, or he'll die."

Good man.

Credan had been with him since they were small children, and he considered Credan as close to a friend as he'd ever had.

Except for Aria. In a few short weeks, she'd become his obsession. *Worshiped or damned, I am yours, my queen.*

Was Aria all he needed? For a fleeting moment, he wondered if his elaborate plan to take over the world still made sense. Did he really need the power?

This is absurd. I must've hit my head harder than I thought. I need rest.

Pravus drifted in and out of consciousness several times, finally waking up in his own bed within his sleeping chamber. The canopy's dark purple fabric stretched tautly to the four bedposts, and white cord tied back dark purple curtains at each post, leaving the bed exposed on its sides and at its foot.

To Pravus's right, a fire roared in the oversized fireplace. Beyond the foot of the bed, the large chamber doors stood closed. To his left, Credan slumped over in a chair next to the bed, fast asleep.

Pravus slowly moved his jaw back and forth without pain but with a great deal of stiffness. He eyed Credan. "Have I bored you to sleep?"

Credan jerked awake and sat up in the chair. He wiped his mouth with his long sleeve. "Lord Rosai. It's good to see you're awake."

Pravus tried sitting up, but his strength failed him, and he collapsed against the bed again. He glared at the canopy. "How long have I been in here?"

"A few hours, my lord. Shall I assist you in sitting up?"

Pravus turned his glare on Credan. Had he the strength, he would've wrapped his hand around the man's throat and relieved him of his life.

Reduced to a drooling babe. Pathetic.

The firelight gleamed on Credan's balding head when he stood. "Please, my lord. No one will ever know of this. I'll help you sit up, and then I'll fetch you something to eat. You need to build up your strength."

Pravus sneered. "So be it, but breathe a word of this, and I'll feed you to the *ferzh*."

Credan nodded and then shuffled around to the left side of the bed. He climbed up on the bed and stacked some pillows for Pravus to lean against. He stood on the bed—over the top of Pravus—and pulled Pravus up by his armpits.

More strength in him than I thought possible.

Credan retreated to the side of the bed again.

Holding his head up felt like a chore and smacking his fist against the bed drained him further. "I told one of the soldiers to get me some meat. Where is he with it?"

Credan wove his fingers together. "Detained—*permanently*. Along with all the other... *witnesses*. Only Ilder and I remain."

The longer Pravus knew Credan the more he appreciated him. Of all the other children within *Fekɛzhn dhä Räd*, Credan was the only one sane enough to befriend.

Worthless, religious zealots.

Pravus stretched his jaw. "Excellent, Credan. Now get me some bloody meat before I'm too weak to chew it."

Credan's brow furrowed. "Bloody, my lord? Are you certain? You do remember that it's forbidden to consume the life blood of another living creature, right?"

Pravus glared daggers at Credan. "Do I look like I care about the ancient laws? Get it for me, or it will be *your* flesh I consume."

"My lord." Credan bowed, backed up several steps, turned, and left the room, shutting the door behind himself.

Ancient laws. Pathetic.

Pravus bound himself to no law of man *or* god. Why should he? Soon enough, *he'd* rule all Centauria and demand they worship him.

He cracked his knuckles, relaxed, and sank into the pillows.

Where are you, my queen? You should've been here by now.

The Inferus Wastelands were known to be brutally harsh with freezing temperatures at night and blistering heat in the day, but he'd protected the horses, the driver, and the carriage from the elements with mezhik. Besides, how could anything go wrong with a pack of gnolls escorting her?

Still, gruesome images of her death stirred in his head.

Do not depart from me, my queen.

CHAPTER SEVENTEEN

Despite it being winter, the sun beat down on the orange sands of the Inferus Wastelands and heated them to the point of being untouchable. Never in her life had Aria seen such a barren and desolate place, and the company she kept only made it worse.

Aria lay on her back and stared up at the tattered green cloth strewn across the top of their makeshift shelter. Karraar lay a few feet from her, fast asleep. The knife on his belt mesmerized her.

Spill his blood. Turn the orange sands red.

Since she'd regained consciousness a few days back, she hadn't spoken a word. Had she the strength, the beast would've been dead long ago. As it were, she plotted his death during every waking moment and would fulfill the desire at the first given opportunity.

He killed your father. Slit his throat and rid yourself of him.

Karraar had cleaned and packed the wound between her shoulder blades. He'd said the metal bar had narrowly missed her spine. She didn't care.

Your survival will be his death.

Not once had Karraar shown any aggression toward her. In fact, he'd saved her life on three different occasions over the past several days. She couldn't wrap her mind around why he continued to help her. She gave him little reason to do so.

Hatred festered in her mind, and she wanted him dead more than she wanted to live.

Take the knife from his belt and drive it through his skull.

They traveled only at night because of the sweltering heat, and the night bore no special path as far as she could tell. Dunes of orange sand and scrub brush littered the landscape in every direction as far as the eye could see. Killing Karraar would certainly end her life as well.

In death, you'll see your family again.

In death, you'll find peace.

Aria sat up, and her shoulders throbbed with pain. She drew a deep breath and pushed the pain from her mind. She'd waited a few hours to make water but could wait no longer. She rolled over on her hands and knees and crawled to the edge of the shelter.

She looked back over her shoulder. Karraar still slept. She dug into the sand with her fingers and made a hole large enough to squat over. She lifted her dress, pulled her undergarments down to her knees, and sat back on her ankles over the hole.

She pushed with her abdominal muscles, but nothing came out.

This does not differ from the cells. You urinated in front of those filthy pigs. Karraar isn't even watching you. Just let it out.

At last, the urine trickled out, but every drop burned like fire.

Karraar stirred and sniffed the air, but he didn't turn her way. "You're dehydrated," he growled. "We need to find water for you soon."

He's sniffing my pee?

Had he only been watching her, she would've felt less violated. She wanted to take the wet sand and throw it in his face. Instead, she lifted herself to her knees and pulled her undergarments back up. She maneuvered around the hole then covered it with sand.

Aria wiped her sandy hands on her yellow dress and left two orange streaks down its front. She wanted to laugh, but she refused to give Karraar the pleasure of hearing it. Instead, she stood and smoothed out her dress.

She rotated her shoulders and lifted her hands as high as they would go. Moving her arms around increased her discomfort, but she couldn't afford to become too stiff to move. She'd need all her strength and dexterity to overcome Karraar, and, to regain that strength, she'd need to rely on him a bit longer.

These aren't the dungeons, Aria. You're not being held captive, and he's not trying to rape you. Speak to him. Get him to lower his guard. Befriend him.

And then plunge a knife into his cold, black heart.

So many questions filled her head: What had happened to the carriage?

Who had attacked her? Why? Why was Karraar there? Why had he saved her and not killed her? Why was he still helping her? Does he work for Pravus?

Does he work for Pravus?

She couldn't get enough air in her lungs. Her throat seized up, and her heart thrashed in her chest. She dropped to her knees and wheezed, clutching her throat.

Aria's head whipped to the side, and blood and saliva flew from her mouth. Pain stung her left cheek. Her eyes rolled backward, and her vision darkened. Her head whipped back the other way, and the pain in her left cheek spread to her right one, then everything came back into view. Her throat opened, and her lungs expanded with air.

Karraar stood over her, ready to backhand her again. "I haven't brought you this far just so that you can die on me."

Aria fell back in the sand and screamed, "Why are You doing this to me?"

Karraar stepped back. "You'd rather I let you die?"

Aria glared at him. "Stay out of it, beast. I'm not talking to you."

Karraar looked all around and then back to her. "There's no one else around, you foolish woman."

Foolish woman? Why do you continue to let him live and breathe? Get up and attack him. Make him pay for your suffering. He's the root of your pain and your hatred. He did this to you.

Aria grabbed fistfuls of sand and threw them in Karraar's direction. "You killed my father!"

Karraar snarled, "That's what this is about? Your *father*? I did no such thing."

He denies it to your face?

Heat rose in Aria's cheeks. She gritted her teeth. "Every time I see your wicked face, my father's head falls from his shoulders again. You sicken me, and you'll pay for what you did."

Karraar reached down, grabbed her by the throat, and lifted her off the ground. Aria looked him in the eye and refused to struggle against his grip. He brought her face within an inch of his. His breath smelled like death, and saliva dripped from the sides of his elongated snout.

Karraar's eyes narrowed, and he growled deep within his throat. "I'm not the one who stabbed your father in the back and made him watch as they slaughtered his friends. I showed you and your father mercy by putting him out of his misery. I gave you closure. You didn't need wonder what might've happened to him. I'm *also* not one of those who took you captive and forced themselves on you."

Karraar lowered Aria to the ground and released her. "You should be thanking me."

Aria coughed and massaged her throat. Hate dripped from her lips. "Mark my words, Karraar, you will die by my hand."

Karraar smiled, and his sharp, yellowed teeth glistened in the light. "I'll look forward to it. In the meantime, you'd better rest. You'll need your strength if you're to overcome me. You'll also need it when our traveling companions come to visit."

Companions?

Aria's eyes widened. "We're being followed? How long have you known? And who or what follows us?"

Karraar gazed into the distance, and Aria turned to see where he looked. "Not long after we entered the wastelands, the nōmed picked up on our trail and have followed us ever since. They hunt in quads and are extremely lethal. They are methodical and cunning foes. They will watch us for days or weeks and will attack once they've established our patterns and our weaknesses."

Aria put her hand over her brow and squinted but saw only sand. "Where are they now?"

Karraar pointed to a distant dune in the west that rose a few feet higher than the others. "Somewhere on the other side of that peak. I can't smell their sweat-riddled hides right now, and that's concerning."

Aria pulled her hair back and tied it into a knot at the back of her head. "If we're to survive an attack, I'll need a weapon."

Karraar didn't reply, so Aria turned and faced him. "Well? Did you not hear me, or are you afraid I'll use the weapon against you?"

Karraar scoffed. He bent down on one knee, pushed his paw-like hand deep in the sand, and withdrew a long, crude spear. He twirled the spear once and thrust it into the ground, point-first. "It isn't much, but you must make do with it."

Aria eyed the spear. *Pick it up and shove it through his throat. He deserves it.* "I was thinking of a smaller weapon."

Karraar swung his arm wide. "Do you see an armory around here? No. You use what's available. Now take the weapon."

Aria glared at Karraar. *Play into his kindness. He won't even see it coming.* "I'm still injured and weak."

Karraar snarled, "Do you think me so ignorant? I know who you are. I've seen the carnage left in your wake. You're a lot of things, but weak isn't one of them. Besides, the nōmed don't care that you're injured. Neither do I. Now take the spear before I beat you with it."

Aria didn't move.

Karraar lifted the battle-axe from his back and took a few steps back. "You're wasting what little time we have, and I need to assess how much of the imminent fight will be mine. Pick it up and show me you can use it. It'll also draw them out."

Karraar gripped his axe with both hands and held it over his head.

"But—"

Karraar lunged at her. Aria grabbed the spear, pulled it from the ground, and somersaulted sideways. Karraar's axe tore through the space her head had previously occupied. Pain tore through her shoulders, but she didn't have time to dwell on it.

This pain pales in comparison to what you endured dangling from the wall at Castle Portador Tempestade. Move!

Aria rolled to her feet and swung the spear like a sword. Its tip skated across Karraar's leather breastplate. He growled and swung his axe at her midsection. She spun away and jabbed the spear at his throat, but he moved out of its path long before it connected.

Karraar's speed and strength exceeded hers, but she knew she could use it to her advantage. He expected her to fight fair, but she couldn't do that and still take him down. They circled twice, each waiting for the other to make a move.

Despite his words, he thinks you're weak. Show him what you're really made of.

Aria stepped back and wiped the sweat from her forehead. Her brow flattened and sank, and the left side of her nose and mouth curled into a scowl. She screamed and ran straight at Karraar, her spear leading the way.

Karraar braced himself with one foot and dropped his axe on the ground. The irrational move caught Aria off-guard, and she stumbled. The spear's pointed end caught in the sand and catapulted her forward.

Karraar turned sideways, grabbed her by the waist as she flew by, and slammed her into the ground. The impact drove the air from her lungs. Her back arched as pain fissured out from the wound between her shoulder blades. She squeezed her eyes and her fists tight and refused to let a single tear fall.

You're a strong woman. Once you've regained your strength, you will defeat him.

"The enemy will do anything they can to throw you off. You must adapt with every passing moment. You fight hard, but your eyes betray you. They project your attack and leave you vulnerable. Fight like this against the nōmed, and you will certainly die."

Aria relaxed her hands and opened her eyes. Karraar stood over her. Strands of saliva hung from his twisted, grey lips.

Karraar stared at her, but not with contempt as before. "Had enough?"

She nodded, and he stepped back. She fought through the pain and sat up. "What happened with the carriage? Why were you there?"

Karraar growled. "It's complicated."

Aria glared at him. "Then simplify it for me."

"Several of my kind have shadowed your carriage ever since you departed from Castle Portador Tempestade. We're the only reason Lord Rosai left you behind. He never would've otherwise."

"And you're the reason he easily dealt with the *zhebəllin*?"

"Precisely. They didn't dare attack him with us surrounding them."

Pravus has been lying to me this whole time?

Karraar crouched down next to her. His knife dangled on his belt, and she needed it. Her hand moved toward it.

Take it, Aria. Use it against him. Bathe the blade in his blood.

Karraar pulled the knife from its sheath, turned it hilt out, and extended his paw-like hand toward her. "Take it. You may soon find it useful."

Aria reached out and touched the hilt of the knife. An image of Karraar's bloody corpse lying at her feet flashed in her mind.

It's what you want.

Aria retracted her hand. "If I take it, I'll kill you with it."

Karraar scoffed. "You may try, but you're not likely to succeed."

Aria raised her right eyebrow. "And you're willing to live with that risk?"

"I can only live in the moment. There's no future for me, so I have no fear of it." Karraar shook the knife. "Take it."

Aria grabbed the knife's hilt, and Karraar released his grip on its blade. She ran her thumb across its blade, and the razor-sharp edge drew blood. She sucked on her thumb until the bleeding stopped.

Karraar removed the belt from his waist and handed it to her. "You'll need this too."

Aria slid the knife into its sheath and stood. She wrapped the belt around her waist and cinched it tight.

"Thank you." The words tasted bittersweet on her tongue.

You'll still kill him when the moment presents itself. He killed your father. You cannot allow him to live.

Karraar's eyes narrowed, his ears twisted, and he raised his nose in the air. He shoved Aria.

A hatchet whistled past her head.

Aria tumbled to the ground but found her feet again a moment later.

Karraar sprang from his crouch, caught one of the nōmed in mid-air, and ripped its throat out with his teeth. Bluish-black liquid sprayed the air, and the body fell limp on the sand.

Aria reached for the spear, but another nōmed threw her to the ground. By the time she rolled onto her back, it was on top of her. The nōmed's rage-filled grey eyes peered through the slit in its orange headwrap. The nōmed snarled and raised its hatchet over its head. Aria freed the knife from its sheath, but the nōmed's hatchet was already arcing downward.

Aria twisted at the waist and curled her body away. The near-miss gave her a burst of energy, and she sat up and leaned into the nōmed. She thrust the knife hard upward and caught the nōmed underneath its elongated jaw. The nōmed hissed, groaned, and stiffened as she drove the knife all the way to its hilt, twisted it, and ripped it back out. Bluish-black blood gushed from the nōmed's wound.

The hatchet's wooden handle slammed the top of her head, and the nōmed let it fall to the ground. The nōmed clutched its throat and slumped to the ground next to her.

Her ears rang, and her head throbbed, but she had no time to let the pain sink in. She wiped the sticky, bluish-black sludge from her eyes and pushed herself to her feet.

Karraar traded blows with another nōmed. The nōmed's hatchet dug into the left side of Karraar's leather breastplate, and they both toppled to the ground, grunting.

Aria scanned the dune that the three nōmed had come from. *Karraar said they traveled in quads. Where's the fourth?*

Karraar and the nōmed held each other by their throats. Karraar had the advantage of long arms, but the nōmed had position and leverage, and Karraar struggled under the nōmed's solid mass.

A bright light flashed in Aria's eyes and she ducked. Another hatchet whizzed over her head. It'd come from the top of the closest dune.

The fourth.

Karraar's roar gained Aria's attention once more. He pulled his long legs up, dug his claws into the nōmed's sides, and pulled the nōmed closer. With the added leverage, he twisted the nōmed's head until it turned unnaturally. Aria heard the *crack* of bones from where she crouched.

Karraar threw the nōmed off himself and lay there. Blood pooled in the sand around Karraar—the third nōmed's hatchet stuck out from his left side. He tried to sit up but fell back against the sand.

Aria glanced back up the dune as she moved toward the spear. The fourth nōmed launched another hatchet at her. She rolled to the side, but the hatchet sliced into the side of her thigh, and she screamed when the pain registered.

You are a warrior. You are a queen. You are strong.

She crawled toward the spear that protruded from the ground just behind Karraar. The nōmed leapt toward her and Karraar from the top of the dune with a loud cry and another raised hatchet in-hand. The nōmed's orange robes fluttered like deformed wings behind it.

You are a warrior. You are a queen. You are strong.

Aria pulled the spear from the ground and hurled it toward the fourth nōmed. Every heartbeat captured the moments like pages from a picture book.

The spear wobbled in the air.

Fragments of sound from the nōmed's cry reverberated against her eardrums.

Her own scream rippled her throat.

The nōmed's eyes widened when it caught sight of the spear.

Aria's trajectory couldn't have been more perfect.

The spear's tip ripped into the nōmed's bare chest and sank in a few inches.

The spear's butt-end came crashing down, caught Karraar on his right side, and ripped into his hide as it slid down and penetrated the sand.

The nōmed slid down the spear's shaft, impaled by it.

The nōmed's hatchet buried its sharp head in the sand right next to Karraar's face and nearly took off Karraar's left ear.

The nōmed slumped on top of Karraar, dead.

Aria's heart raced. Her throat felt raw. Her leg pulsed with pain.

She stumbled over to Karraar and dropped to her knees. The orange sand swam around her, and she shook her head.

Karraar's eyes widened.

She looked down and saw that she held a bloody hatchet to his throat. She couldn't recall grabbing it.

One quick swipe, and he's finished.

Karraar didn't move. "I won't stop you, but it's not as easy to do as you might think."

Her hand trembled.

For your father. For Alderan.

Karraar's eyes mirrored the pain pouring from her own.

Take his life. End your pain.

She released her grip on the hatchet and sank away from him. "I hate you."

She sat back and stared at the ominous orange dunes. Tears welled in her eyes, and she fought them back.

Why did you show him mercy? He'll never show you the same.

Her shoulder blades burned with fire, her leg throbbed, and her arms hung limp at her sides. She drew one leg to her chest and rested her head on her knee. Her heart still raced, and she struggled to get enough air.

She closed her eyes and tried to forget about the pain, but it lingered. How would she survive without Karraar? How would she ever make it back to Pravus without his help? She knew nothing of the wastelands or where they headed.

You should've ended him. Death will find you.

Her tongue clung to the back of her teeth like a leech, and she could barely swallow. "We're not going to survive, are we?"

Karraar groaned and grunted. Aria looked over at him and saw him struggle to push the dead nōmed off himself. She turned over and crawled on her hands and knees to him.

Leave him be. You owe him nothing.

She helped push the nōmed off and then fell back on the hot sand. Karraar sat up and ripped the hatchet from his side. He leaned over and vomited liquid.

Karraar rose to his feet, unstrapped his breastplate, and let it fall to the ground. Blood oozed from his wound and matted his thick, red fur. He raised his head skyward and roared. Aria wished she had the strength to do the same.

Karraar bent down next to her and grabbed the knife that lay in the sand. She didn't move to stop him. She couldn't have even if she'd wanted to. The burst of energy had long since passed, and her body refused to cooperate in any sort of capacity.

Karraar cut away the bottom of Aria's dress. He returned the knife to its sheath on her belt and then grabbed hold of her leg. She winced but then relaxed. He wrapped the strand of cloth around her thigh where the hatchet had sliced it open and pulled it tight. She winced again. He tied the ends of it in a knot.

Aria closed her eyes and bit her lower lip to keep from tearing up. How could a murderous beast like him have moments of such compassion? Had he really killed her father out of mercy?

Don't let him fool you, Aria. You can't trust his actions. You're just a delivery to him, nothing more.

Aria's voice croaked, "We need to find me some water soon, or you'll be delivering a dead body to Pravus."

Karraar grunted. "As you wish, *my queen.*"

Aria's eyes shot open and she looked up at him. "Why did you just say that?"

She *knew* the answer but wanted to hear it from his lips.

"I gave you the chance to kill me—and I would've accepted my death—but you spared my life. I've served only Lord Rosai, and now I will serve you also. My life is yours. Use it. Take it. Do what you will with me."

Aria couldn't move. She could barely breathe. No words could describe her emotional state. Never had she controlled someone else's fate.

The power she'd gained over Karraar intoxicated her. She wanted more.

Is this what Pravus seeks? Is this true power? To decide who lives and who dies?

Karraar's side still bled, and she felt a tinge of guilt, but she had to gauge the sincerity of his commitment to her. She said, "Make haste with the water. I don't want to be alone out here when the sun goes down."

Karraar nodded. "I'll return before the night falls. You have my word."

He grabbed his battle-axe from the ground, returned it to its holder on his back, and dropped on all fours. His face twisted with pain. He held his side with one hand, and raced through the sand like a three-legged, red-haired demon.

Aria crawled over to the shaded area underneath the makeshift shelter and lay back in the sand. She didn't need to dream of Kinzhdm ef Häfn any longer. She belonged with Pravus. Together they'd rule the world.

She deserved the power.

And with your mezhik you'll be unstoppable.

As the prophecies foretold, she would become queen.

You're already a queen, and your reign has begun.

CHAPTER EIGHTEEN

A dull afternoon sun hung low in the east. To the north, the shipping docks of East and West Hotah stretched for miles along the Hotah Bay and up the long, wide mouth of the Hotah River. South, beyond the Hotah Bay, lay the Vastus Ocean—a quiet, desolate world of its own.

Theyn stepped onto the wood-planked dock jutting into the bay, and her legs wavered underneath her, but she welcomed the stability.

Vessels of every shape and size lined both sides of the dock, and numerous fishermen sat next to their boats, working hard to repair their nets in time for the next morning's catch. Others tested and repaired their sails and riggings. Still, others sat on benches at the far end of the docks, soaking in the view and the last rays of sunlight.

Theyn breathed deeply, savoring the dirty, musty smell of the bay and its drenched docks.

It's good to finally be home.

Berggren took the lead as they strolled down the length of the dock, toward West Hotah. Felix followed close behind Berggren, then Nardus and Theyn.

The end of the dock met up with a wide, cedar-planked boardwalk that stretched along the west side of the bay and across the bridge linking East and West Hotah, but it ended there.

Large, carpogenic trees, interspersed with square, seven-foot-tall poles, lined the city side of the boardwalk. Carvings of various fish and animals from the region covered the surface of the poles, and two sconces hung from the top of each pole, parallel to the boardwalk. No two poles were identical.

In summer, Theyn enjoyed walking along the boardwalk and partaking of the various fruits offered by the trees. But the harsh winters left the trees barren of fruit and leaves, and their sky-reaching branches resembled the skeletal remains of giants' hands, begging the gods for mercy and sanctification.

Theyn shook her head. *You're begging the wrong gods. Zhedäƨ ʔʊn would give you fruit even now.*

The beige and brown stone buildings of West Hotah loomed over the treetops like squared-off teeth, and they rose even higher farther west as they climbed the rising hills.

At the first intersection of the boardwalk, the four of them headed west toward a narrow gap between two buildings. The buildings' hand-stacked, stone architecture left the walls rough and sharp in places. Theyn did her best to avoid brushing the walls as they pushed past a steady stream of people coming from the other side of the buildings.

Lapping water and squawking seabirds quickly gave way to the thrum of the city: people talking and shouting about their wares and foods, hooves and wagon wheels scraping along the cobblestone streets, the laughter of children playing, and the crackling of fires cooking food and heating metal.

When they finally popped out on the other side of the buildings and onto the city's main thoroughfare, Theyn soaked in the innumerable sounds and smells.

West Hotah—the commerce capital of the Ancient Realm—housed more than a hundred thousand people and thousands more visitors. People moved through its maze of bumpy, brown cobblestone streets daily, oblivious of the world beyond the outer city walls.

The breadth of the main street spanned more than eighty feet, but more than half of its width went to the various vendors set up along both of its sides. Nearly anything imaginable could be bought along the main stretch: clothing, furs, fresh fish, baked goods, perfumes and beauty products, hand-crafted weapons, art, potions, booze, animals, slaves—the limitation of goods only came by the season.

One could easily get lost or slip into the throng of people, so Theyn kept her eyes trained on Nardus as best she could. Twice she'd lain with him in the past week, and—since she'd drugged him both times—he knew nothing of either encounter. The guilt of it tortured her.

Theyn knew their paths would soon part, but she needed to be with him one last time. Her *condition* demanded it. She'd mapped every inch of his body in her mind and had explored it in detail. Physically, he held no secrets from her.

But what's in your mind and your heart? What stories linger behind the scars you bear?

Because of her condition, the way it fueled her carnal desires, she'd assumed herself incapable of love. But she'd been wrong. She loved Nardus with every fiber of her being and longed to be with him—without deceit. But how would she manage it?

Nardus kept his distance from her, but it was nothing more than a show for Berggren's sake. Every time their eyes met, she sensed his desire for her, but he hid it well under his calm and inscrutable countenance. Every little brush of their skin as they passed each other carried with it secret messages of unbridled passion and desires waiting to be released.

Tonight, we'll be together again.

She wanted to risk everything and tell him the truth about her condition and what she'd done to him because of it. But would he understand her? The thought of him rejecting her and telling her how sick and twisted she was kept her mouth shut.

But I love him.

Berggren led them into a small niche between two beige, stone-walled shops. He put his hand up to halt Felix, glared daggers in Nardus's direction, and then turned to Theyn. "Wait here. I must handle some business before we head to Joriah's."

Berggren turned and slipped into the crowd without waiting for a response. Theyn guessed his business had to do with their next voyage, but she didn't really care to know the details.

A thought struck her and left her reeling. *Nardus will be gone. Who will I lay with to keep my condition under control?*

Panic ripped through her like flashes of lightning.

I don't want to be with anyone other than Nardus. How can I possibly go out to sea again without him? How can I live without him?

Nardus turned his head to the side and shouted over his shoulder, "I don't understand these people."

Theyn frowned. "What's not to understand? They're all busy and have somewhere to be."

"But why haven't they panicked? In fact, why haven't you?"

Why would I panic? Well, besides worrying about not being with you?

"Now I'm the one at a loss for understanding. Are you speaking of the dragon? You know as well as I that we have no idea when that event happens. Why should I panic about it now? And how would any of the people around us know of the vision we shared anyway?"

Nardus turned and faced her. "No, Theyn. I'm talking about the sky. Why does everyone go about as though nothing were wrong with it?"

Theyn looked up at the bright blue sky then turned back to Nardus, her eyebrows scrunched together. "Are you feeling well? The sky's as blue as it always is this time of year."

Nardus's eyebrows arched, and his nose wrinkled. "Are you mad? Ever since I returned from *Ef Demd Dhä* and spewed fire into the sky, it's been blood-red. Haven't you seen the black lightning too?"

Spewed fire in the sky? Theyn shook her head and rolled her eyes. *He's the one who's mad.*

A woman walked by, and Nardus grabbed her by the arm. "Ma'am, can you tell this woman here what color the sky is?"

The woman looked at Nardus with a blank expression.

Theyn smiled at the woman. "Please indulge him. He's new to the city. Please have a look at the sky and tell him what you see."

The woman looked to the sky for a fraction of a second then glared at Nardus. "The sky's blue. Now release my arm before I scream."

Nardus complied, and the woman huffed and walked away.

Theyn crossed her arms. "Are you satisfied now, or do you need further proof?"

Nardus grabbed Theyn by her shoulders. Fear widened his eyes like a hunted animal. "I must go see my friend, Gnaud. Something is terribly wrong with me, and he's the only one who may have an answer."

Theyn relished the touch of his rough hands on her skin. She wanted him to rub them all over her body. She envisioned the encounter and purred. *Mad or not, tonight you're mine.*

Theyn reached up and cupped Nardus's face. "Let me help you, then. Where does this Gnaud fellow live?"

Nardus shrank away from her touch. "You wouldn't understand if I told you."

Theyn licked her lips. *Tell me your secrets, and I'll tell you mine.*

She stepped closer to him and poked him in the chest with her finger. "Try me. I'm much older than you think and have seen things myself that *you* wouldn't understand."

Nardus tried to step back, but she had him cornered. "He lives in Nasduron."

Nasduron? Theyn stepped back, and her eyes narrowed into slits. "The lost city? Impossible."

Nardus raised his hands. "Call it whatever you want. I told you that you wouldn't believe me."

Theyn scoffed. *Nobody would.* "And where is this lost city located?"

Nardus shrugged. "Its location makes no difference. I don't need to know where it is to get there. I just think about it, and then I go there."

"Really?" Theyn blew hot air on her nails and then rubbed them on her white blouse. "And yet you claim to have no mezhik."

Nardus spat on the ground. "There's no *mezhik* in me."

"Normal folk don't just step from one place to another. They also don't incinerate people on contact. What else are you hiding?"

"Nothing. And I swear I don't have mezhik."

Theyn stepped forward, placed her hands against the rough stone wall on either side of Nardus, and leaned close to him. He smelled of sweat and stale ale, but she didn't care. She knew she didn't smell much better since she hadn't showered in weeks.

She purred. "Fine. Let's say what you're telling me is true. How can I help you get there?"

Nardus reached up and grabbed the collar around his neck with both hands. "I need you to take this off. I think it's blocking me from going to Nasduron."

Theyn stood on the tips of her toes and craned her neck so she could get her lips close to his ear. She whispered, "Even if I wanted to, I don't have the power to take it off. But you do."

You have the power to take everything off me. I give it to you. Beg it of you.

Nardus put his hands on her shoulders and pushed her back. "I don't understand. What do you mean *I do*?"

Strip me bare.

Theyn laughed. "Never mind that. Only a wizard or sorcerer can take the collar off."

Nardus frowned. "Then who put this damned thing on me? I thought it was Berggren."

Theyn stepped back, leaned against the opposite wall, and started cleaning under her long nails. She shouted over the noise, "Berggren did, but anyone can place the collar on someone else."

Nardus moved forward, grabbed her hands, and pleaded with her. "I must get this collar off as soon as possible. Please help me find a wizard to do it."

Theyn trembled. *Please don't stop with my hands.*

"Don't you understand? That's exactly where we're headed. We'll stay with an old friend of Berggren's tonight, and tomorrow he'll remove your collar so that you can return to Lord Rosai."

Nardus's eyes brightened. "This friend of Berggren's is a wizard?"

Theyn nodded. "Joriah. He's a nice but strange man. He knows things that one shouldn't know."

Nardus bent over and kissed the tops of her hands. "Thank you, Theyn. That's all I needed to hear."

The touch of his lips on her skin drove her mad with ecstasy. She shivered from head to toe. An urge to pull him against her raged within. *Take me, Nardus. Please! I cannot bear to be without you.*

She fought the animalistic instincts begging her to ravish him right there in the niche. She pulled her hands away and dug her nails into the thick grey mortar of the wall behind her.

Deep within, she sensed her condition awaken—the terrifying, horrific beginnings of her transformation. *Not here! Not now! I can't let him see me this way.*

Nardus touched her shoulder. "Are you okay?"

She swatted his hand away. "Don't touch me."

Nardus reeled backward. "I'm sorry, Theyn. Have I wronged you somehow?"

No, my love, but I've wronged you. Theyn closed her eyes and prayed to Zhedäz Zʊn. *I've followed your rules, my goddess. It hasn't even been seven days since my last coupling. Why are you doing this to me? Why have you allowed my transformation to begin? Do not afflict me this way. I serve you with every breath I take. Still my soul. Keep the beast at bay.*

Theyn opened her eyes, but she couldn't bear Nardus's stare. Somehow, he knew, didn't he? Her betrayal of his trust ached in her heart like a festering wound.

Forgive me.

She pulled her cloak over her shoulders and lifted the hood over her head. Tears swelled in her eyes, and she bolted into the crowd. Nardus called after her, but she quickened her pace.

Don't follow me, my love.

† † †

Nardus looked over at Felix. The deaf mute shrugged and smiled. Nardus raked his fingers through his hair. Wasn't *he* supposed to be the one running away? How quickly the tables had turned.

What do I care? This damn collar will be off in the morning, and I'll never see any of them again.

After all, Theyn meant nothing to him, right? He only cared about his family, not her. She could never be to him what Vitara had been.

Had been? No! My love, I swear she'll never replace you. You're my anchor.

But he *did* feel something for Theyn, didn't he? He'd seen their future, hadn't he? He'd felt the emotions in the vision he'd shared with her. But none of it made sense.

How would we have a daughter together?

"The same way everyone does."

It could never be!

Since resurfacing from the ruins of Mortuus Terra and having fire explode from his mouth, he'd started having brief conversations in his head. Those moments felt like another presence existed in his mind, yet they seemed like another side of himself altogether—alien, yet familiar, all at once. Each episode started with the left side of his chest burning with fire.

How could I ever be with Theyn and pursue resurrecting my family too?

"Why not have them both?"

Madness!

"No more so than raising the dead, right?"

But it could never be. I love my family. Everything I've done has been for them.

"Keep your family. Keep your Vitara. And take Theyn too."

But how? How would that work? Could I really be with Theyn?

"Yes. We can have it all."

The voice left him, and, like his mind, deep fissures of guilt eroded his heart. The burning in his chest subsided.

"Where's Theyn?" a deep voice rumbled. A moment later, Berggren squeezed through the crowd and blocked the niche.

Nardus shrugged. "I'm not sure what happened to her. She seemed fine one moment, then she covered herself with her cloak and ran into the throng. I would've gone after her, but she disappeared before I could even blink."

Berggren scowled at him and breathed deep. "We need to get to Joriah's house as quickly as possible. Theyn may be in trouble, and I need to find her. Keep up, or you'll regret it."

Berggren turned to leave, but Nardus caught his arm. "Wait. I can help you find her. I feel responsible for her running off."

Berggren gruffed. "Not on your best day. Let's move before the rest of the daylight gets away from us."

Nardus released Berggren's arm and followed him up the street to the north, through an unending sea of people. He guessed Felix followed, but he didn't bother looking back.

A few miles down the main street, they took a left onto a narrow street covered by vibrant fabric awnings and chock-full of vendors selling every kind of food imaginable: biscuits drenched in chocolate, nuts and oats crushed into bits and drizzled with black honey, dried strips of boar, rabbit, and deer meat, battered and fried strips of fish, balls of dough fried and rolled in sugar and crushed berries, pan-fried yellow potato cakes covered with a thick layer of butter and goat's cheese, and many other things he'd never seen before.

So many choices. How could anyone choose what to eat?

The variety of odors, scents, and smells wove into an irresistible aroma. His mouth watered, and his stomach rumbled with hunger, but they wouldn't be stopping for food.

Instead, they crossed another street, headed between two fire-kiln redbrick buildings through a dank, musty alleyway that reeked of urine and feces. Then they turned into another alleyway that ran between two rows of buildings. Eventually, the alleyway ended where a long, narrow stone stairway rose to meet a higher crossroad.

Does this city never end?

They ascended the stairs single-file, and by the time they reached the top of the stairs, Nardus could scarcely breathe. Sweat poured from his forehead, and a stabbing pain emanated from the left side of his chest.

He dropped to his knees and pulled up his shirt. The stone glowed red and bubbled his skin like magma.

Fire burned in his eyes, and everything around him took on a red tint. He was himself—yet he wasn't. Hatred and rage swelled in his heart, and each breath exited from his lips and nostrils with red flames and plumes of black smoke.

He looked at the throng with contempt. *Sheep for the slaughter.*

He stood, circled in the street, and spewed a column of red fire at the passersby. Their shrieks fell upon his ears like soft notes of music. Their faces twisted with anguish, blackened like charred meat, and melted from their skulls. Their bodies collapsed in heaps of bubbling flesh on the cobblestone, those heaps turned into piles of ash, and then the ash blew away in the stiff, eastern wind.

Within moments, nothing remained of the people but echoes of their screams.

A sweet symphony.

Nardus lifted his head skyward. Flames spewed from his mouth and reached the clouds. The power—*his* power—transformed him into a mighty black dragon. He spread his arms—his wings—and beat them against his sides, lifting himself into the air. He flew across the city like a shadow of death, setting everything below aflame.

He roared, the sound like rolling thunder, and the sheep scattered. "When I rise again, you will all die."

Two bolts of black lightning ripped through the red sky like jagged claws and shot straight into his heart. He flapped his wings frantically, but they were arms again. He spiraled downward like a fallen angel having lost its wings and slammed into the cobblestone street.

The street rippled like a pond's still surface impacted by a large object. Nardus writhed on the ground, and his body contorted, every bone in his body shattered and every muscle shredded.

"Let me die," he repeated.

"Twelve days," the voice echoed in Nardus's head.

Darkness stalked him, attacked him, and swallowed him whole.

† † †

Nardus lay still on the ground. Berggren stood over him, unsure of what to do. Felix crouched next to Nardus and checked for a pulse. A crowd of people gathered to watch.

Berggren balled his hands. *We don't have time for this. I need to find Theyn.*

Felix turned to Berggren and shook his head. Murmurs erupted from the silence and spread through the growing crowd.

"He's dead," said one woman. Amusement laced her words.

"He probably deserved it," shouted another. "I think he was possessed."

"He said we're all dead," yelled a man. "He must've had it backwards."

Berggren bent down, picked Nardus up, and hefted him over his shoulder. Nardus burned with fever, and the heat radiating from his body penetrated Berggren's clothes and coat. Berggren motioned for Felix to follow, then he turned west and headed down the greyish-white cobblestone street.

Berggren and Felix pushed through the crowd of people, but the crowd circled them like vultures. "Show's over," barked Berggren. "Move along before I get angry."

An elderly woman grabbed Berggren's free arm and stopped him in the middle of the street. "This man is evil. Make sure you drive a stake through his black heart."

Berggren peered into the woman's clouded eyes and shuddered. *Superstitious old fool.*

He ripped his arm from the woman's grasp and forced his way through the crowd.

"Don't say you weren't warned," cackled the woman. "Your inaction damns us all. Damns us all!"

Berggren didn't look back. *These people are cold-hearted. It's no wonder I prefer the open sea to this cesspool of madness.*

Deep, narrow buildings lined either side of the street like massive gravestones. The four-story, grey-and-white marbled granite buildings made the street feel closed-off despite its wide breadth. A few streets down, Berggren and Felix turned right, and the crowds thinned.

Finally, some peace and a path to walk.

Farther up the road, the large, granite structures gave way to smaller ones made of fire-kiln brown bricks and tar-soaked, wooden roofs pitched like steeples, and the cobblestone streets transitioned to crushed red gravel. A mile farther, they made a left onto a steep walkway made up of flagstone and overgrown tufts of brown grass.

They climbed to the top of the walkway and stopped in front of an old, rusted-iron gate that hung slightly off-kilter.

Berggren ran his hand along the top of it. *Gate was brand new when we left. It's been far too long.*

He looked beyond the gate and to the small cottage at the back of the property. Its mud walls and brown thatched roof distinguished it from nearly every other building in West Hotah, as did its fiery-red door.

Felix brushed past him and pushed the gate open. *Screeeech.* They both stepped through the gate, then Felix forced it shut behind them. Its final *screeeech* raised the hairs on Berggren's nape. By the time they made it up the stone path and reached the cottage, a tall, frappant man held the fiery-red front door open for them.

The man wore black, shined shoes, casual grey trousers with pleats over the thighs, a billowing white shirt with a ruffled neck and cuffs, and a fiery-red cape draped over his narrow right shoulder. The cape hung just below the backs of his knees and flowed as though a light breeze disrupted its otherwise tranquil state.

Joriah. Never surprised.

"Cape matches the door. And your hair. And your beard. Intentional, or a coincidence?"

Joriah swept his left hand down the length of the cape and smoothed out the wrinkles. "I never leave anything to coincidence."

"Would expect nothing less from you."

Joriah eyed the body draped over Berggren's shoulder. His kind, teal eyes smiled. "I see some things never change, Iceberg."

Berggren grunted. "My life has no dull moments."

Joriah pushed the cape from his shoulder and swept his right arm into the cottage. "Please, make yourselves at home."

Berggren stepped through the doorway and into the small, single-room cottage. Felix followed close behind, and Joriah closed the door and locked it.

"Welcome back."

Berggren turned and faced Joriah. "Funny choice of words. City feels anything but welcoming these days. Walking through its streets never felt as hostile as it did today."

Joriah nodded. "The city's evolved over the last twelve years, and not for the better. I keep to myself and my business."

A bead of sweat lingered on Berggren's brow, and he wiped it away with the back of his hand. "Don't blame you there. I'm already itching to be out at sea again."

"Oh, where are my manners? I suppose you'd like to set your load down. Hold on just a moment." Joriah swept his arm across his body in a wide arc.

All the furniture in the room scattered to the outer walls. The circular, woven rug in the center of the room rolled itself up and slid across the floor, and then the wooden planks in the floor vibrated, dropped down, and formed a spiraling staircase.

Berggren shook his head. *Wizards.*

He turned to Joriah and pointed at Nardus, who still hung over his shoulder. "Think he's dead."

Joriah chuckled. "Splendid! He won't keep us up all night with his insipid banter."

Berggren scowled. "I'm serious, Joriah."

Joriah's teal eyes twinkled. "To a fault, I'm sure. But your friend's far from dead."

Berggren sighed. "Well that's unfortunate. Guess *Zhedäɛ Ʒʊn* didn't answer that prayer."

Joriah pushed his smarmy red hair over his shoulders. "Take him downstairs and put him in the first room on the left."

Berggren walked over to the staircase and stared down into the darkness. *Like a ship's hull.*

"Where's Theyn? I thought she'd be here too."

If I only knew. "Better be here soon, or I'll have to go find her."

"You sound concerned, Iceberg. That's unlike you."

Berggren scratched his bald head. "It's nothing. Just this damned city. Don't trust her being alone in it anymore."

"Would you like me to help you find her?"

Berggren looked back over his shoulder. "No, but I appreciate the offer. It's not just the city. There are some things about Theyn you don't know and frankly wouldn't understand."

Joriah nodded. "I'm sure you're right. As you know, I'm terrible at reading people and lack any sort of skills in mezhik. How could I possibly know anything about Theyn's *condition*?" Joriah winked at him.

How indeed? Berggren's eyes narrowed. *Never told him, and I'm sure Theyn never did either.*

Berggren turned around, lay Nardus's limp body on the floor, and walked over to Joriah. He crossed his arms and flexed his muscles. "What do *you* know of Theyn's condition?"

Joriah hung his hand on Berggren's forearm and smiled up at him, seemingly oblivious to Berggren's threatening posture. "Perhaps more than you, my friend. But that tale will have to wait for another time."

Berggren grimaced. "Agreed, but we *will* speak more on this later."

Joriah moved past him. "Certainly. Now, let's get you all settled in."

Berggren turned around. Felix dragged Nardus down the steps by his hands. Nardus's head landed on each step with a *thud*, and Berggren couldn't help but chuckle.

I hope you feel that in the morning.

Joriah motioned him toward the stairway, but he needed to find Theyn before sunset. The thought of her being alone in the city at dusk twisted his gut.

City's full of people with evil intentions. Don't need you on the loose either, Theyn.

Berggren walked over to the door and opened it. "I'll be back."

"Suit yourself, Iceberg. Felix, the nearly-dead man, and I will have a riveting conversation in your absence."

Berggren shook his head, stepped through the doorway, and closed the door behind him. He took a deep breath and scanned the city below. How would he ever find her in such a large place?

Where've you run off to, Theyn?

✝ ✝ ✝

Theyn zigzagged through the streets until she no longer knew where she was. Hot tears blurred her vision and streaked down her cheeks. How could she ever go back and face Nardus?

He'll never understand my condition.

How could anyone? She didn't even fully understand her condition. It had been passed down through the females in her family for more generations than she could count.

Each of her family members who'd exhibited the condition had dealt with it in their own way. Some had taken their own lives after the first transformation, others embraced the change but were eventually hunted down and killed, and a few found that a regimen of weekly sexual coupling kept the transformation from occurring.

But never a cure.

At twenty-one name days, when her condition first manifested, she'd allowed herself to give into it and fully transform, but the beast that'd emerged from that experience scared even her. Berggren had been there that night; the scars across his torso were proof. Somehow, he'd managed to subdue her. If he hadn't been there, she might've slaughtered an entire village.

The day after her transformation, Berggren brought Shaul into the situation. The poor kid had been in love with Theyn for years, and Berggren used that knowledge to manipulate him. At first, Shaul shied away from her grotesque, transformed body. Many months later, when Shaul finally came to terms with her condition, Shaul realized he could be the one to save her and be with her.

Theyn couldn't remember that first encounter with Shaul, but their coupling had worked in transforming her back into her human form. Shaul never spoke of it, and he avoided the subject at every request. From that moment forward, she'd coupled with Shaul weekly and kept herself from transforming again.

Years later, Berggren told her that she'd nearly killed Shaul that first night they'd coupled. *And still, I don't even know what I am, Zhedäz ɔʊn.*

She felt so much closer to Nardus than she ever had with Shaul. Shaul had been nothing more to her than a weekly fix for her condition. But she loved Nardus, didn't she?

If I really do love him then why can't I tell him the truth? He'll eventually find out one way or another. It must come from me.

The transformation stirred within her and began manifesting physically. She ran her fingers through the length of her hair, and, by the time she'd reached the ends of the strands, they'd already thickened.

I need to get to Joriah's house. Her pulse raced. *I'll tell Nardus everything and beg him to lie with me before it's too late.*

She fingered the hairs on her scalp. The texture had already changed as well—from wiry strands to a silky fur.

Or I'll have to force myself on him again.

A hard shoulder to Theyn's chest pulled her back into the city and spun her around. A large arm grabbed her around the waist and pinned her arms to her sides, and a hand clamped over her mouth and nose. Theyn squirmed and kicked, but the grip only tightened.

People all around walked by without a glance in her direction, either oblivious or indifferent to her situation. She guessed the latter.

"The more you struggle—" The man's raspy voice vibrated her eardrum. "—the more violent I become. Do you like violence, love?"

The animal within surfaced and begged to be set free.

Don't give in to it, Theyn.

The man pulled her into the narrow space between two grey brick buildings and dragged her to the back of it where no one would see them in the shadows. The man turned her around, shoved her against the wall, and kept his hand clamped over her mouth. He raised a knife in front of her face with his free hand and then held it to her neck.

"Scream and I'll slit your throat. Understand?"

You scream, and I'll tear yours out with my teeth.

Theyn nodded, and the man removed his hand from over her mouth.

Anger raged within and she couldn't keep her mouth shut. "Is this how you treat all your women? You stalk them from the shadows, corner them in the darkness, rape them, and then send them away with your bastard child growing inside?"

The man's guttural laughter soured her stomach. "Oh, they don't walk away, love."

Today, you'll be the one who doesn't walk away.

"What's your name?" she asked.

"Uan," he grunted. "Why?"

Theyn smiled. "I like to keep track of all the names of the men I've killed."

"Oh, really? You're a feisty little thing, aren't ya? How long is this list of yours?"

Theyn growled, "It's about to have its first name."

Uan grinned. "I think I'm in love, love."

Uan lowered his knife and placed the forearm of his other arm across her throat instead. With knife in hand, he sliced open the front of her shirt.

Theyn pulled the sides of her torn shirt open and exposed her breasts for him. *If I let this man take me, it'll stop the transformation.*

Uan slid the side of the blade down the middle of her chest—to her navel—and Theyn purred. Uan dropped the knife, grabbed her left breast, and squeezed it hard. He bent down and shoved his mouth against hers. He repulsed her, and she wanted to gag, but she forced her mouth open and let his probing tongue inside.

Ugh! What has this man put in his mouth? She pushed her disgust of Uan to the back of her mind. *Just let him stop the transformation.*

Uan pulled his head back from hers. "Your eyes are glowing, love. What kind of exotic creature are you?"

"You wouldn't believe me if I told you."

Uan let go of her breast and pulled her hood off her head. She bared her sharp teeth for him, and his eyes widened.

His surprise morphed into a wicked grin. "You're certainly different, love. I might enjoy this more than you."

Theyn grabbed a fist full of his shirt with one hand, pulled him closer, and then grabbed his crotch with her other. Uan groaned and leaned into her grip. Theyn released his shirt and slid her hand down to his belt and unbuckled it.

Theyn panted.

For Nardus.

With both hands, she unbuttoned his trousers and then pushed them down as far as she could reach. He moved his hands down to her waist and fiddled with her belt.

The bones in her hands contorted and her wrists elongated.

Use him, Theyn, like he's used so many before you. The thought repulsed her, but what alternative did she have?

If I let this man take me, would I ever be able to look Nardus in the eye again?

No. I couldn't possibly live like that.

Theyn looked in his eyes. "How many times have you done this, Uan?"

"Been with a woman?"

"No, how many women have you raped?"

Uan finally unlatched her belt. "Hundreds. Every chance I get. That turn you on, love?"

Theyn's stomach roiled. "Oh, it certainly does *something* to me."

This isn't who I am. This isn't who I want to be. Is this what I did to Nardus? Forced myself on him? Theyn knew the answer, and it pained her heart.

Uan slid his hand down the front of her trousers. Images of herself doing the same thing to Nardus flashed in her mind, and she couldn't allow Uan to go further.

What've I done? Tears blurred her eyes. *I'm so sorry, Nardus. I hope you'll forgive me.*

Uan groaned, "You're burning up, love."

Theyn growled and bared her teeth. She grabbed the base of Uan's manhood in her right hand and extended her cat-like claws into his flesh. Uan gasped.

Then she ripped it from his body.

That's for all the women of your past.

Uan grunted, and his eyes burned with hatred. He dropped to his knees and grabbed his crotch. "You bitch!"

Theyn drove her knee under his chin as hard as she could. The *crack* of snapping bones reverberated up her leg.

Uan's head snapped back, and he crumpled against the opposite wall. A short burst of air escaped from his lungs, then his arms and head slackened. His lower jaw hung in an unnatural position.

"Do I look like a dog to you?" She opened her hand, and Uan's flaccid manhood fell to the ground.

She leaned against the brick wall and retched. The thought of what she'd just done sickened her, but he'd deserved it. She retched again. Uan stirred and then wailed.

She flexed her right hand—her fingers were wet and sticky with blood. Her clothes were spattered with blood too. She needed to clean herself up.

What am I going to do now?

The smells of blood, sweat, stale urine, and many others permeated the air. Uan's ragged breathing—even his heartbeat—raged in her head as though her ear were against his chest. Her transformation progressed rapidly.

Think, Theyn!

She moved down the narrow passage a few feet to get away from the carnage and slipped off her cloak. She removed her torn shirt and wiped her hands with it as best she could. She dropped the shirt on the ground and looked back at Uan's slumped form.

Maybe he's got something of use.

Reluctantly, she walked back over to Uan and searched him. A small coin purse hung from his belt, and she took it—payment for services rendered. An ornate leather flask hung around his neck. She grabbed Uan's knife from the ground, cut the flask's leather straps, pulled the stopper from the top, and nearly retched again.

I don't even want to know what this is.

Uan groaned, and Theyn instinctively elbowed him in the side of the head. He fell over on his side.

Stay down.

She poured the liquid from the flask into her hand, tossed the flask in Uan's bloody lap, and rubbed her hands together as she walked away. Back at her discarded shirt, she picked it up and wiped her hands with it again. She tossed her shirt on the ground again and held her hands up but couldn't tell how clean they were in the shadows.

It will have to do for now.

She picked up her cloak, draped it over her shoulders, lifted the hood over her head, and pulled it tight around herself. She walked to the end of the narrow passage and poked her head around the corner. People moved about, but no one looked her way.

Typical city folk. Focused on nothing but themselves.

Theyn hurried through the streets, worked her way up to the highest point she could find, and climbed onto the roof of the nearest building. From there, she saw much of the city and reoriented herself using prominent landmarks. To her left, toward the north, she spotted Joriah's small cottage perched atop a small mound of earth.

But she no longer needed direction. She needed Nardus, and her heightened senses would lead her to him. She lifted her nose in the air and breathed deep.

Nardus.

His scent enraptured her. She leapt from the roof like a cat, rolled as she hit the ground, and sprang to her feet.

Twenty minutes if I move fast. But did she have twenty minutes to spare?

† † †

The Summitto Valley lay in ruin, it's beautiful, yellow-orange hamid grass trampled underfoot, charred with dragon's fire, and bathed in blood. Bodies lay strewn everywhere—some whole, but most severed of limb and head. Scavengers of every kind picked at the dead's flesh.

Cyrus shuddered.

Across the valley to the east, Magus sat atop his mighty black dragon, Cinolth The Dark. Even from where he stood, Cyrus saw the blood dripping from Cinolth's jaws.

Cyrus shook his fist in the air. "This isn't over, Magus!"

Magus's voice thundered across the valley and struck Cyrus in the chest like a bolt of lightning. "Mark my words, Cyrus. You will not live through this night!"

Cyrus flew across the valley like a spirit, seeped between the scales of Cinolth's neck, crawled into his head, and viewed the valley through his red-tinted gaze.

"I'm coming for you, Cyrus," said Cinolth.

† † †

Mezhik tickled Nardus's left ear and cheek with its tingle, and then a sharp pain pierced his left temple like a metal spike. He screamed and swatted the sides of his head as the images of Magus, Cinolth, and Cyrus pulled from his mind like fruit plucked from a tree.

"Stay out of my head!"

The spike of pain withdrew from his temple, and he rolled onto his side, fell off the bed, and landed on the floor. He gasped and sat up. Sweat soaked his clothes, and his head pounded. His surroundings looked unfamiliar, and he couldn't remember how he'd arrived there. He searched his mind but couldn't even recall what'd driven him to the floor.

Argh! What's with my mind? Is it the damned stone, or am I just mad? Surely madness.

A shadow fell across the room. Nardus looked up and saw a thin, unfamiliar man standing in the doorway.

The thin man asked, "Is everything okay in there?"

Nardus rubbed his head, certain that things were *not* okay. "I don't think so."

"I'm guessing many questions are running through your mind right about now."

"A never-ending list. Most importantly, where am I, how did I get here, and how long have I been here?"

The sides of the backlit man's short red beard shimmered. "Well, let's see… you're in West Hotah, by boat, and a few hours. I believe that just about sums up everything you wanted to know, yes?"

A dim light of recollection shone in Nardus's mind's eye. *Theyn.*

Nardus pushed himself up to the bed and sat. The left side of his chest ached, and he rubbed it. "This is your house then?"

"Certainly. An oasis amid chaos. Welcome."

"You're Berggren's friend—the wizard."

The man stepped into the room. "I am Joriah." He dipped his head. "A wizard… of sorts."

Joriah snapped his fingers and the room brightened as though they stood under the afternoon sun. Nardus looked around, but the light had no source.

"I hate mezhik." He turned his head to spit on the floor but thought better of it.

Joriah smiled. "I've gathered as much. You're an intriguing man… what do you call yourself?"

"Nardus Remison. Thought Berggren would've told you as much."

"Iceberg." Joriah snickered. "He was in a bit of a hurry when he dropped you off."

Nardus rubbed the back of his head. One spot, right at the center of the back of his head, hurt when he touched it, and it felt a bit swollen. "Do folks actually call him that? Iceberg?"

Joriah laughed. "Many folks around these parts do. I only call him that because I find it ironic and amusing. Berggren may present folks with a tough exterior, but there's no ice to be found in that big heart of his."

"Guess I haven't seen that side of him yet."

"No, and I'm guessing you won't, either. He sees you as a threat to Theyn, and anyone who threatens her is a sworn enemy of his."

"I'd never hurt Theyn."

"Sometimes events spiral beyond our control, even for those with good intentions. I can feel your sincerity, but he never will." Joriah paused and cocked his head. "Do you love her?"

"Do I love who? Theyn? That's absurd."

Why would he even ask me that?

Nardus lay back on the bed. "I barely know her. Besides, if you knew what I'd endured over the last several months and why, you wouldn't be asking me that."

Joriah wagged a finger at Nardus. "Don't fool yourself. I'm only asking you what you've been asking yourself for some time now."

Nardus closed his eyes. "Don't pretend you know me."

I don't even know myself anymore.

"I never do. As I said, I'm a wizard… of sorts. Some refer to my kind as *Žärz Dhä*."

"Well, I'm sure that means something to you, but I've never heard the term."

"If you were paying attention, I think it'd mean something to you as well. I see things in people that most cannot."

Nardus opened his eyes and stared at Joriah. "And what do you see in me?"

"Pain. Loss. Guilt. *Overwhelming* guilt. You wallow in guilt as a pig wallows in mud."

Nardus swallowed the truth of Joriah's words, and then he quickly dismissed them. "Everyone feels guilty about something. I'm sure you carry guilt as well."

"Yes, but your guilt runs deep inside you—to your core. It stretches far beyond anything you could ever fathom. The loss of your wife and your family hardly penetrates the surface of it. Then there's Bradwr and the guilt you felt after killing him. And now your love for Theyn that you refuse to admit. So much more than that, even. Deep-seeded. How do you manage to get up every morning and carry such a burden?"

How can he know these things about me? "Are you in my head?"

"No, and I don't need to be, Nardus. Your guilt is like a poison that seeps from your pores and permeates the air around you. I felt it like an ominous presence when I entered the room, and I can see it now pouring from your eyes." Joriah moved across the room and sat on the bed. "I could help you some, if you'd like."

Nardus closed his eyes and retreated deep within his mind. Again, the left side of his chest burned with fire.

Should I let him in? What harm could come of it?

"He'll know our darkest secrets if we do."

But he already does, doesn't he?

"How do we know?"

Because he knows me better than I know myself.

"Don't you mean us?"

Why would I?

"Do you think you're all alone inside your head?"

Madness!

"You're not mad, Nardus, but you're deceiving yourself."

Am I? Who are you, if you're not me?

"You already know who I am. You've known me for some time now."

Nardus sat up on the bed and looked at Joriah. "Did you hear that?"

Joriah frowned. "You've said nothing. What was I supposed to have heard?"

Nardus shook his head and sighed. "It doesn't matter. Madness filled my head after my family was murdered, and it tortured me for years. After I finally faced my pain and the guilt of letting my family down, the madness left me.

"But now that I've returned to this world, a different kind of madness has taken hold of me. I keep hearing a voice in my head, and vivid hallucinations plague me. When they happen, I can't distinguish between them and reality."

Joriah sat on the edge of the bed, next to Nardus, and stared him in the eye. "There are things going on within you beyond my skill. *Mezhik derk*. You may need Lord Rosai's help for that."

Mezhik derk… the stone?

Joriah folded his hands together in his lap. "As I said before, I'm a wizard of sorts—a seer. Now, how may I be of service to you?"

Genuine kindness exuded from Joriah's eyes and calmed Nardus.

Can he be trusted? I don't know. But does it matter? No, but maybe I can get him to remove the collar. Yes!

The burning in Nardus's chest ebbed. "If you really want to help me, remove this damned collar."

Joriah smiled. "As much as I'd like to, you'll have to wait. I value my life and know I'd die if I removed it prematurely. Lord Rosai would have my head for it."

Nardus sighed. "It was worth a shot."

"As you said. If you're willing, I could relieve some of your guilt. As a guest in my house, it's the least I can offer you."

"Wouldn't that go against Prav—uh—Lord Rosai's wishes?"

"My friend, I owe Lord Rosai a great debt and accommodate his wishes to the best of my ability, but that doesn't preclude me from doing what I feel is right. My gift—my mezhik—urges me to help those in need. You're one such person. Please, let me help you."

Nardus pulled at his hair. "I guess you can try to help me with the guilt, but you might not like what you find."

Joriah's red eyebrows drooped with his eyes. "We all have our demons, Nardus. Now lay back and relax."

Nardus complied, but his heart raced. *I hope I don't kill him like I did Shaul.*

Joriah moved to the end of the bed and placed his hands on the sides of Nardus's face. "This shouldn't hurt, and it will only take a moment. It may feel longer to you."

† † †

A bright light flashed, and Joriah and the room faded from existence. In its place, a meadow stretched as far as the eye could see. Clusters of sacred-heart trees provided shade throughout the meadow, and a small brook ran through its middle. Nardus breathed deep and took in the aromatic smell of spring.

About a hundred yards from where he stood, an auburn-haired woman leaned against one of the giant trees. As if sensing Nardus's presence, the woman turned and looked straight at him with her penetrating, violet eyes.

Vitara.

His heart skipped a beat, his palms dampened, and a lump formed in the back of his throat. He wanted to call out to her, but he could scarcely breathe, let alone form words. Vitara smiled at him and pointed toward the brook where an adolescent girl played in its waters.

The beautiful young girl looked up at him and her smile warmed him like only a daughter's smile could.

Savannah? Impossible.

He'd never forget his precious little angel's face, but she had to be at least fourteen now. His legs trembled under his weight. He staggered forward a few steps and found his strength again. He raced into the meadow as fast as his legs would carry him.

When he reached Vitara, he scooped her up in his arms and twirled her around. Her laughter filled his ears like songs of angels. Warm tears streaked his cheeks.

"My love. My anchor."

He kissed her lips, and years of guilt fell away like shedding scales. He set her down and stepped back to get a good look at her. She hadn't aged a day. In fact, she might've looked younger than he remembered.

Savannah came up from the brook and put her arms around his waist. "Hello, Papa. I've missed you."

His heart thundered as he wrapped his arms around her. "My precious angel. I've missed you so much."

Vitara squeezed his arm. "We're so happy here, my love. We've never been better. You can let go now, my love. We haven't fallen but risen."

Nardus reached out and pulled Vitara into his arms with Savannah. "Let you go? How could I ever do that? You're my life. You're the only thing I live for, and I've found a way to bring you back."

Vitara swept her hand through his hair and ruffled it. "No, my love. We're happy right where we are. Let us go. Let *me* go. Love another as you've loved me. Nothing would make me happier."

"How could I do that? How could I throw away what we've shared and love another?"

"Nardus, I'm not asking you to stop loving me or to forget the years we shared. I'm asking you to find happiness again. I love you with all my heart and hate seeing you suffer so. You did everything in your power to save us, but it's you who needs saving now. Let go, my love. Just let go."

Vitara's fingers slipped from his hair, and the warmth of hers and Savannah's embrace faded until nothing remained but a ghost of their memories.

Nardus reached out for them, but his hands swept through their transparent bodies without resistance. Like puffs of smoke, they dissipated in the warm breeze.

"Wait," he begged them.

† † †

Nardus sat up in the bed, his cheeks wet with tears.

Joriah moved around to the side of the bed. "Do you feel any better?"

"I'm… not sure." Nardus wiped his face with his sleeve. "What I saw… was that real?"

"I'm not sure what you saw, Nardus. It doesn't work that way for me. I only sense the emotion I'm seeking, like your guilt. When I separated your guilt from the memory it blocked, it allowed you to glimpse the truth of the memory that you truly feel in your heart."

"But is it real?"

Joriah bent down and put his hand on Nardus's arm. "It's the truth for you. That's all that matters."

"Why didn't I see my whole family? And why had Savannah grown so much? Is that how the *Kinzhdm ef Häfn* works? Are there no small children? Do they age quickly?"

Joriah squeezed his arm and then stood back up. "Is that what you believe? The *Kinzhdm ef Häfn*? I didn't realize you believed in Ɂäṭūr."

Nardus pulled on his face. "I don't. Well, I used to. I don't know what I believe."

"Maybe it's what you imagine has happened to them, but I can't answer that. Perhaps the answer will come to you in time. I wish I could give you a better answer, but I just don't know."

Nardus lay back on the bed. "Thank you, Joriah. I believe I do feel somewhat better."

Joriah dipped his head. "You're welcome. Let me know if I can do anything more to help."

"I think you've done more than enough already. If you don't mind, I'd like to get some sleep. This day's been taxing in so many ways."

Joriah nodded. "Of course. I'll see you in the morning."

Nardus reached for his collar and smiled up at Joriah. "I'm looking forward to it. Unless you've changed your mind and want to remove this thing now."

Joriah winked at him. "I value my life, Nardus."

Nardus shrugged. "Was worth trying again."

Joriah chuckled and walked over to the door. He pulled the door closed behind him, and then the muffled *snap* of fingers sounded through the door. For a moment, the room fell into perfect darkness. Then a faint, pulsating light pushed through it, and its intensity grew.

Nardus pulled his shirt over his head, threw it on the floor, and stared at his chest—the source of the light. It burned like fire.

Damn this stone! I will not allow it to control me.

"You think you have a choice?"

Yes. Tomorrow, Gnaud and I will find an answer and it will haunt me no more.

"But how can you be so certain it is the stone?"

Madness.

CHAPTER NINETEEN

Berggren stood in the courtyard outside Joriah's house and scanned the streets below for any sign of Theyn. Vapor plumed from his lips with each breath. The frigid, early evening air settled like fog on the city below.

He'd searched Theyn's usual spots, but she hadn't been to any of them.

Worry knotted his stomach. *This isn't like you, Theyn.*

At times like this, Berggren wished he'd been born a wizard. He could've cast a simple location spell on one of her possessions and would've known exactly where to find her. At least that's how he assumed mezhik worked. Instead, he just stood there—as useless as a stone statue.

Had Joriah been a different kind of wizard, Berggren would've asked him to cast the spell. Helplessness filled him, and that angered him. He needed to channel his anger. A point of focus.

Nardus. This is his fault.

Berggren stormed across the stone path and through the fiery-red door.

Joriah sat in front of the fireplace, watching the fire spit turn. "Please, let the cold air in, Iceberg. I built this fire for that exact purpose—so we could keep the door propped open. Darned thing warms up the entire house if you keep the door closed."

Berggren grumbled under his breath and slammed the door shut. The window next to the door rattled in its frame.

Joriah shook his head. "That door is made to withstand a century's worth of weather, but I fear only a few days of Iceberg attacks will spell its demise."

Berggren glared at the back of Joriah's head. "Don't have the time or patience for your games right now, Joriah. Open the stairway."

Joriah rose from his chair and faced Berggren. "You wear your emotions like clothing, Iceberg."

Berggren clenched his fists. "Open the stairway, or I'll tear the floor apart with my bare hands."

Joriah raised an eyebrow. "I sincerely believe you could." He motioned Berggren over. "Come sit by the fire and tell me what troubles you."

"Don't need your fire or your mezhik. Theyn's still out there, and she could be in trouble. It's Nardus's fault. Open the stairway so I can go down there and make him pay for what he's done."

"Hurting Nardus won't help you find her, Iceberg."

"Maybe not, but it'll certainly go a long way in making me feel better."

"Oh, I'm sure it'd gratify you for a few minutes, but I'm certain Theyn wouldn't see it that way. Besides, this isn't even about her, is it?"

Berggren rubbed his head. "Why do you think you know so much about everyone?"

"It is my gift and my curse, Iceberg. You know that. You're angry with Nardus because of Shaul, not because Theyn ran off. You and I both know he had nothing to do with that."

The weight of Shaul's death hung heavy on Berggren's shoulders. How would he ever find a way to tell his sister? She'd been against the union of Shaul and Theyn from the beginning.

Berggren walked over to the fire and stared at the bluish-orange flames lapping and reaching up toward the spit. The roasting boar smelled delicious, but he was in no mood for food.

Shaul didn't die because of Theyn. He died because of Nardus.

It really boiled down to one thing: his loyalty to Lord Rosai. Shaul could've avoided death had Berggren not been doing Lord Rosai's bidding. He still found it difficult to swallow the truth, though. In his mind, Nardus still carried the blame of Shaul's actual death.

"I'm truly sorry for your loss, Berggren. I know you thought of him as a son."

Berggren felt Joriah's hand on his shoulder. Just its presence there nearly drove him to tears. "Shaul *was* my son. His mother died during childbirth, and I was too young to raise him, so Keerie did. She'd just lost a child of her own and was still lactating, so it worked out well for all of us." Berggren sighed and rubbed his head. "Never told anyone that before, not even Theyn."

Joriah squeezed his shoulder. "I've known for a long time, but I've always kept it to myself. Your sister and her husband are good people, Berggren. Don't wait too long to tell them about his death. You wouldn't want them finding out from someone else."

Berggren turned, smothered Joriah in his arms, and patted him on the back. "You're a good friend, Joriah. Thank you for keeping me from doing something I would've regretted later. I don't like Nardus, and I don't trust him, but he'll be out of our lives in the morning."

"True enough," grunted Joriah. "Can you ease up on the squeezing now?"

Berggren laughed and released Joriah. "I'm still worried about Theyn, though. She's never ran off like this before."

Joriah's teal eyes bore into Berggren's soul. "Theyn's a grown woman. Besides, you know she can take care of herself."

Joriah returned to his chair, and Berggren retrieved another chair from under the table and sat it next to Joriah. He put his left foot on the chair and rested his hands on his knee.

Berggren stared at his hand. "Normally wouldn't worry about her."

"It's her *condition*, isn't it?"

Berggren sighed. "Honestly, that's what I'm afraid of. You've seen the scars, right?"

Joriah nodded. "I have. You said you were attacked by a bear, but it was Theyn, right?"

"Yes, but she wasn't herself. When transfigured, she became little more than a wild animal. We had to keep her caged for many months, and Shaul—"

Berggren leaned over and smothered his face in his hand. *And I did that to my own son.*

Joriah patted Berggren's thigh. "It's okay, my friend. I think I can fill in the details on my own."

Berggren sat down on the chair and stared at the fire again. How Keerie hadn't killed him for what he'd put Shaul through, he'd never know. *She's such a good woman.*

"But those scars of yours aren't nearly as bad as the ones that mark your heart."

Always prying. Berggren's jaw tensed. *Just ignore his probing and move on.*

"Nardus said that Theyn was fine one moment, and then she withdrew, pulled her cloak over her shoulders and head, and ran off. But she's been faithful in coupling weekly. Don't think it's been a week since the last time, but what else could it be? And what does it mean if she's beginning her transformation early? Is the coupling no longer working?" His stomach gurgled.

"There's so little that we know about someone with her *condition*. It could be any number of things. Who has she been coupling with? Do you know?"

Berggren shook his head. Under his breath, he said, "Nardus."

Joriah gasped. "Nardus?"

"Yes, but he doesn't know it. He doesn't know anything about her *condition* either."

"Maybe it's my old-fashioned ideals, but how exactly do you go about coupling with someone without them being aware of it? And why Nardus? Is it because you don't approve of him?"

"After Shaul died, there was no one else to take his place but Nardus. I begged her not to, even warned Nardus to stay away from her, but I knew she had no choice. If she hadn't, I probably wouldn't be sitting here right now."

"Then be happy he was there."

Happy about Nardus? Impossible.

The churning spit mesmerized Berggren, and the slab of boar roasting on it made him salivate fiercely. "When will the boar be done cooking?"

"Oh, I believe it will be done just as soon as Theyn arrives."

"You've always had perfect timing." Berggren chided his growling stomach. "Felix and Nardus are downstairs?"

"Nardus is, but Felix left without saying a word. I called to him as he was leaving, but he acted like he didn't even hear me. The man's quite rude, if you ask me."

Berggren looked at Joriah, who grinned from ear to ear. "It's no wonder you never married. Wouldn't be a woman in the world who'd put up with the likes of you."

"Not a single woman in the world deserves me. I'm one-of-a-kind genuine."

"You're one-of-a—"

The *creak* of the front door sent them both springing from their chairs.

In the open doorway stood Theyn, but she wasn't quite herself. Her cloak hung open in the front, exposing the center of her torso and the sides of her bare breasts, but beige fur covered her skin. Blood stained her trousers and her yellow eyes glowed under her hooded cloak.

Berggren's heart rose in his chest, and he could do nothing but stare at her. The fur. The blood. Memories of the night she'd attacked him bloomed in his mind, his skin grew cold, and his appetite dissipated.

Berggren's hands shook. *My beautiful Theyn, what have you done?*

† † †

Theyn pushed her hood back, and the light stung her eyes.

Joriah moved across the room toward Theyn. "Are you hurt, my dear?"

Theyn growled in the back of her throat. "The blood's not mine."

Joriah sighed loudly. "Oh, thank the heavens. Well, you've come to the right place, my dear. Hold on to yourself just a bit longer. We'll find a way to make this right."

Theyn pushed Joriah to the side and moved to the center of the room. She sniffed the air and then turned back to Joriah. "He's near. Take me to him."

"Theyn... I—"

Theyn whipped around and snarled, "Stay out of this, *father*. Nardus and I will be together. You may as well get used to the idea."

Berggren lifted his hands, palms out. "I only want to help, Theyn. Tell us what we need to do, and we'll do it."

The veins in Berggren's neck bulged and twitched. *Rip into his throat. Make him bleed.* Theyn licked her lips, twisted her neck, and moaned like a feral cat.

No, Theyn! She hugged herself and squeezed her eyes shut. *You can fight this.* But did she want to?

"There's no time for this. I can't hold it back much longer." Theyn opened her eyes and turned back to Joriah. "Take me to Nardus. Now!"

Joriah stood there, immobile.

Berggren yelled, "Just do it, Joriah! I know what happens from here, and it isn't good."

Joriah snapped out of his stupor, swept his arm across the room, and the furniture scattered to the walls. The rug beneath Theyn's feet fought to pull itself from under her. She leapt in the air, and it whizzed away.

The floor shifted, and Theyn dove through the opening as soon as it grew wide enough for her to squeeze through. She hit the lower floor, somersaulted, and came to her feet in one fluid motion.

Nardus's scent filled the area. She moaned and arched her back.

I smell you, my love.

Theyn went over to the first door on the left, opened it, and walked into the room. Nardus lay on the bed, eyes closed and shirtless. Theyn leaned her head back and let the cloak slip from her shoulders and onto the floor.

She shut the door behind her and turned back to Nardus. He sat up in the bed.

Nardus cocked his head. "Who's there? I can hear you breathing—or *purring?*"

"It's Theyn." She barely restrained the ecstasy in her voice.

And I'm here to take you into me.

Nardus stood. "Theyn? Is everything okay? When you ran off earlier I thought I'd said or done something wrong."

Hot tears streaked down Theyn's cheeks, both from love and sadness. Her voice quavered. "Do you trust me, Nardus?"

"Your eyes, Theyn. They're glowing."

Take him.

Theyn sniffed. "Sometimes they do, but that doesn't matter right now. Do you trust me?"

"Trust you? I hardly know you, and our brief history has been sordid at best. What is it that you want?"

You've done it before.

Theyn closed her eyes. "No matter how hard it may be for you, will you do something for me?"

Nardus probed the darkness with his hands. "If it's in my power, yes."

Take him.

No! I won't do that to him again.

Theyn walked over to Nardus and snatched his hands from the air. They were cold and rough in hers. She trembled with desire.

"Are you okay, Theyn? You're trembling." His hands tightened around hers. "Your hands…"

You must ask him, Theyn. And you must tell him the truth about everything if he asks.

"There are things about me that you may never understand. I don't even understand some of it myself." She paused and gathered herself. "I need you to…"

Can I really do this? Can I ask this of him? Or what? Force him again?

"To what? What do you need?"

Even the tone of his voice begs for you, Theyn. Smell him. He reeks with desire for you.

Her heart raced. Her palms moistened. Her stomach clinched. "You."

Unnerving silence filled the room.

Just say yes. I don't want to force you again.

But you will.

Nardus's hands stilled in hers, but he didn't pull them away. "What are you saying? Do you mean—"

"Take me, Nardus." She leaned into him and pressed her furry chest against his.

Every fiber of her being demanded his touch, and her restraint fluttered like a leaf in the fall wind—nearly disjointed from its branch. His heart pounded like a smith's hammer in her ear. She smelled his perspiration even before it ran between his naked flesh and her furry skin.

Take me!

"I…"

She kissed the top of his chest. "I must be with you. Please don't deny me."

"Theyn, this is the one thing I can't do. I have a wife. A family."

You don't need his consent. Throw him on the bed and take him. He won't resist you.

"I understand that, Nardus, but I don't have much time. I can't hold it back much longer."

Nardus let go of her hands and stepped back. "Hold what back?"

"There's a darkness within me. I'm cursed, Nardus. We call it my *condition*. I need you. I need to be with you. No one else can help me."

Nardus shook his head. "I don't understand, Theyn. Why do you need to *be* with me?"

Theyn's skin burned with fire as her transformation continued manifesting physically. She quickly unbuckled her belt and unbuttoned her trousers.

"Are you undressing?" His voice squeaked like an adolescent boy.

Theyn slipped her boots off and let her trousers slide down her legs and to the floor. She stepped out of them and stood before Nardus in the dark, naked. Vulnerable.

You can't wait any longer, Theyn. Take him.

She took his hands and placed them on her swollen breasts.

His hands lingered there for a moment, but then he pulled them away. "I don't understand. What are you wearing?"

"Nothing."

"But—"

She grabbed his hands and placed them back on her breasts—made him squeeze them and feel them. "I'm transforming, Nardus. I need you to go into me. It's the only way to stop this from happening. If you refuse me, I can't be responsible for what happens. I won't be in control for much longer."

She smelled him. His sweat. His breath. His sex. His desire for her belied his words, and she purred. She took his hands from her breasts, pulled them around her waist, and made him feel the stubbed tail beginning to form at the top of her furry buttocks.

"What are you?"

It doesn't matter what I am.

The left side of Nardus's chest pulsed with light. Each beat revealed the desire and agony in his face. He held fast to her but made no moves of his own. His eyes glowed red, like the dragon's.

"Nardus..." She moaned softly. "...you're different too. What are you?"

Nardus seemed too distraught to answer her, and she no longer cared. She had to be with him. She undid his trousers and they fell to his ankles. She leaned against him—against his nakedness. His body raged with fire, just as hers.

His voice trembled, "Theyn, I'm not sure I can do this."

His body said otherwise.

"Yes, you can, Nardus. You want me. I can smell it. I can feel it. I can see it in your eyes."

"But... I still love my wife."

And I love you.

"I'm not asking you to stop loving her, Nardus. I'm not even asking you to love me. But I need you to take me before something really bad happens."

Nardus stepped back and sat down on the bed. Theyn knelt next to the bed and unlaced his boots. She pulled them off his feet and then pulled his trousers off his ankles.

"Theyn..." His voice quavered.

She rose and then pushed him back on the bed. He didn't resist.

He's finally yours.

Theyn climbed onto the bed and lay next to him. She kissed his chest and then nipped at the side of his neck.

"Wait," he begged her, even as he pulled her on top of himself.

She arched her back, moaned like a cat, and dug her claws into the bed.

I cannot.

† † †

Nardus woke, and he wasn't alone. Theyn's arm draped across his chest, and she murmured as she slept. His head felt hazy, but he knew what he'd done—what *they'd* done.

He ran his fingers along the length of her arm. *Soft skin. Like silk.*

Had she really been anything else last night? Had he imagined her a beast just so that he'd feel less guilty about lying with her?

No. I'm certain she was covered in fur. I felt it in my hands. Against my skin.

He'd expected the guilt to overwhelm him, but it stayed contained deep within the compounds of his mind. Vitara's wrath should've rained down on him for such a betrayal of her love, but he felt only a small portion. Nonetheless, it saddened him that he'd done such a thing.

Have I given up on my family? Do I love them less than I thought?

No!

Was this Joriah's doing then? Did he make me lie with Theyn?

If Joriah had had a hand in their coupling, what would've been his motivation? What would he have gained by their union?

Nothing... unless he knows of her condition.

No. No one forced me to lie with her. I've thought about her since the day we met.

He remembered the sorrow he'd felt in the vision he'd shared with Theyn, both in the loss of her and of his family. Thinking back on it, on all the emotions he'd felt in that moment, he'd loved Theyn, hadn't he?

Do I? I just don't know. I don't even know who she is. Or what she is.

His chest burned with fire again, and the voice returned.

"A beast. An animal. Our lover."

Everything about Theyn differed from Vitara: her eyes, hair, skin, lips, breasts, smile. They smelled different, they kissed differently, and they coupled differently. Yet something about the two women seemed similar too.

Being with Theyn and feeling her body against his for the first time had felt strangely familiar—as though they'd been together before.

But that's not possible. It must be my fractured mind.

By the end of the morning, he'd never see Theyn again.

But I've seen our future together. And where had Vitara been?

"Still dead."

How can you think that? What's wrong with you?

"Nothing. Vitara isn't going anywhere, but we haven't much time with Theyn."

Theyn stirred next to him. Even in the darkness, with his red-tinted vision, he relished the curves of her perfect body. He hated himself for looking at her and continuing to lie with her, but he couldn't seem to stop himself.

A fist pounded on the door, and Berggren's gruff voice commanded them to get up.

The burning in Nardus's chest subsided, and the room fell into darkness once more.

I can't do this. I love you, Vitara!

Nardus sat up, but Theyn grabbed hold of his arm and pulled him back down. "Wait a minute."

Nardus groaned. "What is it? I can't do this again, Theyn."

Theyn intertwined her fingers in his. His mind begged his hand to pull away from her grasp, but it just lay there in hers.

Theyn's voice quavered, "It's not that. There's something I must tell you. If I don't, I may never."

A myriad of things swept through Nardus's mind, but none of them seemed relevant. She'd already told him that she loved him. What more could she possibly tell him?

Nardus sighed. "Well, what is it? You're not human?"

"I *am* human, but I have a *condition* that forces me to couple with someone weekly."

"A *condition* that *forces* you to couple weekly? What kind of condition would require something like that?"

"I don't know what it's called, but it gets passed down through the females in my family. Not every female is afflicted by it, and sometimes it skips many generations, but it didn't skip over me. If I don't couple with someone religiously, I start becoming something you'd never want to see."

Ʒäṭūr, what have I done? Is this truly a woman next to me or a beast?

Theyn cleared her throat and continued, "Shaul was my mate for a long time."

"I had a feeling your relationship with Shaul was more than you'd let on."

"For me, it was a necessary one—only to keep my *condition* in check. I never felt anything for him sexually, but he loved me despite what I am."

Nardus frowned. "Shaul died more than a week ago. Who else have you been with? Others on the boat? Berggren or Felix? Ugh, you didn't lie with one of them, did you?"

"Never! I'd kill myself before coupling with one of them. And there was no one else on board that ship that I could've been with. They're all eunuchs."

Nardus sighed with relief, but then confusion settled in his mind. "But you look the same as the day I met you. Even if you'd coupled with Shaul the day he died, you would've missed your seven-day requirement."

"I know, but I didn't."

"You didn't what? Start changing, or you didn't miss it?"

"I didn't miss it."

"How's that possible?"

He *knew* before he even asked. He'd already known before, hadn't he? His stomach twisted in knots.

How could she use me like that? While unconscious?

He crawled over her and stood up.

"Don't hate me, Nardus. You were the only choice I had on that boat. I would've asked you for your consent, but you were unconscious. Both times."

Nardus felt around in the dark for his clothes. "*Both* times?"

Nardus pulled his trousers on. "Did Berggren know about this?"

Theyn brushed past him and rustled with her clothes. "Not until after the first time. He would've killed you if he'd had any other choice."

"He made me promise to stay away from you, and then he allowed it to continue without me even knowing about it? Why would he do that?"

"He knew there was no other way. He knows first-hand what happens if I don't keep my condition under control. Besides, would you have come to me if he hadn't told you to stay away?"

Nardus pulled his shirt over his head and sat on the bed to put his boots on. "No. I never had any intention of being with you. As I said before, I love my wife."

"Then what was I supposed to have done?"

"I don't know, Theyn. It's sad that your first inclination was to couple with me while I lay unconscious. Was it good for you?"

Theyn growled, "You're not being fair!"

"*Fair*? Do you even realize what you've done to me? How will I look my wife in the eye again knowing what I've done with you? And what you've done to me? And how did this happen twice? Did you drug me? Is that what you did?"

Theyn sobbed. "Yes, but I didn't have a choice. I thought you would understand."

Nardus clenched his fists at his sides. "Oh, I certainly understand now. How can I ever trust you after this? You've betrayed me, Theyn."

Theyn grabbed his hands. "There's something you need to see. Please don't make any decisions or say something you may regret later until I've shown you."

Nardus pulled his hands from hers. *Oh, I've already decided. Nothing will change my mind.*

A faint light poured into the room from under the door and silhouetted Theyn's beautiful form. She still wore no shirt. He forced his eyes closed.

Is there no end to my madness? I cannot handle being around this woman.

Berggren's deep voice sounded through the door. "Warned you earlier. I'm coming in."

Nardus opened his eyes. Theyn covered herself with her cloak just as the door swung open. Berggren stood in the doorway, holding a candle.

Theyn looked at Nardus—her cheeks glowed. She rose from the floor, walked over to Berggren, and kissed him on the cheek.

"Good morning, Father." She took the candle from Berggren's hand.

Berggren looked Theyn over. "You're well again, I see."

Theyn grabbed Berggren's hand and pulled him into the room. Nardus couldn't make up his mind if he should continue sitting on the bed or stand up. He hadn't felt as awkward since the time he'd asked Vitara's father for her hand in marriage.

Nardus's chest burned again.

Let me be!

"Relax. Nothing's changed from the way it was yesterday."

Everything's changed! I've gone into her.

"But it wasn't the first time."

Certainly, the last. I will be with Vitara again. I must be.

"But we need Theyn too."

Never again!

Nardus dipped his head ever so slightly. "Berggren."

"Show him, Father. Help him understand."

Berggren's thick, bushy eyebrows met in the middle of his glassy forehead. "Show him what?"

Theyn's chin lowered, nearly to her chest. "What I did to you. Show him."

Berggren lifted her chin in his massive hand. His palm could've covered her whole face. "You *know* that wasn't you, Theyn."

"Show him, Father. Please," Theyn pleaded. "Help him understand the choice I had to make. Help him understand why I had to be with him."

Berggren sighed. "For you, I'd do anything. You know that." He kissed her forehead.

Berggren's gaze hardened when he turned to Nardus. He pulled his shirttails out of his trousers and lifted his shirt as high as it would go. Thick scars laced his stomach, chest, and sides like the roots of a tree breaking through the ground's surface.

Nardus grimaced and looked away.

Theyn did that? What kind of condition does she have? She must be an animal. Nardus's eyes widened. *What does she transform into?*

He turned and looked at her with renewed vision.

Berggren lowered his shirt and tucked it back into his trousers.

"Thank you." Theyn's words were little more than a whisper.

Theyn handed the candle back to Berggren and then sat on the bed next to Nardus. Tears fell from her eyes. "Say something, Nardus. Anything."

Nardus said the only thing he could think of. "Why tell me all of this? Why show me?"

Theyn wiped the tears from her chin. "Don't you see? I'm in love with you. That's the only reason I'm telling you this. We could've parted today, and you never would've known, but I didn't want to keep any secrets from you."

Nardus shook his head. "The strangest thing is that I already knew what you'd done to me. After we—" Nardus looked over at Berggren for a moment.

Berggren's scowl put him on edge.

"—coupled last night—" He glanced up at Berggren again and winced. "—I had the feeling that it wasn't the first time we'd done so."

After an uncomfortable silence, Nardus continued, "My mind wants me to tell you that you've ruined everything. It screams that I should hate you, but I don't. I don't quite understand your condition, but I'm certain that I don't blame you for what you did. I wish you'd been honest with me from the beginning, but I don't know that it would've made a difference. I still feel betrayed, though."

Theyn wrapped her arms around his neck and sobbed in his ear. "I'm so sorry for what I did to you, Nardus. Thank you for not hating me for it."

Nardus embraced her. "I don't think I could ever hate you, Theyn."

Joriah filled the doorway behind Berggren. "Breakfast is ready upstairs. Theyn, I've drawn a hot bath for you and set out a change of clothes."

Nardus released Theyn, and she sat up and wiped her eyes. "Thank you, Joriah. You're too kind."

Joriah bowed. "It was at your father's request."

"Thought you might like that after yesterday." Berggren turned, pushed his way past Joriah, and left the room. Nardus swore he'd seen a tear in the big man's eye.

Iceberg.

† † †

Nardus, Theyn, Berggren, Joriah, and Felix stood in the middle of the one-room cottage—food consumed, items packed, and everyone washed up and ready to head out. Light from the early dawn sky shone through the western windows, casting long shadows across the floor.

Theyn stood across from Nardus and looked radiant, more so than he'd remembered her looking before. The yellow orchid tucked behind her right ear matched her eyes perfectly. She'd worn a similar one behind her left ear the day they'd first met.

I'm going to miss you, Theyn.

The bond he shared with her scared him. How would it change his future? Vitara and his family still lingered at the forefront of his mind, but for how much longer? He couldn't fathom living without them, yet he did so daily.

I'll never give up on saving you, my love.

It'd taken quite some time for him and Theyn—even Joriah—to persuade Berggren to give him back his effects, but, in the end, Berggren folded.

Nardus reached back and touched the hilt of Brinzhär Dädh, felt its mezhik tingle against his skin, and a wave of relief washed over him. Despite his loathing of mezhik, the sword comforted him.

From his neck—beneath his shirt and below the damned silver collar—hung the amulet Tharos had given him. The vision he'd seen when he'd first touched the amulet haunted him still.

Magus. The Dragon King. A god among men. How had they killed him?

Did his dragon, Cinolth, die with him? Or did he survive?

Nardus's pulse quickened. The black claw that had skewered Theyn rose from his memories, and his chest burned.

Could they be the same?

Nonsense. Impossible. Madness.

He looked over at Theyn, and his heart tripped over itself. Her rounded belly, full with another life, pushed from under the lower hem of her white shirt. Movement just below the surface of her stretched skin caught his eye. He couldn't pull his gaze away from her.

How is it possible? How can she already be pregnant and showing?

A single drop of blood ran from her navel, down the front of her belly, and dripped onto the wooden floor. The blood sizzled and seeped into the wood. From her navel erupted the tip of a sharpened black claw.

In his mind, he lunged for her, but his body didn't move. He screamed her name, but she only smiled at him. How did the others not see it? How did she not feel it?

Her lips moved but produced no sound. Had she said something, or had she screamed? He reached for her in his mind, but his arms hung limp at his sides.

His name echoed in his ears as though shouted through a tunnel from a great distance. Joriah's voice? Something latched onto his shoulders, and his body jolted. Twice. Three times.

Something snapped in his ears.

The black claw retracted. Theyn's belly healed itself, shrank, and disappeared under her shirt. Waves of sound and motion swept through his body. His vision refocused, and he found himself staring into the teal-blue eyes of Joriah.

"Are you okay?" Joriah's voice rushed into his ears like a tidal wave.

Nardus blinked several times, but his voice seemed lost. Berggren and Theyn stood on either side of Joriah, Berggren grimacing, and Theyn's face lined with worry.

Nardus leaned his head back and looked up at the ceiling. The burning in his chest dissipated. "What just happened?"

The soft touch of Theyn's skin against his registered as she took his hand in hers. "You grabbed at your chest, and your eyes glazed over."

Nardus lowered his head and rolled it from shoulder to shoulder. "I think I'm okay now."

He knew he wasn't. Precious time continued to slip away from him. Gnaud was his last hope.

Twelve days… or was it eleven now?

The obsidian dragon's timeline burned in his mind, but what did it mean? What would take place at that time? Would that be when he died? Or the entire world? Or was it the amount of time before Theyn died? Or would he become a dragon?

I need your help more than ever, Gnaud.

Felix nodded to each of them and headed out the fiery-red door on his own. He'd be preparing Berggren's boat to sail that night, so he wouldn't see Nardus off. Nardus couldn't care less.

"A man of few words," said Joriah.

Berggren stifled a chuckle.

Joriah clapped his hands. "We'd better set out. Lord Rosai will be very displeased if we're late arriving."

Pravus. Our meeting will have to wait. I must see Gnaud before I do anything else.

The four of them headed out the door, down the stone path, and through the squeaky iron gate. From the gate, they headed down the flagstone path and made a left at the street. Few people moved about at the early hour.

Joriah led them, then Theyn and Nardus. Berggren followed close behind Nardus, and his loathsome gaze burned the back of Nardus's head like a poker just pulled from the fire.

Soon, I'll be rid of you.

They walked along street after street, turning left and then right, traversing several hills on switchback trails, and then across a long and narrow footbridge that spanned the Hotah River and connected East and West Hotah. As the morning progressed, the streets crowded until they found themselves pushing through throngs of people as they'd done the day before.

Theyn reached back and took Nardus's hand in hers. "So that I don't lose you," she yelled over her shoulder.

The hairs on Nardus's arm stood on end, and his pulse raced. Moments from the past evening flashed in his mind like lightning, and guilt seared his conscience. He tried to pull his hand away, but Theyn wouldn't let go. Instead, she dug her fingernails into his wrist and pulled harder. He gave in and closed the gap between them.

"I won't pull away," shouted Nardus over the throng.

"I won't let you." Theyn's grip loosened.

Nardus forced her tender lips and perfect curves from the forefront of his mind and focused on the city and the people around them. *How can so many live in one place?*

Unlike West Hotah, East Hotah catered to the poor and poverty-stricken. Scaled down versions of the grand buildings and houses on the other side of the river lined the streets. Straw, clay, manure, mud, and any other substance they could find and afford comprised most of the structures. None were made of stone, and few were made of wood.

Pale yellow gravel covered the main street that ran along the river and bay, but the streets and roads just beyond contained little more than dirt and a few lumps of rock. Like West Hotah, vendors and shops lined the streets selling wares and foods, but the quality and variety of them were limited.

The experience exhilarated and suffocated Nardus. Voices and shouts came from every direction, indulging them to try or buy. He had no coins to make a purchase, and they had no time to stop anyway.

The group turned down an alley full of weeds and garbage and followed it to its end. They turned right, stepped around a man relieving himself on the building's wall, made their way down some rickety wooden stairs, and headed through a red-brick archway that led them under the main street.

They stopped for a moment in the darkness, and Theyn released his hand. Relief and longing swept through Nardus in alternating waves. She looked back at him, through him, and into his soul.

She winked at him, and he cringed with guilt. *How will I ever face you again, my love? She's ruined me.*

"*Əllíṭ ʊb*." An orb of light rose from Joriah's palm and sent the darkness fleeing to the shadows.

The light accentuated Theyn's perfectly shaped body, and Nardus turned away. *Madness.*

A foul odor crept into his nostrils, and flowing water drew his attention downward. *Sewage tunnels. I'd rather be back in the tunnels under Mortuus Terra.*

Water flowed through the middle channel of the tunnel. It reeked of feces, urine, and death. Rotted carcasses of mice, rats, and other small animals littered both sides of the tunnel. Nardus held his shirt over his nose and willed his stomach to keep its contents.

The arched architecture of the tunnel—its fire-kiln brick walls and ceiling and solid rock floors—seemed out of place.

Nardus scratched his head. "How does a city this poor have sewage tunnels like these?"

Joriah ran his fingers along the brick wall. "Before they built a single structure in East Hotah, they built this sewer system. The plan was to make this and West Hotah the royal capital of the Ancient Realm. But, because of wars and the difficulties in defending a place such as this, the plans were scrapped shortly after the sewers were put in.

"West Hotah continued to thrive, but no one wanted to invest in building here. Eventually, the poor and most of the elderly—except the wealthy—

were forced from West Hotah and made to live over here. Had you not wondered why there were no beggars on the streets of West Hotah and so few elderly people?"

"It hadn't even crossed my mind. Before yesterday, I'd never been to a large city. From the sounds of it, I'd never want to live in a place that treated people like that. Like refuse."

"It truly is a shame." Joriah turned and started down the tunnel.

The four of them huddled to the left side of the channel and walked along its steep edge. On the other side of the channel, a man slumped against the wall. Nardus couldn't tell if the man was dead or passed-out drunk. Either way, the man didn't stir as they passed by.

They walked for miles through the sewage tunnels, turning left, then right, and then left again. The maze seemed endless.

I hope Joriah knows where he's taking us.

Finally, they came to an iron grate that stretched across the tunnel and blocked their passage.

Nardus sighed. *All this way to a dead end. Figures.*

Joriah waved his hand in an outward arc and then stepped right through the grate as though it wasn't there.

Nardus blinked, and then he spat into the flowing sewage. *I hate mezhik.*

Berggren and Theyn stepped through the grate, and Nardus followed. The tunnel stretched straight as far as Nardus could see with the light, but six feet past the grate, Joriah turned to the left and disappeared through a solid wall.

Just like the walls in Ţämball Dhef Däd Dhä. Nardus spat into the flowing sewage again.

Theyn reached out, and her hand sank into the wall. She looked at Nardus, shrugged, and stepped through it. Berggren waved Nardus ahead of him and then followed him through the wall.

The four of them stood in a square room no larger than six feet wide. Four rectangular sconces hung from the walls, tucked neatly into the four corners of the room. The stench of burning pitch overwhelmed the small room, and smoke from the torches stung Nardus's eyes.

A large mirror—it stretched from floor to ceiling—leaned against the far wall. Strange symbols marred its wooden frame, covering every square inch. The mirror held his attention.

Nardus stepped closer to the mirror and stared at the gaunt man before him. His sunken eyes and disheveled brown hair belied his years. Nardus spat at the ground, and so did the man before him. His gaze shifted to Theyn's reflection, and her haunting, yellow eyes met his.

What could she possibly see in me? He returned his hard gaze upon himself. *How could anyone love such a man? How is it that you love me still, Vitara? I'm so unworthy of you. Even more so, now.*

Nardus's reflection rippled and faded as the mirror's surface turned black. Then the inky surface morphed into something more. Something with substance. A swatch of colors burst onto the mirror's surface, twisted into an image like a painting, and then became clear—as though he peered through a window.

On the other side of—no, *through*—the mirror stood a man swathed in black and gold robes. Despite the man's change in fashion and his aged features, Nardus recognized him immediately. He'd never forget those golden-brown eyes and raptor-like gaze.

The man from the Ferzh's Head Inn. Pravus.

Or is it Lord Rosai?

The strong man Nardus had met not so long ago now hunched over like a decrepit old man, clutching his walking stick as though it grounded him to this world and kept him from falling into the next. Strands of silver streaked his raven locks.

How did he age so rapidly? Was his appearance at the inn a trick of mezhik?

Theyn, Berggren, and Joriah all bowed to the man in—through—the mirror, but Nardus refused to show the man the same respect.

After everything I've been through for him, he should bow at my feet.

"Joriah." The small room reverberated with Pravus's voice.

"My lord. It's so good to see you after all these years. It's been way too long."

Pravus's gaze landed on Theyn briefly and then moved to Berggren. "That can't be the same girl you left with. She's *transformed* into a beautiful woman."

From the corner of his eye, Nardus saw Theyn blush. For some reason, the comment irked him. *Does Pravus know of her condition?*

"Thank you, my lord," said Berggren.

Pravus turned his attention on Nardus. His hard gaze felt like that of a father's, and Nardus shifted his weight.

Pravus's thin lips parted and his perfect teeth gleamed. "You've hardly aged, my friend. I'd begun to wonder if you were ever going to return or if you'd be lost forever like so many before you."

A lump rose in Nardus's throat. He swallowed hard to dislodge it, but it remained. Sweat beaded on his forehead, and he felt droplets running down his back. His palms grew cold and clammy, and his heart raced in his chest.

What do I say? "The—I—have."

Brilliant, Nardus. Just brilliant.

"Let's not tarry. I've waited far too long for this moment." Pravus turned and addressed Joriah. "Did you explain to him how this works?"

Joriah nodded. "Yes, my lord, but I will reiterate the instructions as we make ready for the transfer."

Pravus cracked his knuckles. "Excellent. Proceed."

Nardus's hands trembled, and his heart thundered in his ears. Finally, he'd be rid of the collar and would able to go see Gnaud again.

Joriah walked over and stood next to Nardus. "Step up to the mirror, but do not step into it. If you do so with this collar on, it will kill you. Do you understand?"

Nardus nodded, glanced at Theyn, and stepped up to the mirror. Joriah moved behind him, placed his hands on either side of the collar, and slipped it off Nardus's neck. Despite the collar's lightness, a great weight lifted from Nardus's shoulders. He rubbed his neck, happy to be free of it.

I'm coming, Gnaud.

"Wait!" cried Theyn. She moved to Nardus's side and wrapped her arms around his waist.

Nardus leaned over her. The fresh smell of her hair and of the orchid by her ear stole his breath.

She whispered in his ear, "I'm coming with you."

His heart raced faster, and his chest began burning once more. He hadn't even contemplated her coming along. Was it what he wanted? If she didn't come with him, how would she keep her condition under check?

But Pravus will bring Vitara back from the dead. I cannot have Theyn with me. She'll ruin everything.

"But you must. Would you rather someone else lay with her?"

No! ...yes. I don't know.

"You love her."

No. I can't. I must let her go. I cannot allow myself to love anyone but Vitara.

"And yet you flounder with indecision."

His heart bled with sorrow.

Clank!

Theyn cried out and lifted her hands to her neck. Nardus eyed the silver collar wrapped around it, and anger swelled and contorted his face.

He spun and faced Joriah. "What do you think you're doing? What's the meaning of this?"

Joriah's eyes widened, and he stepped backward. "Your eyes... they're glowing red!"

"Silence!" boomed Pravus.

Nardus turned and faced Pravus. "This is *your* doing?"

The corners of Pravus's mouth curled into a wicked grin. "I am... *aware* of your relations. I must say that it did come as a surprise to me, given how deeply you claim to care for your family. I suppose time has faded your memory. Vitara, was it? Do you even remember her?"

Nardus roared at the ceiling. "She's the only reason I'm standing here!"

Pravus raised an eyebrow. "Then why are you so attached to the beast standing at your side?"

Beast? He does know of her condition.

"And why wouldn't he?"

Nardus turned back to Theyn. Tears glistened in her eyes.

"Why do you seek a dead woman when another one stands before you, vibrant and ready to bear your children?"

Shut up! Vitara will come back to me. You'll see!

Nardus grabbed his head and screamed. "I cannot take this madness!"

Joriah held up his hand, begging silence. "She cannot go with you, Nardus, but you already know that. In time, you'll both look back on this moment and realize it was a good thing. Now, step through the mirror, Nardus, or I'll be forced to push her through it and to her death."

"No!" bellowed Berggren. He reached for Theyn's wrist but stopped short. His eyes bulged, and he reached for his throat.

"Enough," said Pravus. "Do as you've been told, Nardus. Or I will crush the life from Berggren. And then from your precious Theyn."

Nardus fumed, but what could he do? Bolt with Theyn? They'd certainly make it no more than a few steps. Pravus had the upper hand with his mezhik. *Nasduron. It's the only choice I have.* With the collar on, she couldn't go with him.

Nardus cupped Theyn's face in his hands and kissed her forehead. He whispered in her ear, "We've seen the future, Theyn. You know I'll come back for you. Even if you've given in to your condition and transformed, I *will* find you."

Tears streamed down Theyn's cheeks, and she grabbed hold of his fingers. "My *condition* be damned. I'll never be with another man. I love you, Nardus."

"I know you do, even if I can't." The words stung him. He could only imagine what they did to Theyn.

I cannot love you. My family will always come first. They must.

"And if she carries your child? Will she not be family then?"

That is madness. It cannot be!

"You already love her."

Nardus's heart hammered, but the burning in his chest faded.

He turned back to the mirror. Pravus stood on the other side, wearing that same smug grin on his face that he had the night they'd met at the inn.

"Release Berggren. I'm coming through."

Pravus's lips moved, and Berggren gasped for air.

Nardus clamped his eyes shut, afraid to see where his step would take him, but he begged for it to be Nasduron. *Here I come, Gnaud.*

The tingle of mezhik engulfed him, and his heart hammered. As he stepped forward and passed through the cold, wet surface of the mirror, the tips of Theyn's fingers still rested against his. A moment later, he felt them no more. He couldn't breathe. Didn't want to.

Warm air caressed his face, and he opened his eyes. The Great Library stretched before him. Gnaud sat at one of the tables, his nose buried in a large book. Nardus breathed in the smells of pine and books, but they quickly shifted to pitch and smoke as the library shimmered.

"No!" He reached for one of the shelves, but his hand passed right through it.

His heart broke. *Why do you elude me, Nasduron? Is my need not great enough?*

The library transitioned into a wide hallway, and the warmth surrounding him faded. The tingle of mezhik ceased, and cold steel slid around his neck. *Clank!*

Pravus stood before him.

Berggren screamed on the other side of the mirror with such venom that Nardus couldn't understand his words.

Nardus turned and looked back through the mirror.

Berggren's face twisted with a rage like Nardus had never seen before, and his grey, deep-set eyes bulged from their sockets. "You're a dead man!"

Berggren lunged forward, but Joriah caught him by the waist. Somehow, despite his disadvantage in size, Joriah held Berggren back just enough to keep him from the mirror's surface.

"Let me go!" Berggren fought against Joriah's grip.

Joriah held fast. "Iceberg, you have no mezhik! If you try to go through it, you'll die!"

Nardus scanned the small room through the mirror. Theyn wasn't there. Theyn. Wasn't. There.

The mirror faded to black, rippled, and then Nardus stared into his own bloodshot, brown eyes. He turned and glared daggers at Pravus. "What have you done to her? Open the portal!"

Pravus's eyebrows raised. "Me? I've done nothing. Maybe it was Joriah's doing." Then his face twisted into that sinister grin. He pointed his finger at Nardus. "Or perhaps it was you."

"Me? I'd never—"

Nardus's stomach twisted with guilt. His legs wobbled, and he collapsed to his knees. He trembled. His mind raced.

Me?

Could the stone have done something to her, like it had with Shaul? Had there been a pile of ash on the floor? Or a silver collar? He leaned over and wretched, but nothing came forth.

Theyn! What have I done?

His next thought struck him like a blow to the side of his head.

If the mirror requires mezhik, how was I able to pass through it and not die?

CHAPTER TWENTY

Four hundred sixty-nine flat, ivory markers littered the sodden ground and flanked the thatched-roof cottage like the skullcaps of a skeleton army rising from a sea of muddied water. Each marker bore the name of the man, woman, or child resting beneath it, their names scratched into the stones like claw marks from an ancient beast.

Alderan sat in the middle of the graves on the west side of the cottage. Two markers, shaped like hearts and intertwined like lovers, stood out among all the others.

His lips trembled. "Redante and Gretchen Somneri." His voice cracked.

Gretchen's marker, worn with age, eclipsed the age of Redante's by a decade. Anguish shook Alderan's bones and blurred his vision. Tension bound his throat.

Mother, father. I miss you both so much. I wish you were here to guide me and tell me what I should do. The world expects me to be a hero, but I just want to be your son again. I know I can't go back and change the past, but I'm not sure how to approach the future either.

My heart tells me that I must do what they ask of me, but my mind taunts me and tells me that I'm weak. A coward. What can I do to strengthen my mind and believe in myself the way you always believed in me? How do I move forward? How do I become something that I'm not?

He raised his hands to the sky and lifted his head. Grey clouds spotted the blue sky, but he looked beyond them.

Ɂäṭūr, my God.

I love Rayah and Aria, but what good will it do me if there's no world for us to live in? Give me strength, Ɂäṭūr. Give me hope. Renew my heart. Renew my mind. Raise me up and make me the man that You've called me to be.

Put courage in my mind where I have none, make me a light in the darkness where there is none, and let me shine so bright that the world will have no choice but to see You through me. Make me Your instrument. Let my hands be an extension of Yours. Use me to exact Your vengeance and Your judgment on those who fall under the gaze of Your wrath.

You are my God. I am Your servant.

Bless me and lead me. Thank You.

He lowered his arms, kissed the tips of his fingers, and then touched his mother's and father's grave markers with them. "May you find rest and peace in Ɂäţūr's arms."

He wiped the tears from his eyes and rose to his feet. A newfound strength surged within him and renewed his spirit. He walked through the field of graves, spoke the names written on each marker, and added, "I will fight for you."

Satisfied that he'd visited every grave, Alderan walked around to the front of the cottage and gazed south, where Viscus D'Silva had stood. Thanks to Savric and Zerenity, nothing remained of the burned-out structures. Given time, no one would even remember the town's existence, save the graveyard.

Alderan faced the cottage and stared at the simple brass doorknob that clung to the brown, weathered door. And the door—*the* symbol of home for him—left his heart tattered and aching.

So many memories.

He lay his hand against the wooden door and traced the coarseness of its grain with his fingertips. He remembered the day that his father—everyone had called him Red—fashioned the door from leftover scraps of burkwood. He'd asked Red if they'd sand the door smooth, but Red said the character of the door came from its roughness.

Everyone knew you were the character, father, and the glue that kept this town together.

Alderan slid his hand down to the brass knob and wrapped his fingers around it.

Tomorrow, Master Savric will tear this house down. His eyes watered, and he wiped them with his other hand. *This will be the last time I'll ever walk through this door.*

How do I say goodbye? He sighed. *It's only a house, nothing more. The memories will remain with me.*

He turned the knob and pushed the door open. A soft roar of conversation expelled from the open door and flitted past his ears like a flurry of butterflies.

Had he heard his name? His heart thumped so loudly in his ears that he couldn't be sure; the veins in his neck leapt with each beat. A bead of sweat slid down his nape and trickled down his spine. Excitement and dread battled within him and left his stomach knotted and jittery.

The doorway—a portal to the future—stood before him. He breathed deep, stepped across its threshold and into the cottage, and into his new life.

It's time I learned how to be a wizard.

† † †

Savric sat at the oblong table with a piece of hard bread in one hand and a chunk of roasted rabbit skewered on the end of a fork in his other. He bit off a corner of the bread and moved it to the left side of his mouth with his tongue.

Breadcrumbs, spittle, and words spewed from the right side of his mouth. "Six consecutive days of hard labor have never felt so rewarding."

Zerenity's bright blue eyes leveled on Savric, but the growing network of red veins muted their usual sparkle. "We do what we must, Savvy."

"Always, Reni." Savric swallowed the last of the bread lingering on the inside of his cheek. "But the boy's demand in burying the dead was spot on. If he is willing to go to such lengths for those who have moved on from this life, imagine the great lengths he will go to save those that are still here."

Savric shoved the loaded fork into his mouth and pulled the meat from its prongs with his teeth. He squashed the meat between his back teeth and groaned as the succulent juices rolled down his throat like small streams of ecstasy.

Alderan's voice flowed from the living area and into the kitchen. "I'll lay down my life for them if I have to."

Savric startled, gasped, swallowed the half-chewed meat, and choked as it lodged in the back of his throat. He beat his chest, but the meat had wedged itself so deep that he couldn't get it to move either direction. His eyes watered, and he pounded the table, desperate for air.

Zerenity thrust her hand toward him. *"Diẕinṭäzhräiṭ."*

The blockage in Savric's throat dissolved, and he gasped. He coughed a few times just to be certain nothing lingered in the back of his throat, and then he lifted a tin cup to his lips and slurped water from it.

Savric wiped tears from his eyes with the backs of his hands. "Thank you, Reni."

Her eyes smiled at him, but she didn't.

Will she ever forgive me? I cannot fathom going so many years again without conversing with her.

Savric, his eyes still watery, turned just as Alderan reached the table. "My dear boy let us hope it never comes down to that."

The resolve in Alderan's hardened gaze both comforted and saddened Savric. *I would take the weight from your shoulders if I could.*

Alderan sat down next to Rayah and across from Zerenity and put his arm around Rayah's waist. "I'll fight to my last breath. I know no other way."

Just in this last week he has shed his youth and become a man. But does he understand what he has signed up for? If so, would he be so brave?

Rayah piped up, "You won't be alone in the fight. I'll always be by your side."

Alderan lifted a fork from the table and pushed a chunk of rabbit meat around the wooden plate in front of him. "I'm ready to become a wizard, Zerenity. When can we start training?"

Savric looked to Zerenity, but her gaze fixated on Alderan.

"Soon, yes," said Savric. "Our business here is done. I fear we are quickly running out of time before the impending war. It aches my bones."

Zerenity blinked rapidly, as though returning from another world. She turned to Savric. "And why do you believe we are running out of time?"

Savric grimaced and furrowed his brow. "You *know* why, woman. We discussed Qotan's findings. It speaks directly to the prophecy."

Zerenity snarled, "Why do you torture me so? I cared for Qotan just as you did. He was like a brother to me. We were both there when he died, Savvy. Do you not remember? We watched them drag him into the darkness—into the Between. He never returned from there. No one ever has. So, stop blaming yourself, and stop blaming me."

Tears flowed from Zerenity's eyes, but Savric knew they were borne of anger and not of sorrow. He pressed her. "But he did, Reni. I caught his arm and pulled him up from the darkness. How did you not see that?"

Zerenity rose from the table and walked over to the fire. "Savvy, you *did* reach into the darkness, and I kept you from going in as well, but Qotan never returned from it. Nothing did. Perhaps some part of you never did either."

Savric cradled his head in his hands. "If that were true, Reni, then why are you the only one who cannot see him?"

Zerenity squeezed her right hand, and the fire's flames intensified. "Oh, let's not play this game, Savvy. I'd venture you'd be pressed to name another soul besides yourself who has laid eyes on Qotan since that day."

"That day changed us all, Reni. You know that." He lifted his head and squeezed the bridge of his nose between his fingers. "Qotan rarely ventures out amongst people. He hardly did before that dreadful day, either."

Zerenity turned from the fire, but the fire's flames blazed in her eyes. "Prove me wrong, Savvy. Name just one person." She shook a finger at him. "Just one."

Savric groaned. *How will I ever get through to this hardheaded woman?*

"As I expected." Zerenity crossed her arms as tears seeped from the corners of her eyes. "You have no answer, yet you still torture me with his name and damn me for caring about you."

A hand squeezed Savric's left shoulder. He turned. Rayah's hazel eyes warmed his heart. *Truly an angel, wings and all.*

Rayah tilted her head. "Who is Qotan, Master Savric? I've never heard you mention him before."

Savric patted the top of her hand with his and gave it a rub. "Qotan is one of the greatest men to ever live. He is a bright, funny, and caring soul. He is my best friend, and my twin brother."

Alderan dropped his fork. It clanked against the wooden plate and tumbled off the side of the table. He leaned over to grab it before it hit the floor, but it floated back up to the table and settled next to his plate.

Alderan gave Savric a sidelong glance, and Savric winked.

Alderan sat up and pushed his hair behind his ears. "Do all wizards have twins?"

"No," said Savric.

Alderan turned toward Zerenity. "Do you have a twin, Zerenity?"

Zerenity rubbed the top of her left hand with her right thumb. "No, darling. Twins are very rare among wizards."

Savric followed Zerenity's silhouetted form back to the table with his gaze. "She is correct, my boy. In nearly every case, the dominant baby starves the other to death while still in the womb. A nasty business, nature is."

Alderan rubbed the back of his neck. "Then I shouldn't be alive. Aria's far stronger than I am."

Savric chuckled. "Indeed. She is a tough one, for certain. I realized that the first time I laid eyes on her. She would do well saving the world."

Alderan rose from the table and walked into the living area. Rayah gave Savric's shoulder a final squeeze and then excused herself.

Zerenity glared at Savric from across the table. "How *dare* you, Savvy."

Savric sighed. "What have I done this time, woman?"

She huffed, "You're supposed to be *building* the boy's confidence, not tearing him down. Have you expelled all that was left of your dignity?"

He rose to his feet and pushed the bench back. "Tar and feathers, woman! If the boy is that fragile, there is no hope. We will all be condemned."

Zerenity's face matched her red cape. "Sometimes I feel as though I never knew you."

"Perhaps not." He raised his right arm out to the side. His staff flew out of the shadows and snapped into his open hand. "I must go check on my brother's condition. When I return, we will pull this cottage apart and send its materials back to the earth. Then I will seal the room below, so no one will ever stumble across it."

Zerenity glared at him. "That's a task you may find yourself doing alone, Savvy. We'll likely be gone before you return from your foolish errand." She crossed her arms and walked away.

So be it. He grunted, slammed his staff's butt-end against the floor, and disappeared in a whirlwind.

† † †

Rayah floated through the living area and settled at the door to Alderan's room. She pushed the door open and walked into the dimly lit room. "Alderan?"

Alderan sat on the end of the bed; his hand raked his head.

She sat next to him and put her hand on his leg. "Are you okay?"

"I don't understand any of this. Why did my parents keep so many secrets from me?"

Rayah stared straight ahead. *I'm sure their reasons were much like mine.*

"They were protecting you and your sister."

Alderan fell back on the bed. "Protecting us? From what? How have any of their secrets improved my life? They're both dead, and people keep trying to kill me at every turn. No one will give me answers. Where did Savric and Zerenity come from? Why do they seem familiar even though I have no memories of them? Were my parents wizards too?"

Rayah had never considered such a question, but she thought she'd heard something about how a wizard must have at least one parent who is also one. Then again, she could be confusing it with herself.

Rayah stared at the floor. "I honestly don't know how that works. I know that drytes like myself must have a mother who's a dryte as well. Perhaps it works the same for wizards."

Alderan pushed his hair away from his eyes. "How could either of them have been? My father was a thatcher, and my mother spun yarn. Why would they have chosen to do those things if either of them had been a wizard?

"Why didn't my father fight back if he could've used mezhik? How did my mother really die? How can I move on with so many unanswered questions? I thought I was ready to save the world, but now I'm more unsure than ever."

Rayah had no answers for him, and she felt helpless. *Ƨätūr, what can I do? How can I help him find what he's looking for?*

The air sizzled, and the smell of pine filled the room. Every candle in the room ignited to life with green flames. Rayah looked up.

Zerenity stood in the doorway. "I didn't mean to eavesdrop on the two of you darlings, but perhaps I can shed a bit of light on your life, Alderan."

Rayah closed her eyes. *Thank You, Ƨätūr.*

Alderan sat up, pushed himself back onto the bed, and leaned against the wall. "Tell me who I am, who my parents really were, how you and Savric know my family, and why everyone keeps trying to kill me. Please leave nothing out."

Rayah scooted back on the bed, grabbed Alderan's hand, and leaned on his shoulder.

Rayah pushed her thought toward Alderan. *"I'll know if she's lying."*

Alderan squeezed her hand. *"As will I."*

† † †

With the flick of Zerenity's wrist, a stool slid across the floor and stopped next to the bed. She plopped down on it and then drew her cape over her legs. She lightly tugged on her earlobe and looked up at the ceiling.

Where shall I begin? Ah, yes, from the books.

She leveled her gaze on Alderan. "Do either of you know what prophecy is?"

Alderan shrugged his shoulders.

"A vision of their future," said Rayah.

"Not quite, darling. Only *Drämärz Dhä* have visions of their future. And, of course, some dragons do too. Pro—"

Alderan leaned forward, his eyes wide. "You've seen dragons? I wasn't sure if they really existed. Wow, they really do live in the—"

"Hold on, darling." Zerenity waved her hand. "Before we travel too far down this path, a decision must be made. We can discuss dragons to your heart's content, or I can tell you of your past and potential future. I'll let you decide, but we only have time to discuss one of them."

Zerenity sat back, crossed her legs at the knees, and took in Alderan's boyish features. His high forehead and square jaw reminded her of his father, but the slight curve of his nose and the petite line of his small, red lips came from his mother. However, his green eyes and blonde hair were unique to him and his sister.

She studied Rayah. The girl's porcelain skin, soft features, and youth niggled her a bit. Her face warmed with a tinge of envy and embarrassment.

The two of them would make beautiful children, but what would become of them? Has there ever been a dryte who was also a wizard? The thought unnerved her, but she couldn't put her finger on why.

Alderan cleared his throat. "I must know everything about my life but promise me we'll discuss dragons later."

Zerenity nodded slightly. "As you wish, darling. Now, as I was saying, prophecy is comprised of visions or dreams of *potential* futures. Each prophecy has several potential branches, but only a single branch will ever be followed."

Alderan frowned. "How is that different than *Drämärz Dhä*?"

Zerenity smiled. "Prophecy is rarely specific to any given individuals and always contains several branches, as I said. The *Drämärz Dhä* will get visions specific to themselves or certain people. They will not contain branches."

Zerenity raised a finger. "However, that's not to say that their visions always come to fruition. The future fluctuates like a rippled pond. Every decision made in the entire world changes the future constantly. With prophecy, one branch *will* be fulfilled."

Rayah pulled at one of her long, chestnut curls. "A prophecy always gets fulfilled by one of its branches? Are you sure, or do some fail to be fulfilled at all?"

Zerenity tapped her finger against her chin. "All true prophecies get fulfilled in some way. However, false prophecies do exist. Sometimes, it's hard to tell the difference between them. Often, more than one prophet will prophesy true prophecies, but that doesn't have to be the case.

"Discernment is required for any prophecy. Some prophecies become self-fulfilling simply because those who know of it force the world down a specific branch. One might argue that these are not prophecies at all."

"Where are you going with this?" asked Alderan.

"Glad you asked, darling. The night you and your sister were born, the stars aligned, and the full moon donned a golden halo, exactly as the prophets had foretold more than two thousand years before. Twins would be born, they'd said. Powerful wizards who could either save the world from the coming darkness or usher it in."

Alderan scratched his head. "But how was it determined that Aria and I were those twins? How can you be certain we're the ones that will fulfill the prophecy?"

Zerenity leaned forward. "Truthfully? It was a simple process of elimination. Twins are rare in our race. And, with a handful of watchers spread across Centauria, it took less than two years to locate you."

"What do you mean by 'watchers?'" asked Alderan.

"Ah, yes, the watchers. Over a thousand years ago, after the dust settled from the Great War, a secret society was born out of the necessity to track prophecies. They called themselves *Feezhärz Dhä*, or, in our tongue, *the watchers.*

"From that point forward, there have always been five watchers—never more and never less. This truth held steadfast until after your birth. Now there are only two watchers left, and the line of succession has been broken."

Rayah leaned forward and rolled her shoulders. "You and Savric are the last, then?"

"We are, darling. If our existence were known to the wrong people, we'd be dead as well."

Alderan pushed himself to the edge of the bed and stood. "Why would you be killed? Are those that would kill you the same ones hunting me?"

"In a word, yes."

Alderan ran his fingers through his hair. "But Aria's safe, isn't she? She must be."

"Safety is in the eye of the beholder. She will not be killed, if that's what you're asking."

Alderan huffed. "Then why are they trying to kill me? I don't understand."

"They believe you're the only person that can stop the darkness."

"But isn't that a good thing?"

"It is, unless you worship the darkness. To them, you're a threat."

"Then why would they want to keep Aria alive? Isn't she a threat to the darkness as well?"

"Only while you live."

Alderan's eyes widened. "But she doesn't know I'm still alive!"

Zerenity reached out and clasped Alderan's arm. "Savric took measures to guarantee her knowledge of your survival. He risked his own life doing so, mind you."

Alderan jerked his arm away from her grasp, vaulted off the bed, and paced the room. "How could the two of you sit back and allow everything to happen to us? To our family? Our friends?"

Rayah rose from the bed and floated to Alderan's side. She whispered something inaudible in his ear and then wrapped her arms around his neck. He pulled her close, and she lay her head on his shoulder.

Savvy held me that way once.

The thought of him vexed her. Anger seeped from her pores like the stench of decay. She uncrossed her legs and rose from the stool. She smoothed out her cape and then walked over to the door.

Why did you leave me this way, Savvy? Death would've been less cruel than this harsh existence. How did we ever come to this point?

Rage shook her. She latched onto the wooden doorframe with her left hand and steadied herself.

This is all your fault, Savvy.

Zerenity drew a deep breath, dug her nails into the soft wood, and allowed her anger and mezhik to flow into the doorframe. The wood vibrated and moaned under the stress, but it didn't splinter.

She looked toward the ceiling. *Forgive me, Father.*

Having regained her composure, she turned back toward Alderan and Rayah. "Darling, do you really think you're the only one who's lost anything in this? All of us sacrificed nearly everything to keep you and your sister alive and as safe as possible. Some gave their lives in service.

"The agents of darkness are everywhere; they hear and see everything and report to their master. Why do you think Savvy and I stayed away for so long? We both loved you so much. Can you not see that?"

Tears blurred her vision. "It broke my heart when I had to leave you two with Gretchen and Red. I knew they'd do their best to raise you as their own, but that didn't make it any easier. Savvy watched you from afar on several occasions, but I couldn't bring myself to do the same. I feared I wouldn't be able to leave you again, and I knew that would put your lives in jeopardy."

Alderan released Rayah and fell to his knees, his eyes wide with fear. "But... I don't understand. You're telling me that Gretchen and Red *aren't* my parents? How can that be?" He looked up at Rayah. "Why would she tell me that?"

Rayah bent down and wrapped her arms around Alderan's chest. "It's going to be okay, Alderan." She kissed his cheek.

Alderan squeezed his eyes shut and sat back on his feet. "Are you saying that you and Savric are my parents?"

Zerenity gasped. "Heavens no, darling. We're merely the ones who rescued you. Had you been mine, I never would've given you up."

Father, I would've given the world to have had children like them.

"But that means… why would…" Alderan's voice cracked, and then he broke down and sobbed.

Zerenity swept across the room and took Alderan in her arms. "I'm certain your parents loved you, Alderan, just as much as Gretchen and Red did. As much as I do. They didn't give you up by choice. They died trying to protect you."

"Did you know them? Or their names?" asked Rayah.

Zerenity closed her eyes as she smoothed back Alderan's hair. Her heart raced; her palms moistened with sweat. The past rushed back from the far shores of her mind like a surging tide, and its undertow pulled her down into its depths.

† † †

Zerenity stood at the base of the Aether Mountains, on their northern side. A stiff wind arose and whipped her hair in her face. She brushed it back with her hand.

Omerus stood across from her, his stare hardened, and his brown eyes narrowed under bushy, peppered eyebrows. He kept his silvered hair cropped short and his beard no more than stubble, and, together, they made his face look narrower than it really was.

He smacked his palm with his fist. "These children are a threat to us all, Zerenity."

She shook her head, knowing it wasn't anger that fueled him. "Why do these precious children beleaguer you with fear, Omerus?"

"Measures were taken to prevent this exact scenario from happening. And yet here we stand, neck deep in its deadly grasp." He shrugged and

raised his hands, palms up. "How did we come to this place?"

"Have there been no other children like them before?" She knew the answer, but it didn't change the fact that her mind refused to accept it.

"Of course not. You know who their parents were. Unzhiftäd."

Zerenity pulled her cloak tight and crossed her arms over her chest. "How is it possible though? How could ungifted parents conceive wizards? Doesn't this go against the laws of nature? At least one parent must be a wizard."

Beads of sweat dotted Omerus's brow. He took a swatch of cloth from within the folds of his greyish-brown robes and daubed his forehead with it. "You know the prophecy, Zerenity. We've been over this before."

Zerenity tapped her fingernail on her chin. "Yes, but perhaps we've made a mistake. Maybe these aren't the children the prophecy refers to."

Omerus shook a plump, sausage-like finger at her. "There are no others, and you know it. Twins cannot be born to the ungifted. It's never happened in the history of our world. Yet these two exist in contradiction."

He fisted his hand. "They are the ones. Of this, I have no doubt. If the council gains knowledge of this… how we're hiding them away… we'll all be dead for failing to inform them."

She reached out and cupped his rosy cheek. His skin warmed her cold fingers. "If the council were to find out, the children would be dead as well, wouldn't they?"

"Yes—" He pushed her hand away. "—and perhaps they should be."

She frowned and shook her head. "They're children, Omerus. I know you don't mean that."

He sighed. "Maybe not, but I beg Zäţūr I did. You know this will be the end of us all."

She looked up at the grey sky and then at the two children huddled together twenty paces away. "Pray that it's not."

† † †

Zerenity gasped for air as she rose from the waters of the past. She wiped her eyes and kissed the top of Alderan's head.

She turned toward Rayah, stared into her hazel eyes, and lied straight to her face.

CHAPTER TWENTY-ONE

S pots of light filtered through the scraggly trees ahead. Rakzar paused, looked back at Amicus and Eshtak, and raised his hand in the air. Amicus and Eshtak stopped, crouched low, and ceased their chatter.

Rakzar lowered himself onto all fours and crept into the clearing. Twenty feet ahead, the ground sloped a bit and then disappeared. He walked over to the edge of the cliff and peered over its edge; its sheer rock face plummeted hundreds of feet before meeting the expansive valley floor below.

He lifted his snout and breathed in. *Smoke.* But within the succulent, smoky aroma bloomed an intolerable stench. It permeated the air like a contagion and stung his nostrils. He snorted.

His hackles rose, and a long growl rumbled deep within his chest. "There are orcs below."

Amicus and Eshtak moved up next to him. Eshtak grabbed a handful of hair on Rakzar's withers.

Rakzar growled deeper. *Perhaps biting his hand off would teach him to keep his other hand to himself.*

Rakzar turned and eyed Eshtak. The little man's thin black lips curled into a smile, but his prodigious eyes couldn't mask the truth within. Rakzar knew that truth well: *fear.* A strange feeling left Rakzar's chest aching and him unable to act.

I'll allow it this once, but, next time, his hand gets removed from his body.

"Are those the ones we're looking for?" whispered Amicus.

Rakzar looked at Amicus. "Only one way to find out."

Snap.

Rakzar sprang to his feet and whirled around. Behind them, a tree branch fell to the ground. Rakzar drew his battle-axes and stepped forward.

Amicus drew his broadsword and pushed Eshtak behind himself.

"Stay behind me," growled Rakzar.

Amicus and Eshtak retreated a few paces.

A deep-yellow eye shone through the trees, and Rakzar recognized the scent. *Borsha.*

The gnoll stepped forward. Shadows lingered across half his face—the good side of it. Words slithered from his slackened jaw, "Ah, the *mighty* Rakzar."

Rakzar snarled. "I know you never travel alone, Borsha. Where are the others?"

A female gnoll stepped around Borsha and stood next to him. Rows of braided yellow fur circled the sides of her head like horns; their ends hung well below her leather-covered breasts. Dozens of tiny strands of yarn and ribbon knotted together and formed a rainbow of colors around her slender neck.

Rakzar knew each strand represented a kill. He'd heard several tales of her ruthless brutality. They called her "The Butcher."

A pair of gnolls materialized from the trees on Rakzar's left. *Yetch and Wibble, the terrible twins.* They spent more time fighting with each other than anything else, but when it came time for battle, they were fiercer and more reliable than any other gnolls Rakzar had ever met.

To Rakzar's right, another gnoll stepped out of the shadows. Rakzar didn't recognize the beast and had to crane his neck just to look him in the eye. The beast's height rivaled that of a young giant. *What've they been feeding you?*

Rakzar stepped back to keep the five of them within his purview. He trusted none of them, and, with the cliff at their backs, he, Amicus, and Eshtak were surrounded.

Tendrils of saliva hung from the side of Borsha's mangled lower jaw. "Find your little boy yet, or is he still getting the better of you?"

Rakzar turned, eyed Amicus for a moment, and then returned his attention to Borsha. "You know I never leave a job unfinished. The boy's dead, and so is his little *dryte* girlfriend."

Borsha turned his head slightly and leaned forward. "Is that so? And how did they die?"

Wibble wound a long piece of wire around the palm of his left hand and then unwound it again. "Talked them to death, just like he's gonna do us." Each end of the wire wound around wooden handles. He pulled the wire taut. "Can we kill them now?"

Rakzar twirled the battle-axe in his left hand. "They burned to death in the castle fire, along with the others. I'd be happy to show you their corpses, Wibble."

Yetch scratched at his left calf with his right foot. A spotted grey tongue hung from the side of his mouth and flapped up and down when he spoke. "Ooh, can I come too?"

Wibble smacked Yetch on the side of his snout. "You're as thick as your head."

Rakzar looked around for an escape route. *How are we going to get out of this?*

The female's movements were subtle, but the *click-click* of the knives releasing and the momentary glint of light off their steel blades as they slid down her forearms and into her open palms didn't escape Rakzar.

Rakzar cocked his head and eyed her. "Make a move, bitch."

Borsha placed his hand over her exposed stomach. "Easy, now, Urza. We're all friends here, right?"

"Eshtak not bad thing's friend!"

Rakzar shook his head. *Does he say everything that enters his tiny brain?*

"How 'bout we peel and eat the little shrimp?" said Wibble.

Yetch scratched behind his right ear vigorously. "Huh?"

Borsha glanced at Wibble. "Can we please keep some semblance of order here?"

Rakzar pointed the tip of one of his battle-axes at Borsha's chest. "If we're all friends, then why have you been following us?"

"Following you?" He wagged his finger. "No, no, no. You've got this all wrong. We're the welcoming party."

Rakzar eyed the five of them. "Welcoming party? Then why do you have your weapons drawn and ready?"

A long tendril of drool glistened like a falling star as it dripped from

Borsha's snout. "I could ask the same of you, *friend*." He dropped his shoulders and sighed. "Urza, put the knives away. Xerp, lower your weapon. Wibble, Yetch, try not to hurt each other. There's no need for bloodshed."

Urza moved her eyes up and to the side as she pushed the knives back up her forearms. With a *click-click*, the knives locked in place. Xerp rested his long-handled hatchet over the top of his massive left shoulder and then flexed his biceps with a snarl.

Rakzar snarled back at him. *There's something off with that one.* He reluctantly returned his battle-axes to his back.

"Don't expect me to lower my weapon," said Amicus.

"Ah, the ebony man speaks." Borsha stepped forward and peered around Rakzar's shoulder. "Feel free to hold your sword up all night. You'll tire at some point."

Rakzar stepped in front of Borsha and shoved him backward. "Leave them be."

Xerp grabbed his hatchet with both hands and raised it above his head. He roared and lunged forward. His hatchet arced sideways and downward, right toward the side of Rakzar's neck.

Rakzar ducked, rolled to his left, and had a battle-axe in his right hand by the time he sprang back to his feet. He swiveled on his heel and swung the axe in an upward arc, but he only caught air.

Amicus cried out and fell backward, narrowly escaping Rakzar's wild swing.

Xerp lay face-up in a heap. Two knives, buried to their hilts, protruded from his dead body: one between his eyes and one lodged in his throat. Amicus's broadsword through the center of his bare chest had sealed his fate. The coppery smell of fresh blood tainted the air.

A loud grunt and a gurgle spun Rakzar to his left. Blood peppered the air and moistened his face as a thin wire sliced through Borsha's neck.

Borsha blinked twice with his one eye, his head turned to the side unnaturally, and then it tumbled off his collapsing body. It landed on the ground with a muffled *thud*.

Wibble stood in his wake, wire in hand and a wicked grin on his face. "No one touches *my* bitch." He grabbed Urza, pulled her close, and nuzzled her.

Yetch snorted. "Oh, I get it. *Shrimp*. It's funny because the little man's so short."

Everyone turned and stared at Yetch.

Rakzar shook his head. "How many times were you dropped on your head as a pup?"

Yetch shrugged. "Anyone else hungry, or just me?"

"Eshtak hungry!" He bounced from one foot to the other and spun in a circle.

"I like the little man," said Urza. "But how does he keep warm without proper clothing or fur? I've got both and still feel the winter air at times."

"Damned if I know," growled Rakzar.

"Eshtak not cold. Eshtak free." He lifted his cloak and twirled around.

Wibble squeezed Urza. "That's what you've got me for—to keep you warm."

Urza shrugged from under Wibble's arms. "You'd better watch it, or you'll find yourself lying face-up in a pool of your own blood like Xerp over there."

Wibble winked at Urza. "Dying by your hand would be an honor."

"No, dying by my hand would be another ribbon around my neck." She shoved Wibble out of her way and walked over to Xerp.

Rakzar growled with laughter. *I like her.*

Wibble glowered at him, and he laughed harder.

Yetch laughed too. "What was funny?"

Wibble backhanded Yetch. "That was."

Urza bent down and freed her knives from Xerp's skull and neck. She licked the blades clean with her long greyish-black tongue and then slid them back into their spring-loaded arm-sheaths.

Eshtak squirmed, danced about, and raked his tongue with his fingers. "Yuck, yuck, yuck!"

Urza slowly licked her grey lips and then snapped her jaws in Eshtak's direction. "Fresh blood, still warm and seeping from an open wound, is better than any nectar. Maybe I'll try yours sometime, little man."

Eshtak coughed and gagged and dropped to the ground. He kicked himself around in circles. "Eshtak hates blood!"

"Leave him alone," growled Rakzar. "We've got somewhere to be."

Urza strutted over to Rakzar and ran her clawed finger down the front of his leather breastplate, stopped just above his leather skirt, and let her hand linger there. "Never any playtime with you, is there, *mighty* Rakzar?"

He grabbed her wrist and twisted her arm. He leaned over and whispered, "Only the gods know what kinds of diseases you're carrying."

Urza glanced at Wibble and then she nipped Rakzar's ear and licked the side of his cheek. "Take a tumble with me sometime, and the gods won't be the only ones who know."

He growled at her. "Not on your best day."

Wibble's glowing eyes narrowed as he pulled the wire taut between his clenched fists. "You even think of tumbling with him, and I'll take both of your heads."

Rakzar released Urza's wrist and glared at Wibble. "Why were the three of you traveling with Borsha and that overgrown beast?"

"Lost a wager," said Wibble. "Turns out he was uglier than the both of us."

Rakzar pointed a finger at Wibble. "That mouth of yours is gonna get you killed one of these days."

"Nah. He's a slow eater and chews well," said Yetch. "Besides, Urza might kill him first if he doesn't keep his snout away from other females."

Wibble backhanded Yetch square in his jaw, and Yetch yelped. "Keep your mouth shut, or I'll use this wire on *you*."

Urza propped her foot up on Borsha's severed head and leaned on her knee. "We've been ordered to stay with those filthy orcs, but you know the difficulty in that, given their stench. This is about as close as we can stand to be."

Rakzar walked over to the edge of the cliff. About five miles out, more than a hundred bonfires lit sections of the valley floor. Makeshift tents sprawled across the frozen plains like giant, wooden-limbed creatures crawling up from their graves.

The horde's grown. The thought unsettled him.

Amicus stood at his side. "What are the chances of finding Murtag and getting him alone amongst all of them?"

"None," he growled. "Now's the time you start praying to your god. Maybe He'll find us a way."

"Never fear, my friend. I'm in constant communion with Him. He'll show us a path if it's meant to be."

Rakzar picked at his teeth and wiped his claw on his leg. "Does he know what he's up against?"

"Who? ʕäʈūr? Nothing escapes Him."

"The White Knight, not your God."

"Ah, Alderan. How could he? How would any of us have seen this coming?"

Better he be damned than me. "If the White Knight's truly some sort of prophesied savior, as the *dryte* claims, he's got one vicious battle ahead."

"So do we."

Rakzar scoffed. "Beyond Murtag's death, there's nothing in it for me. It's not my battle."

"You're absolutely right; it's all of ours. On one side or the other, you'll be fighting. And, for what it's worth, I hope and pray it's ours."

What is it with humans and their gods? "You just keep praying we find Murtag."

Muffled screams of terror rose from the valley below like spirits of the damned begging for repentance. Pain and agony filled those cries and sent his mind back to the White Knight and their first encounter. That night, the White Knight wore fear like a musk; it seeped from his pores and hung in the air like a dense fog, its smell an aphrodisiac for the twisted.

For me.

Now the memory left him hollow and alone, drowning in the depths of the ocean again. Before that fateful night, he'd feared nothing; now it consumed him. His thoughts tortured him relentlessly. *Damn the ocean.*

Despite their differences, he'd bonded with the White Knight. In his miserable existence, he'd never bonded with anyone else. Had he succeeded in killing the White Knight, what would've become of the world? Of him?

So many others still hunted the boy. *Will they fail as I did? They must. If he is the savior.*

His head ached, he needed food, and he needed rest.

The White Knight. This dark world would turn black without him in it.

Like kindling ignited by a spark, understanding filled him, fueled him.

The darkness has a face, but so does the light. But that truth brought with it more questions. *Was I born into darkness, or did I choose it? If it was a choice, can I change my mind, or is there no hope for me? Am I damned? Do I have a soul?*

The last thought unsettled him.

All the questions in his mind faded, but one thought lingered. *Nothing matters without the White Knight.*

Once they dealt with Murtag, he'd find the boy and protect him with his life, wouldn't he? Seeds of doubt lingered still. *Am I capable of being so selfless?* The answer obvious, he purposed himself to defy the odds.

Did he miss the White Knight? The notion unsettled him more than the horde camped below.

What have I become?

† † †

Amicus looked up at the vast sea of stars, and his pulse quickened. *Are you out there, Vonah? Vorene? My heart aches to be with you again. I know my time here's short. I feel it slipping away so quickly. I pray that justice will be served before I depart. Think of me. I'll be with you again soon.*

He stood over Xerp, put his foot on the beast's chest, and grunted as he yanked the broadsword from the beast's still-warm carcass. He wiped both sides of the blade on Xerp's leg, then he slid the sword back into its leather scabbard. He'd become tolerant of Rakzar's odor, but the combined smell of the six of them coated his nostrils and saturated his lungs.

Eshtak plopped down on the ground and lowered his head until his chin touched his chest. "Eshtak dies without food. Eshtak soooo hungry."

Amicus rubbed the top of Eshtak's head. "Let's find somewhere to set up camp. Preferably a good distance from these carcasses."

Wibble wrapped the wire around his left palm and then cracked his neck. "We've already got a camp set up about a mile from here."

Eshtak sprang to his feet and twirled his brown cloth sack around his wrist. "Eshtak likes camp. Camp has fire. And food. Eshtak loves food."

Yetch kicked Borsha's head over to the cliff's edge and followed it. "How far you think I could kick it?"

Rakzar grabbed Yetch by the scruff of his neck and threw him to the ground. "The bodies stay here."

Yetch eyed Borsha's severed head.

"That includes Borsha's head." Rakzar grabbed the head and tossed it back over by its matching body. "Someone might find the bodies if we throw them off the cliff."

Yetch stood and dusted himself off. "Wasn't gonna do it."

Rakzar turned to Wibble and crossed his arms. "Who else knows of this camp other than you three?"

Wibble slid his arm around Urza's waist. "Borsha and Xerp know, but I'm fairly certain they'll tell no one."

Yetch scratched the side of his neck. "Especially Xerp. He never talked. Can't trust those that don't talk. That's what I think. Glad to see him dead. Are you happy he's dead?"

Eshtak skipped around in circles. "Eshtak's happy. Bad thing tried to kill friend."

Amicus raised an eyebrow. *Guess Rakzar's no longer a "bad thing."*

"Fine, lead the way," said Rakzar. "Just make sure your brother keeps his fleas to himself."

"Don't you worry about that. He's never been good at sharing." Wibble got in Rakzar's face. "And neither am I, if you understand my meaning."

Urza squeezed between Wibble and Rakzar. "I'm more female than either of you could handle."

"If you hadn't noticed, I don't follow the pack rules. I don't wanna have anything to do with her." Rakzar raised his arms. "She's all yours."

Amicus shook his head. *Ƨäṭūr, I know You have a plan. I just wish I knew what it was.*

† † †

Rakzar sat next to the open fire, captivated by its orange and yellow flames. The rump of a flayed boar hung over the fire on a spit; its juices sizzled as they dripped into the fire. Why humans cooked meat before consumption baffled him. *They might as well be eating ashes.*

Eshtak leaned back against a log and giggled at the flicker flies each time their wings burst with light. The man-child perplexed Rakzar. How different would his life be if he were to see things again through the eyes of a pup? He dismissed the thought with a snort.

Amicus slowly turned the spit. "Can we trust the others?"

Rakzar shook his head. "No, but we have no other option. Our chance of success is zero without their help."

Amicus poked the meat with a finger and then licked it clean. "Then we should bring them in on it."

"Bring us in on what?" Urza walked out of the shadows and lay next to the fire. Blood caked the fur under her chin and the sides of her snout.

Rakzar ignored the question. "A successful hunt, or did you finally kill Wibble?"

The fire reflected in her lantern eyes. "Don't toy with me, Rakzar. What's going on?"

"Where are the twins?" asked Amicus.

Rakzar grabbed one of his battle-axes from his back and then pulled a whetstone from his leather pouch. He spat on one of the blades and scraped the whetstone against it. "I'm sure they're out marking their territory or something stupid like that."

Urza yawned and stretched her legs. "They've taken the first watch, but they're within ear's reach if we need them. Now, what's this you're bringing us in on?"

Rakzar stopped sharpening the blade and looked at Amicus. "There's no sense in chasing our tails."

Amicus nodded. "We've come to kill Murtag."

Urza sat up. "*Kill* Murtag? You're not serious?"

"You know I don't mess around." Rakzar put the whetstone away and then buried the blade of his axe into a nearby log. "We need your help getting close to him and getting him alone."

Urza pulled a green ribbon out of a pouch on the side of her right thigh and held it up to the light. "I'd like to see him dead just as much as you, but have you forgotten the blood pact?"

Amicus took a knife from his belt, cut off a large chunk of the boar, and handed it to Eshtak. "Rakzar wouldn't be the one to kill him. Maybe Wibble or Yetch, or even you, could take him out while we have him distracted."

Urza scowled at Amicus. *Click! Click!* Her knives slid into her open palms. "Your plan is to eliminate one of us?"

Amicus's eyes widened. "No—"

Rakzar jumped to his feet and pushed Amicus behind him. He put his hand out toward Urza. "Calm down, Urza. There's no need for your knives. Amicus doesn't understand how the pact works."

Urza growled and twisted the knives between her knuckles. "Perhaps you should've explained it to him."

Amicus moved around Rakzar and faced him. "You said you couldn't kill Murtag and that he couldn't kill you."

"That's true, but only part of it. Gnolls and orcs can't kill each other—any of us. The fatal wound would be self-inflicted. Why do you think you're here? It's what we agreed to."

"I know, but then when you agreed to bring them in, I'd hoped that one of them could do it instead. I'm not sure I can." He retreated a few paces.

Rakzar growled, "There's no other way, Amicus. Not unless you want the little man to do it."

"Eshtak not kill. Eshtak run away."

"Well, there it is," said Rakzar. "You're the only option. You *must* do it."

Amicus stormed back, fists clenched. "I don't just kill people like you do. I value life and help preserve it when I can."

"Like Xerp?" snarled Rakzar.

Amicus shouted, "I saved your life!"

Rakzar poked Amicus's chest with a claw. "Don't be a hypocrite, Shadowman. You want Murtag dead, same as me."

"Do I?" Amicus raised his arms. "I'm not so sure anymore. This was *your* plan from the beginning."

Rakzar snorted. *There's only one way to get him back on task.* "Just think about your wife and your precious little girl."

Amicus's left hook caught Rakzar square in the jaw, but Rakzar caught the following right in midair.

Rakzar pushed Amicus to his knees. "Do you think they were shown mercy by Murtag? No. They were burned alive. Can you imagine what that must've felt like?" He released Amicus's fist.

Amicus trembled, but instead of fighting back, he collapsed on the ground and sobbed. "I'll never get their image out of my mind. Every night I close my eyes and relive not being there for them and failing to save them."

Rakzar bent down and gripped Amicus's shoulder. "Then do something about it. Avenge their deaths. Bring justice upon Murtag."

Eshtak wrapped his arms around Amicus's neck and cried. "Eshtak is sorry. Eshtak hurts when friend hurts."

Rakzar stood and rubbed his jaw. *Guess I deserved that one.*

Urza put her knives away and settled by the fire. "Whatever the plan, I'm in. I'm not sure you should tell Wibble and Yetch, though. I'm not sure where their loyalties lie."

Maybe she's not as bad as I thought.

Crack.

The snaps of breaking tree limbs sounded from the south.

Rakzar grabbed the battle-axe from his back and then yanked the other out of the log he'd thrust it into. Urza rolled to her feet with knives in hand and crouched low.

Crack.

Yetch crashed through the trees, tripped, and fell on all fours. "They're gone!"

"Who's gone?" Wibble appeared from the north. The wire in his hand dripped blood.

Yetch scratched the side of his neck fiercely. "The orcs."

CHAPTER TWENTY-TWO

A lone candelabrum sat at the end of the long, rectangular table. Its five candles flickered with energy, but even they couldn't bring life back into the strips of grayed flesh that lay across the bronze platter. Sucked dry and discarded, the short-eared rabbit's meat looked far from appetizing.

Life-giving blood.

Pravus had never consumed the blood of an animal before, but as the minutes passed, he knew he'd do it again. Ancient law condemned its consumption, and the reason behind the law became clear in his mind: if the world knew its power, blood would become the new currency.

Soon enough, blood will flow with war, and my father's kingdom will be reborn.

He leaned into the high-backed iron chair, relaxed, and allowed the blood's effect to fully take hold. The coppery taste lingered on his tongue; a small sacrifice, given the blood's healing power.

He curled and uncurled his fingers without pain, and the pinkish-grey spots on the backs of his hands faded. Strength and life slowly returned to his bones and muscles, a feeling he'd lived without for more than a week.

He cracked his knuckles. *With this blood, Aria will never need to know my true nature.*

He closed his eyes and focused on the other two problems he faced: Aria and Nardus. She should've been back days ago, and he'd returned empty-handed. Both enraged him.

He leaned forward and then stood. His chair screeched as it slid back on the marble floor. He clenched his left fist and whipped his arm out to the side. The bronze platter and its contents flew from the table, ricocheted off the rock wall with a *thunk*, and landed on the floor with a *clang*. The renewed power lightened his mood.

Beast, his wolfhound pup, emerged from under the table and promptly inspected the discarded contents. He sniffed the cold, grey meat, snorted with a twist of his head, and growled at it.

Pravus shook his head. *I'll never understand what you're thinking.* He snapped his fingers. "To me."

Beast trotted over to Pravus's side, looked up at him with big brown eyes speckled with hints of yellow and orange, and cocked his head. Pravus bent down and rubbed the top of his head. His thick silver fur, soft as silk, shone in the candlelight.

"Once Aria arrives, your job will be to protect her with your life. Can you do that for me?"

Beast growled and licked Pravus's cheek.

"That's a good boy. Now, off you go."

Beast whined.

Pravus cradled Beast's big head in his hands and looked at him sternly. "Bed."

Beast walked away a few steps and then looked back. Pravus pointed at the door. Beast whined again, turned away, and then trotted out the door and down the corridor.

Pravus likened the *click* of Beast's nails against the marble floor to that of dragon's claws. *What a glorious age that would've been.*

He stood and summoned Credan.

Credan entered from the far end of the large dining hall and bowed. "My lord?"

Pravus cracked his knuckles. "Make sure my future wife is found, alive and well, or it'll be your head."

"Yes, my lord. I'll send the scouts straight away."

"See that you do." He walked past Credan. "I must go see our guest. Make sure we're not disturbed."

"As you wish."

✝ ✝ ✝

Nardus stood on a wooden crate in the middle of a steel cage. The cage, roughly a twenty-foot cube, sat in the center of a larger room. About ten additional feet extended between the cage's bars and the outer walls of the room.

One side of the room housed large steel doors, at least twenty feet tall and eight feet wide. The two adjacent walls were bare, save for a lone metal bench nestled against one of them, and the opposite wall housed a much smaller, human-sized, black steel door.

The cage contained two round metal posts a foot in diameter each and about twelve feet tall. Eight feet separated them. Heavy chains hung from large steel rings mounted to the top of each pole.

A torture room, perhaps?

"Hello, Nardus." Pravus's voice filled the room.

Nardus turned and stepped off the crate. Across the room, Pravus stood in the shadows.

"How long have you been watching me?" Nardus asked.

"Oh, not long. Have you had enough time to think about your future? We want the same thing, Nardus. Everything we both do is for family, is it not?"

Nardus walked over to the wall of the steel cage nearest Pravus. "You know I'd never do anything that would jeopardize seeing my family again."

"And yet you conceal the stone's location and claim it to be buried within your chest."

Nardus grabbed two of the bars and pressed his face between them. He relished the cold steel against his feverish skin. "I swear, it's the truth. Take the damn stone and bring my family back."

Pravus stepped into the light and folded his arms behind his back. Black and gold robes swaddled him and left him looking frailer than Nardus knew him to be. Though still a shadow of the man Nardus recalled from the inn, Pravus no longer carried the walking stick he'd required just hours before, and the silver streaks in his hair had all but vanished.

Damned mezhik. He spat, but the saliva clung to his lower lip and crawled into his beard.

In a blink, Pravus stood just on the other side of the bars, his face inches away from Nardus's. His hands latched around Nardus's like a smith's tongs grasping a smoldering piece of steel, and his eyes flashed with fire. Pravus's hot breath, drowned in spices and mint, moistened Nardus's face and filled Nardus's flared nostrils.

The familiar tingle of mezhik crawled across Nardus's skin, burrowed into his pores, and left him rigid.

"We had an understanding, Pravus."

Pravus spoke, barely more than a whisper, but his words hammered Nardus's ears. "We did. However, you haven't held up your end of the bargain. I sent you after *Ɂʈōn Dhef Dädh* and you've returned empty-handed."

Nardus shook the bars, but they only moved in his mind. "How many times must I tell you that the stone's inside my chest?"

Pravus removed his hands and smiled. "Do you think I'm so foolish?"

Pressure built against the center of Nardus's chest, dissipated, and then struck him full-force like a double-kick. He heard the cracking of ribs, an expulsion of air from his lungs, and then a guttural moan from his lips. Pain exploded in his chest, and he flew backward.

He slammed into the bars on the opposite side of the cell, slid down them, and slumped on the floor. His vision darkened around the edges and each breath that followed whimpered from his lips. His ears rang, his head throbbed, and the steel-barred cell circled him like the world after turning circles in the middle of a meadow.

Nardus didn't recall Pravus entering the cell, but Pravus knelt beside him and had lifted his shirt. Had he passed out?

He looked down at his bare, concave chest. A dark-red hand print pressed into his skin, and blue and purple marks spider-webbed around it like cracks in dried earth. The left side of his chest burned with fire.

"You're weak, Nardus, but you don't have to be."

Stay out of my head!

Pravus placed his palm on Nardus's sunken chest, and its weight nearly crushed Nardus.

"Don't let him take the stone from us."

I must. It's the only way to bring my family back.

"Beəll ʈäzhädhär," muttered Pravus.

The tingle of mezhik lasted but a moment, and then Nardus's lungs raged with fire as pieces of broken rib retracted into place and melded back together. His sunken chest rose to its original height, his punctured lungs knitted themselves whole again, and he gasped for air. The pain at the back of his skull lingered, but otherwise he felt worlds better.

Nardus sat up. Pravus stood outside the cell and leaned against the bars. Nardus rubbed his chest. "Why did you do that?"

"So that you'd know the power of my mezhik." His voice sounded strained.

"He's weak. We could kill him right now. There are no guards around."

Never!

Nardus pulled himself to his feet. "I don't doubt your power, Pravus, but I haven't lied to you about the stone. It's in my chest. I swear on the lives of my family. I swear on my own life."

Nardus crossed the cell, but Pravus retreated to the back wall of the room and into the shadows.

"I believe you," said Pravus. His admission left Nardus dumbstruck.

Nardus leaned into the bars. "Just like that? You nearly kill me, then you heal me, and *now* you believe me?"

Pravus slowly walked over to the black steel door. Although shrouded under a veil of shadows, Nardus noticed Pravus clung to the wall. "Yes, but it's late. I'll return tomorrow to retrieve the stone. Get some rest. You'll need your strength."

Pravus walked through the open door and disappeared.

"Tomorrow, we'll kill him."

No! He's my only chance of getting my family back.

"Is that really what you want, to pull your family from Kinzhdm ef Häfn and damn them to this existence?"

How could I go on without them? They're all I think of. I need them.

"And what about Theyn?"

Theyn... How can you be so cruel?

The burning in his chest faded, and anguish drowned him in its rising tide. He slid to the floor and wept.

† † †

Pravus leaned against the wall and squeezed his left brow between his thumb and forefinger. Pain pulsed in his head like a flickering flame, and his vision flirted with darkness. *What did that man do to me?*

He stretched out his hand; the skin slowly wrinkled and discolored. How could his energy and power have depleted so quickly? Had Nardus drained them? *Impossible. He wears the collar.*

It must be the stone.

Pravus limped along the wide corridor and hugged the wall to keep his balance. Credan stood a few paces ahead and dipped his head when Pravus approached.

Pravus motioned Credan along. "Walk with me."

Credan dipped his head again. "My lord." He fell in line with Pravus.

Pravus kept his eyes focused ahead. "Have you any word from the scouts?"

"Yes, my lord. They've just left, but they'll be through the forest and into the wastelands within the hour."

"Good. Stay on it and keep me informed. When you receive word of anything, you bring the news to me immediately, no matter the time of day or any matter I may be attending to."

"As you wish. Is there anything else I may do for you, my lord?"

Darkness engulfed him—his vision, his hearing, then his sense of being.

"My lord? Is everything okay?" Credan held his arm, but Pravus couldn't remember him grabbing it.

He glared at Credan. "Release my arm."

Credan sighed but complied.

Pravus began walking again, and Credan followed closely.

"I'm sorry I grabbed your arm, but you were unresponsive for several minutes, and your eyes were clouded over."

Pravus waved his hand dismissively and strolled on. "The rabbit's blood only lasted a short time. I need more blood, but this time I need something stronger."

Credan fell behind and then stopped in the middle of the corridor. Pravus turned and faced him. In the dim light, Credan's turquoise eyes looked grey and lifeless. His narrow shoulders drooped low, and his grey cloak held on only by the cord drawn around his thin neck. He looked sickly.

Credan reached up and wiped beads of sweat from his liver-spotted scalp with a white kerchief. "Do you understand what you're asking of me?"

Pravus studied the man. "I do, but you must understand I have no other choice."

Credan shook his head. "But you've gone against nature. Against the law. What you're doing isn't right and involving me in it makes me just as guilty as you."

Pravus put his hand on Credan's shoulder. "Do you not understand what it is that I'm trying to accomplish? The old law will be abolished once I gain control of Centauria. I will establish a new order. None of this will matter."

Credan lowered his head. "I understand, my lord. I'll do as you ask."

Pravus squeezed his shoulder. "Good man. See that it's done."

Credan bowed and then scurried in the opposite direction.

Pravus turned, grabbed his head, and then dropped to one knee. Pain immobilized him, the walls closed in around him, and darkness pulled him under.

† † †

The crackle of burning wood lifted Pravus from the darkness of sleep. His head pulsed, and his vision was blurry. He felt around to his left and his right. He lay on the cold stone floor, but why?

He sat up and pulled himself to his feet. His fingers slid against his moistened thighs and chest. He wore nothing but a layer of sweat. He wiped at his eyes, but the blurriness remained.

He stumbled over to the bedchamber doors, threw them open, and then stepped into the corridor. The cold air chilled his skin, and his surroundings slowly focused.

Credan gasped and leapt from his chair. "My lord!" His face red, he turned away.

Pravus chuckled. "Come now, Credan. You've attended to me before. Surely my nakedness doesn't frighten you."

"No, my lord, it's not that. It's... the blood."

Pravus glanced down at his chest and stomach—blood smeared them. He wiped his chin with his forearm. *More blood.*

"Is... is it yours?" asked Credan.

Pravus's pulse quickened. *Is it? No, I feel fine.*

He couldn't remember anything. He turned and walked back into the room.

Furniture lay in disarray, some partially dismantled or broken. One footer post of the bed's canopy lay on its side, its dark-purple curtains strewn across the bed and the floor in a tangled mess.

Pravus walked over to the bed, and Credan followed closely. He swept his hand to the side and the curtains fell to the floor. A young woman lay in the middle of the bed atop the white covers, only the covers were no longer white, but stained crimson.

Tilly.

Credan dropped to his knees. "Dear spirits, what have you done?"

Her head lay perpendicular to her body, twisted beyond the natural. Chains hung from the header posts and attached to the seamless silver collar around her broken neck. Two other chains from the footer posts shackled her ankles and spread her legs apart.

A large gash on the inside of her right thigh still seeped, and she lay in a pool of her own blood. Pravus leaned over the bed and took a closer look at the wound.

Had something *chewed* on her leg? Or someone?

Did I? He swallowed hard. The coppery taste left little doubt.

His pulse raced. Had he lain with her too?

He looked down at himself; blood covered him down to his knees. *I must've.*

Before or after I killed her?

He couldn't remember any of it.

What've I done?

His hands trembled, but not with fear. He couldn't take his eyes away from her bloody, broken body.

Tilly, my bronze beauty.

Death suited her, and her blood called to him—aroused him. *Can she still be used?* The thought unsettled his heart, but could he physically resist the lust for her blood? He curled his hands into fists and stared down at himself. *This isn't who I am. I will not lie with the dead.*

Credan whimpered, and Pravus looked back at him.

Credan still knelt, his eyes bulged, his mouth agape, and his face stark white. His lips moved, but he didn't speak. He didn't need to.

Pravus knew Credan's thoughts because they mirrored his own.

What's become of me?

CHAPTER TWENTY-THREE

The chill of nightfall swept across the wastelands, wiggled its way under Aria's clothes, and caressed her skin like the cold hands of a dead lover. She lay in the cold sand and shivered, but it did little to warm her bones.

Death moves in the darkness.

After the attack by the quad two days prior, Karraar insisted they survive the nights without a fire. She didn't like the idea, but she lacked the mental strength to survive another attack. Instead, she quietly suffered the cold each night until the morning sun rose in the west.

Karraar. The killer, the savior, the servant.

He lay close by; had she been blind, she still would've smelled the filthy beast. He'd offered her his warmth, but short of cutting him open and crawling inside his dead carcass, she'd never allow him to be so close.

You should kill him while he sleeps.

She clutched the knife in her right hand as though it were the sole object in the entire world capable of ensuring her survival. Untrue, but it comforted her nonetheless—more so than the prophecies Pravus spoke of.

Why do you succumb to fear? You are the queen of Centauria. You are the center of all prophecy. You cannot die.

Prophecies could be wrong, couldn't they? And how did Pravus know they spoke of her? Besides, what other paths existed? She needed to read them for herself. However, she'd need to get back to Pravus first.

She hadn't slept well in over a week and hadn't slept at all since the last attack. Every noise, every movement, and every step set her on edge. The shadows watched her and stalked her. Tonight, they would devour her.

Urgency swelled in her gut. She sat up, wide-eyed.

Karraar rolled over and faced her. His yellow eyes glowed in the darkness. "What is it?"

She didn't know where her urgency originated, but her breathing shallowed, and she labored for each breath. Beads of perspiration rolled down her nape and wet her brow.

Aria sprang to her feet. "We must move. Now!"

Karraar stood. "We've been over this, *my queen*. You've been through so much. I don't believe you're in your right mind."

He challenges me?

Her grip tightened on the knife. "You question my sanity? Then leave me. I will find my own way."

Karraar gathered the few items they possessed. "You know I can't do that."

"Leave the shelter," she hissed, and then she sprinted across the sand. She reached the top of the second dune before Karraar caught up with her.

"You're going in the wrong direction," he growled.

Her side ached. She bent over and breathed deeply; the cold air stung her lungs. She still held the knife and pointed it up at him. "Don't you understand? It doesn't matter which direction we go. They're everywhere. We're surrounded."

Karraar looked back the way they'd came and surveyed the landscape.

Aria raced down the backside of the dune and up to the ridge of the next one. Her muscles burned, and her legs weighed her down, but she couldn't stop. If she did, the shadows would swoop in and kill her. She crested the dune and started down the other side. Her foot caught, she fell face-first in the sand, and slid to a stop half-way down.

She rolled onto her back and spat sand from her mouth. Her chest heaved as she labored to catch her breath. Large shadows flying in a v-formation circled overhead, blotting out the stars as they passed by. Karraar emerged on the ridge above her and waved his arms in the air.

What is he doing?

Signaling them! Her heart stopped.

"No!" she screamed, but the sound caught in the back of her throat.

The shadows circled once more and then swooped down toward Karraar. Aria scrambled to her feet and ran as fast as her fatigued legs would carry her. She dared not look back but sensed that the shadows homed in on her and quickly closed the distance. Her lungs burned fiercely, almost as much as her legs.

She balled her fists and realization settled in. *The knife!* She must've dropped it when she fell down the slope. How would she defend herself without a weapon?

You're no queen. Just a foolish little girl.

Karraar shouted her name, but his voice sounded miles away. She crested another dune and started down the other side.

A high shrill screech pierced her ears, and wings beat against the air in a thrum. Claws dug into her sides and lifted her off her feet, and the ground pulled away from her.

Her heart jumped into her throat, and she flailed her arms and legs. "Let go of me!"

Higher they soared, far above the Inferus Wastelands. Below, dunes streaked past and disappeared in a matter of moments. The rush of air chilled her bones and blurred her vision.

Don't let go now. She stopped flailing and grabbed ahold of something bony and sinewy.

Long, black talons of death wrapped her sides and squeezed her ribs. She craned her head to the left but saw nothing more than darkness. Who or what were they, and where were they taking her? Did they have Karraar as well?

Surely Karraar would've fended them off, but why had he signaled them? To save you.

Had Karraar's plan backfired, or had it been his plan all along? How could she have trusted him?

You're a foolish girl.

Rage filled her and took the bite from the cold. *The traitor.*

She closed her eyes and relaxed. The wind caressed her hair, and she gave in to the moment. She'd never thought about flying before, in any capacity. Had she done so, it certainly wouldn't have been so breathtaking. She screamed, releasing the fear that she'd stored up over the last week.

At last, she felt free again. She spread her arms and imagined herself flying. Could she use mezhik to fly? *That's absurd, Aria.*

She opened her eyes again. The dunes of the wastelands were gone. In their wake, a vast sea of giant, grey carcasses covered the ground and reached to the heavens, begging for mercy. The dead forest stretched as far as she could see in every direction.

Earlier that week, Karraar had told her about the Carious Forest, but the images she'd conjured in her mind of how it would have looked paled in comparison and left her without words. Never had she seen so much barren land and decay.

Who would want to live in such a place?

Her mind spun with Karraar's tales of mezhik and war that had scorched the earth and left it uninhabitable. Her mind failed to comprehend the power of such mezhik. *One day, you will wield as much power. Even more.*

Far in the distance, a blotch of black rose from the sea of trees. The ground below streaked by ever faster, and they descended at an alarming velocity. Ahead, the blotch of black grew and took shape.

Black walls rose high above the trees. Spires stretched skyward like fingers reaching up to pluck the stars from the heavens. Ramparts stretched between five towers. The castle grew until its enormity overwhelmed her. She'd never seen a structure so massive; it dwarfed Dragnus's castle a thousand-fold, perhaps even more.

To her right, a great black peak rose high above the castle walls, and its rocky arms nestled the western side of the castle. Her pulse quickened, and butterflies stirred in her stomach's pit. *You. Are. Home.* Excitement welled in her throat, and she screamed, but she cut it short when she looked ahead.

Faster, they streaked through the air like a ball of lightning and headed directly toward one of the massive castle walls. She bit down on her lower lip and drew blood. Her hands trembled.

Five…

Four…

She tensed and prepared for impact, but she refused to close her eyes. *You will be queen.*

Two…

One…

She screamed as they flew through a rectangular opening in the wall and into a massive corridor. She swore the opening hadn't existed until they were right up on it. All details were lost as they sped through the corridor, everything reduced to streaks and blurs of color against a black canvas.

They banked left around a corner they should've crashed into and careened toward a pair of large steel doors. Less than a hundred paces away, she jerked backward and upright, to a halt. Her hair flew forward as a rush of wind hit her back, and the thrum of beating wings filled her ears.

A short, balding man stood fifty paces ahead of her, his back turned toward her. The deathly grip of the talons around her sides relinquished. She dropped three inches to the marbled floor and landed softly on her feet.

A whoosh of wings blew her hair forward again. She spun around, hoping to glimpse the shadow creature that had delivered her, but it had already retreated into the darkness of the corridor and had vanished around a corner.

"Good evening, young one."

She'd already forgotten about the man and hadn't heard him approach. She took a deep breath, put on the face of a queen, and then faced him. "Take me to Pravus."

The man bowed. "In due time. First—"

"Do you not know who I am?" Her hands balled into fists and anger blurred her vision.

The man smiled genuinely. "Oh, I know a great many things about you, Aria Somneri."

His kind, turquoise eyes softened her anger and left her words hollow. "And yet you keep me waiting?"

He reached out and took her dirty, broken-nailed hand in his, lifted it up to his lips as he bent forward, and kissed the back of it. "I am Credan Prestar, curator of Galondu Castle, but you may simply call me Master Credan."

Her cheeks warmed. She withdrew her hand from his and moved it behind her back. "I am... honored to make your acquaintance."

"As I am yours. Now, I know Lord Rosai is at the forefront of your thoughts, but he is detained at the present. He sends his warmest regards and regrets that he cannot meet you this very evening."

Aria raged and stomped her foot. "He regrets that he cannot meet me?

I don't care—"

Credan held up a finger. "He assured me that he would meet you in the dining hall in the morning for breakfast." He pushed his spectacle back up his nose and smiled. "I've been told you've had quite the journey. May I show you to your room? I've taken the liberty of drawing a hot bath for you there."

A bath? Her lower lip quivered. "Yes—" When had she last bathed? In hot water, no less? She couldn't recall. "—Master Credan. That would please me very much."

Credan's eyes brightened. "Wonderful." He swept his arm to the left, toward two open steel doors. "Right this way. Your room's a short distance from here."

She followed Credan through the double doors, up three flights of stone stairs, and onto a large landing. To the right, the landing opened to an expansive balcony, but the night shrouded the view. To the left, two wooden chairs and a wooden bench faced an oversized fireplace. A fire blazed even now, and its warmth licked her frozen cheeks.

Directly ahead stood two massive doors, framed in steel and made of hand-carved wood. A single, black-stemmed rose with petals and thorns stained crimson adorned each door, chiseled deep into the wood.

Credan walked over to the double doors, pushed on the one to the right, and it swung into the room. He motioned for her to enter, but guilt and fear and doubt kept her feet rooted on the landing.

All of this for me? She bit her lip to stifle her misting eyes.

Credan motioned her forward again. "Come, come, my dear. This will function as your bedchamber for now."

She took a step forward. "For now?"

"Yes, of course. Once you've wed Lord Rosai you will move into the royal bedchambers with him. I hope this will suffice until then."

There will be a wedding. She took another step. *Am I truly worthy?* Another step, then another. *Of all the women in the world, he's chosen me.*

She stepped passed Credan, through the open door, and into her new life.

No more running. No more fear.

Her eyes could hardly take in the beauty, the enormity, the royalty of the room.

Her legs quaked; it took every bit of her concentration to stand. Her hands shook at her sides, so she clasped them together. "I believe I can manage from here, Master Credan."

He bowed. "Very good. Brema will be in shortly to take your clothes and bathe you."

"*Bathe* me?" Her mind flashed back to Pigman, One-Eyed Jess, and the others throwing buckets of cold water on her and watching her scoop water into her hands to wash with.

"Yes, my dear. She will be your personal handmaid. She will do everything you require, from bathing to dressing to sewing. Anything you need, whenever you need it."

"Thank you, Master Credan. You're too kind."

"It is not I, but Lord Rosai who's kindness covers you." He bowed again and then pulled the door closed as he exited the room.

Aria fell to her knees and let the tears flow. Her body convulsed with relief. Nothing would ever be the same for her again, and she couldn't have been happier.

A knock at the door came quicker than she'd expected. "One moment." She wiped her eyes and her face with her dirty hands. *I must look like death!*

She stood and composed herself as best she could, given her state. "Enter."

A pale, homely girl not much younger than her entered the chamber and closed the door behind her. She walked up to Aria and curtsied. "Mistress Aria, I am Brema. I look forward to serving you." The girl had a thick accent, and Aria couldn't place its origin.

Aria had no idea what to say to the girl. How would a queen address her servant? *You'll learn with time.* "And I look forward to your service, Brema."

Brema clasped her hands. "May I help you out of your clothes and into the bath?"

Aria nodded, confident her voice would squeal with excitement were she to respond vocally.

Aria turned around and faced the four-poster bed. Red and deep-pink curtains hung from its black canopy, tied back against its four posts. Aria glimpsed herself in a full-length mirror to the left of the bed. A haggard young woman stared back at her and took her breath away.

Orange streaks ran the length of her, including her hair and face. The yellow dress she'd been so proud of hung crooked on her shoulders. A large rip crossed its midriff, its front soiled with orange sand and dried, greyish-black nōmed blood, and its last foot torn away, leaving a tattered edge at mid-thigh. Its missing length wrapped her thigh where the nōmed's hatchet had sliced her.

At her back, Brema worked for several minutes unhooking and unlacing the dress. Finally, the dress slid from Aria's shoulders and into a pile around her. Her once-white undergarments now had an orange hue. She imagined how bad she must smell, and embarrassment warmed her cheeks.

"Forgive me, Brema. I've been in the wastelands for more than a week, and they've attached themselves to me. You will not find me in such a state again."

Brema looked over her shoulder and met her gaze in the mirror. "Do not worry yourself, Mistress Aria. I've lived in poverty most my life and have become immune to the smells of the body."

Aria hardened her gaze. "None of this will leave these chambers."

Brema's cheeks blossomed. "Never! May Ɂäʈūr strike me down should I ever open my lips with gossip."

Aria nodded. "Good."

Brema unlaced Aria's bodice, and it peeled away from Aria's skin like an onion layer and fell at her feet. Deep lines pressed into the tops of Aria's breasts, around the sides of her ribcage, and around her hips. Brema pulled Aria's underwear down to her ankles and Aria stepped out of them and the mounded dress.

Aria pointed at the discarded clothes. "Burn those."

Brema nodded. "As you wish."

Brema took Aria's hand. "This way." She led Aria over to a rectangular-shaped, steel tub that sat next to the fire.

Brema held Aria's hand as Aria carefully lifted her wounded leg over the tub's edge. She dipped her toes into the hot water and it stung her flesh. She winced.

Brema gasped. "Is it too hot, Mistress Aria? I'm so sorry."

Aria shook her head. She set her jaw, plunged her entire leg into the water, and then lifted her other leg over the tub's edge and thrust it into the water as well. The water made her legs ache into her marrow, and nothing had felt so good in a long time.

Brema helped her settle into the tub; the water stopped mid-breast.

Brema released Aria's hand and knelt by the tub. "Allow me to remove the dressing from your wound before you lie back. Then, once you've finished bathing, I'll re-dress it."

Aria nodded and leaned forward. Brema made quick work of the dressing and Aria leaned all the way back and slid down until the water rested on her chin. A faint aroma of rotten eggs rose from the water. Aria wrinkled her nose.

Brema moved around to the front of the tub. "I've added several minerals to the water to help you relax and help your skin heal. Once you've soaked for a while, I'll come back in, wash your hair, and scrub you down. Then I'll replace the water, and you can soak some more."

Aria smiled, closed her eyes, and sank all the way underneath the water.

You will be queen.

CHAPTER TWENTY-FOUR

Rakzar stood at the cliff's edge. Amicus, Eshtak, Urza, Wibble, and Yetch flanked him. The valley below lay empty and peaceful. No signs of a recent camp existed.

Damn! Rakzar paced along the cliff's edge. "How could a horde that size move so quickly? A few hours… it just isn't possible."

Urza sniffed the air. "Something's not right. Orcs are incapable of being clean. We should still be able to smell their filth, but it's as though they were never down there at all."

Where have you gone, Murtag?

Rakzar stopped beside Urza. She reached over and touched his front paw with hers and let it linger there for several moments. He shot daggers at her with his glare. *Relentless.*

Amicus came up from behind and stood to his left. "I can't see anything. I wish I had the vision you all have."

Rakzar growled. "We need to get down there and figure out where they've gone."

Wibble squeezed between Rakzar and Urza. "What's the rush?"

Rakzar clenched his jaw. *I hate him. I trust him about as much as Murtag.*

He moved closer to Amicus and fought the urge to shove Wibble over the cliff's edge. He might've read her wrong, but he sensed Urza would be okay with Wibble's death too.

Rakzar glanced at Urza. "An urgent message. What's it to you?"

Wibble pointed to the east, his left. "Several miles over, there's a narrow switchback trail that leads to the valley floor. You'd completely miss it if you didn't know it was there."

Rakzar looked that way and then turned his gaze to the valley floor below.

"Oh yeah. That's a good one. Came up it earlier." Yetch kicked a rock. It rolled over the cliff's edge, dropped about a foot, and then disappeared entirely.

Rakzar shook his head and blinked. He looked at Amicus. "Did you see that?"

Amicus squinted into the darkness. "As I said, I can't see anything."

Urza knelt. "The rock Yetch kicked—it vanished." She swiped at the air.

Yetch snorted and scratched his neck. "Well it's dark. Long way down too. Good place to rid yourself of someone you don't like, ain't it Wibble?"

Rakzar glanced over at Yetch. *Was that a threat, you flea-ridden sack?*

Wibble smacked Yetch on the back of the head. "Shut yer yap and kick another rock over the edge. Or would you rather I threw you over?"

"Off a cliff, anyone can fly—" Yetch made a whistling noise. "—all the way to the ground. It's the landing that's tough to stick."

Wibble swatted at Yetch again, but Yetch ducked out of the way. "Kick the damn rock."

Rakzar, Amicus, and Wibble knelt next to the cliff's edge, and then Yetch kicked another rock over it. Again, the rock fell about a foot and then disappeared.

Amicus whistled softly. "I saw it that time. What does it mean?"

"Eshtak likes games. Eshtak can play?"

The five of them turned around simultaneously. Amicus stood. "Where've you been, Eshtak?"

Eshtak pointed to the south. "Eshtak watch very bad things. Eshtak not like them. Very bad things make women and children unhappy. Make Eshtak unhappy."

"The orcs?" Rakzar moved forward.

Eshtak nodded vigorously and then twirled in circles.

Rakzar placed his hand on Eshtak's head and forced him to stand still. "Where did you see them, little man?"

Eshtak pointed at the valley.

He let go of Eshtak's head and glanced back toward the valley. "You saw them earlier?"

Eshtak hopped from one foot to the other. "Eshtak still sees."

Yetch scratched the back of his ear. "And you think *I'm* crazy, Wibble."

"Mezhik," said Amicus. "Eshtak's immune to its effects. He's seen things before that I couldn't because mezhik blocked my vision."

Wibble stood and unwound the wire around his hand. "Didn't think the little shrimp could get much weirder. Would've lost that bet."

Yetch snorted. "Still funny, because he's short."

"Mezhik?" said Rakzar. "Impossible. Orcs are incapable of wielding such things, as are we."

Yetch scratched both of his armpits simultaneously. "It's true, but they don't need to. They've got wizards with them."

Wibble glared at him. "Don't be stupid. You wouldn't know a wizard from an orc."

"Oh yes I would! I've seen them both. Two women dressed in red robes a few sizes too big. Kind of funny now that I think about it. Why would you wear clothes that are too big? Maybe they both have older sisters who are bigger than them and just borrowed the robes. Or maybe they were bigger once and shrank with old age. But they don't look so old—"

Wibble backhanded Yetch square in the chest. "Stop talking, or I'll throw you over. Not gonna warn you again."

Rakzar narrowed his eyes. *Those two have something planned, but what?*

Amicus rubbed the back of his neck. "I don't think going down there's a good idea."

Rakzar glared at Amicus. "There's no backing out, wizards or not. We have a message to deliver."

Amicus's eyes widened, and his eyebrows rose. "Hey, I'm not saying we *never* go down there. Just not until we find out where Murtag will be."

Yetch thrust his arms in the air and stomped away from the group. "Nobody ever asks me anything." In a higher voice, he mocked, "'Hey Yetch, you wouldn't happen to know where Murtag is, would you?'"

Then, in a normal voice again, he said, "'As a matter of fact, I do. At the far eastern edge of the valley there's a narrow opening in the cliff wall that leads into a rather large cave. The opening is concealed by some large boulders. Murtag retreats to the cave every evening. Calls it his super-secret hideout cave.'"

Rakzar shook his head. *How has he survived this long? I would've killed him long ago.*

Amicus turned toward Yetch. "Is that really true? He retreats to a cave?"

Yetch circled back. "Oh, you were listening? Well, I may have embellished a bit. Really not sure what he calls the cave, if anything. If it were mine, *I'd* call it my super-secret hideout cave. Always wanted one of them. I'd stay in there forever, and nobody would ever find me again."

And the world would be better for it.

Eshtak laughed and twirled in circles. "Eshtak has hideout cave. Eshtak loves cave."

Yetch bent down to Eshtak's level. "Can I see it sometime?"

Eshtak stopped, frowned, and shook his head vigorously. "Eshtak's hideout cave. No bad things allowed."

Rakzar faced Wibble. Even though Wibble smiled smugly, hate spilled from his murderous eyes. *This isn't going to end well for one of us.* Instinct begged Rakzar to part ways, but he knew doing so might be worse. *Keep your enemies close.*

No more games. This ends tonight.

"Get us down there." Rakzar headed east. "I must see Murtag before morning's light."

Urza caught up with Rakzar and grabbed his arm. Her claws dug into his fur. She looked back and then leaned in close. "Must you see Murtag?"

Rakzar glared at her hand. "Nothing will stop me."

She nodded. "Be careful, and trust no one. Murtag knows you're coming."

Why would she warn me? Did she harbor genuine attraction for him? *Or is she the one I should really be watching?*

Trust no one. He never had before, but everything hinged on Amicus. *Can I trust him?* What choice did he have? *None.*

† † †

Wibble insisted they stood at the start of the trail-head but fear blinded Amicus. Its suffocating grip immobilized him too. *Am I the only sane one?* "That's not a trail. It's a death sentence. There must be another way down."

Rakzar grabbed Amicus by the front of his shirt and shook him. Hate seeped from Rakzar's eyes, but not for him. "There's no time to find another way. We must do this tonight." Rakzar released him with an added push.

Amicus peered over the edge and into the perfect darkness. *Dear Ƨätūr, protect us all.* He raised his arms. "Fine, but if I fall my death is on you."

Rakzar leaned close, and his rancid breath nearly surrendered Amicus's dinner. "Our plan only works if you're alive, so make sure you *don't* fall. I'll kill you myself if you do."

Our plan? Amicus looked up at the night sky. *Is this Your plan, Ƨätūr? I pray it is.* It certainly didn't sit right with him.

Rakzar glanced at the others. "Wibble, Yetch, and Urza will lead the way. You'll follow them, and Eshtak and I will follow you."

"No," said Amicus. "I'll go last, and Eshtak will stay up here."

Eshtak bounced up and down on his toes. "Eshtak goes too. Eshtak help friends."

Amicus knelt. "You have the most important job of all, Eshtak. Keep watch from up here. If something goes wrong, run and find Zerenity. She'll know what to do."

Eshtak stilled, and his head drooped. "Eshtak needs friend."

He rubbed Eshtak's bald head. *I need you too.* "I swear we'll be back before you can count to ten thousand."

"Let's go," growled Rakzar.

Eshtak wrapped his arms around Amicus's ribcage and squeezed. "Friend be safe."

Amicus hugged him back. "You too. Use the cloak if you need to hide."

Eshtak's arms slumped to his sides, and he backed away from the cliff.

Wibble circled behind them. "Oh, there's no goodbyes here. The little shrimp comes too."

Now I know this isn't Your plan, Ƨätūr.

Urza stepped into the middle of their hostile circle. "He's not a part of this, Wibble. Leave him be."

Wibble swung his wire in one hand. "All of us, or none of us. Take your pick."

Yetch joined them. "Do I get to pick? I say all of us." He scratched his side.

Eshtak looked up at Amicus. "Eshtak comes. Eshtak will not run away."

Do what You will with me, Ƶäţūr, but keep him safe.

Amicus sighed. "It's settled then."

Urza and Yetch descended into the darkness and then disappeared below the shroud of mezhik.

"I'll take the rear," said Wibble. "Make sure no one gets lost on the way down."

Amicus glared at Wibble one last time and then turned his attention to Eshtak. "You go ahead of us, Eshtak."

Eshtak nodded, bounced from one foot to the other, and then bounded down the path and into the darkness.

Amicus took a deep breath. *Ƶäţūr, keep my feet firmly underneath me and my thoughts on You and my family.*

Rakzar went down next, and Amicus followed right behind. The switchback trail proved treacherous; twice, he lost his footing and nearly fell. Both times, Wibble growled with laughter and cheered for his demise. If Rakzar hadn't grabbed his arm the second time, Amicus would've fallen to his death.

Safely on the valley floor, Amicus bent down and kissed the ground. He glanced back at the cliff wall. From where he knelt, he couldn't see the top. *Never doing that again.*

He stood and looked across the flat valley floor. Miles ahead, bonfires lit the sprawling camp. Virtually nothing lay between them and the orcs; the horde had long since trampled the vegetation or ripped it from the ground.

Amicus joined the others. "How are we going to do this? We've got no cover. They'll see us coming before we even get close."

Wibble looked at him crosswise. "See us coming? You said that as though you're plotting an attack. Are you?"

Rakzar pushed Amicus forward. "Come on." He turned to Wibble. "He's never been around orcs before. He's just a bit edgy."

The orcs' stench intensified with every mile. By the time they reached the edge of the camp, he tasted it. *How do they live with themselves? Do they ever bathe?*

Drums, laughter, grunting, and screams intermixed and created a mild roar across the camp. Females of many species danced around the fires, wearing little more than the chains that hung from their necks. A few males were strapped to boards, and other orcs took turns aimlessly throwing hatchets at them.

Amicus cringed. *I think I see Your plan now, Ɂäṭūr. Therefore, we're doing what must be done. As cruel as the deaths of Vonah and Vorene were, I'd wish it upon them a thousand times over rather than the fate that faces those here.*

They headed east, skirting the northern fringe of the camp until they reached the far cliffs. From there, they had no choice but to walk through the camp. A few of the orcs glanced their way, and others barked obscenities and made lewd gestures, but none made a move to stop or question them.

Tension rose in Amicus's chest and his pulse raced. *Something's not right. This feels too easy.*

Amicus stopped, but Urza pushed him forward. "Keep moving. We're almost there."

"Wait," he said.

Rakzar glared at Amicus and got in his face. "What's your problem?"

Amicus whispered, "What if we're walking right into a trap?"

Rakzar's eyes shifted about, and he lowered his voice. "This isn't the hard part. Getting out alive will be."

Yetch came over to them. He scratched his left ear vigorously, and his eyes narrowed. "To the east. Those three boulders next to the cliff conceal the cave's entrance. You'll find Murtag in there. I'm sure of it." He winked and backed away.

"Go quickly," said Urza. "The rest of us will wait here."

Amicus gasped. "You expect Rakzar and me to go in there alone?"

Wibble unwound the wire around his hand and swung it by one end. "You're the ones who have urgent business with Murtag, not us. What's the problem?"

Yetch scratched behind his ear. "Yeah, life's good out here. I like life."

I can't do this. It's not right.

Amicus turned back, but Rakzar grabbed his arm and pulled him toward the boulders. "You're stalling, and I've had enough of it."

Amicus yanked his arm away and stopped. "You may be used to this kind of thing, but I'm not. I can't just traipse in there. I need to clear my head."

Rakzar glared at him. "Make it quick, then. My patience runs thin."

Amicus knelt and cleared his mind. He thought of Vorene and Vonah and the death they'd suffered, and he drew strength from it.

Ǯäṭūr, I give You my life. If it's Your will, guide my hand that I may strike quickly.

He stood and looked at Eshtak. "We'll be back in a few minutes."

Eshtak looked around. "Eshtak comes too?"

He rubbed Eshtak's bald head. "I'm sorry, my friend, but you must stay here with the others. Rakzar and I must speak with Murtag alone."

Eshtak nodded solemnly. Moisture glinted in his eyes. "Eshtak see friend soon?"

Does he sense something bad? The notion roused Amicus's fear further.

He turned and followed Rakzar over to the boulders and around them. Two orcs stood in front of the cave's entrance. Clubs, hatchets, and knives hung from their belts.

Amicus swallowed hard. *I don't think I can kill one of them, let alone three.*

The orc on the right snarled. "Where do ya an yer pet think yer headed, dog?"

Rakzar towered over them. "Get out of our way. We have a message for Murtag."

"Message is it?" The orc on the left snorted a string of snot back into his porcine nose. "Nobody got no message fer Murtag 'less we say."

The orc on the right crossed his arms. "An we don' say."

Amicus motioned for Rakzar to leave, but he either didn't get the hint or simply ignored him. "Fine. One of you go tell Murtag that Rakzar's here to see him. See what he says then."

The two orcs glanced at each other.

"Rakzar, he says," said the orc on the left.

"Rakzar," confirmed the other.

The two orcs stepped aside. "He's expecting ya," they said simultaneously.

Amicus tensed. *Expecting us?*

He stood there, hoping Rakzar would understand they'd been set up, but Rakzar forced him inside the passage. For a moment, darkness enveloped them, but then a faint light rose from the darkness deep within the passage.

His heart thumped. Sweat beaded his brow, and his mouth became so dry he couldn't swallow. *Turn around. There's still time.*

Courage eluded him. He hissed, "Let's get out of here. We're walking into a trap."

Only Rakzar's eyes glowed against the shadow of his form. "Trap or not, we're finishing this. For both of us. You have a debt to pay, and I'm calling it due."

Amicus sighed. *Strengthen me, Ɛäṭūr.*

He quietly slid his broadsword from its scabbard and nodded. Death hung in the passage like a putrid fog as they moved toward the light. The sound of chanting grew louder as they neared, but Amicus couldn't make out the words or perhaps the language.

How did I get myself into this?

Amicus stopped and lowered his sword. "I can't do this, Rakzar. It's not right."

Rakzar drew close. "Tell that to your wife and your little girl. Let them know your cowardice allowed their deaths to go unavenged. Is that what you want? And how about all the people in your village as well? I'm sure Murtag listened to *their* cries and showed *them* mercy."

"I swore justice, not vengeance. If I do this, how am I better than him?"

"And what about the White Knight's sister? Didn't you kill one of the men that abused her?"

Amicus opened his mouth, but words eluded him. How was it different? He took a life to save another. How many lives would he save by taking Murtag's? Did Vonah and Vorene matter less to him than Aria had? *No! They were so much more.*

Ɛäṭūr, You know my heart. I must avenge them.

He raised his sword back up and nodded. *For all of them.*

As they neared the rear of the passage, Amicus noticed that a light came from an opening to the left. He and Rakzar cautiously peered around the corner. A natural opening, about thirty yards wide and ninety yards deep, lay before them. Its sheer walls rose into the night sky.

Torches set on poles lined the jagged rock walls every ten feet. Red flags with a silver crescent moon at their centers hung from the poles. Two hooded figures in red robes stood toward the far end of the opening with their backs toward Amicus and Rakzar.

The wizards? He looked at Rakzar with wide eyes, but Rakzar had his gaze locked on a third figure.

The third figure knelt between and behind the other two, twice their girth and looked to be more than a foot taller. Red hair, twisted in crude braids, hung down his back. Thick scars marred his dark, drab olive skin. He wore nothing but an ivory loincloth.

Amicus retreated into the passage. Rakzar followed. "Murtag's not alone. Those other two must be the wizards Yetch spoke of. I'm not sure what they're doing."

Rakzar looked back through the opening. "They're worshiping their moon god, *Ɛin*. We go now, as quietly as possible."

"This is suicide!"

Rakzar glanced back and put a furry finger to his lips. "You take care of Murtag, and I'll do the rest."

Amicus exhaled. *There is no reasoning with him. Ɛäṭūr, guide my sword.*

He nodded, and they entered the opening. His heart thundered, and fear nearly immobilized him. The distance between them and their targets shrank as his anxiety grew; ninety yards became thirty.

Think of Vonah. No fear.

They tiptoed up the center of the opening, directly behind Murtag. The chanting continued, and Murtag didn't move. *Twenty feet to go. We have a chance.* Rakzar pulled his battle-axes from his back, ready to strike the two wizards. Amicus focused on Murtag.

Guide me.

Ten feet and closing. Amicus raised his sword, lunged forward, and sliced through Murtag's thick neck with a single blow; Murtag's large head toppled to the ground, along with the ends of his severed red braids.

Rakzar swept around Amicus like a red-haired demon and buried an axe in the side of each wizard's skull before they had a chance to react. The chanting ceased, and they collapsed to the ground without as much as a grunt.

Thank You, Ẑäṭūr.

Amicus exhaled forcefully. "That went as well as could be expected."

"Did it?" The harsh, slurred voice came from Murtag's severed head.

Amicus jumped back and dropped his sword.

Rakzar kicked the head. "What kind of mezhik is this?"

The three bodies melted into the ground and the torch flames burned bright red. Twenty feet back, Murtag emerged from the shadows. The two red-robed wizards flanked him. They'd seemingly stepped out of nowhere.

Wibble approached from the back of the opening. He carried a five-bladed mace with him.

Amicus fell to his knees, anguished. *Ẑäṭūr, what have I done? Your way isn't to kill, is it?*

Murtag crossed his arms. "Did you really think your pathetic plan would work?"

Wibble stood behind Murtag. "I told you they'd trust us once we killed Borsha and Xerp."

How did they know we were coming?

Rakzar stepped forward. "Why didn't you have them kill us when they had the chance?"

Murtag snarled, "Death's too good for a dog like you, but you respond well to humiliation. I think you'll appreciate what I've prepared for you."

Rakzar stepped closer. "Let Amicus go and do what you want with me. I forced him into this."

Murtag looked to his left and then his right. "Ladies, you know what to do."

The two wizards removed their hoods. Each had only half of a silver face, one the left and the other the right. The other sides of their heads were missing. They moved like two shadows, continuously merging and separating from each other as they approached.

Dear Ẑäṭūr, what are they?

Rakzar retreated. "You're no wizards!"

"We are *Käíeƨ*." They swept past Amicus in a blur.

Amicus twisted around, mesmerized by the way they moved. They step into the same space Rakzar occupied, and then they vanished. Rakzar slid backward across the floor and slammed into the stone altar.

Rakzar roared and tore at his armor. "Get them off me!"

Amicus sat back on his feet and trembled. "What in the name of ƹäţūr are they? And what are they doing to him?"

Murtag walked over to Amicus and bent down to his level. A long tendril of thick, yellow mucus hung from his porcine nose. "If you're not a believer in damnation, they'll change your mind. You cannot possibly fathom the level of pain and anguish they're capable of inflicting with a single touch. Imagine them inside your mind—they'll blacken your soul. If you'd like, I'll have them show you."

Amicus glanced back at Rakzar and shuddered. "You're a monster."

Murtag laughed. "Perhaps." He wiped the tendril of mucus from his nose and flung it aside. "Why would you want to kill me? Do you know me?"

Do I know you?

Anger filled Amicus and renewed his strength. He stood tall. "Maybe not, but I know of you. You're a monster. You killed my wife and my little girl."

Murtag stood and looked him in the eye. "And what of it?"

Tremors of rage shook Amicus. "You burned them alive!"

Murtag's cold blue eyes held him hostage. "I'm certain they received what they deserved."

"How dare you!"

Amicus lunged at Murtag, but Murtag sidestepped and used Amicus's momentum to throw him to the ground. The air expelled from his lungs, and he gasped. He scrambled back to his feet.

Behind Murtag, Rakzar tore at himself and raged at nothing. *Hang on, Rakzar.*

Murtag sneered. "Pick up your sword, scrawny man. You've no chance without it."

He and Murtag circled until his sword lay before him. He cautiously bent down and picked it up, keeping his eyes on Murtag. Murtag turned, and Wibble tossed him the five-bladed mace.

Murtag flexed his oversized muscles and swung the mace in a wide arc. It cut through the space between him and Amicus with a *whoosh*. He motioned Amicus forward with a finger.

Even if I fail, at least I tried. The ashes of his family drove Amicus forward.

Every swing of Amicus's blade met the steel of Murtag's mace with a *clank*. Each blow rattled and vibrated through his hands and up his arms until they numbed. He'd drive Murtag back a few steps, but then he'd be driven right back where he'd started.

Rakzar's roars anguished Amicus, but he could do nothing for him but continue to fight. Fatigue quickly set in as he swung the large broadsword repeatedly. His chest heaved as he sucked in air, his lungs on fire and unable to keep up with his furious pace.

His heart thundered. Amicus retreated, and Murtag didn't pursue. *Am I tiring him out?*

Sweat poured from them both in rivulets.

They circled once more.

Vonah and Vorene rose in his memory, holding each other in horrified misery. Flames licked them and burned them, and they screamed. He reached for their greyish-black forms, and they crumbled into a pile of ash.

Their screams strengthened his resolve. *Vengeance is mine!*

Amicus lunged forward and attacked with renewed strength. Three jarring blows drove Murtag back, and the fourth ripped the mace from Murtag's hands. It hit the ground with a soft *thud*. Amicus continued his swing all the way around for a second blow. Murtag anticipated it and dodged to the side, but Amicus's blade caught Murtag's shoulder and sliced through it.

Murtag stumbled and dropped to the ground. Amicus raised the sword over his head, hilt back and blade up in front of him, ready to drive it into Murtag's bare chest. He glanced at Rakzar, who still struggled against an invisible foe.

For the fallen!

"Now!" yelled Murtag.

Amicus brought the sword forward with all the strength he had left, but something caught him around the throat, bit into his skin, and pulled him backward. The sword landed short of Murtag's spread legs and jarred loose from his hands.

Confusion strangled him. *What's happening?*

Wibble's hateful eyes came into view over the top of his head. "I've waited all evening to do this."

How could he have forgotten about Wibble? *Diⱬäfär blinded me with rage.* He reached for the wire as it tightened further.

Wibble stepped back, and Amicus's feet slipped from under him. "No!"

Wibble pulled his arms across his own body with a grunt.

The pain lasted momentarily as the wire slid right through Amicus's neck: flesh, bone, arteries, muscles. Amicus gasped for air but couldn't breathe. He screamed, but it only sounded in his mind. His head tilted forward, and he watched his headless body hit the floor.

Forgive me, Rakzar.

Rakzar's roar faded from his ears and left him in deafening silence. Halos and stars circled the red flames of the torches. His head twisted in the air, held up by Wibble's hand. His vision blurred, dimmed, and then the darkness swept in.

Daddy's coming for you, Vonah.

† † †

Kãíeⱬ filled Rakzar's mind. *"See what you've done to him? What kind of friend are you? You've killed him. How many have died because of you? How many more? Too many to count."*

"Get out of my head!" Rakzar struggled to get up, but something held him down.

"We are one with you now. Tell us your darkest secrets. Let us in."

"You won't get anything from me!"

"Who is this White Knight? Someone close to you? They'll die too, just like all the rest of them."

Rakzar roared, and their presence retracted from his mind.

"Remove the hood."

Murtag.

The hood slipped off his head, and the burst of light from the bonfires stung his eyes. His surroundings slowly came into focus. He lay face-up on the ground, stripped of his weapons, armor, and dignity. Ropes staked to the ground held his arms and legs down.

Amicus's severed head hung over him on a pike, still dripping with blood. Anguish crashed down on him like a smith's hammer. *I'm sorry, Amicus. I brought this on you.* Vomit hung in Rakzar's throat and choked him. He swallowed it back down.

Urza stood over him, one knife in hand. *Traitorous bitch!* Apart from Murtag and Wibble, he'd never hated anyone more than her.

He looked around as best he could but didn't see Eshtak anywhere. *I hope you escaped, little man.*

Wibble and Yetch stood on either side of him, their jaws dripping with saliva. *Bastards.*

"Shave him," shouted Murtag.

"Shave him! Shave him!" chanted the horde.

"With pleasure," said Urza.

She bent down, grabbed a fistful of red fur from his chest, and cut it away with her knife. She stood, held it up for the horde to see, and then threw the fur in the air. The horde cheered with venomous hate.

Murtag snarled, "Remove it all, and make sure you leave him bloody. But keep him alive, Urza."

Urza straddled Rakzar's stomach. She yelled over the noisy crowd, "I've been known to get a bit wild with my knives. I sure hope you put up a fight."

Rakzar spat at Urza. "Do your worst."

"Alive," repeated Murtag. "I know your reputation."

She backhanded Rakzar, and then had both knives in her hands a second later. She raked the blades across his chest. They left bald spots in their wake. She pushed harder on the next swipe and left bloody streaks behind.

She stabbed him in the gut with one of the knives and twisted the blade.

Rakzar ground his teeth but refused to give her the pleasure of hearing him roar. *You're dead if I survive this.*

She worked her way around his torso with the other knife, leaving his flesh bloodied and raw.

An hour later, she finished the hack job, leaving a few tufts of fur here and there. She pulled the knife from his gut and licked the blood off the blade. She stood and ground her heel into his wound. Rakzar twisted and writhed. Urza walked away and disappeared into the horde.

Wibble and Yetch pulled the stakes up that held Rakzar's arms down and yanked him to his feet. Rakzar pressed his paw against the seeping wound in his gut.

The horde surrounded him for miles—beyond his blurred vision.

Murtag stood in front of him, his icy-blue eyes burning with hatred. He grabbed Rakzar's left wrist and raised his arm in the air. "I give you the *mighty* Rakzar."

The horde leered at him and booed and hissed.

"Kill him!" they yelled.

"Death is too good for him." Murtag released his wrist. "Brand him with the sickle."

A hush fell over the horde as word of Murtag's order passed through their ranks.

The sickle? He'd never heard of such a thing. How horrible could it be?

"That's your great plan, shaving me and branding me? Fur grows back, and a brand is nothing more than a flesh wound."

Murtag wiped snot from his nose with the back of his hand. "Oh, this brand is like none you've ever seen. In fact, you won't even see it. It binds to your soul like a plague and slowly kills those around you.

"It'll be your choice as to whether you want to live alone or watch those you care about die a slow, agonizing death. Once infected, your absence will not stop the sickness from running its course. And, even better, it also prevents you from killing yourself."

Rakzar snarled, "Then I'll just hang around here and watch you all die."

One side of Murtag's upper lip rose, and his nose wrinkled. "Oh, I should add that it has no effect on the blood-bound either."

Rakzar's mind reeled as understanding settled in. His stomach lurched, and its contents rose into his throat, burst from his mouth, and splattered when it hit the ground at his feet. He spat the acidic taste from his mouth.

Rakzar thought about the White Knight, the dryte, and Amicus. One thing the three of them shared was an unyielding faith in their God, Ɛätūr. He need help, and he had nowhere else to turn.

I don't know You, Ɂäţūr, but I call on Your name. If I have one, have mercy on my soul. Strike me dead before I send more innocent lives Your way.

Fear rose in him with a vengeance and shook his core. "Don't do this, Murtag. I beg you. Show me mercy. Let Wibble or Yetch kill me."

The two in red known as Käíeᴢ slithered through the ranks of orcs and flanked Murtag. Quietly at first, and then with a deafening roar, the horde chanted, "Sickle! Sickle! Sickle!"

Murtag held his fist in the air until the horde quieted. "You should've known better than to try and kill me. You've brought this upon yourself." He stepped back.

Wibble and Yetch forced Rakzar to his knees and stretched his arms wide with the ropes. Käíeᴢ merged into a single form, removed their hood, and then grabbed the sides of Rakzar's head. Their black eyes turned red, and then silver sickles formed in their centers.

"Please don't," begged Rakzar. "Wibble, Yetch—as brothers, have mercy on me!"

"You're no brother of ours," Wibble said.

"Yeah, we've got different mothers," said Yetch. "But you already knew that."

Käíeᴢ pushed its fingers into his skull. The raw pain paralyzed him. Their words slithered into his mind, *"Būfnd bí dädh."*

The world around him spun and then stopped in front of the pike that held Amicus's severed head. Amicus's eyes opened. They brimmed with anguish. His lips moved, and his words echoed into infinity, "Why did you do this to me? I told you we would fail."

I'm sorry. I'm sorry.

Red eyes of death pulled Rakzar into the depths.

CHAPTER TWENTY-FIVE

Savric stood just inside the open door of the cottage and watched the rain pour. Water streamed from the pitched roof and formed rivulets that converged and ran across the stone path. A frenzy of lightning lit the night sky, the heavens rumbled, and the ground quaked.

Daltura slept, ignorant of the approaching war. Savric's stomach groaned, but not for lack of sustenance. *I am an old man, Ɂäṯūr. Will I see this conflict through?*

He closed the door and leaned against it for a few beats to gather his thoughts. How would they convince King Zaridus that the threat of war loomed on the horizon? Not only did they need proof to present to the king, but they also needed a way to gain an audience with him.

Savric snapped his fingers. "Yes, of course, *Däí Räknƨiǝllääíƨzhn.*"

King Zaridus prided himself on keeping with the ancient traditions of kings, and tomorrow would be no exception for the crown. In the Ancient Realm, the first day of a new moon brought with it Däí Räknƨiǝllääíƨzhn, a day set aside for the common folk to bring their concerns and disputes to the king to be reconciled.

A new moon would rise on the morn. *We must be there.*

Qotan's condition worsened daily. Already, he no longer walked without his staff and limped excessively, and the infection crept up his leg and would soon threaten his life.

How will he endure a trip to the Three Kingdoms? Several hundred miles of travel... and through the Orbis Mountains, no less.

Savric pulled at the ends of his beard. *I cannot manage this alone. He must come, no matter the cost.*

"Come sit by the fire, brother." Qotan's frail voice tugged at Savric's heart.

Please Zäṭūr, do not let him slip away from me. He is all I have. He wiped his eyes and walked over by the fire.

A wool blanket wrapped Qotan's legs, and a shawl draped over his shoulders, yet he shook with chills. Savric lay his hand on Qotan's forehead; his fever still raged.

Savric reached out and his chair screeched across the wooden planks and then stopped next to Qotan's rocker. He settled into the oversized chair; his bones groaned and creaked like an old, squeaky floor.

He placed his hand over Qotan's, little more than bones wrapped in thin skin. "Whatever am I to do with you?"

Qotan rubbed his chin. Pain filled his green eyes, but their sparkle remained. "I daresay I would be of little use as fertilizer."

Savric patted Qotan's hand. "Never sell yourself short. The ground would open wide and welcome you just as it welcomes sunshine on a cool, spring day."

Qotan set the rocker in motion with his feet. "You are too kind, brother. However, we will know soon enough. I fear my demise approaches."

"With Reni's help, we will find a path through this. After all, she is *Fizärd Näíṭezhär*, is she not?"

"You say wizard, I say sorceress. However, I have tried every spell, potion, and incantation I know, and the advice Zerenity gave you has proven fruitless as well. Nothing has made a positive effect. Those vines come from something beyond nature. They are evil."

Savric reached out toward the bookcase. A leather-bound book pulled itself off the shelf, floated across the room, and settled in his outstretched hand. He sat the book in his lap and waved his hand over its cover. "*In əlliṭ Hiz.*"

He opened the book to the first page, pulled a fountain pen from a pocket within his robes, and wrote a message to Rayah: *'Tell Reni that Qotan and I will meet you all at her house in a few days. Right now, we must attend to urgent business in the Three Kingdoms. -Savric'*

He tapped the page with the tip of the pen and the words faded. He returned the pen to his pocket, closed the book, and then tossed the book toward the bookcase. The book righted itself and slid back onto the shelf where it'd come from.

He sat back and rubbed his temples. "Tomorrow marks the new moon. Despite your condition, we must travel to see King Zaridus. Nothing is more important."

Qotan closed his eyes and rocked in the chair. "Travel may very well be the death of me, brother."

Savric eyed Qotan intently. His pale skin looked translucent in the firelight.

You are but a spectre of the man I knew, but I refuse to lose you. Ɂäṯūr will show us the answer. He must.

Savric stroked his beard and mulled over their options. He could think of none that wouldn't involve Qotan in some capacity. "I know you are weak, but I cannot go alone. We must show him what is happening to you, show him the plant that did this to you, inform him of the desolated villages and of the destruction of Castle Portador Tempestade, and advise him on the unfolding prophecy."

Qotan licked his lips and nodded. "I will accompany you to the Three Kingdoms but harbor no expectations of my return to Daltura. The effort will surely take my life."

Savric's eyes misted. "I would never request it of you if another way existed. I would willingly take your place at death's door if Ɂäṯūr would allow it."

Qotan nodded again. "I know, brother. Fear not, though, the completeness of my life could be no greater than it is in this moment. Your love and kindness have outgrown my expectations by lengths beyond measure."

Savric choked back an onslaught of emotions. "Your words are too kind, and, as much as I would like to sit here and talk with you until we expire, I must prepare for our journey."

Qotan opened his eyes and placed his hand on Savric's. "I do have one condition you must agree to before we begin this last endeavor."

Savric's eyes watered, and he looked to the fire. *Will this be our last adventure?* He swallowed hard. "If it is within my power, I will do anything, brother."

"When I transition from this life into the next, you must move. I know how much you care for Zerenity and she for you. Promise me you will make amends with her and finish out your lives together."

Savric pulled his hand away and stood. "Feathers! That woman is confounding. She will never see beyond the end of her pointed nose. Ɛätūr knows I have tried to make her see the error in her judgment and how she has mistreated you, but her complete dismissal of your existence exceeds reason."

He paced in front of the fire. "I fear our relations are beyond repair." He stopped in front of Qotan and thrust his hands in the air. "How can you ask this of me? You, of all people?"

Qotan tightened the shawl around himself. "The disagreement between her and me should never have come between you and her. It is the one regret I cannot take to my grave. I see the way she still looks at you, and you her. Promise me, brother."

Savric reached out, and his staff flew into his hand. He gripped it hard. "She alone contains more venom than a den of vipers. You would hold me to that fate? A life in the serpent's pit?"

Qotan smiled. "Indeed."

Savric huffed. "So be it—" He wagged his finger at Qotan. "—but I cannot guarantee she will have me again."

Qotan shook his head. "You have an uncanny way of making a promise to a dying man, brother."

I will not let you die. Not this way.

"Dying… not if I can help it," he muttered. "I must go prepare for our journey. Now, pull yourself together as best you can. We ride within the hour."

Qotan straightened in his chair. "Ride? Have you commandeered some sort of steeds for us?" His eyes brightened. "Twigglings, perhaps?"

"Twigglings?" Savric chuckled. "No, nothing quite so fanciful, but I cannot tell you now. It would certainly spoil the surprise."

Qotan nodded and gazed at the fire. "Whatever it is, I will be ready."

Savric slammed his staff's butt-end against the floor and disappeared in a whirlwind of fury.

† † †

The theory of collecting lightning seemed sound enough, but in practice it proved more difficult than Savric had anticipated. He stood atop the cottage, at the peak of its pitched roof, with his staff in one hand and a long metal rod in the other.

Rain soaked him through and threatened to drown him at times, but he had a plan: catch the lightning with the rod and redirect it into the crystal orb atop his staff. Had he known his acute fear of lightning beforehand, he might've considered an alternative.

Lightning flashed, and he squeezed his eyes tight.

I am Fizärd Əllíṭ. Lightning is nothing more than intensified light. How can I be afraid of what I am?

Thunder rumbled, followed by another flash. He jerked so hard that he nearly toppled from the roof.

"Bugger-bees!" How could his plan possibly work if he couldn't keep his eyes open long enough to see what he was doing? Savric lifted his face to the sky and the rain pummeled him. He spread his arms wide and closed his eyes.

Ɂäṭūr, You are the Light, and I am Your vessel. Take me in Your hands and comfort me. Steel my nerves and strengthen my resolve. Äímän.

I am Fizärd Əllíṭ.

He opened his eyes just as the dark sky erupted with light, and he willed the light to come to him. As if by his authority, jagged lightning bolts ripped through the darkness and converged on the metal rod he held high.

The light energy hummed as it streaked down the metal rod. It flowed into his hand, up his arm, across his torso, back down his other arm, through his other hand, and up his staff's shaft. The orb atop his staff crackled with energy and shot a beacon of light that reached the heavens and beyond.

Every hair on his body stood erect, save the mop on his head and the rat's nest under his chin. Steam rose from his pores, and his skin turned from a pasty white to a bright red.

Several more times, he pulled the lightning from the sky and stored its energy inside the orb. The experience exhilarated and taxed him. He lowered his arms and took a deep breath.

He pondered the number of bolts they would need for their journey, but no such quantification came to mind. One question weighed on his mind, and he kept circling back to it: how many more strikes could his broken old body handle?

He raised the rod and his staff skyward once again. *Whatever it takes.*

He captured more than a dozen strikes before his legs finally gave up. He stumbled, lost his footing, tumbled down the backside of the roof, and had just enough wherewithal to teleport himself into the living area of the cottage right before he ran out of roof. Somehow, he'd managed to hold on to both his staff and the rod.

Qotan hobbled into the room and looked down at Savric with wide eyes. "I dare not even ask what you have been up to, shall I?"

Savric grinned. "Even if I told you the truth, you would determine it to be a falsehood. Suffice it to say I have formulated a plan."

Qotan waved his hand and flicked his wrist. "You may have me dead *before* we ever arrive in the Three Kingdoms."

Savric sat up and looked down at his chest. Tendrils of steam rose from his robes and tickled his nose. He chuckled. "Perhaps the both of us."

"Indeed."

† † †

Savric's heart raced, filled with a touch of youthfulness he hadn't known in decades. "Do you trust me, brother?"

He and Qotan stood on top of the hill directly behind their cottage. He gripped his staff firmly with both hands and held it above his head.

Qotan looked skyward. "In so many things, you know I do. But in this madness... how could I?"

Savric smiled wryly. "You must, brother."

Qotan reached up and pulled his hood over the top of his head. "Are you certain there is no other way for us to travel?"

"The distance is far too great for us to teleport from here to there, and there are no mirrors close enough to get us there in time for an audience with King Zaridus." Savric spat rain from his mouth. "You know as well as I that there is no time for any other means of travel."

Qotan shook his head. "You squandered our time and have left us with little choice."

"Squandered…" muttered Savric.

Lightning flashed, and thunder boomed immediately, ripping the sky open further. Rain pummeled them in sheets and waves.

"We either live or die together, do we not?" asked Savric.

Qotan shrugged. "I am already dead. Why not go out with a bang?"

"Grab hold of me and let us be off. Adventure awaits."

Qotan stepped behind Savric, wrapped his bony arms around Savric's chest, and held fast to his own staff. "You had better go before I change my mind."

Savric tightened his grip on his staff. "*Ṯrenəbūrṯ bí əllít!*" he shouted.

The world shuddered, and the rain halted midair. Silence enveloped them like a bubble. Lightning hung in the air, its bright, jagged tendrils like gashes in the fabric of time itself.

A cone of yellow light emanated from the orb of Savric's staff and surrounded them. The warmth of mezhik radiated in his bones, and the fresh smell of spring filled his nostrils as pressure built around them.

A jagged trail of light, like lightning, shot up from the orb and into the sky, then eastward across the entire town of Daltura, and far into the distant darkness. Savric's hood and hair blew backward, and his cheeks vibrated with a force unlike anything he'd ever felt before, causing them to go numb.

The sounds and motions of the world roared back to life, and they streaked across the sky like a shooting star, following the path of light that streamed from his staff's orb. Qotan tightened his arms around Savric's chest, and the next moment they landed on the eastern edge of the Daltura Hills, knee-deep in grass and miles away from Daltura and their small cottage.

Savric's heart thrummed in his ears, and he gasped for air. Tremors raced through his body and left his legs weak, and his head spun. A circle of steam rose around them, and the raindrops hissed like vipers as they landed on the heated grass and ground.

Behind him, Qotan wheezed and coughed and released the death grip he'd maintained around Savric's chest. "I daresay, brother, that was enthralling. A much better way to travel than your previous idea. I take back the snide comments I may have made regarding your traveling ineptness in the past."

"Do not be so expeditious in giving your approval. We still have a long way to go before we reach the Three Kingdoms, and Vallah is on the far northern shore of Trivers Lake."

"Indeed, but all the same, this dying old fool needed such a thrill."

"Your consent of my madness heartens me. Further along, we will see if you remain so jovial. Now, grab hold. We have no time to frolic."

Qotan latched onto him once again, they braced themselves for the jolt, and then Savric raised his staff and shouted, *"Ṭrenₔbūrṭ bí ₔllíṭ."* In a blink, they were miles above the ground, streaking eastward across the sky once again.

A dozen more times, he shouted, *"Ṭrenₔbūrṭ bí ₔllíṭ,"* and each time they shot farther into the grasslands, eventually outdistancing the storm. With each leap, the Orbis range morphed from nothing at all to small mounds to distant hills and eventually into sprawling mountains with numerous peaks and hidden valleys.

† † †

The early morning light crept up from the west and slowly pushed the darkness away. Savric and Qotan stood atop Phylarchus Peak, the tallest in the southwestern range of the Orbis Mountains, a good 7,000 feet above the sprawling Valley of Dreshdan.

A fierce wind blew from the north, whipped and snapped his robes like a flag, and chilled him to the core, but the view left him breathless. *Only the hand of Ʒäṭūr could have created so much beauty.*

Trivers Lake spanned the entire valley floor, its sparkling blue waters formed by the runoff and springs from the surrounding ranges. Three sets of ranges comprised the Orbis Mountains, and they cradled the lake to the southwest, the southeast, and across the north.

The lake spawned three rivers: the Hotah to the south, the Tamda to the northeast, and the Hotah/Gala to the northwest. Each river eventually wound its way into either the Gelu Ocean or the Vastus Ocean. The Hotah River, the longest in the Ancient Realm, spanned three quarters of the continent.

"Do we risk one last leap?" asked Qotan.

Savric looked to the east. Far below, the city of Elatos spanned the mouth of the Hotah River. "I fear we have little choice. The sun rises quickly, and the people will have begun gathering in the outer courts. Time has not favored us today."

Qotan leaned heavily on his staff. "I think I can make it on my own, brother."

Savric scowled at Qotan. "We have not come this far only to have you go and do something so foolish. You do not possess the strength in your current condition. You will do no such thing. As your older brother, I repudiate any thoughts to the contrary."

The wrinkles in Qotan's brow deepened as his eyes grew wider and his eyebrows lifted. "Repudiate, you say? I repudiate your claim to be my older brother. You have no proof of such a claim."

"You will not win this argument." Savric lifted his staff in the air. "Now, grab ahold before we freeze to death up here."

Qotan complied, and, three words later, they streaked across the sky again. The waters below whooshed by, and the city of Vallah rushed toward them, but then the orb's light sputtered. They jostled in midair, and then the orb's light fizzled out.

Ɂäṭūr, help us.

The wind lapped at Savric's face as they free fell. The blue waters rushed toward them with alarming speed. *"Ṭrenəbūrṭ bí əllíṭ,"* he shouted, but the orb kept dark.

At their current speed, the water's surface would be as solid as rock.

"Perhaps a light shield is in order?" questioned Qotan in Savric's mind.

Why hadn't he thought of it? *"Brilliant,"* Savric replied.

"Ɂzhäəlld əllíṭ!" A warm, yellow light enveloped them.

Thwack!

They penetrated the water's surface with a mighty splash. The water forked around them as they plummeted deep into the lake.

Savric's hands trembled as mezhik flowed from them. "The travel weakened me more than I had realized. I cannot hold this shield much longer."

"Fear not, brother." An earthy smell permeated the bubble, and Qotan relaxed his grip around Savric's chest.

"What have you done, brother?"

Qotan didn't respond. Savric grabbed Qotan's arms with what little strength he had left and held on as tightly as he could.

Savric grimaced. He couldn't hold the spell further. He took one last gulp of air just as the last of the yellow light faded, and then the cold water rushed in around them. He held fast to Qotan's arms and kicked his legs, but his feet met the lake's silty bottom.

I won't let you go, brother.

A giant hand reached up from the bottom of the lake, grabbed them, and pulled them down into the mud. Darkness encased them like a sarcophagus. Savric exhaled and immediately regretted it as his lungs sank back against his spine. How long could he go without reflexively inhaling?

And Qotan… Ɂäʈūr, save us!

First, a jolt rocked him, then a stiff tug pulled against his entire body, and then he and Qotan slid across the lake bottom. Fire burned in his lungs, and he fought the urge to inhale, but then the darkness dissipated, and they broke the water's surface.

Savric inhaled and extinguished the fire in his lungs. They skimmed across the lake like water skitters, and then they were vomited onto the beige sand beach like bad fish.

The world stilled and darkened around Savric for several moments, and then the day rushed back to life. He lay on his back and stared up at the sky. Hues of purple, orange, and pink painted the sky as dawn arrived. He still clung to one of Qotan's arms.

He released Qotan's arm. "Are you still with me, brother?"

He rolled onto his side. Qotan lay next to him, still and face-down in the sand. Savric pushed himself up, grabbed two fistfuls of Qotan's robes, and rolled Qotan onto his side. Sand filled Qotan's open mouth and nostrils.

Savric leaned over Qotan and pounded Qotan's back, but Qotan didn't respond. He dug his fingers into Qotan's open mouth and scraped out some of the sand, but it kept replenishing itself.

After what felt like an eternity, he stopped digging sand from Qotan's mouth. His fingers ached, and his hands trembled. Sorrow wracked him. He leaned over Qotan and wept.

My dearest Ʒäʈūr, do not take him away from me. He is still needed here.

"*I am not dead yet. Would you like to finish the job?*"

Savric jumped back, and his heart pounded in his chest. "Bugger-bees!"

Qotan rolled on his back and sat up. He spat sand from his mouth and blew it from his nostrils like gritty snot. "Did you really expect me, *Fizärd Ōírdh*, to suffocate in the sand? How ironic would that have been?"

Earth wizard. Savric grabbed his staff and pulled himself to his feet. His bones ground, cracked, and popped. "I feared you had drowned before we reached the sand."

Qotan wiped his mouth with his sleeve and then grinned. "I believe my exact words were 'fear not, brother,' were they not?"

Savric brushed sand off his robes. "The more your lips flail, the more alluring the thought of putting you back in the water and finishing the job becomes."

Qotan stood and favored his staff. "Indeed. My lips have that effect on people."

"We should find some food on our way to the palace. I am quite famished after expending so much mezhik."

"The expenditure of mezhik can lay no claim to your insatiable appetite."

Savric chuckled. "I daresay you may be correct on that."

Qotan retrieved a pipe from within his robes. He turned the pipe upside down, and an impossible amount of sand poured from it. Finally emptied, he placed its end in his mouth.

Qotan gestured toward the north and the milky-white city gates in the distance. "Lead the way, brother. I will do my best to keep pace."

Savric eyed the lake one last time, shook his head, and started toward Vallah.

† † †

Savric craned his neck to get a better view of the thirty-foot-high walls that cradled the lower section of the great city of Vallah against the northern Orbis range. No other city in the Ancient Realm compared to the beauty and majesty of Vallah, and no other palace rivaled the size and grandeur of the

King's Palace, save Galondu Castle.

The city walls, made of greyish-white gneiss stones pulled from the king's quarry deep within the mountain, were built in layers: an outer wall, hollow spaces, and an inner wall. The outer wall measured four feet thick, the inner wall two feet thick, and the hollow spaces between the two walls eight feet thick. The hollow spaces served as housing for the king's royal army.

Turquoise flags bearing the king's coat of arms—a black lion's head on a shield and crossed swords—flew atop each end of the two massive gatehouses. Two pairs of ironwood gates stood open, each gate twenty-five feet wide, thirty feet tall, four feet thick, and reinforced with compounded steel.

Soldiers dressed in black boots, shirts, and helmets, white trousers, and teal leather armor bearing the king's coat of arms stood at the head of the gates and randomly questioned people as they entered the city. The soldiers didn't give Savric and Qotan a second glance as they walked past.

Savric lowered his head and smiled. *We ancients can be more cantankerous at times than the younglings.*

He and Qotan walked underneath the western gatehouse and up the steep-sloped cobblestone road. The road, walled off on either side, rose twenty feet in elevation before leveling off and meeting the main thoroughfare of the lower city.

Savric stood at the top of the road and waited for Qotan to catch up. "At your pace, we may make it to the King's Palace by tomorrow morning."

Qotan wheezed and bent over at the waist when he finally reached the top. "It may do you good to leave me behind. Otherwise, you may never make it to see the king."

Savric reached inside his robes, fingered the leather coin purse that hung from his neck, and pulled out several copper coins. He moved them around in his palm with his finger and then clenched his fist around them. *Only four.* "How many coins do you possess?"

Qotan removed the pipe from his mouth and twirled it between his fingers. "It depends on the constraints of your inquiry. Are you asking what I am currently carrying on my person or generally of my amassed wealth?"

Savric placed his hand on his hip and scowled. "If you would rather I not try to acquire transportation to the palace, feel free to continue with your pointless banter."

Qotan groaned and muttered unintelligibly. He reached into his robes and produced two copper coins, one silver coin, and seven tin bits. He handed them to Savric. "This is a form of thievery, brother."

Savric jostled the coins in his hand. "In that, you are correct. I should not need waste my hard-earned money hauling your scrawny rump through the city, yet here I am doing just that."

He looked about. Deciduous trees lined the southern side of the road, their branches reduced to bones by winter's chill. Greyish-white stone benches, hewn from the same quarry as the wall's stones, sat beneath the trees.

Savric pointed at one of the benches with his staff. "Go rest yourself, brother. I will return promptly with some form of commandeered transportation."

✝ ✝ ✝

Massive marble columns, fifty feet tall, white, and swirled with blues and grays, held up the front entrance of the King's Palace. Perfectly cut, four-foot-square granite tiles created a walkway, and slabs of grey and tan flagstone paved the road.

Savric and Qotan wiggled their way off the back of the hay wagon and bade farewell to the gentleman who drove it. Savric gazed at the steps that led up to the palace doors. *Forty steps.* Had there always been so many? He sighed.

Qotan stood next to the three-and-a-half-foot-tall wall that sectioned off the palace from the city below. Savric joined him. He ran his fingers along the smooth, hand-sculpted railing as he peered down at the bustling city. He could scarcely guess the years and manpower it took to build Vallah and the King's Palace.

Below them lay five distinct levels of Vallah, and each represented a different class of citizen. The lower the level, the lower the class of citizen—at least that's how those in the uppermost level viewed the citizens below them. Beyond the city lay the calming, blue waters of Trivers Lake.

And beyond that, the southeastern and southwestern mountains of the Orbis range scraped the skies. The peaks to the southeast rose in hues of red and purple, and to the southwest, hues of green and yellow. The majestic view rippled Savric's skin with chills.

The undeniable hand of Ɂäʈūr is present in everything.

Qotan trembled, his face far more ashen than normal. He favored his staff heavily. "To be king." His voice trembled as well. "Does this view outweigh the responsibility he carries?"

"If it were so, everyone would be vying for the throne." He offered his arm to Qotan. "Shall we proceed, brother? It is not far now."

"We shall."

Qotan took Savric's arm without another word, and that single act alarmed him.

His condition must be far worse than I imagined. His heart ached with empathy. *Ɂäʈūr, carry us through this.*

The marble steps proved difficult for Qotan, so they rested after ascending every few. At the top of the steps, wide arches ushered guests into the palace. People moved about the palace like worker ants, each focused on their tasks and oblivious to anything happening outside of their small spheres.

The buzz of conversations and transactions filled the hallways as they walked deeper into the palace and into the King's Hall. Intricate patterns wove through the tile floors in waves of blacks and blues, and massive tapestries hung from the walls, each depicting a king from the past.

Large square columns ran parallel to the outer walls of the hall, each decorated in the king's royal turquoise and donning banners with the king's coat of arms. Soldiers, akin to the ones at the city's gates, stood in front of each column, pikes relaxed, but their eyes ever flitting underneath their black helmets.

Several corridors ran perpendicular to the King's Hall, leading to a variety of other halls and rooms. Turquoise carpet runners rose up three deep steps and led toward the Royal Court.

As they progressed through the hall, Qotan's weight on Savric's arm grew. "We are nearly there, brother. Hold on for a bit longer."

Qotan smiled weakly but said nothing.

A small line of people formed ahead of them, each eager to bring their grievances to the king. One by one, the people were ushered into the Royal Court. As each left, some smiled and some brooded. Soldiers dragged a few out by their arms as they struggled and cursed the king.

An hour later, Savric and Qotan stood before the Royal Court doors, waiting to gain entrance. The line behind them had grown beyond Savric's vision. "It is a good thing we arrived here when we did."

The man that stood behind them turned and looked back as well. "Yer right about that. Almost didn't make it here today. Came all the way from Borza."

Savric nodded. "Ah, yes, to the east. Quite a travel, I'm sure."

"Darn right. Two day's travel. Wife's in me ear and up me bum fer draggin' her along. Should'a knew better." He twisted his finger in his ear and pulled out a bit of earwax. A long, grey hair rose out of its middle.

Savric nodded and turned back around just as the doors into the Royal Court parted.

"State your name for the record." The soldier's hand rested on the hilt of his short sword. He eyed Savric's staff.

"Savric Naphor."

"Qotan Naphor."

A man dressed in turquoise trousers, a white, billowed shirt, and black shoes stood next to the soldier. He held a book open with the crook of his arm and scribbled on one of its pages with a quill pen. He nodded, and the soldier said, "Enter."

They stepped through the doors and into the Royal Court. Soldiers flanked the doors, six to each side, and stood with their right hands behind their backs and a pike at their left sides.

Wooden seats, lavishly dressed in a silk, turquoise fabric, lined both sides of the center carpet. Governors and magistrates from across the realm, dressed in an array of attire befitting the Royal Court, filled them.

Hundreds of people stood behind the governors and magistrates, both entourages and advisers of the court. All eyes watched Savric and Qotan walk the thirty yards and then up three deep steps.

A six-foot-tall platform rose ahead of them, and soldiers flanked either side of the seven steps that led up to it, their pikes angled forward. To the left and right stood bleached-wood thrones, each donning a unique carving of a wolf's head above the headrest. Prince Rictar occupied the throne on the left, and Princess Zelanora occupied the one on the right. Between their thrones rose five more steps to the royal throne of kings.

King Zaridus sat forward on the large throne, his icy-blue gaze ever watchful like a hawk's. Unlike the other two thrones, silver spikes surrounded the back of his like sunrays, and wrought-iron armrests, each shaped like a lion's head, replaced the wood of the other thrones.

Large square columns surrounded the thrones and platforms. Turquoise banners streamed down them, bearing the king's coat of arms. Light filtered into the room from the east and west through massive windows that ran from floor to ceiling.

Savric and Qotan bowed low.

"I will address the king on our behalf," said Savric in his mind.

Qotan nodded slightly.

"Rise." King Zaridus's voice thundered through the large room.

Savric and Qotan stood, both on wobbly legs. They leaned heavily on their staffs.

King Zaridus gripped a silver scepter in his left hand and leaned forward. His large fingers dwarfed the silver insignia ring he wore on his middle finger. His silver crown sat crooked on his head, nearly blending in with the curly locks that draped his shoulders. Turquoise jewels lined the crown, centered beneath each of its peaks.

He wore a plain, white tunic, cinched at the waist with a silver belt. Silver sandals hugged his feet, and a turquoise-dyed fur cape rested on his shoulders. Turquoise, silver, and black necklaces hung from his beefy neck. Fifteen feet away, and still his deep-set, icy-blue eyes pierced Savric's soul like daggers.

"State your business." King Zaridus's fingers tapped the metal armrest.

Savric glanced at Qotan and cleared his throat. "Your Majesty, we bring you news from the north and the west with great urgency."

"Proceed."

"Villages have been attacked and completely devastated. Viscus D'Silva and Solasportus to name a few, and Castle Portador Tempestade no longer stands."

"This news is neither new or urgent. I've been made aware of these tragedies, and my advisers have assured me that they were not attacks but merely accidents. A kitchen fire spawned the burning of Castle Portador Tempestade, and a few sparks from that fire set Solasportus ablaze. I know nothing of Viscus D'Silva, but I assure you that we mourn for all those lost, whatever the cause may have been."

Accidents? Feathers! Fury burned in Savric's gut, but he held his tongue.

"Is that all you've come with today?"

"No, your Majesty. There is much more." He pulled on his beard and searched for the right words. "My brother and I have witnessed strange new vines in the Procerus Mountains that are alive with their own consciousness and are highly poisonous. We've brought a sample of the vine for your examination.

"One of them attacked my brother's leg as well. He can hardly walk as the poison works its way to killing him. We believe these events are linked directly to prophecy."

King Zaridus sighed heavily.

Savric continued, "A dark prophecy that will cast the entire world into darkness if it is not stopped. You must gather your armies, your Majesty. War is coming."

Whispers erupted throughout the Royal Court.

King Zaridus held up his hand and waited for silence. "Poisonous vines, attacks on villages, prophecy… and war. Do you realize how mad you sound? Prophecy died with the kings of old, and we've had peace for several decades."

Prophecies dead? Savric's head pulsed. *How can he be so naive?*

King Zaridus adjusted himself on the throne. "As for these *conscious* plants, where's your proof?"

Savric raised a finger. "One moment, your Majesty." He rummaged through the pockets of his robes, withdrew a clay jar, and held it up. "Proof, as you've requested."

King Zaridus stood. "Inspect the jar." Several soldiers rushed forward and surrounded them, pikes aimed to skewer.

One soldier stepped forward. "Lower the jar, and slowly remove the lid."

Savric lowered the jar and placed his hand on the lid. "Be careful. I'm not certain it's dead."

The soldier eyed the jar suspiciously and took a half-step back. "Open it."

Savric removed the lid. Nothing sprang from it. *Thank you, Ƨäṭūr.*

He peered into the jar, and his stomach lurched. Blackened soil filled the jar's bottom, nothing else.

Feathers! It must have decomposed already—but so quickly?

The soldier took the jar from him and examined its contents with his finger. The soldier turned and addressed King Zaridus. "Nothing but dirt."

King Zaridus sat back down. "Is this some kind of farce?"

Savric bowed again. "Your Majesty, I assure you that a poisonous plant resided in that jar. However, I did not realize it had decomposed. Forgive my ignorance."

King Zaridus raised his scepter and pointed it at Savric. "Your story unravels at every corner. And what of your brother? Is he so sick that he couldn't travel, or is he resting somewhere that he can be attended to? Or does he think you are as mad as I do and didn't bother to come at all? Do you even have a brother?"

Are they truly so blind?

The royal court erupted with laughter, and Savric couldn't hold his tongue further. "You accuse me of being mad? My brother stands at my side this very moment!" He turned to Qotan. "Lift your robes and show them your leg. Show them the black veins that threaten your life. That, they will not be able to ignore."

Prince Rictar rose from his throne and held his hand out to silence the court. He looked and dressed like his father, save the crown. His raven hair showered his shoulders.

"You dare make a mockery of this court?" Prince Rictar's blue eyes held nothing in them but contempt. "My father, the king, grants you an audience, and this is how you repay him? With lies? Your madness exceeds any I've laid witness to. What kind of fool talks to himself and gestures at the air as though someone stood there with him? You truly are mad."

Savric's heart thundered in his ears and his legs grew weary. He turned to Qotan, eyes wide and lost for words. Qotan shrugged with a weary smile. *Brother?*

Savric dropped to one knee. *How can this be, Ƨäṭūr?*

Qotan reached down and offered Savric a trembling hand. "Come, brother. We should leave before they throw you out or arrest you."

Savric stood and gathered himself. "My Prince, my Princess, your Majesty. Forgive this weary old man. I have suffered a deep loss, and I am not myself today. I would never intentionally disrespect you and your court. I beg your forgiveness, and I will show myself out if it pleases you."

Prince Rictar looked to his father, and King Zaridus nodded. "Leave us, old man, before our generosity runs dry. Never return here again, or you'll be arrested, tried, and hanged. Have I made myself clear?"

"Yes, my Prince." Savric bowed, took Qotan by the arm, turned, and walked out of the Royal Court. Laughter followed in their wake.

Qotan limped badly as they walked back through the King's Hall. "Perhaps we have misjudged Zerenity, brother."

Reni? Have I wronged you all these years? His chest seized, and his eyes blurred with tears. *What have I done?*

Savric wiped his eyes and then patted the top of Qotan's hand. "Save your strength. You will need it to get back home."

His mind reached into the past and scanned his memories. A common theme ran through every memory that came forth pertaining to Qotan. Each of them, aside from the ones with Reni, were only of him and Qotan.

Had anyone seen him since the accident?

His heart ached with the implications, and he screamed in his mind.

Madness is not possible, is it? Ƨäṭūr, help me understand what this is. I cannot lose Qotan now. I need him more than ever.

CHAPTER TWENTY-SIX

Zerenity stood in front of the full-length mirror in her bedroom, still in her nightclothes. The closet door hung ajar, and an array of clothes lay strewn across her bed and the floor. The morning light shone through the window behind her, reflected off the mirror, and lit her face.

Training starts today, but where shall I begin?

She put her hands on her hips and frowned. She'd never trained a wizard before. Sure, she'd helped a few learn spells here and there, but never full-on trained one. The fate of the world rested on Alderan, but it started with her.

Ʒäṭūr, do not let me fail in this. Give me the words, the knowledge, and the ability to teach him.

"What attire should one wear to train a wizard?" Zerenity muttered.

"Perhaps something in blue."

Zerenity adjusted the mirror. Rayah stood in the open doorway to her far right.

"It'll bring out the blue in your eyes," Rayah said.

"Dearest creator, darling. Have you stood there long?"

"Just so. Alderan's outside taking in the beauty of this place."

"Ah, very good. Let him know I'll only be a few moments longer."

"I will." Rayah turned and walked down the hallway and out of view.

Zerenity refocused on the task at hand. She spun in a circle. Her nightclothes fell to the bed, replaced by a dark-blue, long-sleeved leather top, black leather trousers that hugged and tucked in all the right spots, and black leather boots that rose to her knees.

She snapped her fingers. Her long, silver hair twisted into two braids. Blue ribbon zipped out of the closet and wove its way through her hair. The two braids twisted together and formed one larger braid at the back of her head. Another blue ribbon knotted the braid's end and tied itself into a bow.

Her nightstand opened, and a braided gold necklace slithered from it. The necklace floated over to her and fastened itself around her neck. A small, equilateral triangle hung from the necklace by two of its points. Its blue frame surrounded a silver ring and pulsed with life.

She gave herself a once-over and smiled. *I think this will do nicely.*

"Ūrzhäníz." The clothes strewn across the bed and piled on the floor flew into the closet. The closet door and nightstand drawer closed themselves as she walked out of the bedroom and down the hallway.

From the living area windows, she saw Alderan and Rayah huddled on the bench on the porch. Did they realize how different things would be moving forward?

They will soon enough.

Zerenity stopped at the front door, closed her eyes for a moment, and breathed deep. *I'm all that keeps him from fulfilling his destiny, but not for long.*

She wiped the moisture from her palms, opened the door, and stepped outside. "Grab your things and follow me, darling. Your training begins now."

Zerenity stepped off the porch and strode across the grass. "Rayah, we will be back soon. Snoop around the house if you'd like. I have no secrets."

Rayah said, "I'm coming too."

Zerenity stopped and turned back. "Today is the most important day in Alderan's life. What he learns today will shape his future, and ours. He must be allowed to fully concentrate on this first lesson, and that means you must stay away. In the future, you can watch and possibly participate some. Just not today, darling."

Rayah approached, Alderan at her heels. "Why does it—"

"Rayah—" Alderan cut her short. "—please listen to her. If not to her, then to me. You know I love you and love spending time with you, but she's right. I've got way too much pressure on my shoulders to mess this up. Please understand."

"Fine." Rayah waved her hand. "I'll find something to do on my own." She zoomed over to the house and went inside without a backward glance.

Zerenity looked skyward. *Thank you, Ʒäʈūr.* "Come along, darling. We have lots to discuss and a small window to work within."

† † †

Alderan stood in the middle of a clearing north of Zerenity's house, facing her. Great firs surrounded them like sentinels, but the southern Procerus Mountains loomed over them, their jagged white-and-purple peaks like shards of glass against the blue sky.

Zerenity held out her right hand. "Give me your left hand."

He did, and she pushed the sleeve of his coat up to his elbow. She turned his hand palm up and examined the inside of his wrist.

"A scroll," she muttered. "How interesting."

"You see it too?" Heat rose in his cheeks. *Of course she does, you oaf.*

Zerenity released his hand. "Yes, darling. All of us wizards have a mark. It signifies the type of wizard that we are."

Alderan stared at his wrist. "There were three marks a few weeks ago. Why do I only have one now?"

Zerenity's eyebrows rose, and her eyes widened. "Three? Are you certain, darling?"

Alderan nodded. "But I don't remember what the others looked like."

Zerenity's eyes glazed over. "A mage… is it possible? Not since the Great War has there been one. And fading marks…"

"What does the scroll mean?" asked Alderan.

Zerenity tilted her head back and blinked several times. "You are *Fizärd Mämärä*—a memory wizard. It gives you the ability to see events of an object's past, and it also allows you to manipulate the memories of others."

Mämärä. He thought of Rayah's scarf and Aria's bracelet. "The tingle I feel… is that from my mezhik?"

"Mezhik feels different to each wizard. When mezhik's used, whether by you or on you, you'll feel it in the same manner. It feels warm to me, like sunrays."

Alderan rubbed the scroll. "Why is it grey?"

"The color signifies your proficiency or skill level. Grey indicates that you've just begun. With time and practice, it will change from grey to white. From there, yellow, orange, red, purple, blue, green, and then finally black."

Alderan pushed his hair behind his ears. "How long will it take for me to get to black?"

Zerenity smiled, and her blue eyes sparkled. "Few ever achieve black, darling."

And I'm at grey. How will I ever save the world?

He groaned. "The world's hope rests on me, and I don't know the first thing about mezhik. This is hopeless."

Zerenity scowled and crossed her arms. "We've yet to begin, and you're already giving up? Did you ever think that perhaps your ability to save the world may have nothing to do with mezhik?"

No mezhik? The idea seemed ludicrous. *How could I save the world without it?*

He frowned. "How so?"

Zerenity paced, and her leather boots creaked. "Knowledge, bravery, faith, and hope to name a few. Some of the strongest foes in history should've won their wars, yet we stand here as proof of the opposite.

"During the Great War, Magus had the upper hand on Cyrus. All he needed to do was drive his lance through Cyrus's chest, and the war would've ended. We know how that ended, though."

Alderan sighed and gazed at the ground. *You've made a promise to yourself and all those that have fallen. Stop being the child you used to be. Focus on the future. Be strong and brave, like Aria.*

Alderan pushed his hair behind his ears. "May I see your mark?"

"Certainly, darling." She walked back over to him and turned her left hand up, exposing the inside of her narrow wrist. A bright-green, spade-shaped leaf, veined and with stem, floated on her skin, just below the base of her palm and centered on her wrist.

"A leaf…" Alderan frowned. "What does it mean?"

"*Fizärd Näịtεzhär*. I'm a nature wizard." Zerenity spread her arms, palms up, and smiled.

Alderan watched her intently, but she motioned to the ground with her eyes and head. Dead grass surrounded them. It twitched and vibrated, and from its blackened bases sprouted new life—brown at first, then yellow, and finally green. Skyward it grew, a few inches, a foot, then five.

Alderan inhaled through his nose. "Do you smell that? The grass is there, but a hint of pine is mixed into it as well."

She laughed heartily. "Some types of mezhik have a scent to them, usually akin to what they manipulate. *Näíţezhär* can smell like a variety of plants, and mine smells of pine."

Does mine have a scent to it? He thought back to all the mezhik he'd used but remembered no smell.

"What about *mämä*—whatever it's called? Does it have a scent?"

Zerenity tapped her finger on her chin for a moment, her eyes skyward. "*Mämärä.* I don't believe so, but truthfully you're the first memory wizard I've met."

I am the first? Alderan's heart sank. *How will she teach me to use my mezhik when she's never met a wizard like me before?*

Zerenity gently grabbed his chin and met his gaze. "I don't need to read your thoughts to know what you're thinking. I'm pretty good at reading faces. You're doubting my ability to train you, aren't you?"

Alderan nodded. "I don't understand how you could. We're not the same type of wizard, and you just admitted that you've never met one like me before."

Zerenity released his chin and sat down in the freshly grown grass. She patted the ground in front of her. "Sit down, Alderan. It's time we begin your first lesson."

He ran his fingers through his hair. *This is a waste of my time.* Nevertheless, he sat and faced her.

Zerenity plucked a blade of grass and wound it around her hand. "I may not know all the spells that pertain to *mämärä*, but we'd never start there anyway. You have much to learn before we ever touch on spells and spell casting." She leaned forward. "Do you know anything about the rules of being a wizard?"

Alderan exhaled hard through his nose. "I don't know the first thing about being a wizard, let alone any rules."

She nodded. "Good. The first step to becoming a great wizard is to learn the rules of being one. So, we will start with the first rule of wizardry: always guard your mind."

Alderan scowled. "Why is that a rule? Does it mean to protect my head from an attack?"

"No, but that is also important." Zerenity tugged on her earlobe. "Imagine being in a fight against another wizard. They could take advantage of you should you forget the first rule. They'd be able to read your thoughts, scour your memories, and use that information to gain an advantage over you."

He contemplated it for several moments. He and Rayah shared thoughts, but what Zerenity referred to couldn't be the same thing, could it? *Am I vulnerable to Rayah too?*

Alderan shrugged and nodded. "I guess I understand what you mean. Like when Rayah and I share thoughts."

Zerenity shook her head. "Oh, no, darling. Those two are worlds apart. You're speaking of thought projection. I'm talking about an assault on your mind." She reached out with both hands. "Give me your hands."

Alderan complied.

Her eyes narrowed. "Close your eyes and imagine that your mind is a locked room, and you're the only one that possesses a key to unlock it."

Alderan squeezed his eyes shut. *What does a mind look like?*

He shook his head. *That doesn't matter, you oaf. Picture a room, not your mind.* He did his best to picture four walls and a door. *Probably need a ceiling and floor too. Maybe some windows.*

"Have you pictured it?" asked Zerenity.

Alderan frowned. "Yes, I think so."

"Good. I will try to enter that room."

He squeezed his eyes tighter. The door in his mind's eye opened, and Zerenity stood there. Her presence filled his mind in a way he couldn't describe. Where did he end and she begin? She shook her head and walked out of the room.

Her voice filled his mind, *"Lock the door this time."*

He shut the door and turned the lock. A moment later, she stood with the door opened again, a key in her hand. *"Again. Remember, you're the only one that possesses the key."*

Alderan chided himself. *Apparently not.*

In his mind, Alderan took the key from Zerenity, closed and locked the door once again, and glared at the door. *You will not open.*

The doorknob rattled, the door shook, and then silence. Alderan straightened and pushed out his chest. *Not this time.*

To his left, the window slid open and Zerenity crawled inside. Alderan sighed.

Zerenity shook her head. *"Always be aware of your surroundings, and make sure you've protected yourself completely. You cannot falter in battle like this, or you will die. We will continue this until you've mastered it."*

Alderan nodded, but his confidence weakened.

Repeatedly, he'd lock down the room, but she'd find another way in with little effort. He pulled his hands away from hers and punched the ground. He lay back in the grass and pulled at his hair. "I can't do this."

I can't be the chosen one. They must've made a mistake.

"You mustn't be hard on yourself, Alderan. These things take time."

What does she really know?

"You heard Master Savric. It should be Aria you're training, not me." He grabbed a fistful of grass and yanked it from the ground, roots and all. "The war's coming soon, and I'll never be ready in time." He tossed the grass clump to the side.

Zerenity folded her hands in her lap. "You're right, Alderan. If you don't believe in yourself, you'll never learn. Did you know that self-doubt will hinder your abilities and, in some cases, render them useless?"

Alderan rolled over and stood. "That's what you think of me, isn't it? That I'm useless?" He kicked and stomped the grass as he walked away.

Zerenity's voice filled his mind, *"Never confuse what I think of you with what you think of yourself. I assure you, they're not the same."*

He slammed the door of his mind in her face and locked it.

I can't do this.

† † †

Rayah stood on the porch battling herself. *You shouldn't interrupt them.*
But Zerenity will want to know what Savric said.

She stepped down from the porch and into the yard.

No, Rayah! The message will still be the same when they're done, and Alderan's probably learning so much.

She walked back up the steps and sat down on the bench. *I'll just wait.*

I'm sure they won't be much longer. How long could a first lesson take, anyway?

Rayah rose from the bench and paced in the air. *Why does she want him alone? Does she plan on turning him against me?*

Of course not. Why would she do that? To save the world?

She flew around the side of the house and stopped. *What are you doing, Rayah?*

She spun in circles. *Just a peek. They won't even know I'm there.*

Rayah knew they'd headed north. How far could they have gone? She flew over to the tree line.

No, Rayah! She turned back toward the house and settled on the ground.

She turned toward the trees again, and Alderan brushed past her without a glance or a word.

"Alderan?"

He kept walking toward the house.

What did she do to him? She'd certainly find out.

Rayah headed north through the trees, determined to share her mind with Zerenity.

Alderan's mine. She has no right to keep him from me and upsetting him like she obviously has is unacceptable. Who does she think she is?

"I'm over here, Rayah." Zerenity's voice came from her right.

She moved through the trees and into a clearing. A green patch of five-foot-tall grass stood toward the center of the clearing. Rayah frowned. She didn't see Zerenity.

"I'm in the grass. Come join me."

She floated over to the circular patch of grass and then above it. Zerenity sat at its center. "How did you know it was me?"

Zerenity smiled up at her. "The trees whispered your name as you approached."

The trees know me? She pushed the thought away and focused on her anger.

Rayah settled on the ground in front of Zerenity and got right to the point. "What did you do to Alderan?"

Zerenity's eyebrows rose. "Are you probing, or did he say something to you?"

Her wings fluttered furiously, an outlet for her anger. "He didn't even look at me or acknowledge my existence when he walked past me. Call it probing. Call it concern. Whatever you'd like. What did you do?"

Zerenity shook her head and sighed. "That boy has so much potential, but he lets his self-doubt and lack of self-worth rule his mind. He completed his first lesson, but he didn't even realize it because he concentrated all his energy on his previous failures."

He passed his first lesson? I knew he could do it.

Rayah squealed. "I'll go tell him that he passed!"

"No, Rayah. He must figure it out on his own. Besides, until he does, he won't believe you." Zerenity patted the grass in front of her. "Sit."

Rayah sat down. "I'm sorry I was angry with you. Sometimes I get so jealous of anyone spending time with Alderan other than me. I try not to, but I can't help it. I don't know if it's really me that gets so jealous or if it's my bond to him that makes me that way."

Zerenity smiled wearily. "Bond or not, sometimes we all get a little crazy when we're in love. I believe it does something to our minds—changes something in them, but I'm uncertain of what it is. As you've seen, Savvy makes me crazy sometimes too."

Master Savric!

Rayah scooted closer to Zerenity. "Amidst my fit of jealousy, I'd forgotten that I received a message from Master Savric. He did get an audience with King Zaridus, but it didn't go well at all. The king told him that he'd have him arrested and hanged if he ever returned to Vallah. King Zaridus claimed him to be mad."

Zerenity gasped. "Mad? Did he say why?"

"No, but even in his writing I could tell that he was beside himself with grief. His words made me cry."

Zerenity leaned forward and grabbed Rayah's arm, her eyes desperate. "Did he say anything else, darling?"

Rayah looked at her arm. It whitened around Zerenity's hand. "He said Qotan's near death. The poison's worked its way into his groin and stomach. Savric fears Qotan has little more than a week to live. They're headed here.

He said you're the only hope Qotan has left."

Zerenity released Rayah's arm and stood. "That foolish old geezer. How can I possibly help remedy someone who's been dead for decades?" She placed the back of her hand on her forehead. "I don't understand him. In that respect, he's most certainly mad."

Rayah twirled her finger in her curls. *What would Master Savric do?*

A thought bloomed in her mind. "Maybe we need to look at the problem from a different perspective."

Zerenity's eyes narrowed. "How so?"

Rayah flapped her wings and rose into the air. "Where did Master Savric say this poison came from?"

Zerenity tapped her chin for several moments before answering. "A vine they'd never seen before. He claimed Qotan found it this side of Altus Pass, but high in the Procerus Mountains."

"Have you looked for it?" asked Rayah.

Zerenity looked at her, puzzled. "Why would I, dear?"

Rayah pursed her lips and looked at the ground for a moment. She smiled. "Pretend that the source of the information didn't come from Qotan. What would you do? Aren't you some sort of nature wizard? Wouldn't you investigate it yourself if a new type of vine sprang up and started poisoning everything? Isn't it your duty to investigate?"

Zerenity tapped her chin as she paced. "You're a clever girl. I see why Savvy chose you and why Alderan adores you. Go find your love and bring him back here. We have a quest to embark on."

Rayah giggled. "Master Savric will be pleased if we find something."

Rayah peered up at the looming peaks, and the task daunted her. *How will we find something so small with so much ground to cover?*

She looked at Zerenity again. "Do you think we have a chance of finding these vines?"

Zerenity nodded. "If the vines exist, we'll find them. I'll send a message through the trees. If anyone knows of the vines, it will be them. They know most things. Off you go, now. Hurry back."

"Yes, Zerenity." Rayah flew through the forest, full of hope once more.

We will find your vines, Master Savric. I know you're not mad.

CHAPTER TWENTY-SEVEN

Pravus sat alone in the dining hall and stared at the inside of his left wrist. Not so much at the blue, optical triangle he'd had since growing into his mezhik, but at the purple claw next to it that hadn't existed until last night.

He flexed his hand. He possessed the power to crush someone's skull. *For how long, though? I need answers. Now.*

"Credan!"

Credan shuffled into the hall and bowed when he reached the end of the table Pravus sat at. "My lord, how may I serve you?"

Pravus grabbed the end of the table. His fingers pressed into the hard wood as though it were made of butter. "What did you do with the girl last night?"

Credan's eyes brightened. "I believe she's yet to awaken. Would you like me to summon her?"

"Not Aria, you fool. The *dead* one from last night." *Tilly.* Her broken body flashed in his mind.

"Oh." Credan swallowed hard and pulled on his collar. "I assure you, the situation's been taken care of, my lord."

Pravus leaned forward in his iron chair. "I must see her body."

Credan scratched the top of his bald head. "My lord, that's not possible. We disposed of her body in the boiler room fire last night."

Pravus slammed his fist into the table. *Crack!* The wood splintered, and Credan cringed. "Damn you, Credan. What possessed you to do that?"

Credan stepped back, his face ashen. "It's how we've always managed *delicate* situations, my lord. How could I have known you'd want to see the body again?"

Pravus brooded. *How will I get my answers now?*

But he already knew. Blood lust raged within him. It called to him, begged him to spill more. His hands trembled at the thought of it.

He sat back in his chair and held fast to its arms. "Never mind that. Bring Aria down here. I'm starving, and my patience is wearing."

Credan bowed. "Yes, my lord." He turned and practically ran from the hall.

Pravus stood and stretched his legs. *Enämäəll.*

"Beast, to me."

The dog emerged from under the table and padded over to him.

Pravus bent down on one knee and scratched behind Beast's ears. "Do you like that, my friend?"

Beast barked once and licked Pravus's face.

Pravus grabbed him by his heavy jowls and looked deep into his big brown eyes. *"Do you understand what I'm saying to you? Bark once for yes, twice for no."*

Beast barked once.

"Could be coincidence, right?"

Beast cocked his head and barked twice.

Pravus stood and returned to his chair. Later, he'd retrieve his spell book pertaining to enämäəll and find out what else he could do with his newfound power. A thought occurred to him, and he sat up straight.

Magus. Had blood been the secret to his power? *It must've.* How else could he have taken on Ūrdär Dhef Ɂäfn Dhä and nearly won? Although, he did have Cinolth. Had that been the key, or perhaps a combination of the two?

Tonight, I'll see how far the blood takes me.

† † †

Knock, knock, knock.

Aria rolled onto her back in the warm sand. Sunlight lit the edges of the shelter. She sat up, disoriented. *Where's Karraar?*

Knock, knock, knock.

"Mistress Aria, it's Brema. May I enter?"

Brema?

The events of the previous night rushed back into her memory, and she sank back into the soft, feather-filled comforter. She closed her eyes. "Go away, Brema."

"But Mistress, Lord Rosai requires your presence at breakfast."

Pravus. Gooseflesh prickled her skin.

How long had it been since she'd seen him? She couldn't quantify it. The wastelands had stolen all sense of time from her.

She missed Pravus's charm. His golden eyes. His scent. His intoxicating, mezhik touch.

Aria sighed. "You may enter."

The door unlatched, creaked, and then closed. Brisk footsteps fell against the marble floor. A grunt sounded at the foot of her bed, and then the red and deep-pink canopy curtains pulled apart. Brema tied them back against the bedposts and then did the same with the curtains on the sides of the bed.

Aria rubbed the night from her eyes. "What time is it, Brema?"

"Nearly midday, Mistress Aria." Brema pulled the bed covers down, gasped, and looked away.

Cool air rushed across Aria's naked flesh and left the hairs on her arms and legs standing in its wake. She sat up and swung her legs over the side of the bed; her feet hung more than a foot above the grey-and-white fur pelt stretched across the floor.

She rubbed the gooseflesh from her arms. "It's okay, Brema. You needn't look away. I'm not ashamed of my body. Besides, you bathed me last night."

Brema looked back and dipped her head. "As you wish, Mistress Aria. If I may say so, you are a beautiful woman—more so than any other I've seen."

Aria's cheeks burned. "You're too kind, Brema."

Brema held out her hand. Aria smiled and graciously took it, and then Brema pulled her from the bed and onto her feet. The pelt felt like silk against the bottoms of her feet. She dug her toes into it and squeezed. *Heavenly.*

A red dress with black accents lay across the chair next to the bed.

"Is that for me to wear?" Aria's voice and hands trembled.

Brema squeezed her hand. "Yes, Mistress Aria. One of many."

One of many? The notion left her without words.

She hadn't realized she still clung to Brema's hand until she reached for the dress. She let go and reached out, but Brema pulled her arm back. She glanced at Brema's hand on her arm and then back at the young woman.

She dares restrain you? Backhand her. Let her know you're the future queen. Her queen.

Brema's face flushed red, and she withdrew her hand. She shrank away from Aria. "Forgive me, Mistress Aria. I didn't mean to grab your arm like that. I swear it will never happen again."

Aria glared at her. "See that it doesn't."

Brema eyed the floor. "Yes, Mistress Aria. Thank you. May I dress you?"

"I'm perf—" *You're a queen, Aria. Act like one.* "You may proceed."

Brema helped her into fresh black undergarments and black lace stockings that ran the length of her legs and hugged her thighs. Her mind flashed back to the hatchet that'd sliced into her thigh, but no mark remained. Had it been so long ago?

Brema took the dress from the chair, laid it on the floor, and then had Aria step into it. Brema lifted the dress, and Aria slid her arms into its short sleeves.

Brema moved behind Aria and laced up the back of the dress. Aria grunted as the leather tightened around her waist, midriff, and chest. She expected pain between her shoulders where she'd injured herself in the toppled carriage, but she felt none.

Did Pravus visit me last night? Surely I would've remembered. The bath perhaps?

Black lace gloves slid onto her hands and up to her elbows. Aria sat down in the chair next to the bed, and Brema laced up knee-high, five-inch-heeled, black leather boots.

Brema helped her to her feet. "Let me do your hair, and then we'll select some appropriate jewelry."

Jewelry? The hand-woven bracelet she gave Amicus had been the only thing she'd ever owned that resembled jewelry. She missed Amicus and little Vonah. *I hope you're well, my friends.*

Brema led her over to the vanity in the corner of the room and sat her in the chair. "How would you prefer your hair, Mistress Aria?"

Prefer my hair? She didn't know how to respond. "Whatever you think would look best, Brema. How do women wear their hair around here?"

"Down mostly. But they will soon look to you."

"But why—" She knew the answer. *I am their queen.* She had to reconcile herself to the fact that she'd soon rule over them. "Yes, you are correct. I believe wearing it up would be most suitable."

Brema took the brush from the vanity and brushed Aria's hair. "Very good, Mistress Aria. Your beauty will be the envy of all men and women alike."

Aria's cheeks warmed. *Me, beautiful? Preposterous.* She'd never be the one envied, would she? A simple thatcher's daughter.

She bit her lip hard and drew blood. *No! You are a queen without a past. A new slate.*

Brema took strands of red lace from one of the vanity drawers and then pulled and tucked and twisted Aria's hair. When she finished, Brema turned Aria's head left and then right. "Yes, I believe that's it."

Aria looked at the young woman through the mirror's reflection. "Thank you, Brema."

Brema smiled, revealing a wide gap between her slightly yellowed front teeth. "Wait here. I know just the right necklace for you." She walked across the room and through a door Aria hadn't noticed before.

I'm going to need a guide, so I don't get lost in this place. If Alderan were here, he'd know every inch of it within a week. But he'll never be here… outside of my heart and mind.

Leave the dead in the past, Aria. They have nothing to offer you but pain.

Brema returned. She grasped something in her left palm; thin strands of black leather poked through her fingers and hung down.

Aria frowned. "I don't think that's the kind of jewelry I imagined wearing. Something in gold or silver, or even copper."

Brema bowed. "I beg of you to indulge your servant. Please close your eyes and trust me. If you're dissatisfied with my selection after you've had a look in the mirror, I will find something more to your liking."

Does she not know how a queen should look? Do I? She'd never actually seen a queen before, but she had a good imagination, didn't she?

She sighed and closed her eyes. "Proceed."

Something cold lay against her breastbone, the weight of it more significant than she'd imagined. "Please go look in the full-length mirror and see what you think. I believe it completes the outfit."

Aria rose and walked over to the full-length mirror. The reflected woman's piercing green eyes held her gaze. Her pulse raced as she searched those eyes for traces of the young girl she scarcely recalled. *Are you really me?*

A tight, black leather bodice wrapped her. It dipped low between her breasts and accentuated them. Ruffled red fabric wrapped her shoulders and flowed from the bottom of the bodice, down to her lower thighs in the front and to her ankles in the rear. Red lace edged it.

A single strand of blonde hair hung down the left side of her face. The rest of her hair pulled back into a ponytail at the base of her skull, braided with red lace that matched the dress, and curled into a bun.

A black leather necklace hung around her neck, underneath her seamless silver collar. A large, teardrop-shaped stone wrapped in silver wire hung from the necklace, over her breastbone. The stone pulsed and swirled red-and-black.

The woman before her stole her breath. *You are a queen.*

"Mistress Aria?" Brema's voice sounded distant. "Mistress Aria does the outfit please you?"

Aria smiled at herself. "I think it will do, Brema."

Brema curtsied, and then she straightened up. "Oh, I nearly forgot. The necklace has matching earrings."

Aria turned her head to the side and rubbed her earlobe. *Would a queen have pierced ears? Yes, you would.*

Aria eyed Brema through the mirror. "Grab something sharp, Brema. I will not leave this room without them."

Brema nodded and retreated through the door she'd retrieved the necklace from.

Aria turned her attention back to the regal woman in the mirror and admired her. The tight dress accentuated every curve of her body and defined every muscle. Indeed, the envy of the kingdom; perhaps the entire world.

You are a warrior.

You are a queen.

The world awaits your rule.

† † †

Pravus held the stemmed glass between his thumb and forefinger and swirled its yellow contents. The wine did little for his appetite, but it kept his mind focused. From the moment he'd left Nardus's cell last night until he awoke on the floor of his bedchamber, he remembered nothing.

The stone's the key. No other rational explanation existed, but why did it cause him to blackout?

The stone must've driven him to do what he'd done to Tilly too. *But why?* Did it want him to understand Magus's power?

Absurd. How could a stone have an agenda?

The situation intrigued him, but the thought of Tilly's bloody body being Aria's gave him pause. Aria's death would certainly mean his own. How would he live with himself otherwise? He must distance himself from her as much as possible until he gained control of himself again.

And the stone.

Credan walked through the dining hall doors and bowed. "Lord Rosai, I present to you Mistress Aria." He turned around and exited the room.

It's about time.

He set the glass down on the table and stood. Venom tipped his tongue, ready to be released, but when the woman dressed in red and black entered the room his anger dissolved. Had she not worn the silver collar, he would've sworn her to be someone else.

My queen.

Her boot heels ticked on the marble floor as she approached. Her beauty enraptured him and surpassed his recollection of her. Words escaped him.

How can she be mine?

She stopped before him, removed one of her black lace gloves, and slapped him across his face. *Smack!*

"That's for leaving me to die." She removed her other glove and slapped the other side of his face. *Smack!* "And that's for not coming back for me."

Pravus's cheeks stung, but he didn't care. He took Aria's hands and kissed the tops of them. "You have my word that I will never leave you alone in the wastelands again."

The steel in her eyes aroused him.

Aria crossed her arms. "You will never leave me alone again. Anywhere. Where you go, I go, or you won't go at all."

He dipped his head and smiled. "Yes, my queen. I live to serve only you."

"See that you do."

Pravus grabbed Aria by her waist, pulled her close, and pressed his lips against hers. She stiffened for a moment, but then wrapped her arms around his neck. He kissed her deep, and she pressed in harder.

She pulled back, and they both panted. "The thought of not sharing your bed pains me. When are we to be wed?"

Tilly's twisted neck flashed in Pravus's mind. He pulled away. "Soon, my love. The preparations are nearly complete."

Aria placed her hand on his chest. "Can we not gather a few people now, say our vows, and return to your bedchamber to consummate it?"

Anger shook his arms. "No." He stepped back. "I'm sorry, Aria. I don't mean to be short with you, but certain steps must be followed. Also, you cannot imagine what I've been through since we've been separated."

Aria's collar glowed red and matched her face. "What *you've* been through? How can you be so insensitive? Have you not heard what *I've* been through? From the moment you left me in that carriage, I had to fight for my life. If Karraar hadn't shown up when he did, I'd be dead. Do you not understand that? Do you not care? Several times I teetered between life and death."

He grabbed her hand. "Yes, my love, and I'm sorrier about that than you'll ever know. I'm struggling to be a good man to you—I really am. Not because you don't deserve it, but because it doesn't come easily for me.

"As I've said before, until you came into my life, nothing mattered more than myself. I do my best to keep from pushing you away. Bear with me, my love, and don't be angry when I fail to meet your standards. I will fail, again and again."

Aria stared at Pravus intently for several moments, then her gaze softened. "I understand, and I will try as well."

A man walked into the dining hall carrying a silver platter topped with a domed lid. He placed the platter at the end of the table, next to Pravus's seat. He removed the lid, bowed, then scurried away. The platter held piles of eggs, cheeses, and slices of various meats—more food than any two people could ever hope to eat in a single sitting.

Pravus led Aria around the table and to a chair to the left of his own. "Shall we eat?"

Aria sat down. "Yes, and then we can begin my training?"

Pravus sat down, placed some food on the silver plate in front of Aria, then filled his own. He took the vial of wine and filled her glass half full. "We will start your training soon, but not today. I have several matters to attend to today that cannot be delayed."

Aria eyed Pravus. "Then I will join you." She picked up her fork, stabbed it through one of the eggs, and took a bite of the egg.

Pravus shook his head. "That's not an option, my love."

Aria tensed and set her jaw. "You agreed there'd be no more secrets between us."

He gazed into her alluring green eyes. "I did, and we shall have none. Nardus, the man I told you about, is here. He's extremely dangerous, and I don't want you near him."

Aria frowned. "How dangerous could he be?"

Pravus cracked his knuckles. "He nearly killed me last night. That's all you need to know."

Aria took a sip of her wine, sat the glass down, and placed her hand over his. "If he's that dangerous, then maybe you shouldn't be around him either."

Pravus grabbed several slices of meat and cheese and stuffed them in his mouth. He chewed them on one side of his mouth. "Perhaps not, but I've no choice. He still has the stone and refuses to give it to me."

"Refuses?" Aria scoffed. "Why can't you just take it from him? You are stronger than him, are you not?"

Pravus sighed. "As simple as that sounds, mezhik doesn't always work that way. That stone contains mezhik more powerful than you and I combined."

Aria shrugged. "Then we must wait until he gives in."

Pravus leaned forward and rested his elbow on the table. "Until he gives it up, we cannot be wed. Do you understand now why I must go see him?"

Aria's brow furrowed, and the ends of her mouth curled downward. "No. Should I? What does the stone have to do with our wedding?"

Pravus cupped her chin. "Everything, my love. Our entire kingdom depends on that stone. We cannot marry until it's in m—our possession. Believe me when I tell you that I salivate at the thought of bedding you. I've thought of little else since our first encounter."

She smiled. "And I you. I find myself lacking restraint every time your skin caresses mine. I need you, Pravus. More than the air I breathe or the food I consume."

Pravus smiled and leaned back in his chair. "Then you understand the importance of getting the stone from Nardus?"

"I suppose I do, but what would you have me do the rest of the day?"

"Credan will show you around the castle. Anywhere you'd like."

"The library. I want to know more about the prophecies."

"Very well." He shoved a whole egg in his mouth, chewed it twice before swallowing it, downed the rest of his wine, then stood. "I will see you tomorrow, my love." He bent down and kissed her.

She scowled at him and continued eating.

He smiled. *I do not deserve such beauty.*

He walked out of the dining hall and met Credan in the corridor. "Do what you must to appease her, but don't let her anywhere near Nardus."

Credan bowed. "Yes, my lord. She will not see Nardus, but she'll have the run of the castle, otherwise."

Pravus nodded. "That's my fear. Be sure you tell the entire staff to steer clear of Nardus as well. I've business to attend with him, and I'll not tolerate being disturbed. Am I clear?"

Credan dipped his head. "Your will be done."

Pravus walked to the end of the corridor, turned right, and headed toward the dungeons.

That stone's coming out of Nardus's chest, whether he's dead or alive.

Pravus quickened his pace. "Preferably dead."

† † †

Elatos lay in ruins, its wooden structures burned with dragon's flame. A mighty dragon perched atop the remains of the white castle wall. His black scales glistened, wet with blood.

A man stood at the dragon's side and held up the severed head of the king. He shouted down at the remaining people and soldiers, "Bow to me, and I'll end this war today. Continue to resist, and I'll slaughter every one of you. Make your choice now."

One by one, people fell on bended knee until only one man stood.

"You dare stand against your new king? Tell me your name so that I may erase it from history."

The man in the crowd shook his fist at the man. "I am Cyrus, son of Ashram. While I live, I will fight for the people."

"And I am Magus, Lord of the People and King of the Dragons. This very day, you'll die by the hands of the people you claim to fight for."

Magus addressed the crowd. "Rise, my children, and slaughter this fool. Fail, and you will all suffer his fate."

As one, the people rose. Soldiers with lances and swords pushed through the crowd.

"We will not die for one man," cried the people.

Soldiers charged at Cyrus from all directions.

Cyrus stepped forward and out of existence.

† † †

Nardus lay on the floor, drenched in sweat. The left side of his chest burned with fire and glowed red under his shirt. Mezhik tingled in his head, and then pain ripped through his left temple like an arrow. In his mind's eye, the black dragon gazed at him with contempt, and then the details of the dream eroded from his mind until nothing remained.

Nardus roared at the ceiling. "Remove this thing from my chest!"

"Nine days," echoed the voice in his head, "or the sickness will remain with you forever and everyone you care about will die. You'll be left with no one."

I'm already alone.

"Leave me," said Nardus.

"But I've just arrived." Pravus leaned against the steel bars and peered between them.

Nardus sat up. "Unless you've come to remove the stone and bring my family back, you can leave too."

Pravus frowned. "If not me, then to whom were you speaking?"

Nardus stood and pulled his shirt open, but the fire and glow in his chest had already faded. He pointed at his heart, or at least where his heart used to be. "This damned stone."

"And why would you be speaking to a stone?"

"Because it speaks to me."

Pravus's eyebrows rose. "Does it? And what does it say to you?"

Nardus rubbed the scars on his left bicep. "That I should kill you."

"And will you? Or at least try to?"

Nardus spat. "All reason says I should. What you've put me through exceeds the price of the bargain we made."

Pravus smiled deviously. "Does that really make sense to you? You've asked me to resurrect your family. Could any price I require of you, even your own life, match that request? I think not. What price have you put on your family's lives?"

Nardus closed his eyes and shook his head. *He's right, my loves. I'd give my life to save all of yours. Even for one of you, I'd pay with my life.*

Vitara, I know I've wronged you with Theyn. But I beg you, lend me your strength once again. You are my anchor. The love of my life.

Nardus opened his eyes and walked over to face Pravus. "No price is too great for my family. If it's within my power, I will not harm you. I give you my word."

Pravus cracked his knuckles. "I will make no such promise. Taking that stone from your chest might kill you. If it does, I will consider our deal finished."

Nardus grabbed the bar with one hand. "Then you'd better pray I survive." He poked his chest with his forefinger. "I came back with this damned stone. Don't think I won't claw my way back from *Ef Demd Dhä* to end your life if you cross me."

"Enough talk, my friend. Grab onto the bars, and don't let go."

Nardus did, and Pravus reached through the bars and placed his right hand on Nardus's chest.

Nardus's chest tingled as mezhik flowed from Pravus's hand.

I hate mezhik. He turned his head and spat on the floor.

Pravus's nails grew into claws and punctured Nardus's flesh. Deep within Nardus's chest they sank, cracking ribs and tearing muscle and tissue. Nardus screamed but held fast to the bars. Nardus's chest ignited with fire and his vision burned red.

"We kill him now!" exclaimed the voice in Nardus's head.

Nardus roared, and Pravus screamed.

Pravus's hand shriveled and blackened. His skin wrinkled, and his raven hair turned white.

"Get it away from me!" screamed Pravus, his eyes wild with fear.

No! I need him alive.

"You need nothing. You were warned. He dies."

"No!" screamed Nardus.

He ripped his hands from the bars and shoved Pravus with all his might. Pravus's hand slid out of his chest and Pravus flew backward and collapsed to the floor.

Nardus leaned against the bars, his chest heaving. The wound burned with fire and seeped blood. Nardus grimaced as his flesh knitted itself together again.

Pravus lay still, face-up.

Did I act too late?

"You'd better hope you did."

Pravus's chest rose and fell. Once. Twice. He stirred and moaned.

He lives, and you've failed. Now get out of my head.

"You'll regret this!"

The burning in Nardus's chest ceased, and his red-tinted vision normalized. He slid to the ground and spat on the floor. "You don't control me, you bastard."

He looked at his chest, but no wound remained. Only sweat covered it. He closed his eyes and focused his mind on his family.

I'm still fighting for you, and I'll never give up.

CHAPTER TWENTY-EIGHT

Crudely shaped dirt walls surrounded Rakzar and stretched to the greyish-blue sky above. He lay on his back in a cesspool of urine, feces, and other bodily fluids, paralyzed with pain. The stench gagged him, but he couldn't escape it.

Orcs, both male and female, stood or squatted along the edges of the pit and took turns urinating and defecating on him. Some did other things far worse—some so horrific and grotesque he'd never be able to unsee them.

They mocked him, laughed at him, and spat on him. "*Mighty* Rakzar, the feces king!"

Stripped of his dignity, his clothing, and even his fur, he begged them to kill him, but they only laughed harder.

Ɂäṭūr, the dryte's God, I don't know You and I'm not even sure You exist, but if You do, I beg You to show me mercy. Stop my heart. Strike me dead. Do whatever You must to end my life. I cannot live this way.

He waited impatiently, but nothing happened. Had he really expected anything? Ɂäṭūr wasn't his God. He didn't believe in any of the gods. Did he believe in anything at all?

The curse.

After nearly drowning in the ocean, he wanted to believe in something more, an existence beyond the cruel world he knew, but it lay beyond his grasp of understanding. Did he need a soul to understand the afterlife?

Do I have a soul? The question dominated him of late. *Blackened, perhaps? Damned? More so with this curse.*

Marked with the sickle, death followed in his footsteps. Save the blood-bonded, anyone who crossed his path would die, no matter them a friend or foe.

I have no friends, not even the White Knight.

A lone shadow fell across the pit, then Murtag's ugly face appeared above its rim. "You're a traitor to your own kind, dog. I should've let Urza or Wibble kill you, but my mercy is boundless. Claw your way out of this pit, and you'll live. Don't, and you'll eventually starve to death. Your choice. If you manage to survive, pray we don't meet again. The things Käíeʑ could do to you exceed nightmares."

Despite the piercing pain in his side, Rakzar pushed himself up on his elbows. "Death will find you, Murtag, and I'll be there to watch you suffer."

Murtag sneered. "I look forward to it, dog." He turned and walked away.

Rakzar lay back. *How did we fail so miserably?* They'd had Amicus's God on their side, hadn't they? *Where's the justice in his death, Ɂäʈūr? Where's my justice? Our vengeance?* Murtag deserved to die.

Rakzar forced himself to sit up. Dried blood, dirt, feces, and other substances crusted his side where Urza had stabbed him. She could've killed him, but she didn't. Had she not done so out of mercy or to torture him?

Definitely torture. She's a merciless bitch and killing me would have been merciful.

He looked at his bloody hands and feet. She'd ripped out his claws. *Claw my way out? Maybe in six months when my claws have grown back.* He grabbed fistfuls of mud and feces and flung them at the wall. He roared until he coughed up blood, his throat raw and shredded.

The end of a thick rope, tied in a large loop, dropped into the pit next to him. He looked up.

Urza?

She peered over the edge. "Slip the rope under your arms."

Rakzar hesitated. *Is she here to finish the job?*

"Hurry up! We don't have much time."

He fought through the pain and slipped his arms and head through the rope's loop. "Okay."

The rope jerked taut and tightened around him. Urza grunted. "I'm strong, but you're gonna have to help me."

Rakzar growled, "Hold on." He breathed quickly three times and then pulled himself to his feet. The pain blinded him and shook him to the core. He staggered but remained upright. "Go!"

The rope jerked taut again, and then he rose from the ground. He grasped at roots and rocks, anything that jutted out from the dirt walls, to help Urza pull him up.

"Whatever you do, don't let go of the rope," he growled.

Urza grunted.

He reached up, grabbed hold of the rim of the pit, and tried to pull himself up, but the rim crumbled and broke away. He slipped and fell several feet before Urza caught the rope and stopped his fall.

She called down to him, "I think I can hold the rope, but you're gonna have to climb the rest of the way up."

Rakzar growled, gritted his teeth, and climbed the rope. His outstretched arms ripped his side open again. He grimaced but kept climbing until he reached the top of the pit and crawled over its edge.

He panted, and his vision swam. "Why are you helping me?"

"There's no time." She grabbed him and pulled him to his feet. The rope loosened and slid to the ground. She put her shoulder under his arm and led them west.

Rakzar looked around. "There's nothing out here. They'll see us for miles."

She held her free hand over her nose. It made her voice sound funny. "They're orcs. They can't see more than a couple hundred yards."

"Maybe not, but Wibble and Yetch can."

"Your little friend has them occupied right now."

Rakzar stopped. "You mean Eshtak?"

She forced him forward. "Of course. This plan was his idea."

No! What were you thinking, little man?

Guilt rose in his throat like bile. "We must go back."

"Are you mad? There's no going back. I just forfeited my life to save yours."

"I didn't ask you to do that." He stopped again and glanced back toward the horde. "I can't leave Eshtak behind."

"Of course you didn't, and you didn't need to." She removed her arm from around him, grabbed him by the jaw, and turned his head to meet her gaze.

He glared at her. "How many times do I have to tell you that I'm not interested?"

No semblance of a ruthless killer remained in her yellow eyes—only love. "You don't remember, do you?"

Remember? Were we together? The thought didn't sit well.

He jerked his head away. "What am I supposed to remember?"

She grabbed his head again and forced his attention. "I'm here because I care about you, *brother*."

Brother? He couldn't have heard her correctly.

He shook his head. "That's not possible."

"Yes, it is. You saved my life when I was a pup."

His head spun. "No…"

Flashes of Murtag snapping the necks of his mother's pups pummeled Rakzar's mind. He'd defended them and told them to run, but none of them had survived, had they?

"I went by another name back then."

Rasha? She couldn't be.

She smiled. "You do remember."

A burst of strength returned to him. "That doesn't matter right now. Amicus is dead, and I cannot leave Eshtak with them!"

"The little man will be fine. He'll meet us on the other side of the valley where it's safe." She pulled on his arm. "Let's move."

He took a few steps and then remembered the promise he'd made Amicus. "I must recover Amicus's body and bury him with his family."

He turned back toward the horde. Still, no one pursued them, but for how long?

How can I get to Amicus's body without being recaptured?

"Rakzar, don't make my sacrifice meaningless. Come on. The little man has already retrieved the body."

He's retrieved the body? He looked back at Urza. "How?"

She shrugged. "I don't know, but he's the strangest, sneakiest little man I've ever met. So much more resourceful than you'd imagine. And loyal. I told him to run long ago, but he refused. He insisted on helping his friends. Helping *you*."

Why would he help me after I led Amicus right into a trap and got him killed?

"Fine." Rakzar dropped on all fours. "When we meet up with him, I'll take the body and then we'll go our separate ways. All of us."

Urza dropped on all fours too. "We'll discuss this later." She turned and headed west through the trampled, dead grass.

His side still bled, and the pain nearly debilitated him, but he fought through it and did his best to keep pace with Urza. They ran more than ten miles before his legs finally gave out. He collapsed and slid face-first across the dead vegetation.

He pushed himself back up on his hands, but the world spun circles around him. His arms buckled, and he collapsed. "I think I've lost too much blood."

Urza slid to a halt ahead of him and padded back over to where he lay. "We can't stop here. There's nowhere for you to hide, and I won't be able to defend you."

Rakzar closed his eyes. "Leave me, then."

He felt her breath on his ear. "Stay still. Someone's approaching."

"Run. I can't let you die for me too." He opened his eyes and tried to move, but she held him down with her knee.

"It's Wibble and Yetch." She looked him in the eyes. "Do you trust me, brother?"

How can I? He'd never trusted anyone in his life before, but what choice did he have?

I'm already dead. "Do what you must to stay alive."

She nodded. *Click-click!* Her knives slid into her hands. She shoved one of them into the wound on his side. Blistering pain swept across his body, and he did everything he could to keep from screaming.

His vision blurred and doubled, and then the world became shades of grey, only shadows. His head jerked twice, pain splintered from his temple, and then the darkness swept in.

✝ ✝ ✝

The smell of smoke lifted him from the depths of darkness. Rakzar leaned against a large rock next to the fire. Bandages wrapped his waist. His body ached, but it paled against the pain in his heart.

Eshtak sat on the opposite side of the fire, quiet, distraught, motionless. Rakzar had never seen him so still. Eshtak cradled Amicus's severed head in his arms like a baby. Tears streamed down his cheeks.

I've killed them both. Rakzar thought he might vomit.

No words would bring Amicus back. No words would ease Eshtak's pain. No words would ever repair their friendship. Sadly, none of it mattered. The sickle would kill Eshtak if they remained together.

I must take the body and leave. It's for his own good. He still has friends.

Urza circled the fire, her knives twirled in her hands. Bandages wrapped her neck and her right leg. Had she worn them earlier? *No.*

Rakzar groaned. "What happened?"

She averted his gaze as she walked past. "Nothing happened. Just rest."

"I remember you pulled me out of that pit, but nothing after that. How did you injure yourself?"

She stopped and glanced back at him. "We do what we must to survive."

He looked over at Eshtak. "And him?"

"We'd both be dead if not for him."

"You said he caused a distraction so that we could escape."

She came back around the fire and sat next to him. She slid her knives home with a *click-click*. "He did. But he saved us too."

"He saved us..." He stared into the fire. "What happened to your neck?"

Urza fingered her bandage. "Wibble and Yetch came after us. I tried to make it look like I'd captured you again, but they knew I'd helped you escape.

"Yetch attacked me from behind, tore into my leg with his teeth, and pulled me to the ground. Then Wibble wrapped that wire of his around my neck. He tightened it just enough to cut into my throat. Never had I seen so much hate in his eyes.

"He accused me of choosing you over him. He said he'd make you watch him take me right there, and then he'd cut off my head when he finished with me."

"I'll *kill* him." Rakzar moved to get up, but she held him down.

"Wibble's already dead. They both are." She looked over at Eshtak. "The little man stabbed Wibble in the back of the neck and paralyzed him. After that, I fought Yetch off and then buried my knife in his thick skull. Then I took Wibble's wire and used it on him, starting between his legs where it would hurt him the most. He might've been paralyzed from the neck down, but he cried like a child."

Rakzar lowered his head. *It makes no sense. Why would they fight for me? I'm not worth saving.*

He peered into the fire again. "Help Eshtak find his friends. I'll take the body and bury it."

"We'll go together," she said with finality.

"Eshtak can't be around me, and he'll need protection."

Urza huffed. "Perhaps you don't know the little man as well as you think. He can hold his own when needed. He has many tricks in that sack he carries."

Rakzar pushed himself to his feet. His side throbbed. "It doesn't matter. The curse will kill him if he stays with me. I'll make my peace with death soon enough, but I cannot allow anyone else to die on my account. Especially not him."

Eshtak looked up at him. "Eshtak not leave friend."

How can he still call me friend after what I've done?

Rakzar hobbled over to him. "Hey, little man. About Amicus... I just want to say I'm—" The word *sorry* seemed so inadequate. What good would it do him anyway? "You must warn the others, Eshtak. Their lives depend on it—on you."

"Eshtak must help?"

"Yes. You'll be a hero. It's what Amicus would want you to do."

Eshtak looked down at Amicus's head. "Eshtak will never forget friend."

Eshtak wiped the tears from his cheeks and then placed Amicus's head into his brown cloth sack. He pulled the green scarf out of the sack and laid it down. He took off the brown cloak he wore and offered it to Rakzar.

Rakzar scoffed. "That won't fit me."

Eshtak slipped the silver ring off his finger and handed it to Rakzar. "Bad thing becomes lizard man. Then cloak fits."

Bad thing. Never truer words.

He turned the ring over in his hand. "I don't know what this would do to me." He looked at Eshtak. "Why didn't you turn into a lizard man?"

Eshtak shrugged. "Mezhik not change Eshtak. Eshtak change mezhik."

Urza came around the fire and stood next to Rakzar. "I'm not sure putting that ring on is a good idea."

Eshtak smiled. "Ring keeps friend safe. No one will find bad thing if bad thing is lizard man."

If the ring killed him, would that be so bad? He had nothing to lose. He looked at Urza, shrugged, and slipped the ring on his littlest finger.

At first, nothing happened. But then the ring tightened around his finger, and its silver tail grew and slithered across the back of his hand and wrapped around his wrist. The bones in his hand popped and cracked, and his fingers shrank.

What have I done?

Urza reached for the ring on his hand, but a spark of white light arced between them, and the energy threw her backward. He tried to grab her, but his body contorted and writhed.

His flesh burned and bubbled and sprouted scales, and what little hair he'd retained fell away. His bones cracked, shrank, and reformed. His tail widened at the top and grew to the ground like a whip.

His ears shortened and melded into his head and his neck elongated. Sharp, hooked claws sprouted from the ends of his fingers and toes. His eyelids shrank back around his eyes.

His side no longer hurt. He looked down at it. The bandages had fallen to the ground. *No more wound. I guess mezhik has its benefits.*

He held his scaly hands out. They looked different, but they didn't *feel* different. He turned to Urza, who lay on the ground, propped up on her elbows.

"Well?" The word slithered from his lips.

"I've never seen mezhik like that." She stood, walked over to him, and sniffed him. "I thought you smelled bad after I pulled you out of the pit earlier, but now you smell like a saurian." She wrinkled her nose. "Disgusting."

Before, she'd stood about six inches shorter than him, but now he had to look up to meet her gaze. His forked tongue whipped the air. "I smell nothing but you."

Eshtak clapped. "Now friend safe." He offered his cloak to Rakzar again.

Rakzar took it and whipped it around his back and over his shoulders. He pulled the front of the cloak shut and lifted the hood over his smooth head. He looked down at himself but didn't see a change.

Urza gasped. "You've disappeared, along with your disgusting stench."

She reached out, and he moved backward. She pawed the air.

Guess it works.

He pulled the hood back off. "Thank you, Eshtak. This means a lot to me. One day I'll return these to you."

Eshtak grinned, but he didn't dance about like normal.

Urza pulled on the necklace of colored strings around her neck. "I still think we should stick together."

"I'll see you again, sister."

"Soon, or I'll hunt you down."

He turned back to Eshtak. "Take whatever you need from the sack, little man. I'll have to take it with me so that I don't have to carry Amicus's body all the way across the world."

Eshtak nodded. He reached in the sack, withdrew his favorite mirror, and then handed the sack to Rakzar. "Eshtak find lady in mirror."

"It's settled then." Urza gave him one final look and walked away.

Eshtak grabbed the scarf he'd laid down and wrapped it around his neck. Rakzar shook his head. *Ridiculous.* "Until we meet again."

"Eshtak miss friend."

I'll miss you too.

He lifted the hood back over his head and headed northwest through the Reis'Duron Grasslands and toward the Discidium Sea.

Time to take you where you belong, Shadowman.

CHAPTER TWENTY-NINE

The descent from the King's Palace to Vallah's lower city took most of the day, and now the sun perched atop the Orbis range to the east, painting the western range in shades of red, orange, and purple. Had circumstances been different, Savric would've enjoyed the spectacle.

Instead, Qotan clung to his arm, hung from his shoulder, and weighed him down.

Have I lost reason? Would I be asking myself the question if I had?

No, it is not possible. My faculties are intact. But would I not come to that conclusion either way? A mad person doubtfully thinks themselves to be mad.

They walked along the cobblestone street, toward the city gates. They stopped many times along the way, Qotan barely lucid enough at times to put one foot in front of the other.

So why can no one see him but me?

Qotan slumped against him and pulled them both to the ground.

An older woman walked in the opposite direction. She scolded him, "Drunk at this hour? Have you no dignity? You're in the king's city. What kind of example are you setting for the children? Shame on you."

Savric ignored the woman and patted Qotan's cheek. "Stay with me a bit longer, brother. We only need to reach the harbor. It is not much farther now."

The woman huffed. "Talking to yourself and gesturing lewdly. You are most certainly mad, sir. I shall report you to the king this very day."

Savric raged within. *I should get inside that woman's head and give her nightmares for a month. That would teach her to hold her tongue.*

Instead, he turned and smiled at the woman. "I assure you, the king is fully aware of my lewdness and my madness. Now move along before you glimpse my bare backside."

The woman's face reddened. "Well, I never!" She stormed away.

Qotan's head rolled to the side. Black veins crept up the side of his neck and reached for his lower jaw.

Dear Ƶätūr!

Savric placed his hand over the black veins. *Deathly cold.* He closed his eyes and allowed the warmth of his mezhik to flow out of himself and into Qotan. He held his hand against Qotan's neck until his arm shook with fatigue and his head floated on his shoulders.

Savric pulled his hand away, his breathing labored. He opened his eyes. The black veins on Qotan's neck receded.

Qotan's eyelids fluttered, and then he opened his eyes. "Why must you hover over me, brother? Do we not have matters to attend?"

Savric smiled wearily. "I wondered if I had lost you."

Qotan frowned. "The harbor is a striking place during this season. I would nary miss such a scene. And where shall we go from the harbor?"

Savric stood and helped Qotan to his feet. "North, up to Aberporth. There is a mirror located there that we can use to get back to Zerenity's house."

Qotan blew air from his mouth, and his lips vibrated violently. "Aberporth? Quite a distance from here. You would carry me all that way on your back?"

Savric held his hand over his eyes to block the sunlight and peered down toward the docks. "If I had to, yes. However, I have found a riverboat heading up there this evening."

Qotan nodded. "Yes, yes, that makes much more sense. Your swimming skills were never stupendous, and I am in no condition to chance it on my own."

Savric chuckled. "At least you have yet to lose your humor, brother."

"It will be the last thing to go before death takes me."

Together, arm in arm, they headed down the road and through the city gates. Fifty yards ahead, the harbor docks stretched across the sand and out into the water. Boats and ships of various sizes lined the docks. Men worked furiously on several of them, loading and unloading cargo of various kinds.

Why are there so many boats docked?

They sought a boat called *The River Maiden*, recognizable by a wooden mermaid figurehead below its bowsprit. The third boat to their left fit the description, and the name across its side confirmed it. A narrow gangplank extended from the dock up to the boat's deck.

A stocky man stood at the foot of the gangplank, scowling. An orange strip of hair separated the left side of his head from the right, and two, small, golden hoops hung from each ear.

"Must be the old man. Lucky you didn't get left behind," he barked, his voice rough.

Savric smiled. "Yes, yes. I am said old man. The name is—"

"Don't care." The man held out his hand. "Four coppers, or you stay put."

Savric frowned. "But we agreed on three copper coins."

The end of the man's flat nose lifted and twitched. "You've cost me time. The new price is four. Keep flapping those lips of yours, and it will be five."

"Feathers! Four is all I have."

"Then we have a deal. Hand them over."

Savric reached into his coin purse, withdrew the four copper coins it held, and shoved them into the man's greasy hand. *High seas robbery.*

The man dropped the coins into his trouser pocket. "A pleasure. Get on board before you're left here."

"Hold my waist, and I will walk in front of you with our staffs," said Qotan.

Savric glanced at Qotan. "Do not even think about pulling us into the water."

"I might do just that if you don't get moving," said the man.

Savric ignored the man. He and Qotan slowly walked up the gangplank and made it onto the deck without incident. They settled into one of the corners of the deck and leaned against the bulwark.

Savric looked around. No mast rose from the deck. In fact, no sails of any kind existed. *How does this boat move?*

The man from the dock pulled the gangplank away from the boat. He whistled loudly and twirled his finger in a circle above his head. The boat lurched backward and drifted away from the dock.

Is he not the captain?

The boat's bow swung around unnaturally fast, and then they headed north, along the northern leg of the Hotah River. The boat sped up, and the landscape flew by in a blur of colors. Savric stood, and the wind rushed through his hair. "I will be right back."

Qotan nodded and closed his eyes.

Savric held onto the bulwark and walked toward the stern of the boat. He climbed the stairs to the upper deck. No one steered the boat. He looked across to the bow of the boat. *No crew?*

"What have I engaged us upon?"

He walked to the back of the quarterdeck and knocked on the door of the captain's quarters.

"Enter."

A woman's voice. Peculiar.

He opened the door and stepped inside. High windows lined the port and starboard walls and lit the small room. A hammock, strung between two central beams, rocked back and forth and cradled the woman lying in it. The woman swung her feet over its edge and rose to her feet.

Dark-blue curls dominated her disheveled hair and offset her stark-white skin. Pointed ears sliced through her hair, capped in silver. A thin black line traced her pale-blue lips. Her large, deep-set eyes were blue ice but didn't seem cold, and they accentuated her narrow nose. Her high cheekbones angled higher with her v-shaped jawline and pointed chin.

She wore a sheer-white blouse with bell-shaped sleeves and an open collar. Half untucked, it hung below her waist in spots. Baggy beige trousers descended into calf-high brown boots. Silver bands wrapped her wrists, and a silver chain hung from her neck. An ivory-handled dagger hugged her left hip, its black sheath strapped to her waist with a brown leather belt.

She stood tall, her feet spread hip-width. Her hand casually rested on the hilt of her dagger.

"State your business, wizard." Her thick accent bit off the ends of her words.

Savric looked down at his light-brown robes and chuckled. "I do suppose these old rags tell a tale of their own."

"What is it you seek?"

"I am simply curious as to what makes this vessel move so quickly through the water. Is it mezhik, or something else?"

Her nostrils flared, and her lips curled. "Have you come to enslave me and harness my mezhik?"

Savric gasped. "Feathers! Under no circumstance would I ever perform such a monstrous deed. Who would ever think to commit such treachery?"

She turned the bracelet on her wrist. "Others like you have come before, always under the guise of friendship."

He staggered backward. *Żäţūr, is this true?* An image of Aria and her silver collar slithered through his mind. He shuddered. "I swear on my life, I present you no harm."

She glared at him. "Your words are nothing more than wasted breath. We live in dangerous times. One such as myself can never be too careful."

He dipped his head. "I completely understand your caution."

"Good. Then you won't mind removing your cloak and your robes."

Her request caught him off guard. "Remove my robes? Are you mad?"

She unsheathed her dagger and pointed it at him. "Do as I command, or you'll find yourself at the bottom of the river."

Savric shook his fist at her. "I came in here out of simple curiosity and now you command me to disrobe and threaten my life? I will do no such thing!"

"Then you've left me no choice."

And you have left me none, either.

He gazed into her eyes, reached out and touched her mind with his, but she blocked him. Moreover, she attacked him with her mind. He deflected her blows, but she proved strong. How long could he keep it up? Healing Qotan earlier had drained him.

He raised his arm in surrender. "Wait. I will do what you ask."

She lashed out at him one last time with her mind and penetrated his outer defenses. Her voice echoed in his mind, *"Now."*

In all his years, he'd never felt a mind like hers. He sensed she toyed with him and could easily take him down with a single thought. The implications of such power shook his core.

He removed his cloak and tossed it at her feet. "What do you hope to gain from this?"

She sheathed her dagger. "Your robes too." She picked up the cloak and rummaged through its pockets.

He glanced at the ceiling. *No one has seen me disrobed in ages other than You, Ƶäţūr.*

He sighed, removed his robes, and handed them to her. Her lingering eyes warmed his cheeks. *You are far too old to allow your skivvies to embarrass you.*

He rubbed the chill from his bare arms. "Perhaps you could tell me what it is that you are searching for. It might hasten the process."

She searched through the layers and pockets of his robes. *"Ƶäbräƶär."*

He shook his head and sighed. "You are certainly a stubborn woman. I would never place one of those wretched collars on anyone."

She eyed him. "Maybe not, but you are hiding something. I can feel its mezhik."

She held his robes in her left hand and placed her right over the top of them. Her blue eyes turned white. She mouthed something he couldn't hear and then raised her right arm. A leather-bound book rose out of the garment and sat on top of it.

Savric gaped at her. *Feathers! That is impossible.*

The blue in her eyes returned, and her gaze penetrated right to his soul. "Why do you possess this book?"

The accusation in her tone curled his toes. *Why do I possess it?* His heart raged with anger, but he kept his tongue in check. "You know what it is, then?"

She traced a circle on the cover with her thumb. *"Ƶäɘll Dhef Ƶäfn Dhä.* Do you see it?"

"How could I not?"

She circled him. "It doesn't belong to you." Her words chilled the air, or so he imagined.

He stroked his beard and pulled hard on it. "I vehemently disagree with you on that account."

"After the Great War, these books were given to members of *Feɘzhärz*

Dhä."

His eyes widened, and he glanced away. *How can this be? No one should know of Feɜhärz Dhä.*

She leaned forward. "You know of the watchers too. We were told they were all hunted and killed centuries ago."

He nodded. "As was I."

She tapped the book with her blue nails. "Where did you find this?"

Why must she continue to press me?

He turned away from her. "I did not find the book. It was given to me."

She grabbed his chin and forced his attention. "*Given*? Are you implying you are one of the watchers?"

Feathers! Ɂäʈūr, help me out of this.

He pushed her hand away. "As you said, they were all killed centuries ago."

She took the book in her right hand and tossed him his robes. She paced while he squirmed back into them. "If you're one of the watchers, there'll be proof."

"Proof?" He scowled at her. "Please enlighten me as to exactly what this proof would be."

She sat the book on a table at the back of the room and walked back over to him. "Show me your wrist."

He held out his left arm. "My wrist reveals nothing but the type of wizard I am."

"Your other wrist."

"My other wrist? I assure you that there is nothing on my right wrist." He lowered his left arm and raised his right one. "See?"

She grabbed his elbow with one hand and his hand with her other, then she lifted his wrist up to her lips. She spoke a word he didn't recognize and breathed on the inside of his wrist. Despite her icy appearance and demeanor, her moist breath warmed his skin.

She lowered his arm, and they both stared at his wrist intently. His wrist warmed and glowed bright red, and then little sparks of light rose from his skin and skittered in the air like ashes from a fire.

Parallel to his arm, an image of a golden spyglass materialized on the inside center of his wrist. Underneath the spyglass, four black lines emerged, twisted, and then formed a "W."

Savric's heart pounded.

Dear Ɛäʈūr, this must be Your doing. Why have You brought us together? For what purpose?

She let his arm go and paced again. "What does this mean? How can this be? They should not exist."

He raised his hand. "And yet here I stand, one of two."

She stopped mid-stride and eyed him. "There are *two* of you?"

"Yes, but that is insignificant." He rubbed his wrist, but the mark remained. "How did you know about this mark? I am of *Feɛzhärz Dhä* and never knew of its existence."

Her gaze bore into his soul. "The answer is simple, watcher. My race created those marks. We're responsible for all of them, including those of wizards."

Could it be? His mind doubted her, but his heart yearned for her words to be true.

He took her hand, bowed, and then kissed the top of it. "I am sorry I let my ill manners best me today. I am Savric Naphor, known as The Wise. Who are you, and what race do you come from?"

She dipped her head. "It is a pleasure, Wizard Naphor. My name is Morcinda, and I am of the silver-eared clan. I am *äəllfin*, and, more specifically, *äəllf äkfeʈik*."

The myths are true! The aquatic elves exist.

He released her hand, held one hand behind his back, and pulled on his beard with the other. "It seems we have both been misled."

"As you say." She walked over to the table and picked up the book. "My race does not believe in coincidence. You and I have crossed paths for a reason."

He joined her at the table. "As you know, my race tends to exchange beliefs and traditions on a whim. However, I answer to a higher power. One not of this world. Ɛäʈūr. He is my guide. My path through Him does not waver."

"You may call Him by a different name than I, but I believe we serve the same God." She held the book out to him. "I believe this is yours."

He raised his hands. "You keep it. My heart tells me that one day soon I will need your services again, and this will afford me the luxury of contacting you."

She stared at the cover and nodded. "I will guard this with my life."

"See that you do. Now, to my original request. Can you entrust me with your secret as to how this vessel moves?"

She smiled. "In a way like your use of mezhik, I speak to nature. I command the water to push this boat, and it obeys."

He picked up his cloak and wrestled it around his shoulders. "You have delighted me this day. I shall not forget it." He dipped his head. "Thank you for your time, Morcinda. I must go check on my brother. He is unwell, but he will find your story fascinating."

She dipped her head in return. "Until next we meet."

Savric smiled and then showed himself out.

✝ ✝ ✝

The healing wears off quicker each time.

Qotan huddled in the corner of the deck, his light-green cloak tightly drawn. Black veins crept up the side of his face. He trembled, and his forehead burned with fever.

Savric knelt next to Qotan and stroked his cheek, distraught by his condition. How much more could his heart take? "We will reach Aberporth soon."

Qotan's teeth chattered, and his words tripped over his graying lips. "B-brother, you must l-let me go. I have b-burdened you far t-t-too long."

Savric took Qotan's hand and held it between his. "Never have you been a burden, brother. *Never.* I urge you to keep fighting and hang on until the last moment possible. I will never stop searching for a remedy."

Qotan closed his eyes. "I have ch-cherished our t-time together. N-n-never a moment of regret."

His hand slackened.

CHAPTER THIRTY

Savric squeezed Qotan's hand. *No, no, no! Dear Ɂäƫūr, please do not take him!*

Tears welled in the corners of Savric's eyes and rolled down his cheeks. His heart ached and raced, and his chest tightened. Sorrow lumped in his throat and then escaped in a long wail.

This cannot be. This cannot be Your plan.

He lifted his head and cried out to the dark sky, "We are Your servants, Ɂäƫūr. We may never understand Your holy plan, but how can this serve Your purpose? Does this world not need more of us to reflect Your light? How will we survive the coming darkness if none of us remain?" He let go of Qotan's hand and beat his chest with his fists. "Answer me!"

The orb. He had little choice.

Is this my desperation, or Your plan? He set his mind to it, caution be damned.

He grabbed his staff and raised it in the air. Lightning flashed several times, striking his staff with each bolt. White-hot light raced the length of his staff and into his body. The hairs on his arms rose, and light burst from his eyes like beams.

He pressed his free hand against Qotan's chest. *"Bí əllíƫ Hiz!"* Light energy—his mezhik—surged through him, down his arm, and poured into Qotan. His staff's orb shattered into a thousand shards of light and fizzled in the air like embers.

Qotan spasmed, his entire body lifted off the deck, and then slammed back against it. He sat up, gasped, and his eyelids shot open. His green eyes glowed in the fading light. The black veins receded once more.

Savric collapsed on the deck, exhausted.

Thank You, Ɂäƫūr.

Qotan stood, leaned on his staff, and looked down at him. "What have you done, brother?"

Savric closed his eyes, his head splitting. "What had to be done to save you. You left me short of an alternative."

"Your staff cannot be repaired. You have rendered yourself defenseless."

Savric shrugged. "You live. What more matters?"

"Everything. We both know what you have done will not last. The poison will return, and I will perish. Furthermore, the world still teeters on the cusp of war."

"But we have more time to save you."

"And if we fail, what have you gained?"

Savric looked up at Qotan. "Another week or two with the one I love more than anything else in this world."

Qotan shook his head. "You are a damned fool, brother."

He nodded. "Indeed, but that is no surprise to either of us."

Qotan turned his gaze north. "The dim lights of Aberporth approach."

Savric lifted his arm, a thousand-pound weight in his weakened state. His hand trembled. "Well, do not just stand there, give me a hand up."

Qotan reached down and pulled Savric to his feet. "How much energy did you have stored?"

"It matters not." He reached out with a trembling hand, and his staff rattled on the deck.

Bugger-bees. I guess I will have to do some things like the unzhiftäd for a time.

Savric sighed. "Would you be so kind as to retrieve an old man's staff?"

Qotan eyed him. "You have broken your staff *and* expended your mezhik?"

He flexed his hand and nodded. "A good summary of the situation."

Qotan blew air from his nostrils. "If we perish because of your antics, I will most definitely hold you accountable." He bent down, picked up the broken staff, and handed it to Savric.

The boat lurched to a halt, and the lights of Aberporth to the east and north shined upon them. Workers hustled up and down the docks, unloading cargo from some ships and loading cargo into others. A gangplank slid up to the deck from the dock below.

A squat man climbed the gangplank and hopped onto the deck. "This is as far as you go, old man. We've a schedule to keep. Take your leave."

Savric dipped his head toward the man. "Give our thanks to your captain."

The man said nothing but motioned toward the gangplank with his head and eyes.

They exited the boat and had barely stepped onto the dock when a rush of wind rocked them, and a spray of water doused them. They looked back, but the boat had vanished.

Qotan looked at him with a raised eyebrow. "I surmise you have a tale to tell me about our boat?"

Savric chuckled. "Indeed. We have a bit of a walk ahead of us, and it will make the time pass quicker."

Qotan swept his hand forward. "Then let us be off."

Savric eyed the top of his staff and grimaced. "Perhaps you should lead the way."

"A wise choice." The end of Qotan's staff lit the docks with its pure white light. "And dare I ask where we are headed?"

Savric peered into the dusk light. A single building stood atop a lonely hill. *A hermit's true friend.* He swallowed hard. "The lower room."

Qotan lowered his head. His chin nearly touched his chest. "I was afraid you might say that."

"The alternative is far beyond your capability."

Qotan turned to him, an eyebrow raised. "Alternative? I am listening."

Savric chuckled. "You carrying me to Viscus D'Silva."

Qotan scratched his chin. "If I had that kind of strength, the ladies would come swooning."

Savric shook his head, the thought preposterous.

Qotan pulled out his pipe and shoved its end in the side of his mouth. With the touch of his finger, a slender stream of smoke rose from its bowled end. He toked on it a few times then nodded. "The lower room it is."

Qotan led them along the docks, dodging the hustling workers as best they could. "Pray that we find ourselves quickly this time."

Savric stroked his beard as they walked. "I recall you being the one lost, not I."

"I am troubled by your lack of recollection, brother." A ring of smoke rose above Qotan's head. "We will see who is still lost in the end."

Savric cringed. *I pray it is not both of us.*

CHAPTER THIRTY-ONE

Fear—a wretched trait shared among the weakest beings and creatures. Pravus loathed it more than any other. In the past, his pride prevented him from succumbing to it, but touching the stone in Nardus's chest had changed him. Fear strangled his heart and crippled his mind.

Aria. How could he face her in his current condition? *She'd leave me. Or kill me and take my kingdom for herself.*

His head ached. *She'd never.*

Regardless, the blood oath they'd take at their wedding would prevent her from doing so. But would it be the only thing that held her back? Would she still marry him?

She isn't like any other. I'm being paranoid.

He groaned. *Pathetic.*

He drew his cloak's hood over his head and stuffed his white hair into it. He held his shriveled right hand tight against his body and pulled himself from the floor with his left. He leaned against the wall.

He closed his eyes, but the red eyes of death he saw when he had touched the stone followed him into his own darkness. Such hatred, loathing, and contempt filled them. They wanted him dead but not just him. *The entire world.*

What has Nardus brought into this world?

No book he'd read about Ʒţōn Dhef Dädh ever mentioned anything about it having such power, nor a will of its own. But did it, or did that will stem from Nardus? How could it come from the stone?

Some demon must've come back with him. It's the only rational explanation.

Pravus glanced back at Nardus; he laid on the bed in the cell with his back to Pravus. Every passing moment increased Pravus's loathing of Nardus.

He tightened his jaw. *You'll not survive this.* If all went as planned, either Aria or he would kill Nardus. *Together, nothing will stand in our way.*

Blood. A lust for it filled him. A deep, uncontrollable urge like gasping for air after being underwater too long. His thoughts flailed like fish on hooks, fighting for their lives. Only his thoughts of blood flourished. Not only of blood but of spilling it.

His heart raced, tendrils of sweat slithered down his nape, his vision narrowed, then everything grew black.

† † †

Despite his weakened state, Pravus charged through corridors and down stairways like a man possessed. The scent of the zhifṭäd—of their blood and their mezhik—drove him forward.

He stopped in the middle of a corridor many levels below the surface and faced one of the black stone walls. To his left hung a tapestry depicting a scene of savagery and slavery from the Great War.

Fitting.

He stepped through the wall and into the hidden passage beyond. At the end of the passage, he descended thirty-three steps and entered the place he called the transformation chamber.

An eleven-foot-wide, white marble walkway stretched sixty feet toward the center of the room. Impenetrable darkness lined the walkway. Massive wooden chandeliers hung above the walkway, a thousand candles burning bright on each of them. Their bronze chains rose into the void, anchored to oblivion. The candlelight lit the walkway like daylight, but the light didn't stretch beyond the walkway.

At the end of the sixty feet, the walkway spread into an octagonal shape, eleven feet on each side. Suspended in the darkness, three feet beyond each of the seven other sides of the octagon, sat glass-walled cubes, each measuring ten feet on every side.

Ambient light filled six of the cubes, and their contents were similar, yet unique. The seventh cube, opposite the walkway, lay dark, ominous, and empty.

Pravus paced the perimeter of the octagon like a caged tiger, contemplating which cube to open. *Middle left, or middle right?*

He looked down at his shriveled, blackened hand. How much blood would it take to restore his strength? *Both.* His pulse quickened, and his mouth watered. Their scent nearly drove him mad.

He reached out toward the middle cube on the left. It slid toward him and came to a rest against the side of the octagon. He stepped through the glass—an illusion of security for others—and into the cube.

A young woman lay on a bed of glass.

"Rise," he said.

The young woman's eyelids fluttered, and her soft-grey eyes opened. She swung her legs over the side of the bed, stood, and awaited further instruction. A seamless, silver collar circled her neck. A piece of red silk stretched across her breasts, crossed at her back, and wove through and around the tops of her legs and waist, much like a loin cloth.

He stretched his left arm toward her and held out his hand. "Come, Yora."

She took his hand in hers. The warmth of her tanned skin quickened his pulse. The vein at the side of her slender neck leapt with her pulse and begged him to puncture it. He nearly ravaged her on the spot.

With forced restraint, he led her out of the cube and to the center of the octagonal platform. The cube slid back into place, and the ambient light within it faded.

"Wait here," he said.

He let go of her hand and reached out to the center cube on the right side. As with the first, the cube slid over to the edge of the octagonal platform. He walked over to it and stepped inside. A dark-skinned woman with long yellow hair lay on the glass bed.

"Rise," he said, and she obeyed.

Like Yora, Triza wore a silver collar around her neck. A piece of yellow silk that matched her hair wrapped her body the same way Yora's did. Pravus took her hand, led her out of the cube, and then the cube slid back in place. Again, the light within the cube faded.

Pravus led Yora and Triza out of the transformation chamber and up to one of his bedchambers deep within the castle. He threw the doors open wide, stepped into the large room, and beckoned Yora and Triza to follow.

A massive, four-poster bed hugged the far wall, and a lounge chair sat next to it. A fire blazed in the fireplace to the right of the entrance, lighting and warming the room. A long brown couch faced and paralleled the fireplace, and two brown stuffed chairs flanked the couch. An inner room of the castle, it had no windows. Shadows danced about the room, cast by the firelight.

Pravus took Triza and sat her in the lounge chair next to the bed. He led Yora over to the bed, hoisted her onto it with his good arm, and bound her to the bedposts by her wrists and ankles; she didn't resist.

Triza watched intently, her yellow eyes wide with wonder. Pravus moved around the bed and to her side. She bit down on the inside of her lower lip and looked up at him.

Pravus stroked Triza's cheek. "You'll be next, my dark angel."

Triza's face brightened, and her eyes sparkled. "Yes, my lord. I look forward to the service I will provide you."

Pravus nodded then turned his attention back to Yora. Her blood teemed with mezhik and called to him—begged him to take it. He shed his garments and climbed onto the bed.

"I am yours, my lord," said Yora.

As is your blood.

He breathed deep and dove into the madness.

CHAPTER THIRTY-TWO

A week had passed since Savric met with King Zaridus, and Zerenity hadn't heard from him since. Usually, she wouldn't worry about him, but he'd seemed distraught in his last message to Rayah. However, if she'd learned someone she cared deeply for was nothing more than a figment of her imagination, how would she cope with it?

I daresay, not well at all. I pray you're stronger than I, Savvy.

She stood in the middle of a clearing north of her house, awaiting Alderan's arrival. The sun hung overhead and warmed the fresh mountain air. Spring awaited just around the corner, and she looked forward to its arrival.

Zerenity, Alderan, and Rayah had spent four days in the forest northeast of her house searching for the villainous vines that Savric insisted grew there. However, they'd turned up nothing; she'd expected as much. The exercise proved fruitful in one regard: it further solidified her resolve that building a life with Savric had no future while he still clung to Qotan and the past. She must move on. *For both our sakes.*

Normally, a pupil would master the first rule of wizardry in the better part of a day, but Alderan still struggled with it. Rayah had asked her how the first week's lesson faired, and she'd described it as abysmal at best.

Alderan's potential exceeded her own tenfold, but how would she help him unlock it? Stubbornness and self-doubt plagued the boy. *If only he'd get out of his own way.* But could he?

Can we rely on him to save the world? Zerenity doubted it, but she'd never voice her concern. Doing so would profit no one. In fact, she'd chided Savric when he'd voiced a similar opinion.

Alderan trudged from the trees like a walking corpse. He wore his tan trousers tucked in one boot and over the other, and his once-white shirt contained more hues of yellow and brown than the dead and dormant foliage surrounding them, especially in the armpits. His blond hair stuck straight up on one side of his head and lay totally flat on the other, a perfect example of his attitude.

She crossed her arms and shook her head. "Tsk-tsk. If you have so little respect for yourself and our lessons, how do you expect to learn?"

Alderan looked down at himself and shrugged. "Didn't realize it mattered." He pushed his fingers through his hair and tucked the ends behind his ears.

She sighed. "I suppose it's a good segue into the second rule of wizardry."

Alderan lifted his chin. "And what is that?"

"Pride is a double-edged sword." *Clearly not something he possesses.*

He frowned. "And why is that a rule?"

The grass crunched under her feet as she circled Alderan. "It's quite simple, darling. On one hand, if you don't look the part, you won't feel the part. If you don't feel the part, you won't be the part. And if you're not the part, you're as good as dead."

She raised a finger. "However, too much pride in your skill and wit can make you overconfident and sloppy and can also get you killed. Therefore, it is a double-edged sword."

Alderan's brow furrowed, and the left side of his mouth pulled back. "I'm dead on both counts then. What's the point?"

Zätūr, is this Your idea of a cruel joke? I know You use the weak to conquer the strong so that both sides know the impossible victory is by Your hand. But what if the weak have no faith in Your hand strengthening them and bringing victory? Will You still use them to save us, or will we all be condemned?

She closed her eyes. *Forgive me. I am one of those who are weak. Strengthen me that I may help and not hinder.*

Zerenity sighed and opened her eyes. "We'll start with the simple things. When we train, you'll dress appropriately. Do not show up again with disheveled hair and dirty clothes. Respect me. Respect your training. Am I clear?"

Alderan looked down at his clothes. "And what would you have me wear? I don't have a closet full of clothes like you must. What you see is all I have."

She tapped her chin with her finger. "A proper wizard wears robes. I'm sure I have something that would do you justice."

"Robes? Pfft." Alderan folded his arms. "You mean like the dress Master Savric wears?"

"Don't be so quick to judge, darling. They say, 'Once in a dress, you'll never wear less.'" She winked at him. "It's a fashion statement, to be sure. However, it called a 'robe' or 'robes,' not a dress. They're quite comfortable."

Alderan pushed his hair behind his ears and looked down. "I don't know. Wouldn't certain parts just... roam around in there?"

Zerenity's cheeks warmed, and she scowled at Alderan. "You may discuss such vulgar things with Savvy if you like, but never with me. Do you understand?"

Alderan's face flushed bright red, and he shied away. "Did I say that out loud? I'm sorry."

She waved her hand. "Never mind that, darling. I think I know just the right thing. I'll be back in a flash."

Zerenity twirled out of the clearing and into her bedroom. From under the bed, she pulled out a long, flat brown box. She opened the lid and folded back the yellow tissue paper. Light-grey robes and a dark-grey cloak lay inside it.

Tears filled her eyes, and she blinked them back. "Thirteen years..." *Has it really been that long?*

She pulled the garments out of the box, lifted them to her nose, and breathed deep. Never worn, they smelled fresh. She eyed the second box that lay under the bed. Would its contents ever be unboxed? Moreover, would she ever see her precious Aria again?

Her heart ached, and she trembled. *You've no time for this, Reni.*

Zerenity took another deep breath and focused her mind on Alderan and his training.

She twirled back into the clearing in an instant, robes and cloak in hand. Alderan sat on the dead grass and picked at the ground with a stick. She dropped the garments in his lap. "Try these on."

Alderan stared at them, and his brow furrowed. "Did you just buy these?"

She scoffed. "Of course not. I bought them when you were hardly more than a baby."

Alderan tossed the stick into the brush. "They're definitely out of fashion then."

Zerenity raised her eyebrows. "I didn't realize you had an eye for fashion. Nevertheless, robes are forever fashionable for a wizard. Now give the robes a try before I strip you down and put them on you myself."

Alderan grabbed the garments and stood. "I'll go try them on in the house."

She smiled. "Good idea. Rayah will be able to see you in them as well."

Alderan grunted. "Fine. Turn around so I can put them on."

She turned away. "You can leave your skivvies on or take them off, either way. Savvy would never be caught without them, but Qotan never wore them again once he switched to wearing robes."

Several moments later, Alderan said, "Well?"

Zerenity turned around, and her heart leapt. Alderan reminded her of Savvy when he first donned his robes. She circled Alderan, a smile frozen on her face.

Behind him, she pulled the shoulders of the robes taut and smoothed the sleeves. *A perfect fit.* However, the robes hung a few inches too long around his ankles.

Zerenity knelt. She turned her finger in a counter-clockwise motion, and the robe's bottom hem unstitched itself. Then, she opened and closed her hand and the robe's bottom turned under itself and rose until it reached the perfect length for Alderan's height. Finally, she turned her finger in a clockwise motion and the robe's bottom stitched itself back together.

Zerenity rose and nodded as she circled back around and faced Alderan. "Those will serve you well." She pointed at the discarded garments. "Grab your belt from your trousers and cinch it around your waist."

Alderan complied, his expression still sour. "I feel like an oaf."

She reached out and squeezed his shoulder. "Give it time, darling. Soon, you'll have forgotten the feel of trousers."

Alderan shook his head. "Don't count on it."

She waved her hand, and Alderan's clothes vanished.

Alderan spun around. "Hey! What are you doing?"

Zerenity raised her hand. "Relax. I've sent your clothes to the wash."

He folded his arms. "And what are we to do now?"

She circled him. "How about I teach you some combat moves while you're in your robes?"

He looked down at his robes and then back to her. "Combat moves? In this? And how will I do that?"

She smiled. "Gird your loins."

† † †

Hey, Rayah, why don't you go have fun by yourself? Rayah shook with rage. *He's my future husband, not hers!*

How much longer would Alderan need to train? None, if it were up to her. Hadn't he saved them enough times to prove his skills? Did it really matter how his mezhik worked, as long as it did?

Ɂätūr will guide him. He doesn't need her.

She had no idea where she'd flown; nothing looked familiar. Mace pine trees huddled around her like predators closing in on their prey, their mace-like branches stretched out and poised to pummel her into the ground. She flew high in the air, but the tall trees still outstretched her by dozens of feet.

This is her fault too.

Frustrated, she screamed. Black birds squawked their displeasure and took to the sky. She shielded her face as they darted dangerously close. She spun in the air, fists balled at her sides. "Watch where you're flying, you daft birds!"

She buzzed aimlessly through the trees, still fuming. A fallen, mace pine tree lay on the ground below her. She settled down on the massive trunk to collect her thoughts and get her bearings back.

At first, she thought nothing of the ends of its branches still green with balls of needles, but the longer she sat there, the harder it became to ignore. She ran her fingers through the needles of the branch closest to her. They still sprang back with life.

Strange. Why would a healthy tree fall?

She walked the length of it, back to its massive base. Its roots, pulled from the earth, splayed out.

How could a tree this mature be ripped from the ground? She fluttered through the entangled roots to investigate further.

The black soil around the roots and the gaping hole left by the overturned tree reeked of death. Unlike the brownish-tan earth around it, the soil teemed with life, but with nothing she'd seen before.

Ꝛätür, what is this?

Several slender, dark-grey vines slithered in the bottom of the hole like serpents, and they hissed at her when she leaned in for a closer look. Their orange thorns raked grooves in the soil, and their orange leaves dolloped a gelatinous yellow substance into them.

Are they… breeding?

One of the vines struck at her with its thorns. She flew backward and screamed, narrowly escaping its reach, but she scraped through some branches from another tree. She fluttered higher and searched for more of the vines but found none.

Those must be the vines Master Savric said his brother found!

How would those little vines topple such a massive tree though? Were they *that* strong? She shuddered to think of the damage they would cause if left unchecked.

Kill the wildlife… nature… poison our water supplies.

"I must warn Zerenity."

She beat her wings hard and zoomed through the forest. Zerenity's house lay just ahead, so she pushed herself harder. By the time she reached the yard in front of the front porch, she could scarcely breathe. She dropped to the ground and tumbled through the dried grass.

She sat up and spat bits of grass from her mouth, shook it from her hair, and brushed it off her dress. She stood and faced the house. The front door hung wide open, and a nidorous odor permeated the air.

The hairs on her arms stood. *Rakzar?* No, she knew his scent well enough, but the similarity could only come from one source: another gnoll.

Or gnolls! They seem to travel in packs.

Already labored from flight, her breathing deepened and turned ragged.

She stood there, shaken and petrified. *What should I do? Is Alderan inside, or are they still training?*

If she flew back to where they trained and they weren't there, would she be too late coming back for them? If she went inside now, would she find Alderan and the others dead? Or would the gnolls kill her and wait for Alderan to return?

"You must be the infamous dryte everyone speaks of."

Rayah jerked her head to the right. She'd been so consumed with herself and the open front door that she hadn't even noticed the gnoll lying in the grass. She beat her wings, but fatigue kept her feet rooted to the ground.

Please, Ẑäṭūr, not again! No matter their planning, trouble sought her at every turn. Her stomach soured. *Am I the one who puts Alderan's life at risk?*

The gnoll sat up, her yellow fur twisted in rows of braids. "Relax, dryte. You'd already be dead if that were my intent."

Rayah swallowed hard. "Why are you here then?" Fear shook her voice. *Stay calm, Rayah.*

The gnoll hooked a claw on her rainbow-colored necklace of ribbons and yarn. "A delivery for a *mutual* friend."

"Rayah meet Urza?" Eshtak stood in the doorway, his eyes gleaming. "Urza sister of Rakzar. Urza friend now. No more bad thing."

Rayah glanced between Eshtak and Urza. "How did you find this place?"

Urza pointed a clawed finger at Eshtak. "The little man's more resourceful than you might think."

Eshtak held up his small mirror with the brass handle. "Eshtak find lady."

Rayah tensed. *If they can find us, so can others!* She looked at Eshtak. "Where are Rakzar and Amicus?"

Eshtak's chin dropped to his chest, and then he turned and disappeared into the house.

"Amicus is dead," said Urza, her voice flat.

Ẑäṭūr, no! Rayah dropped to her knees. Tears blurred her vision. Sorrow overwhelmed her, and she sobbed.

"Rakzar still lives," said Urza.

Rayah cried harder. *Why are You so cruel, Ẑäṭūr? You take the good ones from the world and leave the evil ones. Have You no mercy? Do You hate us all?*

"He's gone to bury Amicus with the rest of Amicus's family."

Rayah sniffed and wiped the tears on her dress. "Rakzar?" She couldn't comprehend the beast showing compassion of any kind. "Why would he do that?"

"Despite what you may think of him, Rakzar isn't a cold-hearted killer. There's more good in him than he lets on. He's saved more lives than he's taken. I'm certain of it."

Can it be true? Rakzar, the one who hunted them for months, a savior? She'd witnessed him take two lives. But how many had he saved or at least attempted to save?

Amicus… Alderan… Eshtak… Rakzar had nearly drowned trying to rescue Eshtak in the ocean.

"Your hatred of him doesn't blind you, does it?" Urza cocked her head. "No. I think you see the good in him too."

Good in Rakzar? Rayah shook her head. "It isn't possible."

Urza stood and stretched her legs. "Deny it all you want, but it's irrelevant."

Rayah looked up at Urza. "And why is that?"

Urza rubbed the front of her neck. "You'll never see him again."

Rayah scoffed. "No? And why not?"

Urza's gaze bore into her. "Because he cares for you and your *White Knight*. Honestly, I don't understand the appeal. Perhaps it's the boy he really cares for." Urza looked around. "Where is he, anyway?"

Rayah crossed her arms. "None of your business. He *will* save the world, you know."

"So I've been told. The *emotional* wizard." Urza growled with laughter.

Rayah's fists balled at her sides. "Rakzar underestimated him once too."

"I believe it had little to do with underestimating the boy. Rakzar's far more complicated than you'd imagine. He claims to work solely for money, but sometimes the job isn't worth its payoff. The boy isn't the first job he's left unfinished."

"You're a liar. From his own mouth, he's said just the opposite."

Urza's eyes flashed, and her mouth curled into a grin. "He says many things to distract from the truth. He's grown to believe some of the lies himself. If you do ever see him again, ask him about the little orphan *dryte*. Now there's a tale you wouldn't wanna miss hearing."

Rayah's eyes widened and her heart pounded. *Ɂäṭūr, is it true? What does Rakzar have to do with me?*

✝ ✝ ✝

The beast held Rayah with a knife to her throat, and Alderan's rage consumed him.

"Rayah!" Alderan bounded through the last trees and into the yard, his sling in-hand, loaded, and whirling in a circle. "Let her go!"

"Easy, *friend*." The beast released Rayah.

Rayah flew toward Alderan, her arms raised and hands waving. "It's not what you think, Alderan. Urza's not an enemy."

Alderan stopped short; the sling still whirled over his head. *Why would she defend that beast? Why did the beast let her go?*

Alderan's mind raced back to the dungeon cell and the fireball he'd nearly killed Amicus with. His arm slumped to his side, and the rock fell to the ground.

Alderan shook his head. "I'm sorry. I didn't know. After everything we've been through, I couldn't stomach the thought of losing you again."

Rayah wrapped her arms around his neck and kissed his cheek. "Never apologize for wanting to protect me."

Zerenity whirled into the middle of the yard, her silver locks whipping the air. She thrust her arms forward. "*Əllzïä!*"

Thick green vines twisted up from the ground and wrapped around Urza's legs. Urza hacked at the vines with her knives, but more of them sprouted and worked their way up her torso, ensnaring her arms too. Urza growled as they wrapped around her snout and muzzled her.

Alderan ran his fingers through his hair. *At least it wasn't me using mezhik on someone this time.*

Eshtak ran out of the house, jumped off the porch, and sprinted across the yard. He grabbed Zerenity's arm and yanked it down. "Eshtak's friend! Eshtak's friend!"

Zerenity looked down at Eshtak and then back at Urza. "When did you arrive?"

Alderan walked over to Zerenity. "She's not our enemy today. Let her go."

"You know her?" Zerenity's glare chilled Alderan.

Rayah moved around Alderan. "I do."

Zerenity huffed. "Fine." She swept her arm toward the ground, and the vines restraining Urza fell away like ash.

Urza snarled, "Do any of you *think* before you act?"

Hesitation is what gets you killed. Alderan shook his head. *No. Don't think that way anymore. You're the savior of the world.*

Alderan stepped forward. "Our experiences with your kind have been anything but pleasant. However, that doesn't excuse our behavior toward you. I ask your forgiveness."

"As do I," said Zerenity. "These uncertain times have left me quick to judge between a friend and a foe."

Urza wiped her knives on her legs and then slid them back into their sheaths on her forearms. *Click-click.* Urza eyed Alderan with her haunting yellow eyes. "So, you're the White Knight."

"Alderan." He stuck his hand out.

Urza eyed Alderan's hand but didn't take it. "How does it feel knowing the weight of the entire world rests on your shoulders?"

Crushing. Devastating. His stomach gurgled.

"You believe then?" asked Rayah.

Urza released her knives and sheathed them again. *Click-click.* "My opinion is irrelevant." She moved close enough to Alderan that her nose nearly touched his. "The only thing of importance is whether or not *you* believe it."

Alderan swallowed hard but held his ground. "I can't afford not to, but, more importantly, why are you with Eshtak? Where are Amicus and Rakzar?"

"The first is dead, and the second is gone," said Urza.

The weight of her words crushed Alderan and drove him to his knees. *Amicus dead?* Tears formed and streaked his face. *How can it be true? And Rakzar...* Had he not become an ally?

How can I hope to save the world when I can't even protect my friends?

Rayah touched the back of his hand, but it brought him no solace. Alderan wiped his eyes. "What happened?"

Urza unsheathed her knives again and twirled them in her hands. "They were foolish to go after Murtag and his red-robed demons. Amicus lost his head, literally. Rakzar lost even more. They should've killed him too, but what they did was far worse."

Alderan stood. "What could be worse than death?"

"To be cursed with the touch of mezhik derk."

Mezhik derk? Alderan glanced over at Zerenity, but her gaze fell to the ground as she shook her head. The amount of knowledge he lacked astounded him. *How will I ever understand it all?*

"Where's Rakzar gone?" Alderan faced Urza again. "Will he return?"

Rayah reached for his hand and squeezed it. "I'll tell you about it later."

"Are you staying?" he asked.

"Not a chance." Urza dropped on all fours. "I only waited to meet you, the *emotional* wizard." She turned and padded toward the forest.

Alderan called to her, "Urza, wait. Now that you know where we are, will you send others?"

"My allegiance lies with my brother, not the pack. If others come for you, it won't be my doing or Rakzar's." She stepped into the trees and vanished.

Her brother? Why had Rakzar never mentioned her? Then again, Rakzar wasn't one for deep conversation, or conversation at all for that matter.

Amicus. He'd saved Aria's life but couldn't save his own. *I owe you mine, friend.*

Alderan realized all the death that surrounded him had the opposite effect on him than what he would've thought: the deeper the sorrow for the loss, the greater the strength and courage he gained from them.

You will not be forgotten.

Nothing stood between him and his destiny but himself. How could he continue to be so selfish and not give everything he had, no matter the task? Resolve strengthened his heart and steeled his mind.

Amicus, I will avenge your death. He pulled Rayah close and kissed the top of her head.

I will train hard and avenge them all.

† † †

Fissures spread from the fist-shaped indentation in the mirror's surface and refracted the white light emanating from Qotan's staff. Savric stared at several reflections of himself, some whole and others mercilessly severed.

Savric leaned on his staff, worn in every sense of the word by the mind game they'd nearly lost in the lower room. "Must adversity stalk us at every opportunity?"

Qotan stroked his chin. "A quest is not truly a quest without opposition, brother."

Savric stared at Qotan's numerous eyes. "I am quite worn of questing."

"Indeed. At some point, the torch of adventure must be passed along. Someone far younger than us, I believe. Calen, perhaps. However, we can ill afford to stop at this juncture."

"To be certain." Savric turned and looked at Qotan directly. "And what do you make of this?"

Qotan reached out and touched the fractured glass. "Only mezhik could damage one of these mirrors, but who would do such a thing?"

Bugger-bees. Who would have the strength?

Savric pulled on his beard. "Dare we traverse through the lower room again?"

"You know as well as I that we cannot."

"Are you privy to knowledge of another option that I am not? We cannot simply teleport ourselves out of here, nor could we have even in our youth."

"No, the barrier prevents us from that." Qotan's brow furrowed and his lips pursed. "However, there is another way. You will not like it, nor will I."

Savric dreaded asking, but they were out of options. "Pray tell, brother."

"It will certainly shorten my life, but I could attempt to repair the mirror."

Savric's chest tightened, and his legs wobbled. "Are you mad, brother? We do not understand the first thing about the mirror's mezhik." He stomped his foot. "I will not risk losing you over such a foolhardy task. Our chance of survival is far greater traversing the lower room a thousand times more."

Qotan placed his hand on Savric's shoulder. "Do not deceive yourself, brother. We narrowly escaped the lower room getting down here. You will not survive it again in your condition, and especially without a functioning staff."

Ꝣätūr, are we trapped here to die?

Savric squeezed his eyes shut for a moment. "I must sit down." Qotan helped him to the dirt floor. Savric sighed and stroked his beard. "How shall we proceed? I have never unwoven a spell before."

Qotan smiled. "Nor I, but you tend to assess situations harsher than I."

"How so?" asked Savric.

Qotan shrugged. "You see the answer to be one of repairing a broken spell."

"And you do not?"

Qotan rubbed his chin. "Perhaps it is not the spell that is broken, but simply the mirror."

The mirror? Savric chuckled and shook his head. "Brother, you are a genius in your own right, even if not by the world's standard. However, how do you propose repairing it? You cannot simply cast a healing spell on an inanimate object."

Qotan nodded. "You are never lacking perception, but it *is* a mirror, brother."

Must I pull the thoughts from his head? "Proceed to your point, brother, before we both perish of starvation or boredom or both."

Qotan shook his head. "Glass. It is all about the glass. I am *Fizärd Ōírdh*, and glass is made of sand."

Feathers, he is right.

"But doing so will sap your energy, and the poison will take hold once more." Savric balled his fist. "I cannot allow you to do it. The risk is too great."

Qotan smiled down at him. "It is not your choice, brother, and there is no other way for us to proceed."

The light faded from Qotan's staff and cast them into an inkwell of darkness.

"*Əllíṭ ʋb.*" A small yellow orb rose from Savric's open palm, its dim light barely strong enough for him to make out Qotan's features. "Be careful."

Qotan nodded, pressed his palm against the fractured mirror, and breathed deep. *"Beəll ṭäzhädhär."* The mirror's surface rippled. *"Beəll ṭäzhädhär,"* he repeated, this time louder. A musty, earthy potpourri bloomed in the room.

Qotan's hand glowed against the mirror. The ground trembled, and then the dirt rose. Slowly at first, and then with fervency, the dirt funneled in the air and poured into the fissures in the glass. One by one, copies of Savric's reflection merged as the glass healed itself.

Savric tensed his shoulders and held his breath. *Easy, brother.*

The last of the fissures repaired themselves, and then the indentation rose to meet the rest of the mirror's surface. The seam around the indentation erased itself until none of it remained. Qotan looked down at Savric and smiled.

A bright light filled the mirror's surface, so brilliant Savric had to shield his eyes with his hand. The air shook like thunder without noise, and its violent concussive force shot the light into the room, threw Qotan across the room, and knocked Savric backward. Darkness rushed in as the light evaded.

Dear Ɂäṭūr!

Savric's orb snuffed out and left him blinded with darkness.

Feathers, feathers, feathers!

"Qotan!" Savric crawled across the dirt floor, found Qotan's outstretched arm, and grabbed his hand. "Talk to me, brother."

Qotan moaned, and Savric's spirits soared. *Thank You, Ɂäṭūr.*

Savric pulled close to Qotan and put his ear near Qotan's mouth. "Brother, can you hear me?" Qotan reeked of singed hair.

Qotan wheezed. "Did I repair it? Does the mirror work?"

He patted the back of Qotan's hand. "You did well, brother. So very well."

"*Əllíṭ ʊb,*" said Savric. Qotan's staff lit the room.

Savric took the staff and pulled himself up with it. He leaned over to help Qotan but froze. Black veins reached up the side of Qotan's face like skeletal fingers grabbing at his brain.

Savric cried out to Ɂäṭūr, "Have mercy on him, Father, and strengthen me."

Savric reached down and lifted Qotan onto his shoulder with one arm.

The weight nearly crushed him, but his legs held fast. He grunted with each step but managed to make it over to the mirror.

He held his hand against the mirror. The warmth of mezhik flowed into his hand and up his arm, and the mirror's surface softened and became wet. *Tyrosha*, he thought, and he hauled Qotan through the mirror.

† † †

"Reni…"

Zerenity gasped, opened her eyes, and sat up in the chair. A blanket wrapped her, and the heat of the fire warmed her face. Still, she pulled the blanket tighter.

I'm not strong enough to lose you, Savvy. Where have you gone?

Eshtak lay on the floor, his legs drawn to his chest, just inches from the yellowish-red flames. The pain she'd witnessed in his eyes over the loss of Amicus tore her flesh and ripped her beating heart from her chest. Sorrow ravaged her still. She wiped warm tears from her eyes, but new ones formed instantly.

"Reni…"

She lifted her head and closed her eyes. *How can I do this, Ȝäṭūr? How do I bring comfort to those around me when my sorrow runs just as deep as theirs? How do I give them hope when I have none to spare? Speak to me. Guide me.*

"Reni help me."

Her eyes shot open. Had Savric's voice not been a spectre of her dreams? "Savvy? Where are you?"

"Your closet." Even in her mind, Savric sounded near death.

Zerenity sprang to her feet, tossed the blanket in the air, and spun out of the room before the blanket had touched the floor. She reached for her closet's doorknob even before she finished materializing in her bedroom. She threw the door open wide.

A large pile of clothes lay on the floor of the closet; a wrinkled hand protruded from the pile. Her heart thumped, and her breath caught for a moment. Rational thought evaded her. She frantically tossed clothes to the side, her mind in no frame to use mezhik.

Under several layers of dresses, she unburied Savric's wiry white hair.

She pushed the dresses aside and pressed her hand against his forehead. He burned with fever. "Stay with me, Savvy."

She grabbed his hand and pulled, but he didn't move. "Alderan!" She screamed for him until her voice became hoarse.

Boots thundered down the hallway, and the bedroom door creaked as it swung inward.

"What's happened?" Alderan entered the closet and knelt beside her. "Master Savric?"

She wiped tears on her sleeves. "Help me get him on the bed."

Alderan put his hand on her shoulder. "Move out of the way. I can handle this."

Zerenity backed out of the closet. Alderan grabbed Savric under the arms, pulled him free from the pile of clothes, and dragged him out of the closet.

"Eshtak help." He moved around Alderan and grabbed Savric's legs.

Together, the two of them lifted Savric onto the bed. Zerenity moved around to the far side of the bed and sat next to Savric. She took his hand and kissed the back of it.

What have you done to yourself this time, you old fool?

Rayah floated at the foot of the bed. "What can I do?"

Zerenity wiped tears from her eyes. "Fetch a cold rag and a glass of water. He's burning with fever."

Rayah nodded and flew out of the room.

Savric moaned and pointed toward the closet. "Brother…" he whispered.

Alderan and Eshtak both turned and peered into the closet. "Can't see anything in here with all the clothes."

Dear Ɛäţūr.

"You won't find anyone in there." She gathered her wits and swept her hand to the side. *"Ūrzhäníz."*

The clothes in the closet sprang to life and put themselves back in place.

Alderan turned back toward the bed and pushed his hand through his hair. "You're right, there's no one in there."

She sighed, half-hoping she'd been wrong. *Of course not. We cannot see spectres.*

Eshtak tugged on Alderan's trousers. "Eshtak sees old man. Man sick too.

Needs help."

Zerenity's breath caught in her throat. She shared a long glance with Alderan, and then Alderan followed Eshtak into the closet.

Rayah zoomed back into the room, rag in one hand and a wooden cup in the other. She handed them to Zerenity and then settled at the foot of the bed.

"Thank you, darling." Zerenity laid the rag across Savric's forehead and lifted his head just enough to drip a few drops of water in his mouth.

Savric swallowed. "More…"

Rayah gasped. "Dear Ɛäţur! With all the action and confusion earlier, I forgot to tell you that I may have found the vines Master Savric spoke of."

Zerenity's gaze snapped to Rayah. "You must show me."

Alderan stepped out of the closet, his face ashen, his gaze distant, and his eyes lightning. He clutched an old staff. "Qotan's indeed alive, and we must save him."

Zerenity gasped and dropped the cup of water. She hadn't possibly heard him correctly. She looked at Savric, horrified. *Is it possible, Ɛäţur? Does Qotan truly live?*

"You've seen him?" Zerenity's voice trembled.

Alderan's eyes flashed and then returned to normal. He turned the staff in his hand. "Yes. When I picked this staff up I saw its last events. Savric came here with Qotan. He looked deathly sick with black veins spread up his neck and cheeks. I'm unsure how much time he has left."

Zerenity rubbed her arms, chilled to her bones. *Can this truly be?*

Eshtak poked his head out from the closet and motioned Zerenity to come. "Eshtak show lady sick man."

Zerenity stood on shaky legs and walked around the bed. Eshtak took her hand and led her into the closet. Toward the back of the closet, to the left of the mirror, they knelt.

The floor before them lay barren. Zerenity shook her head. "I don't understand."

"Eshtak show." Still holding her hand, he reached out with his.

Her heart thundered. Her eyes blurred. And then it happened.

Qotan?

CHAPTER THIRTY-THREE

A single shelf in the library held more volumes of books than Aria had read in her entire life. Tens of thousands of books lined the shelves floor-to-ceiling and wall-to-wall.

They covered a vast array of subjects and themes, from *The History of Etiquette* to *Common Remedies for the Common Man*. She found tomes dedicated to *The Breeding of Canine Subspecies* and *The Arts of Horticulture and Agriculture* and other subjects she couldn't fathom, but none of them related to prophecy or mezhik.

She sighed. *This is pointless.*

She closed the book she'd started flipping through, scooted her chair back, and rose from the table. "Master Credan?"

Credan walked in through the double doors. "How may I be of service, Mistress Aria?"

She smoothed out the wrinkles in her blue dress. "I've been poring over these books for the past week, but I haven't found what I'm looking for."

He clasped his hands behind his back and smiled. "And what is it you seek?"

"Pravus told me he possessed several books on prophecy and mezhik. Where will I find those?"

Credan scratched his nose and cleared his throat. "Those, my dear, would be in Lord Rosai's personal library."

She swept her arm in a wide arc. "These books are of no interest to me." She strolled over to him and held out her elbow. "Take me there."

Credan eyed the floor, averting her gaze. "Some areas of the castle are currently off limits... due to complications. Lord Rosai's personal library happens to be in one of those areas." He shook his head slowly. "I am deeply sorry."

Complications? Anger rose in her throat and tightened her neck. *Why does he insist on forgetting who I'm soon to be?* She bit her lip and waited for her anger to settle before she spoke.

She chose her words carefully. "Master Credan, I'm far more perceptive than you credit me. As I see it, one of three things have occurred: Either you're forbidden to grant me access, you're unwilling to grant me access, or you simply fear what I may find in there." She leaned in close and searched his eyes. "Which option is it? Personally, I think it's the last."

Credan averted her gaze once again. "It's far more complicated than that, young one."

She ran her finger down the side of his cheek, tempted to dig her nail into it but refrained from doing so. "Please do your best to simplify it for one such as me. One whom you deem so thick."

Beads of sweat formed on the top of his balding head. "I would never imply such falsehoods of you! I've misspoken if that's what you heard. I have a deep respect for your wit and understand the draw Lord Rosai has toward you. Forgive me, Mistress Aria."

She lifted his head with a single finger and waited until his gaze met hers. "You haven't answered the question."

Credan's cheeks bloomed red like blood roses. He adjusted his shirt collar with a finger and swallowed hard. "Simply put, it may be a combination of all three."

Aria crossed her arms. "Let's see if I understand. You're forbidden *and* unwilling to take me there for fear of what I might find?"

He wiped the top of his head with a white kerchief. "Agreed, mostly."

She furrowed her brow. "How can you agree 'mostly?' Either you do, or you don't. There's no ambiguity to be had."

Credan nodded. "Right you are. It's not a fear of what you might find so much as it is of what might find *you*."

She walked back over to the table and rapped her knuckles on it. Her mind traversed her brief but violent past. How could anything be more dangerous than what she'd already endured?

Play the politician, Aria. Address his concerns and find common ground.

Aria faced Credan once more. "I will concede your ruling… on one condition."

Credan clasped his hands behind his back and leaned forward. His eyebrows arched over the tops of his spectacles. "And what condition might that be?"

Aria motioned toward the door. "Retrieve some of the books from Pravus's personal library for me."

Credan shook his head. "What you ask of me is impossible." Aria glared at him, but he continued, "It's not that I'm unwilling to do so, but physically unable. Lord Rosai has set several wards to prevent unauthorized access into his library. Entry without his presence and approval would kill me."

Aria raised her arms and thrust her hands forward. "Please speak Centaurian, Master Credan. What is a 'ward,' and how would it kill you?"

Credan frowned and looked toward the ceiling for several moments. "I am no expert in such matters, but I can give you my basic understanding of it. A ward is a type of woven mezhik that can be placed on or around things, like a room for instance. I think of it like a fisherman's net."

Credan smiled and continued, "If you try and cross through the ward, its mezhik will spring to life, so to speak, and conjure or fire off the mezhik spell contained within its fibrous net."

Aria opened her mouth to speak, but Credan raised his hand. "I know, it's not the kind of explanation you seek, but it's the only one I can offer you. Lord Rosai is far more equipped with the knowledge of such things, so you should question him about it."

Aria crossed her arms and paced in circles. *He has answers for everything, so how can I get what I need?* The castle teemed with servants, guards, and others of whom she didn't know their purpose.

Others. She smiled and turned toward Credan. "Would anyone else have access to his library?"

Again, Credan's gaze averted hers for a moment. "No, I don't believe so." *He has a tell when he lies.*

Anger fueled her and drove her across the room. She drew so close to Credan that she almost tasted his lunch. Wide-eyed, he stepped backward.

She jabbed his chest with her finger. "There's no point in lying to me, Master Credan. Take me to whomever has access, or I will find my own way to the library. Would you want my death on your conscience? What would Pravus do to you if I were to die?"

"If you died, he'd destroy the foundations of this world and leave me alive to witness it."

"And is that what you'd want?"

Credan sighed and shook his head. "No, Mistress Aria."

"Of course not." She held out her elbow for him. "We've wasted enough time. Let's be on our way."

"Very well." Credan hooked his arm though hers. "We will talk with Wizard Wrik, but I assure you he is a cross man and not fond of anyone disturbing him. He will certainly deny any request you may bring to him."

She smiled. *No one denies me.*

† † †

As she had done in the dungeons underneath Castle Portador Tempestade, Aria mentally mapped every door, hallway, corridor, and stairway they walked, crossed, or traversed through Galondu Castle.

Aria walked down a long stretch of corridor, alongside Credan. "At the peak of its usage, how many soldiers were housed here?"

"One can only speculate, but I'd venture a guess of at least 250,000. Plus, there would've been several thousand chancellors, counselors, advisers, and other political figures. A thousand wizards and sorceresses too."

She gaped at the tapestry-lined walls and soaring ceilings. "Why were the corridors built to such massive scale? Doesn't it seem inefficient?"

Credan laughed. "If this castle was only made for humanoid creatures, then yes. However, when they built this castle before the Great War, they also considered the size of dragons. Some dragons are small, tiny even, but many are so large that a single claw matches the size of you and me."

Dragons. Aria's head swam with images from the castle tapestries.

She stopped and pulled Credan to a halt as well. "Dragons roamed these halls?"

"Certainly! With their trainers, of course."

Aria pictured people leading dragons around with leads like horses. *Could I have owned one?*

Her stomach tickled with excitement. "Are they friendly?"

Credan pulled her along the wide corridor. "Some, perhaps. But they were fiercely prideful creatures and didn't enjoy being caged, chained, or forced to do the bidding of anyone but themselves."

Aria stopped again. "'Were?' Have they all died off?"

Credan shrugged. "Tales arise now and again of dragon sightings, but I've yet to meet one myself."

Aria peered back at some of the tapestries they'd passed. "Some of the tapestries depict men and women riding the dragons."

"They certainly do." Credan pulled on Aria's arm. "Come along. We can talk as we walk."

Aria sighed but complied. "As you wish."

Credan led them down the corridor, passing several intersections and stairways. "Those you mentioned were ones they called *Rídärz Drezhn*. The Dragon Riders. With their help, the tides of the Great War began to turn in Magus's favor. Had it not been for *Ūrdär Dhef 2äfn Dhä* and the strength of Cyrus, Magus would've won. The world we live in would certainly have been different if he had."

Aria closed her eyes and imagined soaring through the sky, but not in the clutches of their claws. She'd experienced that already with the scouts and would be happy never doing so again.

Credan led her to the right, down a narrow and poorly lit hallway, and to a plain, honeyed-oak door set deep in the wall. A brass knocker hung on the door at eye-level, a front-facing dragon's head with a ring clutched between its teeth. Credan took the knocker and rapped on the door three times.

"Leave me be," said a deep, masculine voice.

Credan turned to Aria and smiled. "We've tried our best. Better not to disturb him further."

She scowled at him, grabbed the knocker, and rapped hard thrice more.

Credan's eyes bulged, but he held his tongue.

She pressed her ear against the door and listened. Rustling papers. A chair screeched on the floor. Footsteps. *A large man?* The door vibrated, and she pulled her ear away. A lock turned, and the door moaned as it cracked open.

A dim light filtered through the doorway, and a pair of golden eyes, set under bushy grey eyebrows and behind wire-rimmed frames, peered around the door's edge. "Did you not comprehend my words, or does your self-importance supersede my wishes?"

Credan dipped his head. "Forgive our intrusion, Wizard Wrik. We were just leaving, I assure you."

Aria clenched her jaw, pulled her arm from Credan's, and glared at him. "*We* are not leaving, but you are free to excuse yourself, Master Credan. In fact, I insist you do." She turned her gaze on the eyes behind the door. "Wizard Wrik and I have several matters to discuss."

The cracked door opened wide, and the dark-skinned man filled the opening, both in width and height. His pearly-white teeth brightened his wide smile, and his bald head afforded him more youth than it should've. Only the lines around his eyes and across his forehead betrayed his true age.

Wrik turned sideways but kept his gaze trained on Aria. He swept his arm into the room. "Please, make yourself at home."

She smiled and stepped past him and into the small room. A large bed nestled the corner of the room catty-corner to the door. At the foot of the bed, directly opposite the door, sat a desk obviously too small for Wrik's large frame.

A table with two chairs shoved underneath its edge hugged the corner to the right of the door. Papers and books covered its surface. Several square, iron sconces hung on the walls; their yellowed candles flickered in rhythm. A fire blazed on the hearth inset in the wall between the table and the bed.

Aria pulled a chair out from under the table and sat down. Hushed whispers between Wrik and Credan met her ears, the words indistinguishable. She didn't care what they discussed. She'd get her way regardless of any arrangements they made.

She snatched a sheet of paper off the table and held it up to the light. Strange symbols lined its edges, and the writing—if one could classify it as such—resembled nothing more than childish scribbles. *How does one read this?*

She set it back down and slid one of the books to the table's edge. She leafed through it, but its text resembled the writing on the paper.

How will I learn anything if I can't even read the books?

Wrik closed the door and walked over to the table. "Credan's informed me that you are the future queen. My congratulations. Lady Aria, yes? May I call you by that name, or would you prefer I call you something else?"

Lady Aria. She rather liked it, especially the way his silky baritone voice caressed the words. "Lady Aria is perfect. And how shall I address you?"

He adjusted his spectacles. "I will gladly answer to any name you bestow upon me, but simply Wrik will suffice, if it pleases you."

"Simply Wrik." She laughed.

He smiled and chuckled. "How may I be of service?"

Master Credan, you're a liar! Wrik's anything but cross.

Aria looked up at him and channeled as much charm as she could muster. "Lord Rosai has had little time for me as of late. I'm desperately seeking knowledge of the prophecies and of training in mezhik. Any time you can afford me will be greatly appreciated and will be remembered when I've taken the throne as queen."

"I assure you that I'll do everything in my power to help you." He pulled out the chair next to hers, angled it toward her, and sat down. "As you may have guessed, Master Credan outlined some rules I am to follow regarding you."

Here it comes. Will I find no one in this castle willing to help me?

His golden eyes collected the candlelight and churned like molten liquid. "However, I am my own man and have my own agendas and opinions. I work for Lord Rosai, not because I owe him a debt or because he holds something over me, but because I am an expert on prophecy. How could I possibly live without being where the action is to take place?"

Aria smiled. *Is this the real reason Credan didn't want me to meet Wrik?*

He leaned forward, took her hands and kissed her knuckles, and then released them back to her. "Unlike the faltered opinions of some of those surrounding us, I know you're anything but fragile. Nothing will prevent the prophecies from being fulfilled. Ask anything of me. I am your servant."

One thing eclipsed her desire to know the prophecies: who was Nardus? The man and his stone stood between her and Pravus marrying, and she didn't like it. Pravus had already wasted a week trying to get the stone from him. She didn't want to wait further.

She also didn't like the fact that Pravus thought her to be too weak to handle a man like Nardus. How dangerous could he be? She could handle herself in any situation. She'd proven that in the dungeons.

She ground her teeth. *Pravus doesn't own me. I'll move things along on my own.*

She smiled at Wrik. "Do you know the man Pravus holds here?"

Wrik shrugged. "You must be more specific than that. Hundreds of men are held in the dungeons at any given time."

Aria smoothed her dress, more to wipe the perspiration from her palms than to straighten any wrinkles in the fabric. "Nardus."

Wrik leaned back, and his lips curled into a wicked grin. "I do. A very dangerous man."

She stood. "Take me to him."

Wrik rose from his chair, a giant next to her. He smoothed his silver robes and adjusted the black belt around his waist. "Wasn't sure you'd ask. I cannot take you to him, but I will get you close and tell you where to go from that point."

"Why can't you take me there yourself?"

"Only Lord Rosai is allowed in that section of the castle. There's only one way in, and a squad of soldiers guard the entrance." He winked at Aria. "I will create a diversion for you."

Her hands trembled. "I will be indebted to you."

He took her hand between his thumb and finger; they nearly covered the palm of her hand. "Yes, and one day I will ask a favor of you."

Aria straightened and looked Wrik in the eye. "Then we're in agreement."

"Good." He turned, opened the door, and motioned her forward. "After you, Lady Aria."

She walked out of the room and into the hallway. She wiped the perspiration from her palms again and took a deep breath.

What makes you so dangerous, Nardus?

She must know, even if it killed her.

† † †

Pravus stood on top of the southern rampart and leaned over the stone parapet. More than a hundred feet below lay Atrum Moenia, a once-bustling city, now a graveyard of structures inhabited by the beasts of the world and the lowest of the lowly.

He squeezed his left fist tight. *Eradication will come soon enough.*

The wind whipped his robes and his silver-and-black hair. He pulled back his sleeves and studied the three marks on the insides of his wrists. A week ago, he'd had a single mark on his left wrist, but now his left had two and his right had one. The one on his right intrigued him the most.

Triza, a Fizärd Erzíe, gave her life for the cause. *For the kingdom.* Unlike Tilly's blood, he'd remember hers.

Four parallel black lines ran perpendicular to the veins on the inside of his right forearm. The outer two lines were slightly shorter on one end than the others. To the right of the lines, the side where the four lines were even, a black, cloud-shaped mark marred his skin. *A gust of wind. Erzíe.*

He stepped back from the parapet and stretched his right hand. His fingers still curled unnaturally, but the blood of Yora and Triza had healed his blackened and shriveled skin and had returned his strength. He held his arms down at his sides and flattened his hands as best he could, palms down and parallel to the rampart he stood on.

"Fallí." Mezhik's cold touch flowed down his arms, and the smell of spring blossomed in the air. A great wind arose from nowhere, howled, swirled, and encircled him. The air vibrated, and small rocks bounced along the top of the rampart. Below his palms, the air rippled and quaked and twisted like tiny cyclones.

The bottom of his robes fluttered, and his feet lifted off the ground. At first, he ascended only a few inches, but then he applied resistance with his open palms and soared twenty feet above the rampart.

Excitement bubbled up from his stomach and burst from his lips in a fit of laughter. *I am a god!*

He tilted his left hand to the right and spun himself in circles. He over-corrected and pushed himself out well beyond the parapet wall. Fear seized him for the briefest moment, but that instant severed the spell and sent him plummeting.

The ground raced toward him ever faster. Another second and he'd meet the ground.

"*Fəllí!*" He thrust his hands toward the ground and demanded that the air slow him down.

A strong draft rushed up from the ground and brought a cloud of dust with it.

Amidst the dust and chaos, Pravus lost sight of the ground, but then his feet met it with jaw-jarring force. Pain tore through his shins. He tucked his head and rolled forward, but his downward momentum cracked his head against his right knee. He cried out as he rolled over his left shoulder and came to a stop on his back.

Pain pulsed in his temples with every heartbeat. He reached up and checked his forehead; a lump had already formed over his right eyebrow. He sat up, and the world tossed him about. He squeezed his eyes tight for several moments and then blinked a few times to slow his spinning head.

Once his vision settled, he looked around. To his left and right, no more than twenty feet in either direction, razor-sharp rocks jutted up from the ground. An image of himself impaled on the rocks formed in his mind and ignited his anger. He punched the ground, and his knuckles cracked on the hard rock.

He brooded over the failed flight. *I'm pathetic. No matter how much blood I consume, I'll never rival Magus's strength.*

At least not without Aria's.

Pravus pulled himself to his feet and stood still until the pain subsided enough for him to think again. He dusted off his robes and checked his aching shins. He moved about, but the pain persisted.

He shook his head and clenched his jaw. *Shin splints.* He forced air through his nostrils, and then stepped from where he stood outside the castle and into his bedchamber in a single step.

Pravus uncinched his belt and let it fall to the floor. He pulled his robes over his head and tossed them to the side. Then he stepped out of his shoes and crawled onto the bed.

He sank into the goose feather comforter face-first and let his exhaustion pull him down into sleep.

† † †

Aria stood alone in the dark corridor, frozen with fear. Demon shadows stretched down the walls and across the floor and melded into the darkness, their elongated bodies undulating to the rhythm of an inaudible source. They beckoned her into the darkness.

Not long before, she'd separated from Wizard Wrik so that he could distract the guards from their post while she snuck by. In the better part of two hours' time, she'd grown fond of him. She longed for his company and the strength and comfort she drew from his imposing presence.

You're the future queen. Fear does not control you. If only she had faith in her thoughts. The hairs on her arms and nape stood on end, her pulse quickened, and her throat tightened. She swallowed hard and crept forward.

Unlike the other corridors in the castle, this one's breadth exceeded the others tenfold, and the flooring transitioned from dull black rocks to large slabs of swirled black-and-grey marble. Cylindrical columns lined both sides of the main thoroughfare, and beyond those columns lurked monsters.

Aria shuddered and rubbed her arms with her hands. Several moments later, she realized she'd stopped moving again.

Wizard Wrik referred to the corridor as the Hall of Dragons, and for good reason. He'd explained that the derro dwarves, stone masters of the old world, had carved replicas of dozens of the dragons that resided in the castle before the Great War. Each carving stood to scale, and the stones and gems used to create each masterpiece perfectly matched the dragons they represented, right down to the translucent membrane covering the wings of the winged ones.

Some of the dragons would've fit in her palm, and others had claws the size of her torso. Like other species, their diversity spanned all colors, sizes, shapes, and skins. She surmised male and female specimens were represented in the lot of them, but how would one determine the sex of a dragon? She also wondered what they ate.

Probably me.

Aria moved forward again. In the dark, the dragons' eyes followed her. *They're not real, Aria.* Knowing so did little to bolster her courage.

Each step echoed on the hard floor like the beat of a familiar song, weaving tales of her treachery. Had anyone been around, she imagined they would've heard her coming for miles. She stopped in the middle of the hall and plopped down on the floor. With a great deal of effort and several grunts, she removed her knee-high boots.

How does Brema do it so effortlessly?

She stood and carried her boots. The cold floor froze her bare feet, but at least she no longer filled the hall with the sounds of a cavalry riding into battle. Instead, her heartbeat hammered her ears.

A fair trade-off.

At the far end of the hall, she turned left underneath a rounded archway and headed down a spiraling stairway that seemed to have no end. When she arrived at the lower landing, she walked down the attached corridor, made two lefts, a right, then descended another stairway—a straight one this time and far shorter.

A three-way intersection of hallways met at the bottom of the stairway. She went straight ahead twenty feet, turned around and went back, then turned to the left. *Keep it straight, Aria, or you'll never find your way back.* The hallway took a sharp left and ended at a doorway. The black steel door stood wide open.

She stopped and listened. The smell of burning pitch tickled her nostrils. Her pulse soared.

Don't do this, Aria. If Pravus finds him so dangerous, think of what he could do to you.

She bit down hard on her lip and drew blood. *You've come all this way. Just go in there.*

She needed to know. She must know. The unknown would haunt her otherwise.

She swallowed her fear and walked through the doorway. She hugged the wall where shadows collected and maneuvered over to a metal bench. She quietly set her boots on the floor and then sat on the bench.

Inside the steel cage, the man she knew to be Nardus lay on a bed of straw, his back to her. From what little of him she could see, he looked no different than any other man she'd seen before. She couldn't be certain, but she thought him to be asleep.

A silver collar wrapped his neck, a match to hers. *Is he a wizard?* Pravus had never alluded to him being one, so she'd never considered it before. If he were, wouldn't the collar prevent him from using his mezhik? And the steel cage contained him, didn't it?

What else could make him so dangerous? She thought of no explanation.

Two steel posts with heavy chain stood at the center of the cage, but he wasn't bound to them. Had he been as dangerous as Pravus led her to believe, wouldn't he have been restrained as well? Something felt amiss.

She frowned. *Why is Pravus so adamant about me staying away from him? Is it really because he's dangerous, or is it something else entirely?* She disliked secrets and lies, even the ones she kept from others.

She stood and crept over to the cage to get a better look at him. *Why are you special?*

Cold steel bars met her cheeks as she leaned closer. Nardus moaned softly, but she couldn't determine if he'd said anything intelligible. He rolled over, and faced her, his eyes closed.

Aria gasped and pulled away from the bars. *How can it be?*

She retreated farther until the bench pushed against the backs of her calves. She sank down onto the bench.

Her chest tightened, and her stomach knotted. She'd seen his face before. Her mind reeled, unable to fathom the depths of Pravus's betrayal. Why would Pravus have kept this from her?

Does Pravus know? She closed her eyes. *How could he?*

She shook her head, opened her eyes, and stared at Nardus.

But Pravus must.

Memories of Daltura and the old man at the café flooded her mind. The note. The words. Those precious, significant words: *He lives.*

In her heart, she'd known those words had never referred to Alderan, but still she'd clung to that hope, no matter how thin the thread. However, the man in the steel cage removed all doubt as to the meaning of those two words, and it crushed her soul.

He's the one that lives, not Alderan. Already, she hated him.

Nardus. The name left her bitter, and her collar glowed red.

How much has Pravus kept from me? Had anything from Pravus's lips ever been the truth? He had an explanation for everything she'd gone through, but were they too calculated and perfect? *Is Pravus really the man I've come to love?*

She needed a friend she could confide in. She'd give anything to have Amicus at her side again. She missed his big smile and the kindness he'd always showered upon her. Vonah too. Her big bright eyes and innocent wonder always brought Aria joy and laughter.

But Nardus… The man from her memories. Or were they dreams? *What does it mean?*

She trembled, and the cold room enhanced her tremors. She drew her knees to her chest and chewed on her lower lip.

He's dangerous… Had Pravus referred to emotional danger and not physical? Or had he implied a danger to their relationship? Would anything ever change her feelings for him?

No. Pravus saved me. My life is his. I will die loving him.

And what about Wizard Wrik? He'd called Nardus dangerous as well. He knew nothing of her past, didn't he?

Regarding Nardus, she needed answers. She must know why his face haunted her memories. *Will he even remember me? Or is it all in my head?*

Are they someone else's memories? As a wizard, maybe the past presented itself to her like the future does a prophet. She knew nothing of mezhik or of her capabilities, so the possibility seemed viable.

Should I wake him? Her pulse increased. *What would I say to him if I did?*

Moving forward, she'd need to find her voice. A queen had to address her subjects, so some practice wouldn't hurt.

She cleared her throat. "Nardus." Her voice came out so weak, she doubted the sound reached Nardus's ears.

✝ ✝ ✝

"*Nardus.*" Vitara's voice roused him from sleep.

Nardus sat up and rubbed the sleep from his eyes. Steel bars surrounded him and pulled him back into the present. *If only I was with you, my love.* "Soon."

From the corner of his eye, he glimpsed a form in the deep shadows, huddled on the bench. He shook his head. "What do you want from me now,

Pravus? Have you found another way to torture me?"

No response. He waited a few more beats. *Something's different.*

He walked across the cell and peered into the shadows. The torchlight flickered just right, giving him a hint of the person sitting on the bench. Not a man, but a woman. His heart thundered, and his mind raced, irrationally, but he knew what he'd glimpsed in that brief instant.

He closed his eyes. *She isn't there, is she?* His chest didn't burn, and the voice in his head failed to respond. *It's impossible.*

He opened his eyes, but the woman still sat on the bench. He clutched the bars in his hands, an anchor for his sanity. *You're my anchor.*

"Vitara?" Uttering her name buckled his knees, and he slid to the floor. "Is that you, my love? Have you come to haunt me?" Hot tears streamed down his cheeks, but he didn't care. She needed to see his sorrow. "I'm so sorry. Forgive me, my love."

The woman didn't move or speak, but her gaze never left him. He shook the bars. "Why must you torture me? Have I not suffered enough already? Speak to me or be gone!"

He grabbed his head and screamed. *What have I done to deserve this madness?* His chest and throat convulsed with sobs, and snot hung from his nose. "Leave me!"

Still, the woman didn't move.

"Vitara, my love, I beg of you… give me leave. I seek your presence every moment of my existence, but I cannot take your silence. Do you still not forgive me for Theyn? What must I do to win back your heart? Require anything of me, and it will be done."

He reigned in his emotions, wiped the tears from his eyes and the snot from his nose, and leaned into the bars. "I never intended for you all to perish. Forgive me for failing to protect you and our children as I should've. I live a life tormented in damnation every moment we're separated. I still fight for you, my love."

He pulled himself back to his feet. "Please, I beg of you, say something."

The woman leaned forward, but her face remained in the shadows. "I am not her."

Not her? Nardus staggered backward, stunned. The air in the room thinned, and Nardus couldn't breathe deep enough to catch his breath.

"N-not her," he stammered. He closed his eyes for a moment and collected his thoughts.

No, of course not. How could she be her? This madness still plagues me.

Nardus stepped back up to the bars and motioned the woman over. "Come out of the shadows so I can see your face."

The woman leaned back and sat silent for several moments. Then, in a voice faint enough to be a whisper, she said, "Stand back... and I will."

Her voice reminded him of Vitara's, but he wouldn't mistake them again. He retreated to the other side of the cage and motioned her over again. "Please, I wish you no harm."

The woman lowered her legs from the bench and stood. She stepped forward, just into the light and no farther. Curls of blonde hair framed her slender face, and her green eyes bore into him. Familiarity bled from her soul and filled his, but he couldn't place its source.

Risking her retreat, Nardus took a step toward her. "Do I know you?"

She smoothed her blue dress and clasped her hands in front of her. "I—I don't know. I was about to ask you the same thing."

"I feel we must, but from where, I couldn't say." He took another step forward. "What's your name?"

"I am Aria. Aria Somneri." She reached up and twirled a finger into her blonde curls.

Aria? Do I know that name? He pondered it for several moments, but no recollection came to mind. "I'm sorry, but that name doesn't mean anything to me."

She stepped forward, her finger still wrapped in her hair. "I have memories of you... or maybe visions. I don't know which they might be."

Nardus rubbed the scars on his left bicep, and his heart ached for Vitara. "Please tell me. Maybe they will free my memories as well."

Another step. She stood just beyond the bars. "They're just glimpses, really. I believe I was very young at the time. You sat nearby, watching my brother and I play on the beach, building sandcastles."

Sandcastles? His knees weakened, and it took all his strength to stay upright. *How can it be? Why does she have my daughter's memories?*

He moved over to the crate at the center of the cage and sat down.

Don't all children build sandcastles on the beach? Yes, of course they do.

He needed further proof. "What else can you tell me of it?"

She lifted her head and closed her eyes. The corners of her mouth raised into a smile. "I always enjoyed when the tide would come in and wash away everything I'd built. It was like getting a clean slate to work with again. But my brother would usually cry about it and refuse to play after it happened."

Proof enough.

"How do you have my daughter's memories?" He stood, his face hot with anger. He pointed at her. "Did Pravus send you in here? Did he put you up to this? What kind of cruel game are you playing at?"

Aria retreated to the shadows. "This is no game! Pravus doesn't even know I'm down here. He forbade me to see you, but I had to know. Do you have any idea what he might do to me if he finds me down here?"

Nardus put his hands on his face. The left side of his chest burned. He pulled at his hair and groaned. "Not now."

"Give her the stone."

I told you to stay out of my head.

"We want the same thing. Give her the stone."

Never!

† † †

Pravus heard Nardus screaming before he reached the end of the hallway. He walked through the doorway and into the large room with the cage. Nardus stood in the middle of the cage, fists balled, muscles taut, and veins bulging, screaming at the ceiling.

Pravus looked to his right and couldn't believe his eyes. Aria stood by the bench. *She's disobeyed me!* Fury raged within him.

Why would she do this? How did she get down here? He knew the answer. She must've had help. He snarled. *Credan will pay for this.*

He reached out toward Nardus and twisted his hand into a fist.

Nardus grabbed his own throat and gasped for air. Pravus pulled his fist down hard and Nardus dropped to the floor. Pravus unclenched his fist and turned his attention back on Aria.

"Did I not make myself clear when I *forbade* you from coming down here?" He pointed at Nardus. "That man's more dangerous than you could ever imagine!"

Aria's hands balled into fists. "I am sick of being treated like a child! You have no authority to forbid me from doing anything. I make my own decisions about what I should and shouldn't be doing. If you're unwilling to accept that, then find someone else to be your *queen*. You once told me that you liked that I was a strong woman. I am far stronger than you know. Neither you nor anyone else will control me anymore. Am I clear?"

Pravus fumed. *She dares to yell at me?* He opened his mouth to respond, but words failed him. She'd infuriated him, humiliated him, and disrespected his authority. He could've ripped her heart from her chest in that moment, but in the next, he wanted to confess his undying love for her.

How does she do this to me?

Nardus coughed then spat on the floor. "Serves you right."

Pravus glared at Nardus. "I'm in no mood for your insolence. Press me further, and I'll make you the focus of my wrath."

Aria walked over and placed her hand on Pravus's arm. "How is it that I know this man?"

That single touch calmed Pravus. He searched Aria's eyes for several moments. Like his, her anger had faded. "You *know* him?"

† † †

Nardus stood and walked over to the bars closest to Aria and Pravus. "She has my eldest daughter's memories. Explain that, wizard. Is it mezhik, or something far darker?"

Aria crossed her arms and furrowed her brow, her gaze on Pravus. "Don't even think about lying. I'll know if you are, and I'll walk out of here and never return."

Pravus rubbed his hands together and cracked his knuckles. He gave Aria a sidelong glance. "What if I told you that you're his daughter?"

My daughter? Nardus punched the bar. "I'd say you're a liar. You know that's impossible. I buried my sweet Shanara when she was only three and my angel Savannah when she was one. Savannah died in her mother's arms. Even if I hadn't buried Shanara, Aria's far too old to be her."

Pravus ran the back of his finger down Aria's cheek. She flinched. "And how old do you think Aria is?"

"Fifteen? Sixteen? How would I know?" Nardus studied Aria's soft features. *She does have Vitara's cheeks and eyes, but it's not possible for her to be Shanara.*

"I'm sixteen." Anger and tears filled Aria's eyes.

Nardus massaged his left bicep. "Bah, sixteen. See? An impossibility."

Pravus leaned back and frowned. "Impossibility? On what grounds?"

Nardus raised his arms. "Oh, I don't know—maybe the fact that the numbers don't add? Shanara was three years old when she died. You approached me little more than a year afterward. I was gone six to eight months in that godforsaken place, and now I've been back another month or so."

Nardus did the math in his head. "If she were five or so, I'd be more inclined to believe you, but sixteen—bah."

Pravus's brow rose. "Six to eight months? Is that really what you believe? What did that place do to you?"

Drove me mad!

Had he the power, he would've pulled the steel bars apart and strangled Pravus. "How about you go there and find out firsthand, like I did. Damned mezhik." He spat on the floor.

Pravus shook his head. "There's no other way to tell you this but straight out. You were gone *twelve* years, my friend."

Nardus glared at him. "We're certainly not friends, and there's no way I was down there twelve years."

Pravus looked at Aria and stroked her cheek. "Tell him the year, my love. He won't believe it from my lips."

Nardus raged inside. *If she were my daughter, I'd never let you lay a finger on her!*

A drop of blood moistened Aria's lower lip. *Shanara used to bite her lip too. But I'm sure many girls do. She can't be her.*

"P.G.W. 1219. I was born in 1202."

"1219..." *But I left at the end of 1206. This cannot be. It's madness!*

He pressed his head against the bars. "No, no, no. I buried her. She cannot be Shanara."

Vitara, my love, and my anchor, tell me the truth! How is this possible?

Nardus roared and beat the left side of his chest. "You said this damned stone would bring my family back from the dead! Why did you send me to that hellish world if part of my family still lived? This is madness! She cannot be her!"

Pravus took Aria's arm and pulled her closer to the cage. "Look at her, Nardus. I mean *really* look at her and admit it. You knew she was your daughter the moment you saw her."

Nardus's mind reeled. How could Aria be her? *Shanara… Aria has her memories. Why else would she have those memories? Building sandcastles.*

The anger passed, and hope burned in his soul. He reached for her through the bars, but she retreated. "Shanara, don't be afraid. Is it really you?"

Tears streamed down her face, and the silver collar around her neck glowed red. She shook as though she might explode, and, when she did, her rage targeted Pravus. "You *knew* he was my father, and you kept that from me? What kind of monster are you?" She ripped her arm from Pravus's grasp.

My daughter lives. Vitara, our daughter lives!

Pravus reached for Aria's arm again, but she twisted away and backed farther from them both. "Keep your hands off me, you bastard! You've lost your right to touch me."

Pravus moved toward Aria. "Aria, I can explain."

Rage grew within Nardus again, and he swiped at Pravus through the bars. "You touch my daughter again, and I'll kill you myself!"

Aria's fists balled at her sides. Tears still streaked her face, but her cheeks glowed with anger. "How long have you known?"

She didn't wait for an answer. Instead, she ran out the steel door and disappeared.

No!

"Shanara, wait!" Nardus slammed himself against the bars and grabbed at Pravus. "How dare you do this to her, you twisted bastard!"

Pravus backed away from the cage. "Calm down. We'll get this misunderstanding worked out in the morning."

"Misunderstanding? And I thought *I* was mad!" Nardus turned and kicked the crate in the middle of the cage.

Damn.

Another thought filled his mind. *My family!*

Nardus charged the bars again and slammed them with his fists. "Whose body did I bury with my family if it wasn't hers?"

Pravus shrugged. "How would I know?"

"How would you know any of it? Oh, I have the answer right in front of me." He shook his fist at Pravus. "This is all *your* doing."

Pravus held his arms out. "All I ever wanted was to help you, Nardus. I swear on my mother's grave. After you left for Mortuus Terra, I heard rumors of missing children. A wizard with the right skills can uncover many things, and I knew one such wizard. With his help, I discovered the truth about what happened that day with your family."

Nardus quaked with rage. *Does anything come from his mouth but lies? Madness!*

Nardus shook the bars. "You're a liar, Pravus. How did I ever trust you? You stole thirteen years of my life from me and my daughter. I'll be damned if I ever let you take this stone from my chest. Do you hear me? You'll burn in *Ef Demd Dhä* first!"

Pravus glared at Nardus, and his jaw hardened. "Tomorrow, you die," he said slowly, "and that stone will be mine." He turned and left the room.

Nardus pressed against the bars. *My daughter lives!* He screamed her name until his voice gave out. Exhausted, he lay on the floor and stared at the ceiling. The left side of his chest raged with fire, hotter than ever before.

"You should've listened to me. Had you done so, he'd be dead already."

Had I listened to you, I wouldn't know about my daughter.

"What difference will it make tomorrow?"

What significance does tomorrow hold?

"Have you forgotten already?" Laughter echoed in his mind.

Had he forgotten?

"Your days were numbered, and tonight is your last. Tomorrow, we'll kill them all."

The countdown! How could he have forgotten?

"So you do remember. Good."

The burning in his chest faded, but the pain in his heart remained. How much more foolish could he be? Would he ever see Shanara again? Losing her a second time would surely cause him more pain than he could handle.

I cannot let her go. If we separate, it will be her doing, not mine.

Thoughts of Theyn bubbled to the surface of his mind and reopened the wounds of her loss. *How beautiful you were.* Had his hand participated in every loss he'd suffered? *Am I the cause of everything?* He knew the answer in his heart, but his mind wouldn't accept the fault.

The obsidian dragon rose in his memory again, its terrible claw thrust through Theyn's midsection. *Our daughter.* How would their child save him? With Theyn gone, they'd never have one. *None of this makes sense.* All hope died with Theyn.

The sickness will come.

But now he had Shanara. *Aria? No!* How could he ever be around her? The sickness would take her too.

Wait! He sat up, his mind finally clear. How could he have been so daft?

Knowing the dragon Tharos, Nardus should've realized he'd been looking at the vision with the obsidian dragon completely wrong.

Damned cunning dragons! The obsidian dragon never said our daughter, Theyn. He always looked at me and said, "your daughter." He must've meant Shanara! She'll be the one to save me from the sickness.

Dread set in. He covered his face with his forearms. *But I've driven her away. And why would she help me even if I hadn't? How could I ask it of her?*

Tears wet his arms. *But I'm lost without her. I must ask it of her if I get the chance.*

He grabbed wads of his hair and pulled. *What if the stone crawls inside of her like it did me? Would she then carry the sickness? How could I do that to her? To my daughter...*

What could he do? He lay back on the floor and brooded. *Ẑäṭūr help me. I'm damned either way.*

What would you have me do, Vitara?

✝ ✝ ✝

Aria lay in one of the corners of The Dragon's Hall and wept. Her life crumbled around her once more. Strife followed her like thunderclouds. Had she brought it upon herself?

You're just a stupid girl. Pravus never loved you, did he? Maybe he only wants to use you for your mezhik? How could you have thought otherwise? Blinded by love. You don't even know what love is. How could you?

Why would anyone love a simple girl like her? She didn't even know who she was. It didn't seem possible. *How pathetic am I?*

To think she'd believed she'd be a queen enraged her. *Pravus isn't even a king!*

How would she ever face him again? *How could he do this to me? Why would he lie to me about everything?* He must've known her from birth.

He said he'd dreamed of me before we had met. What a liar! He must know Alderan too.

What else had Pravus kept from her? More importantly, where would she go now? She couldn't possibly stay, could she? *How unpleasant would that be?*

And what about Nardus, or her father, or whoever he really was? Should she listen to his side of the story, or let him stay dead like everyone else in her life?

No matter what, he isn't my father. But could he be again? *No. He had his chance.*

But what had really happened? What caused them to be separated? *Did he just leave us to die? Another woman?* Who was her mother? He'd mentioned someone named Vitara. *Is she my mother? What does she look like? Where is she, or what happened to her?*

She needed answers. She needed closure. She had to speak to Nardus again. Beyond getting answers, how would she move forward?

If she possessed the stone, Pravus would have little choice but to marry her, wouldn't he? *Why would I want to be with a liar?*

Because I love him.

She wiped the tears from her eyes. *But how can I love a man I can't trust?*

She thought of the seven-pointed piece of paper and sighed. *But I lied to him too.*

Do I still want to be queen?

Yes! More than anything. But how?

She chewed on her lower lip as she recalled the numerous conversations she'd had with Pravus over the last three weeks. Only one thing separated him from ruling the Ancient Realm: the stone.

It must be the key.

I must talk to Nardus and do whatever it takes to get the stone from him. It's the only hope I have left for a future.

Aria rose, wiped her face on her blue dress, and smoothed out the wrinkles. Hidden in the deep shadows, Pravus hadn't noticed her when he'd stormed through the hall earlier, so she safely headed back down to see Nardus.

He may not be my father, but I am his daughter. If he loves me, he'll do anything I ask of him.

She walked through the black steel doorway, into the room, and right up to the inner cage that held Nardus. Palms sweaty and heart racing, she sat on the floor and pushed her arms through the bars. "Give me your hands... father." The word "father" felt foreign on her lips. "Let me feel them so that I might remember how they once held me."

Nardus wiped his eyes and looked over at Aria. "You came back," his voice rasped. "I didn't think I'd ever see you again." He crawled over to her and took her hands in his.

Emotions flooded her mind as memories rose from her past. Nardus's hands soothed her aching heart and overwhelmed her. She leaned her head against the bars and sobbed. Nardus leaned forward and kissed her forehead through the bars. How much had she missed that? She sobbed harder, and her chest convulsed.

Nardus whispered in her ear, "I've dreamt of this moment since the day I lost you, but I never imagined it to be like this."

Aria pulled her hands back and wiped her eyes with the hem of her dress. *Pull yourself together, Aria. Look where your emotions led you with Pravus. Focus on the task at hand. He's not your father. Get the stone.*

She took a deep breath. "Tell me our story. How did we come to be separated? Did you search for me?"

His brown eyes bore his heart and soul, and the story he wove moved her like none she'd heard before. No doubt remained as to the authenticity of his claim on her, and she desperately wanted his love and approval, but she couldn't allow herself to feel anything for him as a father.

She had a mission: get the stone and rule Centauria. Father or not, she had no room in her rent heart to love another. Loss stalked her like a tiger and losing another father would kill her for sure.

Nardus reached through the bars and patted her leg. "Thank you for returning, Shan—Aria. You've given me more joy in the last hour than I've had in the last thirteen years combined. I'll never forget this time we've spent together. I love you more than life itself."

Aria's mind spun. Had she missed something? Was he saying goodbye to her? *Surely not!*

She swallowed her fear and smiled. "I'll come visit you again tomorrow."

"You *can't*." Nardus's terse response seemed to have surprised even him. "Forgive me, I didn't mean for that to come out so harsh."

Her heart jumped in her throat and squirmed like a rat in a tube. "You don't wish to see me again? Have I done something wrong, father?"

Pain filled his brown eyes. "No, my precious girl. You could never wrong me. I want nothing more than to see you again, but it's not that simple."

Comfort him. Bring him back around.

She took his hands again. "Then explain it to me. Help me understand why you'd refuse to see me again. You say that you love me. Do you not?"

A single tear fell from Nardus's eye. "I love you to the stars and back." He looked down at his chest. "But... it's this stone."

The stone? Her heart raced. "Is something wrong?"

He rubbed the tops of her hands with his thumbs. "I know this sounds crazy, but the stone talks to me."

A talking stone? How strange is that? Not strange, but mad. She played along in his madness. "And what does the stone say to you?"

Sorrow flowed from his eyes. "If it stays in me, I'll develop a sickness that will kill everyone in Centauria."

She shrugged, the solution so simple. "So then take it out."

He let go of her hands, backed away, and shook his head. "It's not that simple. It's been telling me to give it to my daughter for a few weeks now.

Until today, I didn't understand why it told me that. How could it have known you still lived when I didn't?"

How could this not be fate? Take it from him.

She leaned forward and stuck her arms through the bars. "You must let me do it, father."

He retreated farther. "I can't let you do that. What if it kills you?"

Kills me? How could a stone kill me?

But what if it really talks to him?

It doesn't matter. You must take it, or you might as well be dead.

She motioned him closer. "I don't believe it will."

He stood and paced. "And why not?"

Lie to him. Do what you must to get it. Weave the lies into truth, and he will believe.

Aria rose and held the bars. "There's something you should know too. I came back down here for the stone. It's also why I came down here in the first place. Not to defy Pravus, but because I've had dreams. The only way we'll survive is for you to give me the stone. Don't you see? This isn't *your* destiny but *ours*, father."

Does he believe me? Of course he does. Why would he expect me to lie about it?

Nardus pulled on his hair and gazed at the ceiling. "Is there no other way?"

She reached through the bars again, as far as her arms would stretch. "Please, father. Let me help you."

He turned back to her. Tears glistened in his eyes. "ʕätūr, if I lose her again, I will pull asunder the gates of Kinzhdm ef Häfn and remove You from Your throne. Do you hear me?"

He walked over to her. Her pulse quickened. Could she go through with it? *I must! But how does this work?*

He ripped his shirt open. The left side of his chest pulsed with a reddish light, and his eyes changed from brown to red. He grabbed the bars and roared. "Tear it out before I change my mind."

She lightly pressed her hand against his muscular chest. His smoldering skin warmed her cold hand. She felt dirty touching him, her father, but she had no other choice. "What do I do now?"

Nardus's lips moved, but the voice that came forth wasn't his. "You only need ask, child."

She hesitated. *For my future.* "Give me the stone."

Nardus roared again, grabbed Aria by the shoulders, and arched his back. He tilted his head back, and fire spewed from his mouth. She cringed and tried to recoil, but she couldn't break free from his grasp.

He pulled her close, and her hand plunged into his flesh. Hot, steamy wetness enveloped her hand. The smell of blood, sweat, and sulfur rose in her nostrils, an aroma that should've repulsed her, but instead she inhaled deeper and longer and then exhaled with a soft moan.

She bit her lip, enraptured. The taste of blood caressed her tongue. In Nardus's chest, a hard and smooth object met her fingers and then her palm. She wrapped her fingers around it.

The stone is mine.

Her entire body raged with fire, and the entire room washed red. She yanked her hand from his chest, and he exhaled deeply.

He released her, stumbled backward, and collapsed on the floor. He lay still, blood smeared across his chest.

Crimson drops fell from her closed fist and spattered the floor. She trembled, knowing the power she held exceeded any other. She turned her hand over and slowly opened it. A reddish-black stone lay in her palm, beating like a heart.

She smiled, her future secured. *Thank you, father.*

She lifted it up for closer inspection. In the entire world, she'd never seen another one like it. Its power, an intoxicating mezhik greater than any she'd ever experienced before, flowed into her. Her eyes rolled back, and she groaned like a cat in heat.

Pravus be damned. I'll never give you up.

† † †

Pravus stood in the center of the octagonal platform in the transformation chamber. Seven glass cubes surrounded him, three of them cast in darkness. Four young women, each in stasis, lay on glass beds within the other four cubes.

The zhiftäd. Perfect specimens. Ripe for bloodletting.

He reached out to each of the four cubes in succession, and they slid across the expanse and settled next to the platform. His moistened hands opened and closed at his sides. He breathed in their scents and reveled in them. He swayed to the rhythms of their beating hearts, a symphony of ecstasy in his ears. Their veins called to him.

Footsteps thundered down the path behind him. Pravus turned and met Wizard Wrik's steel gaze.

Wrik stopped just short of the platform and bowed slightly. "Lord Rosai."

Pravus tented his fingers. "I assume you've good reason for this intrusion?"

"I'm aware of your recent—" Wrik's gaze shifted up for a few moments. "—*experimentations*. To be truthful, I neither condone or condemn them, but I ask that you ponder what it is that you truly desire. Already, you've reduced our candidate pool for the ceremony to its minimum. If you proceed down your current path, we'll need to postpone the ceremony. *Indefinitely.*"

The blood. Pravus's mouth watered. *I need their power.*

He stepped to the edge of the platform and met Wrik's gaze. "I must have both."

Wrik ran his tongue across his teeth and smacked his lips. "As you're aware, we've no other prospects to speak of." He held up a finger. "Unless you'd like to start using male subjects as well. Keep in mind that we would need to clear several hurdles for that to work. We're possibly talking years to bring something of that nature to fruition. Young men can be difficult to mold."

Pravus needed the stone. To get the stone, he needed more strength. *Blood is the key.* His need for it grew and set him on edge. "Without the stone, there will be no ceremony. What I'm doing is necessary to obtain it."

The corners of Wrik's mouth curled upward. "Your experimentation with the blood is only to acquire the stone?"

Pravus tensed as rage coursed through his veins. "Of course it is! Do you think I *enjoy* consuming their blood?"

Keep pressing me, and I will consume yours next.

Wrik shrugged. "I've read plenty of books detailing the effects of blood lust. There comes a point where the need for the blood supersedes all other thoughts and desires. Eventually, every subject who practiced it went mad."

Pravus looked back at the four lit cubes and the women they contained. *Have I reached that point?* Their blood called to him still, and his ability to converse with Wrik diminished.

He closed his hand and rubbed his thumb on the side of his finger. *I'm stronger than this.*

He forced his attention back to Wrik. "And what would you have me do to acquire the stone without their blood?"

Wrik folded his hands behind his back. "The problem is already solved."

Pravus stepped back, his mouth agape. *Solved? How could it be?*

The questions dissipated as his need for blood peaked. His hands trembled, and his mouth watered. *I could use all four of them. Take only the blood I need from each of them.*

Pravus staggered backward. *No! My entire future hinges on the ceremony. I cannot be so pathetic.*

Pravus dropped to one knee and closed his eyes. *This will not control me.* With his mind, he pushed the cubes away from the platform.

For several moments, he didn't move. Perfect silence surrounded him. He breathed deep, but the air held no scent or aroma other than the zhifţäd blood.

Pravus opened his eyes, rose, and met Wrik's gaze. "And what did this solution of yours entail?"

Wrik's eyes gleamed. "Your betrothed, Aria. I spoke with her just before coming down here to find you. Aided by my knowledge, she's retrieved *Ʒţōn Dhef Dädh* from Nardus."

Pravus's breath caught in his lungs. *Aria has the stone…*

His heart hammered, and the blood lust intensified once more, surging beyond his capacity to control it. Saliva drooled from his mouth, and he wiped it with his sleeve. He pushed past Wrik and hurried down the white marble path.

I must have her and her blood.

CHAPTER THIRTY-FOUR

Improperly dressed, Zerenity's bare arms, legs, and cheeks stung from the cold morning air, but she had little time to fuss over it. She followed Rayah through the forest, unaware of where they headed and too distraught to question her.

Qotan clung to life by the thinnest of threads, and his fate rested firmly on her shoulders. She prayed that a thorough examination of the vine that had poisoned him would help her concoct a remedy. Administering said remedy would be another feat in itself.

One problem at a time.

She'd let decades pass without once contemplating why Savric insisted Qotan lived. *Why did I not see it, Ɂäṭūr? How could I have been so stubborn and blind?* As with most of their wild adventures, mirror-jumping had been her idea. *Perhaps that guilt shielded me from the truth.*

Rayah stopped a few paces ahead of her. "The felled tree is just over this ridge. We should probably be careful. There's no telling if the vines have grown or not. They could be concealed underneath the layers of foliage and debris."

Zerenity came up next to Rayah and stopped. "This is close enough, darling, I'll take it from here. We cannot risk you getting poisoned as well."

Rayah twisted her chestnut curls around her fingers. "You won't get an argument from me. Is there anything else I can do?"

"You've done well here." Zerenity tapped her finger against her chin. "Would you go back to the house and see if you can get Savvy to eat something? He needs to build his strength back up, or he'll be of no use to anyone."

Rayah scratched her side. "I can go back and do that, but is it safe for you to be out here alone? What happens if the vines attack you? How will we know?"

Zerenity feigned a smile. "I will use every precaution, darling. Nature is my specialty. I will not let it best me. If I haven't returned to the house by lunchtime, come find me."

Rayah nodded and flew off in the direction they'd come from.

I envy her youth.

Zerenity stood still for several minutes and dwelt on the past. *Had I the chance, I'd go back and do things differently, Savvy. I hope you'll forgive me one day. I didn't know.*

She shuddered the past away and focused her mind. *Now, for the task at-hand. Ɂäțūr, guide me.*

She knelt on the cold, hard ground, pushed up her sleeves, and placed her hands on the roots of the nearby trees. *"Ɂbäk."* Her eyes rolled back inside her head, but her vision widened and deepened as her mind flowed through the trees and sped over the ridge.

The trees groaned, and the ground quaked. *"Save us, mistress. Death approaches."*

The fallen foliage churned like a bed of maggots. She reached out, swept the ground with her long branches, and uncovered the source of the churning foliage. Dark-grey vines spotted with orange thorns and leaves slithered across the ground.

"Kill her," they shrieked. *"Pull her into the darkness."*

They gnawed at her roots, clawed their way up her trunk with their thorns, wrapped themselves around her limbs, and choked the life from her. She fell to the ground with a thunderous boom. Others around her fell as well.

She gasped as her eyes rolled forward, and she sat back on the bottoms of her feet. Her heart galloped in her chest, and she couldn't fill her lungs with air. *Dear Ɂäțūr, Savric was right. Those vines cannot be from our world.*

I must get a sample. She searched her pockets but had nothing with her to cut or contain one of the vines. How could she have come so unprepared? She knew the answer, but it made little difference.

I'm Fizärd Näíțɛzhär. Improvise.

She stood and crested the ridge. The large tree Rayah spoke of lay on the forest floor just ahead of her. Already, the needles on the tree had browned and fallen off in clumps.

This was green yesterday? It's a wonder Qotan still lives.

Zerenity grabbed one of the tree's branches and broke it off at its base. With her hands and a touch of mezhik, she sculpted the branch into a deadly weapon easily capable of cutting through vines and the like. She took a chunk of the tree's trunk, scooped out its middle, and created a large bowl. She fashioned a lid for the bowl from another section of the trunk.

She inspected her handiworks. "These will have to do."

She took the container and her wooden sword and cautiously proceeded toward the root-end of the felled tree. As she walked, she swept the ground with the sword and pushed the leaves and pine needles aside.

Where are you, you little devils?

Movement to her left spun her in its direction. She slashed with her wooden sword and severed a foot-long section of the vine. The vine hissed and writhed on the ground, and then stilled.

Leaves rustled, and the ground moved under her feet. A sea of vines rose around her like a wall, encircling her completely. Yellow, gelatinous pus dripped from their orange leaves and sizzled when it hit the debris on the forest floor.

Ɂäţūr, help me!

Zerenity scooped up the length of severed vine into her container but dropped the lid in the process. The vines danced around her like serpents, and several of them struck at her with their thorns. As one, the vines arched back and then came at her full-force, striking and spitting pus.

Zerenity spun out of the forest and into her yard, narrowly escaping the attack. She tossed her wooden sword into the trees and walked over to the front porch. She sat down on one of the steps and set the container down next to her.

The vine lay still at the container's bottom, but she suspected it still lived. She huddled over the container to get a closer look at the vine. As she did, she scratched the back of her left hand with her right. Something wet and sticky gummed her fingers. She looked down at them, and her breath caught.

Blood.

A two-inch-long gash crossed the back of her left hand and still seeped blood. Her heart knocked in her chest. Had she cut herself while crafting the sword? *I would've noticed, wouldn't I? Maybe not. The vines held my attention quite well.*

The answer lay in the container next to her, but she couldn't accept it. Wouldn't accept it. She'd spun away before they'd reached her. But that hand had held the container. The *open* container.

Zerenity peered into the container again and scrutinized every inch of the vine. One thorn stood out, darker than the others. She peered closer. *Is that blood on its thorn?*

The door behind her creaked and moaned as it swung open. "You're back, Zerenity."

She slid her wounded hand underneath her other and sat up. "Just so, darling."

Alderan plopped down on the step next to the container and peered into it. "I see you were able to get a sample of one of the vines. Hopefully you didn't run into any trouble like Master Qotan did."

Her hand throbbed, and heat radiated from it. "A simple extraction. No issues at all."

He pushed his hair behind his ears. "That's a relief. I'm not sure what we would've done if you'd become infected as well."

She smiled through the mounting pain. "Well, you've nothing to worry about. I'm just fine."

Alderan looked at her. His green eyes matched the surrounding evergreens, but the only thing Zerenity saw in them was her own reflection and her lying eyes. *It's for his own good.* How many more lies would she tell him? In the end, they'd catch up with her. They always did.

Alderan stared into the container. "Now that you have a sample of the vine, do you think you'll be able to find an antidote for the poison?"

She closed her eyes for a moment and swallowed her pain. *Give me strength, Ʒätūr.* "I'll spend the rest of my life working on it if I must. I need to examine this vine before it withers away like Qotan's sample did, so perhaps you should run along."

Alderan nodded and stood. "I know my training must wait, and I understand."

She looked up at him. "You don't need me to be there for you to practice the lessons I've taught you. I expect you to study and perfect them. I know Rayah's felt a bit left out, so practicing with her will do you both a world of good."

Alderan smiled. "I think Rayah will appreciate that very much." He turned to leave, but then swung back around. "I nearly forgot. Master Savric's conscious once more and is asking after you. Something to do with the quality of the food. I believe he enjoys your cooking far more than Rayah's. I do too, but please don't mention that to her. I'm in far too much trouble with her already. No need to stoke the fire."

"Very well." She pretended to look back down at the container, but squeezed her eyes shut. "Please let Savvy know that I'll come check on him in a few minutes."

"Sure will."

The door creaked and moaned, then it latched shut with a final *click*.

She exhaled. "Dear Ɛätūr."

She looked down at her throbbing hand. Now, a thin layer of pus covered the wound, and it produced a rancid smell that gagged her.

Zerenity swept her other hand over the wound. "*Häall.*"

The wound burned like acid, and the pus bubbled and turned into a blackish-red sludge. She wiped the sludge away with the back of her other hand. The burning subsided, and the wound faded, but underneath the skin she surmised the poison had worked its way into her veins.

How long could she keep the secret from the others? *Hopefully long enough to find a remedy.* But could she find one in time to save her and Qotan both? She couldn't allow herself to ponder it.

Ɛätūr, help me. Help us all.

† † †

"The between…" Alderan scratched his head. Nothing came to mind. Zerenity had mentioned it the night before, after she saw Qotan, but had been too distraught to talk further of it.

Zerenity walked through the front door, and Alderan cornered her. "What's the between?"

She turned and stared out one of the front windows for a few moments. "Just as it sounds, darling. A conjured existence between here and the afterlife." She demonstrated with her hands, each representing a place.

"Those in the between—neither here nor the afterlife—are trapped in between a state of life and death, their souls torn from them and their flesh left to dwell in unrest until the Great Separation. They roam about, separated from Ɂäʈūr and lost in darkness. Can you imagine how horrific that must be?"

Separated from Ɂäʈūr? Is that possible? Alderan looked at his hands and turned them over. *Am I capable of creating such evil with my mezhik?* His heart ached, and his chest tightened *I must be. I nearly killed Amicus.* "Maybe I shouldn't learn to use my mezhik."

Zerenity's blue-eyed gaze focused on him through the window's reflection. "Wielding any power you don't understand is far more dangerous than learning how to use it and control it. Without knowledge of it, how would you understand the risks and consequences of your actions?"

He raked his fingers through his hair, walked over to the couch, and sat down. "I don't know. I guess I wouldn't. But I don't want to hurt people with my mezhik."

Zerenity stepped away from the window and joined him on the couch. "As with most things, there are two sides to mezhik: *allíʈ* and *derk*. The true difference between them is intent. Most mezhik can be used for both good and evil.

"As a wizard, you must always be conscious of how you use mezhik. Not only how you use it, but *if* it should be used at all. Sometimes you can reach the same result without it. It should always be a last result, never a first choice."

She smiled. "This brings us to the third rule of wizardry: the greatest mezhik is that which isn't used."

"I didn't think we were having a lesson today."

"Life gives us lessons daily. We so often choose to ignore them. A true sign of death is when one stops learning altogether."

He scratched his head. "What does the third rule mean when it says, 'that which isn't used?'"

Her eyes brightened. "Good question. Mezhik is a type of energy that flows within us and is expended when we use it. Every wizard has a limit to the amount of energy they possess. As it's used, it weakens us. In battle, your decisions as to when to use your mezhik can be the difference in winning or losing.

"Small spells cast here and there may seem harmless in and of themselves, but their costs add over time. The last thing you'd want would be to lose a battle because you expended your mezhik doing mundane things you could've accomplished without its use."

He frowned. "But I see you do things all the time that shouldn't require mezhik."

Zerenity smiled, and Alderan swore her cheeks turned a shade or two redder. "I admit, I'm a repeat offender of the third rule. Were I going into battle, I would certainly need to shore things up.

"As you grow with age, mezhik tends to become a crutch. Your body becomes less cooperative while your brain insists things can still be done as usual. Eventually, you resign yourself to using bits of mezhik here and there to compensate. Next thing you know, mezhik has become a first response and not a last resort."

"What about me? I used mezhik countless times before ever knowing I was a wizard. How can I abide by the third rule if I have no control of it?"

She patted his knee. "Control will come with practice. Now, I must go check on Savric." She got up from the couch and proceeded down the hall that led to her bedroom.

He sighed. *And when will practice come?*

Rayah walked in from the kitchen, her small curvy lips curled into a devious smile. Like when they'd first met, Alderan swore the room brightened with her presence. Her translucent wings shimmered with colors.

As always, her beauty transfixed him. *How can she be mine?*

She giggled. "Snap out of it, silly. If your eyes grew wider, they'd pop right out of your head."

Had he not blinked since she entered the room? His dry eyes burned, confirming his suspicion. He blinked several times. "I know that smile. What've you been up to, Rayah?"

She giggled again and stretched her arm toward the kitchen door. "I present to you, Sir Eshtak."

The door jerked open, and a short, dapper man walked into the room. From his black shoes, charcoal-grey trousers, and white lace-up shirt to the long, black, split-tailed coat and black brimmed hat he wore, he looked everything a gentleman and nothing like the Eshtak Alderan knew.

If not for the green scarf around Eshtak's neck and the bulbous nose that hung over his thin black lips, Alderan might've mistaken him for someone else. "Wow, Eshtak!"

Eshtak spun in a circle and bounced from one foot to the other. "Eshtak likes clothes. Rayah makes for me."

Rayah beamed. "I thought them more appropriate, given his current company." She scratched her side.

Until that moment, he hadn't known that he could love her more than he already did. "Amicus would be so happy if he were here."

She giggled. "He is happy. I'm certain of it."

He's with his family again.

Alderan's thoughts drifted to Aria, and his elation faded. *Will I ever see you again, sister?*

† † †

Zerenity sat in a chair next to the bed and smoothed back Savric's wiry white hair with her fingers. He looked so old and frail—much more than usual.

Savric leaned back in the bed, propped up by several pillows. His hands shook the cup of water he held, but he refused Zerenity's assistance. "Bugger-bees, woman. I am not dead yet."

"Maybe not, but you're certainly working hard at accomplishing just that."

"If my intentions were to shorten my existence, I would find a more elegant way of doing it." He sipped water from the cup and then handed it to her. "Now, if you would kindly move aside, I need to go find my brother and tend to him."

He tried to sit up farther, but she held him back with just two fingers to his chest. "You're not going anywhere. I assure you that Qotan is stable for now and resting, as you should be."

His bushy grey eyebrows congregated over the top of his nose and the corners of his mouth sagged. "Stable and resting? You have not seen him in several decades, refer to him as a figment of my imagination, and now you say he is stable and resting?"

His terse and accusatory tone tore at her heart, and she deserved it. *Zätūr, I'll gladly take all his anger if You'll help me find a way to heal his brother.*

She took his liver-spotted hands and brought them to her lips. Strength remained in them, and she longed for them to hold her once more. "I saw him, Savvy. Last night."

His eyebrows rose. "You dreamt of Qotan?"

She squeezed his hands. "No, Savvy. I saw him with my own eyes."

His eyes widened. "You did? Where?"

If allowed, she'd gaze into his kind blue eyes for an eternity. However, fate seemed to have a different plan for them. "In the closet, on the floor. I saw him only for a moment."

To think, I would've given you up had it not been for last night. But will you ever forgive me for all the pain I've caused you and Qotan?

He pulled one of his hands away from hers and stroked his beard. "Then I am not mad." He smiled. "Never believed I was, truthfully. But why did you see him only for a moment, and how do you know that he is still okay if you cannot see him now?"

She glanced toward the hallway. "Eshtak. He's a strange little man and a mystery all his own. Mezhik doesn't affect him the way it does the rest of us. He's been keeping an eye on Qotan."

Savric groaned and leaned back into the pillows. "I feel so disadvantaged at the present. What does Qotan have to do with mezhik and this Eshtak fellow?"

Her neck ached from being held in an awkward position for so long. She massaged it for a few moments and decided it best to move to the bed where she could face him better. She stood, pushed his bony legs toward the other side of the bed, and then sat down in the vacated space. She pulled her feet under her thighs.

"It has everything to do with them. Do you remember the day the three of us were mirror-jumping?"

He scratched his chin and searched the ceiling. "If I recall, there were several of those days."

She waved her hand. "Yes, yes, but I'm referring to the last of those days. The day everything changed."

He coughed and reached for the cup of water. She leaned over and retrieved it for him.

"Bits and pieces, but I have never wielded a memory such as yours. A refresher would be welcomed." He sipped the water.

Zerenity tapped her chin with her forefinger. "You must remember, Savvy. It was the last jump we were going to make that day. Qotan touched the mirror, and the surface rippled, but only darkness lay beyond it.

"We decided it was unsafe to proceed not knowing what might meet us on the other side, but Qotan kept his hand on the mirror. Something grabbed his hand and pulled him into the mirror, but you grabbed his other hand and fought to pull him back. Your arms went through the mirror as well, but I held onto you and managed to pull you back from it."

He nodded. "I remember that. When you pulled me back out of the mirror, I held onto Qotan and pulled him out as well."

She took his hand again. "You see, that's where our memories of that event differ. You saw Qotan come back through the mirror, but I never did. I never saw him again until last night."

Savric shook his head, and his brow furrowed. "But why? What happened?"

She rubbed the top of his hand with her thumb. "A few years ago, I ran across a book in the room below Alderan's house called *Intus: The Scourge*. Do you recall that book?"

He looked to the ceiling, frowned, and shook his head. "I cannot say that I do, but I did not read every book in that library either. Several of the books were gathered from other locations and stored there by fellow wizards."

Zerenity waved her hand again. "Never mind that. It's unimportant. Intus was a cave town buried deep within the southern range of the Sol Deus Mountains. Because of its location, the inhabitants consisted mainly of short-statured humanoids with pale skin and virtually no hair. Their mining skills were second-to-none. Some called them albino dwarves, but most referred to them as dwellers.

"Years before the Great War began, Magus Carac and his legion of wizards went to Intus to test a spell they called 'scourge.' Prior to conjuring scourge, they cast a containment web over the entire town.

"With the web in place, they took a single specimen from the town and wove a special spell around him to protect him from scourge. The spell adhered to his skin like tattoos and rendered him unconscious. Satisfied with their test subject, the wizards surrounded the town, just beyond the containment web, and began the conjuring of scourge.

"Unfortunately for the rest of the world, Magus didn't participate in the conjuring. He stood back a great distance from the town and watched. The conjuring went as planned, creating a plane of existence they called 'the between.' Inside the between, flesh and soul were separated, leaving the flesh to wander aimlessly until the Great Separation.

"The containment web held the between, but its edges frayed out just enough to reach the wizards surrounding the town. Nightmarish shadows pulled the wizards through the containment web and ripped their souls from them, evidence the scourge would continue its cycle indefinitely.

"I believe the place Qotan got pulled into was Intus, and I believe he's trapped in the between."

Savric stroked his beard. "If that were true, then how can I still see him? How is he not trapped inside the town like the rest of them?"

"My theory is that a small part of you is trapped there with him, and that part of him remains with you. That is why I believe you see him."

"If it worked as planned, why did Magus refrain from using the spell during the Great War?"

"After months of waiting for the test subject to emerge from Intus, he deemed the experiment a failure. If he couldn't keep himself safe from scourge with a protection spell, how would he be able to conjure it and survive?"

"I see. Back to the between and Qotan. If this theory of yours is correct, how do we rescue him from it? How do we remedy the poison?"

She scratched the top of her hand. Black veins spiderwebbed under her thin skin.

Dear Ɂäʈūr! I'll need to wear gloves until I can find a remedy.

She moved her hand under her leg. "I've managed to retrieve a sample of the vines. I'll need to thoroughly examine it and use mezhik to determine its makeup. From that, I hope to find a remedy. Since your sample deteriorated so quickly, I fear I have little time before mine does as well."

Savric pulled on his beard. "This Eshtak fellow. How does he fit into all of this?"

"When you meet him, you'll understand. I hadn't put all the pieces together until last night."

"May I meet him now?"

"Of course. I'll go get him. Don't go anywhere." She smiled at him, and he rolled his eyes.

Zerenity rose from the bed and made her way into the living area. Rayah and Alderan lay on the couch, fast asleep. Through the front windows, she saw Eshtak in the yard, twirling and launching his hat in the air like a boomerang.

He's suffered so much loss. How does he manage to find such joy in everything he does? If only we were all able to live as he does.

She opened the door. "Eshtak, could you please come inside? Master Savric would like to meet you."

He grabbed his hat from the air, jammed it on his head, and bounded up the steps. "Eshtak likes new friend."

"Qotan?"

He nodded vigorously. "Eshtak laughs with Master Qotan."

"I'm sure you will find Master Savric just as pleasing." She removed the hat from his head and handed it to him. "Remember, hats are for outdoors, not indoors."

He nodded and skipped inside. She closed the door behind her and nearly fell over him. "Don't just stand there. Go and see Master Savric. I've got a vine to dissect."

He hopped down the hall and out of sight.

She leaned against the door. Her hand trembled; the poison was taking a stronger hold. *Haste is the key. I must get ahead of this before it renders me useless.*

She folded her arms tight and walked over to the kitchen door. She hated keeping secrets, but worrying everyone would do little good, especially Savric.

How would he handle losing us both? She dared not think on it lest she became overwhelmed by it.

She pushed through the kitchen door and stopped in front of the small table. The vine still lay in the bottom of the container, undisturbed. With her good hand, she set to work. *No more sleep until I've found a remedy.*

† † †

Rayah frowned at him. "Alderan, I know that look. You're contemplating doing something stupid again, aren't you? We shouldn't have listened in on their conversation."

He circled the couch. "You heard her. I say we go find that book and see if there are any more clues about that scourge spell they used. If there's anything we can do to help Master Qotan, I say we do it."

Rayah grabbed his arm to stop him, but he pulled her along. "Stop a minute and think about what you're saying. Remember the last time we used one of the mirrors without help? We both nearly died."

He stopped, and she ran into his shoulder. "Yes, but you're wrong to blame the mirror. You were taken by that lizard man, not the mirror, and I had no choice but to follow after you."

"No matter the circumstance, those mirrors are dangerous. Look what happened to Master Qotan."

Alderan ran his fingers through his hair. "You're right, they are dangerous. That's why I should go alone."

"Alone?" She huffed and pointed her forefinger at him. "If you even *think* of going alone, you'll have an even bigger problem to deal with than Master Qotan."

He smiled. "Do you know how beautiful you look when you're all angry? Your lips pucker just so."

I could kiss them right now.

Alderan leaned toward her, but she pressed her palm against his chest and held him back.

"You think your boyish charms and compliments will render me docile? Don't even try to change the subject."

The corners of her mouth quivered, and then she burst with giggles.

The sound of her laughter warmed his heart. How long had it been since he'd heard her truly laugh? He couldn't remember.

He grabbed her, wrapped his arms around her, and then fell back on the couch. She squealed and squirmed, but he held fast. He chased her lips with his, but found her nose, eyes, and cheeks instead.

"Stay still so I can kiss you properly."

Rayah pulled back a bit, her hazel eyes misty. "Promise me you'll never stop loving me."

Alderan cupped her heart-shaped face with his hands, her silky porcelain skin radiant. "My love for you grows stronger daily. Every moment we're apart is an eternity of agony."

He kissed her nose, and she giggled. She reared back, and they tumbled to the floor, him on top of her. Her eyes bore into his soul, the laughter in them replaced with a love so deep he couldn't fathom the depths of it. *How could I ever love anyone else?*

The world around them faded into oblivion, their eyes locked for an eternity. His hands trembled, and he ached to be with her.

His heart hammered. *No one would know.* He breathed deep. Her hair smelled like lilacs.

Ɂäţūr sees everything. You must pull away.

But how could he? In their hearts, they were married already.

The warmth of her breath caressed his skin, and chills skittered down his neck and back. Her chest heaved underneath his, labored, but not from his weight.

Let her go.

Alderan leaned into her and let his lips rest against hers, never breaking eye contact with her. She licked her lips, and his. Her fingers slid through his hair, kneading and pulling lightly. Her soft little nose rubbed against his.

Respect her.

Rayah nipped his lower lip and pulled on it playfully. Their foreheads touched, hers an inferno against his. He closed his eyes, kissed her deeply, and then rolled away.

We'll be together soon.

His hands shook, desperate to touch her and hold her again. He sat up and rubbed his arms. Never had controlling himself proved so difficult. *Ƹ̵̡ātūr, give me strength to withstand these urges a little longer.*

He opened his eyes. Across the room, Eshtak watched them.

Alderan's skin crawled. *How long has he been there?*

Eshtak sauntered over to the couch, his eyes glistening, and his cheeks wet. "Eshtak had special friend once."

Rayah settled back on the couch. "You had a family?"

Eshtak nodded. "Eshtak misses."

Eshtak had a family. I suppose everyone must at some point. "Are they still alive?"

Eshtak shrugged. "Eshtak can't find." He walked off toward Qotan's room.

Alderan plopped down on the couch, a fair distance away from Rayah. He didn't trust himself to be too close to her now.

"How do we become so self-absorbed that we forget there are others around us as well? How will I save the world when I can't even take the time to get to know the people around me?" Alderan sighed. "You'll be the ones who help me. Shouldn't I know your strengths and weaknesses so that I'm never caught off-guard by your reactions, no matter the situation?"

Rayah scooted closer. He cringed inside. *Ƹ̵̡ātūr, keep her from me.*

She scratched her side. "Speaking of knowing people, do you trust Zerenity?"

He breathed deep and calmed himself. "I suppose so. She seems genuine enough."

"The other night, when she talked to us about you and Aria, I kept getting the feeling that she was either lying to us or holding something back. Did you feel it too?"

He pulled on his fingers. "No, but I tend to assume the best of people. What do you think she lied about?"

She shrugged. "Nothing in particular, I guess. I just wondered if she held back information from us."

"I guess she could've, but to serve what purpose?"

"Forget it. I'm sure it's nothing." Rayah floated off the couch. "I'm gonna go sit with Master Savric for a while."

Alderan stood and kissed her cheek. "I'll keep it in mind to scrutinize every word she utters." His stomach rumbled. "In the meantime, I think I'll go check on lunch."

She shook her head and scratched her side. "Lunch? Is it a male wizard thing to constantly think of food? You've become nearly as annoying about it as Master Savric."

He grinned. "Like my heart, my stomach wants what it wants. I've no control over either."

She rolled her eyes and flew down the hallway. Her sweet smell still lingered, and he breathed deep. *My winged angel.*

He walked through the kitchen door and stopped just inside. Several cabinets hung open, their contents emptied onto the wooden counters and table. Zerenity sat on a stool next to the kitchen table, hunched over an open book.

Several piles of books towered over and surrounded her. Papers lay strewn across the floor, scribbled with illegible notes in the margins of discarded plant diagrams. Chaos ruled the kitchen with no sign of lunch in sight.

Maybe I should come back later.

Zerenity slammed the book shut. "How can it not be in any of these? Surely someone's come across these baleful vines before."

Alderan walked over to the table and stood next to her. "Is there something I can help with?"

She waved her hand. "Leave me to it, darling. The answer must be staring me in the face. I only need open my eyes wider."

Did her hand look so dark earlier? He couldn't recall, but it certainly didn't look well. "What happened to your hand?"

She quickly pulled her hand from the table and hid it underneath. "Oh, it's nothing. I hit it on a branch earlier this morning while I was out in the woods. It's just a little bruised. I'll be fine."

Rayah's right. She's hiding something.

"It looked worse than any bruise I've seen before." Alderan reached for her arm, and she shrank away.

She glared at him. "I said it's nothing."

He raised his arms. "Fine. It's nothing then."

He picked up a book and flipped it open. The words on the page bobbed up and down, as though set out to sea, their letters jumbled and foreign. "How can anyone read this?"

"A few of these books are at least a millennium old and were written in Ancient Centaurian. Sadly, few people who can read the language still live."

He flipped through a few more pages. "But you can read them?"

She sighed. "Certainly not, darling. I rely on the drawings in those books. I only pick up a word or two here and there. I'm certain I've missed many useful things in them."

Alderan squished his face and squinted at the page. "Why do the letters swim about?"

"I've never noticed them 'swim about.' Let me see it."

He handed her the book, and she examined it.

"Hmm. No, there's definitely no swimming about that I can see. Perhaps you're in need of some reading spectacles."

Alderan took the book back and focused on the letters. The longer he stared, the clearer they became. They stilled and then lifted from the page. The tingle of mezhik tickled his hands, and the inside of his right wrist burned. He turned his right hand palm-up and stared at the purple light beaming up from the square on the inside of his wrist.

"What the…" He dropped the book, and it smacked against the floor.

Zerenity rose from her stool. "If you won't—Dear Ӡӓṭūr!"

An opened, transparent-purple book hovered over his wrist for several seconds and then shrank as it lowered to his wrist. The book, now an inch square, seared his skin like liquid fire, and left a grey brand behind.

Zerenity grabbed his hand and examined his wrist. "Do you know what this mark means?"

Do I ever know what anything means? "No, but I'm guessing you do."

"Yes! This is the mark of *neallӓzh*. It means knowledge. Even among mages, it is a rare gift."

Alderan stared at the mark on his wrist. "I don't understand. Why did that just happen?" He looked at Zerenity. "I wasn't even trying to do anything but read the book."

Zerenity frowned. "I admit, you perplex me. I've never known a mage firsthand, so I'm not sure how your abilities manifest. Us wizards only have one focus of skills, so there's never anything to obtain outside of our concentration. You must learn to adapt to and control your skills as they manifest."

Zerenity's eyes brightened. "In the meantime, you may have just saved us."

Alderan scrunched up his face. "Saved us? From what?"

She searched his eyes and then showed him the back of her hand. "The vines attacked me this morning, just as they did Qotan. They've poisoned me as well. Please don't tell the others. They needn't worry."

I knew it! "Zerenity, how can you keep this from the others? Especially Master Savric?"

How could I keep this from Rayah?

Her eyes pleaded with him. "Savvy's still recovering. Knowledge of this would only drive him to do something he hasn't the strength to do."

Alderan looked down at his right wrist again and then back at her. "And how does this knowledge mark save you?"

Her eyes sparkled. "The books, darling. I believe you can read the ones I cannot."

He bent down and picked up the book he'd dropped. The words lay still on the page. "And what would I do to read it? Is there some spell I should cast?"

She placed her hand on his shoulder. The tingle of mezhik flowed from her. "Not everything requires a spell. Some mezhik is natural, like breathing. Relax and focus on the individual letters. As with all mezhik, you must believe it's within your power to read the text, and instinct will kick in."

He squinted at the page. "The letters rose from the page just before I dropped the book, but now I don't see anything at all. They aren't swimming about anymore, either."

She released his shoulder and the tingling ceased. "Don't think about it, just read the words, darling."

Read the words. Don't think. I'm good at that.

"Wait… I was concentrating so hard on the individual letters that I didn't realize the words were written in *our* language. Maybe I'd been trying to read it upside down before."

She laughed. "No, darling. It's still written in Ancient Centaurian. What does it say?"

He read from the book: *"The sting of a horned dialix (sketched below) may cause the feet and tongue of the stinging victim to swell and itch, but the liquid from the stem of an orange drooper (diagrammed below) will reduce the swelling and calm the itchiness. Administer two drops in each eye and wait a few hours. If the symptoms persist, repeat treatment."*

"Interesting, but not helpful right now." She tapped her finger on her chin. "Because of Qotan's condition and the one I'm developing, we shall suspend your training until we've found a remedy for this poison, Ẑäṭūr willing of course."

No training? How will I ever be ready to face the coming war? I don't even know what we're up against. Then again, I won't have a chance if Zerenity and Master Qotan are dead.

Alderan sighed. "I think you're right." He closed the book and set it on the table. "I do have a question for you though. On a slightly different subject."

She sat back down on the stool. "Anything, darling."

He stood and paced. "There are so many things about mezhik that I don't understand, and many I probably never will, but I was wondering if it's possible to reverse a spell?"

Zerenity tilted her head back and eyed him under a furrowed brow. "Reverse a spell? As in, countering it? Like a water spell to deflect a fire spell?"

He shook his head. "No, I mean actually reversing it. Undoing its effect."

She sucked in her lower lip and tapped her finger against her chin. "In all my years, I've never heard of such a thing. Never even contemplated it, truthfully. Why do you ask?"

He pushed his hair behind his ears. "I was thinking about the scourge spell that binds Qotan to the between. How will we ever bring him back from the between if we can't reverse the spell?"

She folded her arms. "You were eavesdropping on my conversation with Savvy, I gather?"

Alderan grinned sheepishly. "Not purposefully, but I found your story fascinating. I think I should go back to my house and look through all the books in the library. Maybe I can find a solution to both problems."

"Perhaps, but we should exhaust our resources here first." She pointed at a stack of four hefty books. "Take those, and the one you read from, and pore through their texts. They're all written in Ancient Centaurian and contain only a handful of pictures between them. Hopefully one of the books will provide a solution."

He looked at the stack of books. *Plants. Ugh. Why can't they be on an interesting subject, like Intus?* "I'll start looking over them now."

She bent down and gathered the papers from the floor. "Divide and conquer. It may be the only chance we have."

He picked up the five books and grunted. "It might go faster if I knew lunch would be on the way soon."

Zerenity looked up at him and shook her head. "If I didn't know better, I'd assume you and Savvy were cut from the same stone. The man never misses a meal."

His stomach rumbled, and he laughed. "No one should."

She stood and shooed him with the papers in her hand. "Remove yourself and those books from my kitchen, and I'll whip up some lunch."

Alderan hurried into the living area and dumped the books on the couch. *Maybe Rayah can help me look through these. She knows what the vines look like.*

He thought about her and the moment they'd shared on the floor. *Maybe being alone with her isn't such a great idea right now.*

He settled in on the couch and picked up the first book. "*A Field Guide to the Plants of the Ancient Realm, Vol. 3.*" He ran his fingers through his hair and exhaled loudly. "It's gonna be a long morning." He flipped the book open and set to work.

† † †

Alderan stood in the center of the city, rooted with fear. The walls of the obsidian palace reached ever upward, caressing the blackened sky. A woman, both familiar and unrecognizable at once, stood atop the southern rampart. Her red-and-blonde hair whipped in the wind, and massive, black, leathery wings spread behind her. Two red orbs pierced the darkness above her.

People pushed past Alderan, headed toward the palace gates. He screamed at them, but they continued their march without even a glance. He grabbed one of them, an old woman, and he turned her around so he could face her, but her inky-black eyes left him nowhere to focus his attention. Her pale skin highlighted a network of black veins running beneath its surface.

Each person he stopped had the same black eyes, pale skin, and black veins. None of them resisted his interference, but each continued toward the palace when he released them.

Alderan climbed onto a nearby rooftop and watched as thousands of them funneled into the city and marched toward the palace. He turned back toward the palace and looked up at the woman.

A presence entered his mind, and he knew it was the woman. Her words filled his head, "The black tide rises. The end draws near. Join, or be swept away."

† † †

Alderan! Rayah flew into the living area, her heart racing in her chest and her breath caught in her throat. Alderan lay on the couch amongst a pile of large books.

"Turn back!" Alderan's head tossed side-to-side and sweat poured from his brow.

Rayah grabbed him by the shirt and shook him. "Alderan, wake up!"

Alderan's eyes snapped open, their whites and green replaced by wells of inky-black. "The black tide rises." The high-pitched voice sounded nothing like his own.

Ɂäṭūr, what's happening with him?

Rayah reared back and smacked his cheek, hard. His head jerked sideways, his eyes rolled back in his head, and then he sat up and gasped.

His eyes rolled forward again, their green color returned.

Rayah hugged his neck. *Thank You, Ɛ̄ṭūr.*

"I thought I might've lost you. Are you okay?" She released him and moved back.

Alderan rubbed his temples and then his eyes. "I had another one of those nightmares with the obsidian palace. I thought I was over them since it'd been so long since my last one, but I guess not. They're so real when I'm in them."

She pushed the pile of books on the couch to the side and sat next to him. "Maybe you should talk to Master Savric or Zerenity about them. Just before you woke, your eyes opened, and they were all black."

"*Black*?" His eyes widened. "The people in my nightmare had black eyes too."

She scratched her side. "That sounds frightening."

He massaged his cheek and jostled his jaw. "Did you hit me?"

She giggled. "I couldn't get you to wake up, and I didn't have any water handy."

"What is all the ruckus in here about?"

Master Savric! She zoomed from the couch and offered him her shoulder. "You're not supposed to be out of bed."

Savric scowled. "Feathers. I have been relaxing in there for weeks now." He winked at her, but his smile faded quickly. He placed his hand on her shoulder and steadied himself.

Alderan set the book aside and stood. "Let me help you, Master Savric." He walked over to Savric's side, placed his arm underneath Savric's and around Savric's back, and nearly lifted Savric off the ground.

She and Alderan led Savric across the living area and stopped in front of the couch, but he urged them on. "I must check on Qotan. My mind says he will be gone soon, but my heart cannot bear the thought of it."

Rayah kissed Savric's cheek. *Nor can mine, though I've never even met him.*

† † †

Savric grimaced as Alderan and Rayah shuffled him down the hallway. He'd never experienced weakness quite so debilitating before. *How will I help Qotan in such a state as this?*

From the doorway, the bedroom opened to the left. Three wooden chairs lined the far wall, the closest of them occupied by Eshtak. A single-sized bed, centered and perpendicular to the wall on the far left, filled most of the small room. Qotan lay on the bed, his eyes closed, and a tan wool blanket raised to his chin.

Alderan and Rayah helped Savric settle into the chair closest to the bed. He leaned forward and rested his elbows on top of his bony knees. Qotan's chest slowly rose and fell, so shallow, nearly undetectable.

How peaceful you look, brother. The sentiment, he knew, lie far from the truth.

How long will you remain with us? He leaned over and felt Qotan's forehead. *Cooler than before. But is that good or bad?* He gently lifted one of Qotan's eyelids and then the other. Both eyes, corner to corner and top to bottom, were dull and black as night.

He reached out to Qotan with his mind but couldn't make a connection. "Can you hear me, brother?"

Qotan lay still.

Dear Ẑäṭūr, be gentle with him when You take him.

Alderan stood on the opposite side of the bed. "How's he doing?"

Savric scooted back in his chair. "I forget you cannot see him. How strange it must be to watch me interact with nothing. Do you see a form under the blanket?"

Alderan bent down and looked closely at the bed. "No. I don't believe so."

How do two things occupy the same space at the exact same time? He shook his head. "This *between* is quite peculiar. Beyond my understanding."

"And his condition?" Rayah sat on the chair next to him.

Savric stroked his beard again. "Yes, of course. It is much the same as yesterday. However, he has become unresponsive even to thoughts, and his eyes have turned completely black. Even beyond the iris. There is no more white in them."

Alderan and Rayah gasped and looked at each other with wide eyes.

Savric's brow furrowed, and he looked between the two of them. "This has meaning to you? What is it? What are you keeping from me?"

Alderan raked his hair between his fingers. "I've had a few dreams—well nightmares, really. I'm sure they mean nothing."

Savric pulled on his eyebrows and twisted the ends. "Tell me of these dreams of yours, and leave no detail out, no matter how insignificant you think it to be."

Alderan first told him of the five black towers and the one white tower and how the white tower turned grey and then black. Then, he told Savric of the necromancer who rose an army of the dead from the ground. Last, he told him of the woman and the leathery wings and red orbs, and how the people with black veins and black eyes flooded into the city and the obsidian palace.

The obsidian palace. Only one place in the Ancient Realm fit the description: *Galondu Castle.* Magus Carac had cursed the surrounding land at the end of the Great War, and no one had lived there in twelve centuries.

Could it be the epicenter of prophecy once more?

Savric pulled on his beard. "We will need to consult the texts for clarification, but I believe what you are seeing in your dreams are bits and pieces of nightmares and prophetic future. I believe you may have the gift of prophecy.

"With proper guidance, your dreams could give us insight into what is coming. No prophecy currently exists beyond the currently unfolding events."

He looked back at Qotan. *The black eyes and veins. Are they related? They must be, but how?*

Savric grimaced. "I would enjoy being found mistaken, but I fear we will find no answer to the poisonous vines in any horticulture book. I believe we must look elsewhere."

Alderan moved around the foot of the bed. "Like in the library under my house?"

Savric chuckled. "That would be a fine starting place, but there are many holds for books. Most highly secretive and extremely dangerous."

Alderan pushed strands of hair behind his ears. "Show me how to find these holds, and I'll get us the answers we need."

"My boy, I appreciate your enthusiasm more than you know, but getting into these places, finding the books, and surviving are only part of the equation. The books themselves are often dangerous, and so many are written in languages that have been lost for centuries. Some unknown even before the Great War."

Alderan held his right arm out, inside up. "Look, Master Savric. I've received the gift of knowledge. I helped Zerenity look through books she couldn't read."

Savric grabbed Alderan's wrist and examined it. *Nealläzh.* His bones tingled with excitement. "Tomorrow, we will begin a new quest."

His stomach rumbled, and he patted it. *Easy, old girl. I have not forgotten you.*

"Now, if my nose serves me correctly, lunch is about ready. I could use some good food and a bit of rest. I do not recover as quickly as I used to."

Rayah stood and stretched her arms. "Speaking of old, Zerenity said that Master Qotan looked as old as you."

He frowned. "Thinks I look old, does she? Not the catch she once knew?" He stared at the liver spots on his hands and sighed. "I daresay, there is no repudiating the truth. This old sack of bones has certainly witnessed grander days."

Rayah patted his leg. "Aren't you the one who told me once that age was nothing more than a matter of perspective? Old and young are only determined by the way you feel and act?"

He sat back and pulled on his beard. "Those words contain far greater wisdom than anything this old man could ever dream to have." He winked at her.

Alderan helped Savric up and put his arm around him. "Does everyone age in the between?"

Savric breathed heavily. "I daresay, I have yet to ponder such a question. Qotan certainly has, but his circumstance might be different than those that are trapped in Intus."

Rayah took Savric's other arm. "Eshtak might be 1,300 years old, but he still looks quite young."

Savric winced, his back sorer than he remembered. "True, but if he is an albino dwarf, I have heard they often live several millennia. So, his age is not necessarily a good point of reference."

Eshtak stood and crossed his arms. His thin black lips arched into a frown. "Eshtak young, not old." He shuffled out of the room with his head hung low.

They laughed heartily.

Alderan pulled them forward. "Let's get some food before I die of starvation."

Cannot argue with that. Savric glanced back at Qotan as they exited the room. *Hold fast, brother. We will find a way to remedy the poison tomorrow. I am certain of it.*

CHAPTER THIRTY-FIVE

Aria lay on the hard floor, curled in front of a cold, lifeless fireplace. She needed no fire though, for the stone warmed her. She nestled it between her bare breasts and cuddled it like an infant. *I'll protect you, my love.*

Last night, after she'd made her way up to the top of the southernmost spire, she'd stripped out of her clothes, piled them at the door, and locked herself inside. Naked, she'd rubbed the smooth stone down her arms and legs and circled her stomach. Its intoxicating mezhik enraptured her and left her breathless.

Sunlight shone through the southwestern window; its rays caressed her bare skin. As wonderful as it felt, the sun's touch paled compared to the stone's.

Aria uncurled and rolled on her back. The stone rested between her breasts as she stretched her arms and legs. Transfixed by its pulsing red glow, she imagined it to be the heartbeat of a baby inside her womb.

Is that what you want?

She slid the stone down her abdomen, below her belly, and applied pressure to the stone. It sank beneath her skin with ease. Its intoxicating touch faded, and then a fire raged in her belly. Her entire body tensed, and she gasped for air.

What have I done?

The stone spoke to her in her mind. *"What's necessary."*

Necessary? But what must I do now?

"Take steps to ensure our survival."

Pravus. The wedding. The ceremony of the stone.

"Yes, the ceremony. It is far more important than anything else. Do as I ask, and you will rule the world."

Pravus has instructed me on the steps and words that must be used in order to release the stone's power.

"I'm sure he's told you what he knows to be true, but he understands far less of the stone than he knows. I will guide you through the ceremony."

How can I trust you? I don't know you or understand what you are. Maybe you're only a voice in my head. A sickness of the mind.

"And you trust Pravus?"

No… I don't know what to believe.

"I want the same thing you do. You were born to rule, and I will serve you."

I… I will trust you.

"Good."

What will happen after the ceremony?

"We'll kill the man who claims you as his daughter."

Nardus… Why must he die?

"He's fulfilled his purpose, and now his existence threatens our future. Do you still wish to rule Centauria?"

Yes.

"Then it must be done. He'll stop at nothing to take the throne for himself, even if it means killing you."

Would he? She knew little of him.

The fire in her belly subsided, and a deep sadness filled her. Could she really kill Nardus? Did the sandcastles mean nothing to her? *Father…*

Hot tears streaked her cheeks. *Once perhaps, but he abandoned us. Alderan would still be alive if he hadn't.*

She let her anger blossom and her hope for a father fizzle, and her memories of Nardus became tainted. *He deserves to die for what he did to us, and, if he's a threat to my future, there's no way I can allow him to live.*

She rose to her feet, wiped her cheeks, and slid back into her clothes.

I am the future queen. She balled her hands and set her jaw. *No, I am the queen. Liar or not, it's time to make amends with Pravus and build our kingdom.*

She unlocked the door and traversed the spiraling stairs. An urgency, founded or not, quickened her pace further.

We must marry today.

† † †

Pravus's hands quaked inside his robes' sleeves, but not from nerves. The blood lust still raged within him and drove him toward madness, yet he clung to his sanity, if only by fingernails.

He'd spent several hours during the night searching the castle for Aria, but she'd hid well. Had he found her, there would've been nothing left of her and nothing to celebrate. All his years of hard work would've been lost in a few irrational moments to fill a need that would never be satisfied.

Damn this weakness! It will not rule me.

He stared at the diversity of lavish foods spread across the long tables, but his mind looped over the events hours before. How had Aria managed to take the stone from Nardus when he couldn't?

What does it mean?

The grand clock mercilessly ticked away moments from the day. They neared the noon hour.

Where is she?

Dozens of constituents, dignitaries, and lords filled the massive hall, the air abuzz with conversation. They gathered in small groups, huddled over tall tables, sipped wine, and consumed an assortment of delicacies. Considering the lateness of the invitation, their numbers surprised him.

Pravus looked around the room. As if on some sort of secret rotation schedule, each of them periodically eyed him with scrutiny. *Like vultures, they wait for their prey to die. But tomorrow, they'll see that Aria and I are gods. They'll be waiting forever.*

Credan stood to Pravus's left, and Wizard Wrik to his right. "Keep them occupied and make sure the wine continues to flow. I must go find my future queen."

Credan leaned over. "My lord, I believe she was spotted heading toward her bedchamber not long ago."

Pravus fumed. "And you found it unnecessary to inform me of it?"

Credan lowered his head. "I apologize, my lord. I fear I've allowed myself to become preoccupied with our guests. Forgive me. Shall I fetch Mistress Aria?"

Pravus snarled, "Far be it from me to interrupt your preoccupation of *my* guests. I will fetch her myself."

He walked through the hall, ignored the guests that called out to him as he walked past, and stepped into the corridor. He nearly teleported out of the corridor and into the waiting area outside Aria's bedchamber, but he caught himself.

No mezhik until the ceremony tomorrow. I'll need my full strength.

He groaned. *Such a long trek. But this will be the last. Tonight, she lies with me.*

Twenty minutes later, he arrived outside her bedchamber doors. He knocked loudly and waited. Several seconds later, the lock disengaged, and the door on his left opened slightly. A homely young girl peered through the opening.

The girl's eyes widened, and she quickly pulled the door open. "Lord Rosai." She curtsied. "Mistress Aria's not quite dressed yet. If you could give us a few minutes—"

He pushed her aside and entered the room. "Leave us."

She curtsied again and then pulled the door shut behind her as she exited the room.

He moved through the entranceway and around the corner. Aria stood in front of a full-length mirror, naked from the waist up and her back to him. She held her eyes closed and her hand against her abdomen. Her lips moved, but she made no sound.

Her breasts were fuller than he remembered, and her beauty transcended her scarred flesh. How long had it been since he'd healed her at Dragnus's? *A lifetime ago.*

An impulsive urge to ravage her as he had Tilly, Yora, and Triza pulled him across the room. He stood behind her, could smell her, her zhifţäd blood. Still, she refused to acknowledge his presence; only her lips moved.

I am here, Aria.

Her slender neck tilted slightly and gave him perfect access to her blood. He leaned in, ready to bury his teeth in her flesh, and glimpsed himself in the mirror. Gaunt, frenzied eyes met his own. He stumbled backward, horrified by the monster's reflection.

That cannot be me!

In the mirror, Aria's eyes opened, red as blood. Her steel gaze met his. "Is your father's kingdom worth my blood?"

Is it? Thoughts twisted his mind. *How could it not be? Her blood will make me a god.*

He gazed at the monster again. At himself.

Would it end with her? Hadn't Tilly's blood satisfied him? *Only for a moment. But Aria's...*

He grabbed his robes at the neck and ripped them to his navel. He fell to his knees and screamed at the ceiling. "I will not let you take this from me!"

Aria turned to him and pulled his head against her belly. Her bare skin warmed his face like sitting close to a fire. He exhaled, and, with that breath, his blood lust subsided. He trembled, and tears soaked his cheeks. How would he ever live without her?

He stood and lifted her into his arms, her skin against his. He peered into her eyes; they were green again. Had he only imagined them red before? *It doesn't matter.* He kissed her forehead, her cheeks, her lips.

Aria wiped his face with her thumbs. "Tonight, we marry."

She stunned him. "Yes—did Credan tell you? Or Wrik?"

She frowned. "Tell me? No, that was a demand."

Pravus backed up to the bed and sat down, her on his lap. "It's why I came to find you. Several guests have arrived already."

Aria's eyes sparkled. "Then our timing is perfect. And tomorrow we hold the stone ceremony to cast the spell."

Has she read my thoughts?

He ran his fingers through her hair and down her bare back. "Give me the stone."

She kissed his lips and shoved him back on the bed. She took his left hand and placed it on her belly. Her eyes glowed red again. "This is as close to the stone as you're gonna get."

"Ouch!" He pulled his hand away from her scorching belly. "What's happened to you?"

She leaned over him and put her hands around his neck. "Ask for it again," she growled, "and I won't hesitate to snap your neck." She shook her head, and her eyes turned green once more.

Pravus scowled. "Does the stone speak for you, or have you become that calloused?"

She backhanded him, hard.

He grabbed her neck, just above her silver collar, but quickly released her. *Don't do anything that can't be undone.*

Her left nostril rose and twitched, and her venomous gaze struck at him like a viper. "From the moment I met you, you've done nothing but lie to me. How could I be anything but calloused? To think, I actually loved you. Even worse, I thought you loved me too."

She loved me.

He placed his hands on her bare sides. "Aria, you're mistaken."

She backhanded him again. "Don't think I can't replace you."

"I admit it. I have lied to you... about many things." She swung at him again, but he caught her wrist. "Stop and listen to me."

She scowled at him. "Why should I? You're a liar. You'll just lie more."

Her anger aroused him. *She still loves me.*

He grabbed her other wrist, rolled over, and pinned her to the bed. "As I've said before, I'm terrible with relationships. I trust no one. I lie and manipulate to get what I want. I always have.

"Most everything I told you in the beginning were lies, but the one thing I never lied about is loving you. At first, the thought sickened me. How could I possibly love anything more than myself? You were a means to an end; a tool I could use to accomplish my goal.

"After we met, your strength and courage astonished me. You're fearless, like me. I didn't think I'd ever find another person that complemented me so well. Being cooped up with you in that carriage for so long opened my eyes to possibilities I'd never dreamed of.

"You upended my life and warmed my cold heart. I love you, Aria Somneri, more than my father's kingdom. More than revenge. My love for you supersedes everything else."

Her voice feigned anger, but her eyes softened. "And when you've tired of me? Will you cast me aside for another?"

Pravus stared into her eyes for several moments. "Tonight, we'll be married, bound by blood and soul, and then we'll consummate our marriage. I'd do those things for no other."

She smiled wryly. "I'm half-naked now. I won't stop you if you want to finish the job. I'm no virgin, and I doubt you are either."

Her warm body and exposed breasts aroused him further. He closed his eyes, but her nakedness remained in his mind's eye. *Control yourself.*

Pravus opened his eyes and kissed Aria's forehead. "You don't know how I've longed to be with you, but we must wait until tonight."

She pulled her hands free and slid them inside his torn robes. "Tonight's far too long to wait, and it doesn't feel like you want to."

He went rigid as he searched her eyes. *Does she know the binding will only take hold if we've not lain together? Is that why she insists?*

He kissed her deeply and then rolled away from her. "Tonight, my love."

She sat up and covered herself. "Take your chances, then. I may not be so giving tonight."

He swallowed hard. *She must know, but how? Who would've told her about the binding? Wrik? The stone? We must consummate our marriage tonight, or the soul bond will be invalidated.*

He got up from the bed and pulled his robes closed. "I'll send your servant back in to assist you. I'll send several more as well."

Aria uncovered her breasts again, pushed them up with her hands, and bit her lower lip. "Last chance."

He reached over the bed, took her hands in his, and kissed the tops of them. "Soon, my love."

Pravus quickly left the room before she succeeded in seducing him.

She knows.

† † †

Nardus had no idea how much time had passed since he'd given the stone to Shanara, but she hadn't returned to see him. *Will she?* Nasduron awaited, but he stood still, torn with emotion. The air shimmered around him, ready to teleport him.

One thought. One step. I'd be there now.

He'd relinquished the single most important item he'd possessed, and he'd do it time and again without hesitation. *Shanara lives.*

But still, the decision toyed with his mind. Had he given up on the rest of his family? Did Shanara mean more to him than the rest of them?

No, I cannot think that way anymore. She still lives. How could she not mean more? I lost her once when I put my rage and revenge ahead of protecting her and Shardan. I won't allow anything to come between us again.

He rubbed the scars on his left bicep. *She lives, but they do not.* Now that she possessed the stone, would Pravus still honor their agreement? *I doubt he ever would've. The bastard.*

The vision he'd seen of Vitara and Savannah crept into his mind. Realization of its meaning drove him to the floor. *Had I always known Shanara lived? But what of Shardan? He wasn't in the vision either.*

Does he still live too? Neither Pravus nor Shanara had mentioned him. If he lived, wouldn't he have been there with them? *It's possible he lives too.* Would having almost half of his family alive satisfy him? Could he be happy? Did he even have a choice?

No.

How could he possibly be selfish enough to go to Nasduron? What if Shanara came back to see him again only to find him gone? *How could I abandon her again?* Even if she forgave him for the first time he'd abandoned her, she'd never forgive him a second.

He shook his head. *It cannot be. I'm sorry, Gnaud. Perhaps one day I'll return.*

Vitara, my love, and my anchor, I'll see you again one day as well, even if I must plead and reconcile with Ɂäʈūr to do so. I'll pay any price.

Pravus entered the room through the black steel door. He circled the steel cage and dragged his dragon's-head cane across the bars. *Thunk. Thunk-thunk. Thunk.*

Nardus sat on the crate, arms folded. "Did you come down here for a reason, or only to drive me mad with your shiny new cane?"

Pravus stopped in front of him and leaned on his cane. "Do you know what today is?"

Nardus rubbed his left bicep and stared at the outer scar. "Did you mistake me for someone who cares? Take your news elsewhere."

Pravus lifted the cane and placed it under his right arm. "Don't be so hasty to dismiss me, my friend. My news involves your daughter."

He stood and glared at Pravus. "You so much as lay a finger on Shanara and I'll kill you."

Pravus cracked his knuckles. "Believe me when I tell you that I plan on doing far more than that with her tonight."

Nardus charged the bars and grabbed hold of them. "Don't think these bars will stop me!"

Pravus held his ground. "Aria and I will be married in a few hours."

"Married? Impossible! Why would she marry you after everything you've done to her?"

Pravus smiled smugly. "Love's a strange emotion—foreign to me until recently. Did she not confide her love for me to you, her *father*? No, I suppose not. She does suffer from severe abandonment issues."

Nardus reached through the bars, but Pravus stepped back, just beyond his reach. "You're a dead man! Mark my words." Spittle peppered the air.

Pravus smoothed out the sleeves of his long coat. "I'll keep that in mind. In the meantime, get yourself cleaned up. You can't attend the wedding dressed or smelling the way you do. You'd drive away our guests. And possibly spoil the food."

Nardus's knuckles whitened around the bars. "And what would make you believe I'd attend such a blasphemous affair?"

So that you can watch me suffer?

Pravus leaned on his cane with both hands. "How often does a father see his daughter married? Once in a lifetime?"

Nardus groaned. *Not like this. Not to a monster.*

Pravus stood tall. "It doesn't matter what you think of me. Your daughter and I *will* marry whether you approve or not. Think of what it would do to Aria if she knew you refused to attend one of the most important events in her life. Given your history, she's unlikely to forgive you as it stands. Stay down here, and you'll guarantee it."

How can I not be there? How could I deny you anything, Shanara?

"You'd uncage me for this wedding?"

Pravus moved into the shadows and became one of them. "The cage never existed." His words echoed like spectres in the night.

The steel bars dissolved in Nardus's hands, and he stumbled forward. He spat on the floor. "Damned mezhik."

Four guards filed in through the black steel door, their glaives down and ready to gut him. Two of them moved around and behind him, and the other two flanked him, one on each side.

Welcoming party. How thoughtful.

He slowed his breathing and calculated the number of moves it'd take to overpower them. *Seven. Perhaps twelve with less risk.* But how many more guards stood outside the door or down a corridor or waited inside a room to ambush him? *Too many unknowns to risk it.*

Something hard pressed against his spine, between his shoulder blades. One of the guards behind him said, "Keep your eyes forward and follow my instruction. Do you understand?"

Nardus nodded. What would escaping buy him, anyway? Wasn't his objective to win back Shanara's trust and love? How would resistance accomplish that? What choice did he have but to go along with them? *None. Shanara's love means more than any freedom I might gain from it.*

"Good. If you deviate from my instruction, we will shackle your hands and feet and give you something worth thinking about. Understood?"

A beating. Physical pain had befriended him long ago, their relationship oft strained and nearly deadly on several occasions. Even so, he'd take it over any other kind. "I only want what's best for my daughter."

The flanking guards raised their glaives and walked through the black steel door.

"Follow them," said the guard.

He moved forward, through the door, and down the hallway to the right. "Where are we headed?"

"The only place you're fit to go—the baths."

Nardus had no arguments. Several turns and hallways later, they rounded a corner and traversed a corridor that reeked of mildew. Steam billowed at the far end, distorting the view. When they reached the end, an enormous room materialized through the clouds of steam.

Girthy square columns surrounded several pools of steaming water and held up a soaring roof of glass. A few men and several women sat in the pools, perched around their edges on ledges a few feet below the water's surface. Even with the steam rising, his eyes took in more of their naked bodies than he desired.

"Strip everything off," said the guard.

Nardus looked around. "Here?"

The point of one of the glaives dug into his side and tore his shirt. "Now, or we will do it for you, piece by piece."

He quickly stripped down and climbed into the nearest pool. The hot water quickly melted away his aches, and he slid farther down.

An older woman sat several feet away, her eyes locked on him. She smiled at him with brown, yellow, and black teeth, several of them missing.

Nardus shuddered and turned away.

He dunked his head and pulled the water through his hair. When he rose back up, the woman sat next to him. The tops of her long, wrinkled breasts bobbed on the water's surface like albino alligators, their cyclops eyes surveying the waters for easy prey.

Out of all the horrors I've witnessed and all the trials I've endured, I'll never be able to erase those wretched beasts from my memory.

Her hand slid to the inside of his thigh and she squeezed. He nearly cried out, but her boldness frightened him. Her nails dug into his flesh, and her strength astounded him.

Moreover, the tingle of mezhik flowed into him and rendered him immobile. She placed a finger over her mouth with her free hand and winked.

Damned mezhik!

With her hand firmly planted between his legs, she leaned over and whispered in his ear. "Now is not the time to stir the pot. She will not be swayed this day. Do so, and your days end quickly. Stave your anger, hold your tongue, and opportunity will present itself."

He rose to confront her, but the pool lay empty. He smacked the water with his fist. *Damn this eerie place.*

Two younger women from a pool caddy-corner to his giggled and batted their lashes.

He threw them a rude gesture with his middle and third fingers and then sank back in the water. *Madness is a disease here.*

A basin sat beside the pool, full of fresh herbs and oils. He scooped up a handful, rubbed them between his hands, and then scrubbed his face, under his arms, and between his legs. Satisfied, he rose out of the water and doused himself with rosewater and cloves.

One of the guards tossed him a small, damp towel and he made the most of it. Nardus still dripped with water when the four guards led him away from the pools and into a much drier and less musty room. Across the room, a fire blazed and popped. The guards took his clothes and tossed them on the fire, his boots included.

He seethed. "Those were my only clothes, and the boots could've been repaired."

Only one guard of the four ever spoke. "The clothes on the chair are yours. See that they fit."

He looked at the pile of black clothing and then back at the guard. "And if they don't?"

The guard shrugged. "Go naked, I suppose. Makes little difference to me. I'm sure some of the other guests would find it offensive, though."

Were I a woman, they'd be ogling me.

Nardus stood in front of the fire and let the heat dry him. He pulled his hair back; it nearly fit into a ponytail. How long had it been since he'd last cut it? He pulled on his chin and the four inches of coarse beard.

My love, would you even recognize me?

He returned to the chair and dressed. The clothes fit perfectly. *Mezhik, I'm sure.*

Once ready, the guards led him through a myriad of hallways, stairs, corridors, and rooms. *How would one ever find their way in this place?*

They brought him into a small room with only a wooden chair in the corner and a bookcase with three books.

"Wait in here," said the guard. "The time is not quite upon us."

The guard left the room and closed the door behind him. No lock engaged. He waited a few minutes and pondered if he should try the door. *Where would I go? Become lost and starve to death?*

He took one of the books from the bookcase and settled in the chair. *The Ferzh of Dashner. Sounds interesting.* Two pages in, his eyelids grew heavy. He leaned back in the chair, lowered his brimmed hat over his eyes, and dreamed of Theyn.

† † †

Nardus stood in the middle of an expansive hall, surrounded by a horde of strangers. Like him, the men wore all black: brimmed hats, collared shirts, button-up vests, long ties, long coats with tails, skin-tight trousers without pockets, and ankle boots. He still wore the silver collar, the only difference between him and them, but his coat hid it from view.

The women dressed in ensembles of black as well: small black hats with veils, black dresses that hugged every curve and bulge from their shoulders to their knees. Fur pelts wrapped their necks, and they wore black evening gloves, knit stockings reaching up beyond the length of their dresses, and heeled shoes. Everyone wore their hair up and under their hats as well, leaving no strands untucked.

Cult of the damned.

Guards, stationed throughout the hall and in the corridors leading into it, also wore black: helmets, gauntlets, breastplates, shirts, belts, boots, and armor. Black iron and steel even made up their weapons.

Black banners hung from the ceiling, and black curtains draped the walls with no section left uncovered. Black tables hovered over the floor yet stayed in place. Only two items in the entire room weren't black: the lavish assortment of food and the dark-amber ale; even the wine was of a dark vintage.

The room, bright as a summer day, contained no candles or torches to speak of. From what he could tell, the light just existed.

Damned mezhik. He caught himself just before he spat. He looked around, but no one paid him any attention.

He walked the hall, nodded to those who eyed him, and exited into the corridor. His tight trousers rode up in places they had no business touching and itched something fierce.

He grimaced and adjusted himself. *How does anyone wear these damned things?*

People lined the corridor in both directions, captivated by the large tapestries that hung on the walls. One captured the bulk of their attentions. Curious, Nardus made his way over to it.

The tapestry depicted a starry night sky and a black dragon he found curiously familiar. A rider dressed in black robes sat in a leather saddle strapped on the dragon's back just below the base of its neck. Plumes of smoke rose from the dragon's nostrils, and the rider's black cape billowed in the wind.

The tapestry drew him in, as it had the others. Air rushed through his hair, and the whoosh of wings beating the air filled his ears. They soared over the dark land, ever faster, banking this way and that, and then spiraling downward. Just before crashing into the earth, they swooped upward once more and climbed into the clouds.

The cold, upper air chilled him, but the thrill of the flight kept his focus. Downward they plummeted again, his stomach in his throat and screams of joy in his ears. They shot across the plains and then skimmed across the waters of a great lake.

Upward they soared again, until he swore he could reach out and touch the stars. His heart raced as he broke free from the saddle and lost his grip on the reins. For a moment, the earth stilled below him, and then he scorched the sky as he streaked toward the earth.

He breathed fast and heavy, and his heart shook his chest. Fear strangled him. *I'm gonna die.* The ground rushed up to meet him, and the stream of air burned his eyes. His knees bent, and he choked on his own breath, his feet nearly to the ground.

He closed his eyes and braced for the jarring impact and bone-cracking pain that would follow, but neither came. He opened his eyes. Nardus still stood in the corridor, his brow damp with sweat and his nerves frayed. His gaze remained locked on the tapestry. Those around him clapped and cheered.

Damned mezhik. He would've spat had he not been in such close quarters.

"Have you ever seen or felt anything like it?" asked one man.

"I most certainly flew on a dragon," said another in response.

"How does Lord Rosai do it?" asked a woman.

The man next to her shook his head. "I couldn't even begin to figure it out. His powers are devastatingly marvelous. To the grave, he has my fealty."

Not wanting to get sucked into any more scenes, Nardus cautiously traversed the corridor and averted his eyes from the other tapestries and guests. Everywhere he looked, doors, hallways, intersecting corridors, stairways, and rooms branched off.

Escaping from the castle would prove difficult. He imagined one could walk the corridors for weeks without seeing the same place twice.

Farther ahead, the corridor opened wide. As he neared, a tall, thin man bowed. "Good evening, sir. Ahead lies the Hall of Dragons. I caution you to keep watch of your heart if you dare enter. I assure you, you've never seen anything like it."

Nardus looked ahead but only glimpsed a darkened hall lined with pillars. "I assure you, I've seen things no man should ever see, and I lived to tell of it."

The man swept his arm to the side. "Enjoy the spectacle."

Nardus stepped into the hall, and the air sizzled with energy. To his left and right, rows of columns stretched the length of the hall, and beyond the columns towered majestic sculptures of dragons. One looked familiar. *Perhaps the same kind of dragon as Tharos.*

The room faded to black, and then a world beyond time roared to life. Dragons of all shapes and sizes roamed the land and filled the skies. The variety of dragons astounded him. Every type imaginable, from fire-breathing dragons to water dragons to air dragons to ice dragons. Tiny, gigantic, ferocious, and cute.

His loathing of mezhik stayed intact, but even he couldn't deny the grandiosity and splendor of it. Had he been a child, his mind might've expanded beyond his head. *Shardan would've loved this.*

He walked around for a while, caught up in the moment, his cares obliterated. The world faded away, and he found himself at the center of the hall. Several guards ushered people back through the corridor and into the main hall once more, him included.

Now I understand what Shanara sees. He didn't know the circumstances she'd grown up with, but if they were anything like this, how would he ever be able to compete?

No, it's not a competition. I am her father. She will come around. She must.

A large, dark-skinned man stood at the front of the hall. He towered over most of the crowd. "Please make your way out the double doors to my right." His booming voice filled the hall. "The wedding will begin momentarily."

Nardus stood still, his feet firmly rooted to the floor. The crowd jostled around him and filtered through the doors. How could he stand by and watch his precious daughter make the biggest mistake of her life? *This can't happen. I won't allow it!*

In one blink, the large man stood next to him, his golden-eyed gaze a weighted force. "Mr. Remison, I presume?"

He eyed the big man. "I am. Who are you?"

"Wizard Wrik." He extended his hand.

Nardus took Wrik's hand. It swallowed his and part of his forearm as well. He thought about Shanara and holding her tiny little hand right after her birth. *So precious.*

"A pleasure, I'm sure. What can I do for you?"

Wrik released his hand. "As the father of the bride, I'm sure you're aware that it's your privilege to walk her down the aisle."

Is he serious? Words evaded him.

Wrik adjusted his spectacles. "This union will take place, with or without your blessing. The choice is yours, but keep in mind Aria's thoughts and feelings. She is a special young woman, and very hard-headed. If she were my daughter, I'd do everything in my power to make her happy, even if it didn't sit well with me."

Nardus clenched his fists and set his jaw. "You'd have me go against every instinct I have to protect her from that monster?"

Wrik smiled, calmer than any other man he'd met. "Monster or not, he loves your daughter more than you'd imagine. If you knew the lengths he's gone to give her the world, you might reconsider."

"Pravus is a *liar*." Spittle peppered the air.

"Is he? How much family do you need to be happy? Is Aria not enough for you? Has she not risen from the dead, as he promised?"

Nardus shook his finger. "Don't mince words, *wizard*. And don't pretend to know or understand me. Shanara means the world to me!"

Wrik lifted his hands, palms up. "Then prove it to her. Walk her down the aisle despite your loathing of her betrothed. Win her heart back."

Nardus closed his eyes. *You know he's right. You can't push her away and expect her to love you again. Damn you, Pravus!*

He rubbed his left bicep and forced air through his nostrils. He looked up at Wrik. "I can't argue with your logic. I'd do anything to make Shanara happy."

Wrik slapped him on the shoulder. "Good. You could probably start by calling her Aria."

Aria. How could he call his precious little girl by any other name than the one that he and her mother had given her? *Because she only knows herself as Aria. Is it so much to ask?*

"Aria…" The name tripped over his tongue, but he'd get used to it with time. "May I see her before the ceremony?"

"I'm sorry, but there's no time for that." Wrik ushered him toward the double doors. "We must go and take our places."

Through the doors, they immediately teleported to the top of Atrum Peak, high above Galondu Castle. He looked back, but no doors remained behind them. He stood on the western edge of the caldera's rim with sheer cliffs at his back.

A light breeze from the east burned his eyes and set him on edge. How easy it'd be for a strong gust to throw him to his death. *Perhaps not a terrible death.*

In his mind's eye, shards of rock jutted up and impaled him, missing vital organs and leaving him to slowly bleed out. He shuddered away the image, but the memory of Theyn impaled by the dragon's black claw replaced it. Tears moistened his eyes; he blamed the wind.

The caldera, a massive bowl of black rock, lay below. The eastern third of the caldera's wall no longer stood, and its altered shape created an amphitheater with a breathtaking view of Galondu Castle below. *A perfect place for a wedding.*

Benches, carved straight from the rock, layered the angled walls and stretched from one end of the caldera to the other, save the steps in front of him that led down to the floor. White carpet, lusher than any furs Nardus had ever laid eyes upon, covered the steps—a stark contrast to its surroundings. Red petals covered the center of the carpet.

The people that'd filled the hall minutes before now filled the benches. No spot remained vacant, save one at the very front. *Must be mine.*

A natural stage skirted the lower eastern edge of the caldera, raised about four feet from the floor. A black marble altar, erected at the center of the stage, nearly swallowed the short man standing behind it. The man wore black robes, and grey hair ringed the top of his bald head. Light glinted off his spectacles and his head.

A single, black-stemmed rose lay on top of the altar, its red petals stark against the marble.

Pravus stood to the left of the altar, his commanding presence undeniable. His black-and-silver hair bathed his shoulders and splashed down below his chest. He wore black robes, but thin silver stripes streaked them vertically.

Nardus's teeth ground in his ears, his jaw tight with tension. His fists balled at his sides, every muscle in his body tense with rage. So many years stolen. *It may not be today, but you will pay.*

He breathed deep and looked to the heavens. *This is Shanara's day.* The stars shone in the dark night sky like diamonds and filled him with sorrow. Vitara, Savannah, Shardan, and Theyn surely looked down upon him, but so did the eyes of Ɂäţūr.

Is it too late for me? His heart ached, and his soul mourned.

"Rise." The small man's voice filled the caldera.

As one, the people rose from their seats and turned to Nardus. No, not him, but beyond him. He turned and matched their gaze. His heart, a galloping stallion, thundered in his ears. He wiped his sweaty palms on his miserable trousers.

Far in the distant sky, a white speck appeared. It grew and approached with heart-wrenching speed. A thunder, like drums, shook the air, and grew in volume. He squinted and then blinked with disbelief as the white blob took shape.

White, leathery wings spanned a hundred feet and beat the air—the source of his drums. The giant white dragon, bearded with spikes and horns that extended from his skull, towed a white carriage behind.

The wheel-less, heart-shaped carriage floated behind the dragon on a bed of air, a sight all its own. Nardus tried to glimpse Aria, but opaque panes of black glass surrounded the carriage.

The dragon and carriage headed straight for Nardus, and then the dragon banked to the left at the last moment, sweeping over the rim of the caldera. The crowd gasped and cheered and awed as the dragon and carriage cruised over the expanse above Galondu Castle, around the other side of the caldera's rim, and came to a rest just beyond Nardus, to the west.

The dragon and carriage hovered in the air and the crowd quieted. Only the beating of the dragon's wings sounded.

Nardus's heart leapt, and his legs trembled. *This is for Shanara, not Pravus.*

In his mind, he stepped toward the carriage, but physically he remained still. His legs weighed a ton, his feet caught in quicksand. *Damn you, legs, move!* He nearly picked them up with his arms.

Everyone's watching. She's watching. Are you not foolish enough already? These events will move forward, with or without you. Now move!

Like breaking from a stone shell, Nardus lurched forward. He reached out and touched the white handle on the carriage door. His heart jumped and caught in his throat, the tingle of mezhik overwhelming. He pulled down on the handle.

Click!

† † †

Every moment in her life led to this one. When the carriage door opened, she'd step out and into her new life. *Am I ready?* The stone burned in her belly and calmed her.

"You were born for this moment."

Predestined. Prophecy. I am a queen.

"And so much more."

The carriage door swung open, and the night air rushed in. Nardus stood before her, hand held out for hers.

Rage rose within her. *What is he doing here?*

"His duty as your father. Fear not; he won't live through tomorrow."

But why must he be here?

She closed her eyes for a few moments and breathed slowly. *He cannot change the fates. Pravus and I are destined for each other.* A comfort in some ways and a burden in others, she didn't want to navigate her wedding with any outside influence. She needed to experience it on her own.

Leave me for now, and let me take this night in. I will never have another.

"As you wish but remember what must be done." The burning in her stomach faded.

She took Nardus's hand and stepped down from the floating carriage and onto the caldera's rim.

"Aria." Nardus kissed her gloved hand. "I've never seen anyone as beautiful as you. Not even your mother compares."

He dares speak to me!

She glared at him. "Father." Had it manifested physically, her voice would've ripped a hole in his throat. "Refrain from speaking. This is my night."

Nardus nodded, a weary smile on his weathered face. His eyes, wrought with sorrow, and perhaps love, left her conflicted. She saw Alderan in him, a constant reminder of what she'd lost. Maybe it played into the anger she drew from his presence, but there had to be more.

Nardus took her arm in his and guided her to the edge of the steps. The ground swayed beneath them. Aria thought she might fall, but Nardus held her tight. *Don't let me go, father!* Her weakness enraged her. How could she share this moment with him? *But how would I navigate the steps without him?*

She pushed Nardus from her thoughts and set her focus on the stage far below. Pravus stood below and to the right of the stage, his gaze focused on her. His white teeth gleamed.

I am his bride.

She looked over the throng of people gathered on the benches. They looked at her with wonder.

I am their queen.

Pole torches roared to life all around the caldera and down its eastern sides. Drums thundered, and then a symphony of sounds and music ignited the night. *The March of the Bride.* A song of tradition, Wizard Wrik had told her.

Carefully, they descended the steps. Halfway down, she glanced back up. Her long black train still poured from the carriage. She hardly noticed its weight.

The closer they came to the bottom of the caldera, the faster her heart beat. Pravus, her destiny, patiently waited for her, his golden eyes brimming with passion. An overwhelming urge to run and jump into his arms filled her. *Still a girl at heart, but that's not bad.*

At the bottom of the steps, they halted, along with the music.

From their vantage, she only saw the top of Credan's head behind the altar, but his voice boomed, "Be seated."

The crowd obeyed.

Credan spoke to Pravus. "Take your bride from her father and step up to the altar."

Nardus gave her arm a final squeeze and released her.

Aria cringed. *Never yours again.*

† † †

Aria stood before Pravus, her beauty beyond measure. Every blonde hair on her head placed perfectly, braids wrapped around her head from her temples like a crown, and the rest flowed down her back. A white lace veil hung over her face, banded at the top with diamonds. A single diamond sparkled against her forehead, and diamonds hung from her ears.

White lace trimmed the top of the dress and wrapped her slender neck. Silk and lace comprised the entirety of the dress from the neck down, every inch lavished with intricate beads and stitching woven into floral patterns. Lace sleeves hugged her arms, and the bodice wrapped her tightly. From the waist down, the dress spread wide, and the train at the back stretched into infinity.

The multi-toned dress complimented all her features and transitioned from stark white at her shoulders to a light-grey bodice to a charcoal-grey waist and then to a deep black by the time the dress reached the ground. The colors transitioned seamlessly.

Her green eyes radiated from underneath her veil. Every fiber within Pravus ached for her. How the gods had smiled upon him.

He took her white-gloved hand in his. He yearned to touch her skin, but that single piece of fabric prevented him from doing so. *Damn those gloves! They'll burn in the fire tonight.*

Pravus escorted her up the four steps, onto the stage, and to the front of the altar. They turned and faced Credan, who stood on the opposite side.

Credan's brow glistened with sweat, and he dabbed at it with a cloth. Then he removed his spectacles and wiped them with the same cloth.

Get on with it. I've got a marriage to consummate.

Credan returned his spectacles to his face and then addressed the crowd. "You've all been summoned here to bear witness of this union between Pravus Rosai, lord of Atrum Moenia and the rightful heir to the throne of our fathers, and Aria Somneri, princess of Viscus D'Silva."

Aria squeezed his hand, and he smiled. *A slight embellishment, but soon she'll be queen of the Ancient Realm.*

Credan continued, "Any who wish to contest this union are free to voice their opinion but be aware that you sign your own death warrant. Dissent will not be tolerated."

Come on, Nardus. Stand up and say something. Tell us your heart. Contest this union and die now. Satisfy us all.

Silence prevailed.

Pravus shook his head. *Coward.*

Credan went on, "As many of you know, this day is momentous, not only because of the union between the two people who stand before me, but because of the fulfillment of prophecy this union creates. *Fädinzh dhä Ballek.*"

"*Fädinzh dhä Ballek,*" the crowd repeated.

The Black Wedding. Pravus glanced down at Aria. Her eyes, full of confusion, met his. He winked at her and squeezed her fingers. Her ignorance amused him.

Credan looked between them. "Face each other." They did. "Lord Rosai, give her the words of your heart."

He looked deep into Aria's eyes, an endless universe he'd never fully traverse in a thousand lifetimes. He took both of her hands in his. Warm through the gloves, yet they trembled. *Be at peace, my love.*

Pravus cleared his throat. "Prophecy and predestination speak of many things, but never of love. I've known for many years that we would eventually come together in marriage, but the idea of loving you was ludicrous at best. I'd never loved before, other than myself, perhaps, and I never wished to love anyone either.

"The concept of love escaped me until the day we met at Castle Portador Tempestade. Love at first sight would be rash in most any circumstance, yet you took my heart right from that moment. I cannot imagine life without you by my side.

"You are the light to my darkness and a warmth to my coldness. My black heart is yours alone, and I surrender it to you for eternity. You filled a void in my soul I never knew existed. I hope to be your lover and your friend, forever. I love you, Aria."

Under her veil, tears streaked her cheeks. He heard sniffing from the crowd too. *The perfect response.* Pride swelled within his chest.

Credan wiped his cheek and turned to Aria. "And yours for him."

Aria closed her eyes. Blinded without them upon him, he struggled to know her heart. *What is she thinking? Am I unworthy of her? No, now you're being pathetic. How does she manipulate me so?*

Aria's eyes opened, and they bore deep into his soul. Her words spoke to his heart. "I was no one. A nomad, born into a hopeless world. Everything I knew crumbled around me, an existence surrounded by walls of deceit. With every facet of my life ripped away, I was left cold and alone.

"Beaten, raped, abused, and chained, I'd lost all hope of normalcy. When I met you, I was at the bottom of a deep pit with no hope of freedom. But you came to my rescue, pulled me from the pit, and set me on a pedestal I never could've attained otherwise.

"You are flawed, as am I, but I accept that. I give you my heart, free of strings, and my love, without obligation for reciprocation. You are what I could never be, and you lift me and my heart to the heavens. We will certainly struggle, but my love for you will remain tempered steel. I am yours, heart, soul, body, and mind, for eternity. You are my king, and I am your queen."

Several in the crowd cheered and whistled.

Unease gripped Pravus. *Would they love her more than him? Shouldn't they? Love her but fear me.*

Credan quieted the crowd with his raised hand. "This union will not only be bound by prophecy and the gods, but also by blood." He cleared his throat. "Wizard Wrik, please come forward for the binding ceremony."

Finally, the second-most important part of the night.

Wrik ascended to the stage in two bounds, gracefully stepping around Aria's train. He removed a long strand of black silk ribbon from his coat pocket and hung it over his shoulder. Credan picked up the black-stemmed rose from the altar and extended it across the altar. Wrik reached out and took the rose.

Wrik smiled at Aria. "Please remove your left glove, Lady Aria." She did so. "Now, hold out your left hand, palm up. You do the same with your right, Lord Rosai." They both complied.

Wrik took the rose and sliced their hands open with its sharp red thorns, right across the meat of their palms. Aria winced, but Pravus stood stoic. From top to bottom, Aria's dress darkened: her veil, neckline, and sleeves transitioned from stark white to a light grey, her bodice from a light grey to a darker charcoal-grey, and the lower part of her dress from a charcoal-grey to a deep black, matching her train.

"Join hands," said Wrik.

Pravus and Aria intertwined their fingers. Her hand stuck to his, and their blood mixed. Wrik took the long ribbon, wound it tight around their hands and wrists, and then tied the ends together in a knot.

Wrik retrieved a cloth pouch from within his coat and walked around to the other side of the altar. Credan moved out of his way. He slowly emptied the contents of the pouch and formed a circle of grey sand on the altar. Then he drew a knot across it, from one side to the other, with more of the sand.

"Place your hands over the circle," said Wrik.

Aria looked at Pravus, and he gave her a smile and a nod. They reached over the altar and placed their bound hands over the circle.

Wrik placed his hands over theirs. "With your blood, and by the powers of the universe, I bind your souls, one to the other. Let it be done!"

The circle ignited with red flames, and the drawn knot rose from the altar. The knot wrapped around their hands, just as the ribbon had, and then it turned into black smoke. The circle fizzled, faded, and disappeared. The ribbon that bound their hands fell away like ash, and their hands separated.

Aria looked at her hand, her eyes wide. "The gash is gone," she whispered.

Pravus smiled. *But never forgotten.*

Aria's dress darkened further.

Wrik moved to the side and Credan took his place behind the altar once again. "Face each other one last time."

They did so.

Credan pushed his spectacles up. "Lord Rosai, take the band fashioned for her and place it on her middle finger."

He took Aria's right arm and pulled her glove off. Wrik handed him a simple gold band.

So that it will never detract from your beauty. Pravus slid it onto her finger. "Beyond death."

"Beyond death," cried the crowd.

Credan looked to Aria. "Mistress Aria, take the band fashioned for him and place it on his middle finger."

Wrik handed her a larger silver band. Her hands trembled as she slid the band in place on Pravus's finger. She said, "For eternity."

"For eternity," shouted the crowd.

"By the gods, I claim you wed!" shouted Credan.

Every inch of Aria's dress turned black as she slid her black gloves back on.

"Seal it with a kiss," said Credan.

Pravus lifted the black veil over Aria's head and peered into her eyes. *My wife.* His heart thundered. He bent down and kissed her deeply, and their tongues intertwined.

The cheering crowd faded into the background, and nothing remained but them, alone on the top of the world. Eternity came and passed as they held each other, neither willing to pull away and break the bond that bound their lips.

Out of breath, they separated. The noise of the cheering crowd rose in Pravus's ears again, and the world zoomed into view. She panted, and he couldn't help but smile.

Credan climbed up on the altar and stood. "I give you Lord and Lady Rosai!"

The likelihood anyone beyond the stage heard him was abysmal at best, but it made no difference.

Now to the most important part of the night: consummating our marriage.

He took Aria, lifted her in his arms, and carried her down the four steps. Before they reached the steps that led up to the top of the caldera, Nardus blocked their path.

Pravus glared at him. "Remove yourself, or I'll remove you."

Nardus rubbed his left bicep and looked at Aria, his eyes red and wet. "I know you don't require it, but you have my blessing, Aria. I wish you a full life." He took her hand and kissed it. She didn't pull away. He smiled wearily and then moved out of their path.

Tomorrow, he dies.

Pravus carried Aria up the steps, through the heart of the cheering crowd. Those nearest bowed as they passed. At the top of the caldera, he turned around and addressed the crowd. "Tonight, you drink and dine in our halls without restraint. Tomorrow, you will witness the beginning of the future—the rise of House Rosai!"

The crowd cheered, and he turned and carried Aria over to the floating carriage. The carriage and the dragon had both transitioned from white to black and nearly blended into their surroundings. Aria climbed from his arms and into the carriage, and then Pravus climbed inside.

He closed the door, and they jetted through the night. They circled the caldera several times and egged the crowd on. Then they headed down the sheer cliff and to the castle below.

Down into the heart of Galondu Castle they flew, through the atrium and the easternmost steel doors, through the corridors, and to the stairs that led to the upper castle and the royal bedchamber. Pravus helped Aria from the carriage, and then the carriage and dragon evaporated.

Aria gasped. He held her and kissed her.

She wrapped her arms around his waist. "I must learn everything you know."

He kissed her forehead. "The power of illusion."

Tomorrow, they'll all be deceived by the truth.

† † †

Pravus lifted her into his strong arms and carried her across the threshold and into the bedchamber. His gaze never left hers, his golden eyes brimming with passion. He kicked the door shut with his heel, carried her over to the couch, and laid her down on it.

"Wait here, my love." He disappeared behind her and the couch.

A fire blazed in the hearth, its heat more than adequate to fill the large room. Hundreds of candles lit the room, set about on nearly every flat surface and inside the ornate wall sconces. The room dwarfed the one she'd been sleeping in, and its beauty surpassed anything she'd ever imagined.

Her chest tightened, and her palms moistened inside her gloves. Her pulse raced. *Is this really happening? Am I really to be the queen of the Ancient Realm? No, all Centauria.*

Aria sat up on the couch, her black dress spread out like a fan. A four-poster bed, grander than any she'd ever seen, nestled the far corner of the room. Dark, royal purple curtains hung from its canopy, drawn closed. Red petals from the roses in the atrium spread across the floor in a trail that ended at the foot of the bed.

Pravus returned with a long-stemmed glass in each hand. A dark-red liquid filled them—she assumed wine. He sat next to her on the couch and handed her one of the glasses.

He held up his glass and so she raised hers. "To our future, and the future of our kingdom."

She nearly giggled, her nerves frayed. *Maybe this wine will calm me.* "To the future."

Their glasses clinked, and she downed the liquid in a single gulp, barely appreciating its sweet, buttery taste. Pravus drained his glass a bit slower, savoring it. He took the glasses and set them on the table in front of them.

He stood and held out his hand.

Is it time already? Did she need to pee? Had she already?

Her mind gummed. The room swam. No, the room not only swam, but spun around her.

Did he put something in my drink? Her stomach ached. She thought she might vomit. *Wouldn't that be attractive? How do you like your new bride, now that you wear the contents of her stomach?*

Her belly burned, and the stone spoke to her. *"Do not lie with him tonight. Use every excuse necessary."*

He's my husband now. I must.

"If you must, lie with him in the—"

The fire in her belly dissipated. "In the what?"

Pravus smiled, his perfect white teeth nearly glowed. "I didn't speak. Are you not feeling well?"

"Yes, I think…" *What do I think?* The room no longer spun, and her stomach settled. "No, I'm okay. Just a bit of nerves."

His eyes sparkled. "I assure you, I'm a bit frazzled as well. We can take our time. The night is still young."

Aria gave him her hand, and he pulled her to her feet. He led her down the trail of petals and to the foot of the bed. Her breath caught again. *Resist him.*

He still held her hand. "May I remove your gloves, my bride?"

She nodded, her voice lost in the moment. He slipped them from her hands and tossed them on the floor, near the couch. He removed his brimmed black hat and tossed it as well. It spun through the air and landed on the couch. Had it been a good shot, or had he used mezhik?

A good shot, I think.

His eyes undressed her and left her vulnerable. "If you'd turn around, I'll unlace your dress."

"No!" Her cheeks burned, and she covered her mouth. His seductive gaze never faltered. "Can we dance for a while first?"

His eyes widened. "Dance? We've no music to dance to."

She took his hands. "My papa used to dance with me, and we never had any music. He'd hold me close, we'd spin around the room, and all my fears and doubts would melt away."

Pravus drew her close and put his arms around her back. She put hers around his waist and leaned into him. His scent aroused her, and she breathed deeper. How long had it been since they'd been so close? Earlier that day, but this was different.

Moments from their journey in the carriage swept through her mind: each touch, each look, and his *mezhik*. She moaned softly and tightened her arms around him.

They rocked together for an eternity, moving little more than a few inches. Every passing moment weakened her resolve to resist. He lifted her off the floor, spun them in circles, and pressed his lips against hers. She opened her mouth, and he kissed her deep.

I cannot deny him. I cannot deny myself.

He set her back down, and she turned around and pulled her hair out of the way. "I think I'm ready now."

His hot breath caressed her neck, and his lips sent chills racing. He continually kissed her neck and earlobe as he unlaced her dress.

She bit her lower lip and suppressed a moan. *Hurry.* She almost reached back to help him.

The dress loosened on Aria's shoulders, and she let it fall to the floor. She stepped out of it, and Pravus tossed it to the side. She turned around and unbuttoned his outer coat and vest. He shrugged out of them and tossed them on the floor. She unlaced his shirt, first the sleeves and then the front.

She ran her hands over his muscular chest and abdominals and kissed his stomach. "Tell me your secret. How do you always smell so good?"

"It's the one thing you'll never know." His hands fumbled at her back. "The damned thing's knotted."

She turned around and waited for him to work the knot free on her corset.

"Rip it off me if you must." Had she ever wanted anything so much?

"No need." The corset fell to the floor, and she kicked it aside.

Pravus bent down and pulled off each boot as she steadied herself with his shoulder. Then he kissed her thighs, her knees, her shins, and the tops of her feet as he rolled her stockings down her legs.

He stood and pulled off his boots and socks. She unlaced his trousers, and they fell to the floor. She nearly jumped with surprise. *He wears no undergarment?*

It'd never crossed her mind that someone would dress in such a way. Urgency forced her mind back to the task at hand. She quickly pulled her own undergarment off, and then they both stopped.

They held each other's gaze. Her heart hammered. Her mind returned to the dungeons and the abuse she'd endured inside their walls. Phantom pains manifested as she recalled the injuries she'd suffered.

She shuddered them away and focused on the day he came for her. *He healed me. He saved me. He loved me.*

"Take me," she said, "but be gentle. I've known nothing but abuse."

He cupped her chin in his hand. "I'll always be gentle with you, my love."

Although he'd never raised a hand against her, the rage he'd shown in Daltura belied his words. *How will he relieve his anger, if not through me?*

Pravus bent down and picked her up, one arm under her back and one under her knees.

She wrapped her arms around his neck and laid her head against his chest. "I love you."

He carried her around the side of the bed and pulled the canopy drapes apart. He laid her on the bed, and she scooted over to the middle. He crawled up next to her and drew her to him. They kissed for several minutes, never taking their eyes from one another.

They rolled, and he wound up on top of her. His weight crushed her, yet she pulled him tighter. He parted her legs with his.

She reached between the two of them and touched her belly. Fear seized her. "Wait."

Pravus rose and sat back on his legs, her thighs in his hands. "What is it, my love?"

Her mind frantically searched for the root of her fear. Had the stone warned her about something? *Yes, but what?*

She closed her eyes for a moment and the stone's words returned to her: *"Do not lie with him."*

But why? No reason came to mind.

She shook the notion away. "It's nothing. I thought I'd forgotten something. Lie back down with me. Consummate our marriage."

He lay on top of her again, and she wrapped her ankles around his legs. He steadied himself on his elbows and kissed her chin, her lips, her nose, and then her forehead.

"Before we continue, I think I'll remove your collar. You'll never have another night like this, and I want you to feel and experience everything the way it should be."

Her eyes widened, and fear swelled in her throat. "Remove my collar? But I've had no training. You said it wouldn't be safe."

He stroked her cheek. "I trust you with my life. Besides, our bond will protect us both. Up to this point, your experience with mezhik has been one-sided. When I go into you, we'll both release some of our mezhik. It's natural, and it's something you'll never forget the first time. The memory of it and its feeling will stay with you forever."

She recalled every intoxicating moment that his mezhik had touched her in the past and the inner struggle she'd battled with her lust. She bit her lower lip and moaned softly. *No more holding back.*

She peered into his eyes. "I trust you, husband. Remove the collar and take me before I go mad with desire."

He took the collar in his hand and pulled. It slid right through her neck like vapor. He tossed it across the room, and it clanged on the floor. She braced herself, but for what she didn't know.

Moments sped by, but nothing changed. Had she expected too much?

Pravus took her hands in his. She arched her back as the intoxicating touch of his mezhik trickled into her hands, up her arms, and swept across her body like an ocean wave across a sandy beach. She moaned softly.

He went into her, and her mind exploded with emotions and feelings. Her hands squeezed his, and her toes curled as she squeezed her legs and pulled him farther into her.

Her body spasmed uncontrollably. Her wrists burned with fire, and light emitted from them.

For the first time, her mezhik flowed, distinctly different from his, yet still intoxicating. She panted, nearly out of breath. *Don't stop. Never stop.* She tried to express her love, but words evaded her.

She kissed him deeply, and the canopy over them burst into flames. She gasped. A warm rain drizzled over them and intensified their passion, moving together ever faster.

Vines snaked up the bedposts, and yellow and red flowers bloomed from them. Sand piled on the bed, slid together, and formed sandcastles, and then the soft rain beat them back down. A mighty wind swept through the room and snuffed out the candles, casting them into darkness.

Still, they moved together, their rhythm never lost.

Don't ever leave me! Lie with me forever.

They rose off the bed and floated in midair. His thoughts crashed into her mind with fervor, pummeling her like waves from the ocean. None lasted long enough for her to grasp their meaning, but their ghosted images trailed behind and slowly faded from existence.

Bolts of lightning shot from her hands and arced around the room. The rent air crashed back together with the sound of rolling thunder, and all the candles burst to life with flame once more.

How much more of this can I take?

They dropped back down on the bed, drenched in sweat and rain. They shuddered together, he collapsed on top of her, and then they fell still and silent, save for their labored breath. Her heart roared in her chest as the intoxicating mezhik dissipated. She shuddered again, an aftershock of pleasure.

Her hands relaxed, and his slid away. She unwrapped her legs from his waist, and he rolled to the side.

Aria asked, "Have you—"

"Never." He reached over and stroked her sweaty hair. "Never, my love."

She needed him again. More than air in her lungs. She rolled on top of him and stroked his sweaty, muscular chest, her fingers entangled in his mass of curly hairs. "Again."

He moved his hands to her waist. His golden eyes sparked with passion. "You'll be the death of me."

She arched her back. Mezhik flowed from her, and the room fell into darkness once more.

He took her again.

† † †

Pravus lay asleep in Aria's arms, his head on her left breast. He breathed heavily, exhausted from their consummation.

Across the room, Aria's silver collar lay on the floor, its shiny surface gleaming in the candlelight. After so long, it'd become a part of her, and she didn't trust what she might do without it.

Should I put it back on? Would I be able to? She ran her fingers through Pravus's hair. *I think it can wait. The morning will come soon enough, and I'll give birth to our future.*

She sank into the bed and took in the previous day's events. The stone's retrieval, the lavish wedding, the earth-shattering consummation. She smiled. *I am Aria Rosai, Queen of Centauria.* She smelled Pravus's hair and wanted him again, but she'd let him sleep.

She drifted in and out of sleep several times, but in the late hour of the night, emotions stirred within her—deep ties of a familiarity she'd nearly forgotten. Tears formed in her eyes and spilled down her cheeks.

She thought of the old man at the café. The seven-pointed star. The single piece of paper. Two words.

Her heart, mind, and soul had but one purpose and one thought: *He lives!*

She finally understood that those two words had never referred to the man named Nardus. No, they spoke of the one dearer to her than any other in the world, and the one reborn.

Alderan.

In her mind, she raced through forests, across wastelands, over grasslands, traversed hills and mountains, forded rivers, and swam oceans to meet him. Joy smothered her with tears.

Can he feel me too?

CHAPTER THIRTY-SIX

A ghostly voice pulled Alderan from his sleep. *"Alderan."*
He sat up in the rocking chair, and his skin prickled. Darkness swaddled him, save the glowing embers in the hearth. He wiped sleep from his eyes and yawned. Had he heard his name, or had it simply been the night? Fully awakened, he rose from the chair.

Squeeeak!

He grabbed the arm of the rocking chair and settled it before the entire house woke. He stood still a few moments and let his eyes adjust. Rayah slept in the rocking chair next to his, undisturbed. Eshtak snored lightly, sprawled on the couch like a mutt. His legs twitched and kicked softly.

Alderan smiled. *A good dream, perhaps?*

Alderan walked over to the large window left of the front door and peered out at the moonlit yard. The silvery light bathed everything it touched: the dead grass, the bushes, the trees. Nothing stirred about but him, his heart, and his mind.

He closed his eyes and recalled the voice he knew he'd heard. *So familiar. Aria?*

His fingers wrapped around the bracelet on his right wrist. His throat tightened and caught his breath. Her presence, so faint but undeniable, touched his mind, and he wept.

How could he resist seeking her out? Did anything else matter? Could the world not find another savior? Or couldn't it at least wait for him to reach her?

She's the real savior. If I find her and bring her back, she can save us all.

What other choice do I have? Everyone knows I'm no savior. I can't even use my mezhik.

He grabbed his hair, pulled it back into a ponytail, and then let it fall back in place. *Does Aria even need my help? Wouldn't I feel it if she did? And how can I leave with Zerenity poisoned? What if she dies because I abandoned her?*

He needed space. He needed air. Alderan gathered his belongings and checked on Rayah once more. She still slept. He crept down the hallway and slipped through the ajar door into Zerenity's room.

The deep darkness blinded him, but he felt his way around to the closet door without incident. He paused for a moment. Zerenity snored softly, and the window rattled against its frame as the wind gusted.

Alderan turned the doorknob and pulled the door open. The metal hinges moaned softly as the door arced open. He squeezed through the small opening and closed the door behind him. His hands guided him through the closet, probing the darkness like two antennas. Layers of clothes hung from wooden bars that stretched across the closet, and he pushed his way through them.

A few steps beyond the last row of clothes, his fingertips met the slick, cold, wet surface of the mirror and plunged into its rippled surface. He hadn't determined a destination, and the pitch-black world through the mirror didn't entice him as a pleasant one. On the other side of the mirror, cold air chilled his fingertips.

He retracted his hand, but something grabbed it and pulled him through the mirror. A cry rose in his throat, but another hand clamped over his mouth and nose before the sound breached his lips. Fear swelled in his mind, and the hairs stood on his nape.

He fought to free himself, but their strength tripled his. The darkness and the hand covering his mouth and nose suffocated him. He gasped for air but succumbed to its elusiveness, his last thoughts as fleeting as wisps of air in spring.

Aria…

CHAPTER THIRTY-SEVEN

Pravus lay in bed and stared up at the tattered canopy. Aria rested in the crook of his arm, her head against his chest. Her warm breath caressed his bare skin. Throughout the night they'd made love several more times, but none were like the first time. *None will ever be.*

He reached out with his free hand and the silver collar he'd tossed on the floor last night shot into the air and into his open palm. The collar slid right through and onto Aria's neck without resistance.

Aria stirred, yawned, and then her eyelids fluttered, and her eyes opened. She kissed his chest and then propped herself up on her elbow.

She wore a smile that could've seduced a eunuch. "Good morning, husband." She nibbled on her lower lip.

Pravus leaned over and kissed her forehead. "Thank the gods you're awake. The ceremony will be upon us in a few hours, and we haven't discussed the part you will play in it."

Aria sat up, and the sheets fell away from her, exposing her nakedness. She turned in the bed and faced Pravus. She walked her fingers down the length of his chest and underneath the covers that covered his groin.

Pravus reared up and snatched Aria's hand from his groin. "As much as I'd like to lie in bed with you forever, we don't have time. If the ceremony doesn't go according to plan, all will be lost. Would you choose to make love to me again and risk living in poverty, or would you rather discuss what you are to do so that we can rule Centauria?"

Aria huffed, "A single night, and you've tired of me already." She reached for him with her other hand. "Can we not do both? I'm certain *I* can handle it."

He pushed her arms away and then slid off the side of the bed. The cold, wet floor froze his feet and shook his shoulders.

He looked back at her. "You certainly made a mess of this place last night."

She fingered the collar around her neck. "I'm not the one who took this collar off am I?"

"That is true, but how would I have guessed what you were capable of?" He shook his head and then headed toward a set of wooden doors to the far right of the fireplace.

Through the doors, a row of robes and dresses hung from wooden rods on either side of the closet. The rods went back a good ten feet before ending at the back of the closet. Pravus retrieved a set of black robes for himself and a pair of white trousers and a white, button-up shirt for Aria. He returned to the bed with them.

He placed the trousers and shirt on the bed. "Put these on."

She wrinkled her nose. "The entire community is here to see our kingdom reborn and you want me to wear those?"

"Yes. Those and nothing more. No stockings or undergarments. No jewelry. The blood will use you as a conduit, so you cannot wear anything that will restrict its movement."

She sighed. "Fine. I will dress like a barbarian if it pleases you. Along with this stylish collar."

"Good." Pravus put on his robes and smoothed them out. "You may style your hair if you wish."

Aria slid off the bed and landed on the floor with a soft *thud*. "And wreck my ensemble? I think not. I will wear it down."

"The ceremony itself will not take long. You will stand in the center circle and I will cut your palms with a ceremonial dagger that has been blessed by the gods. Once done, I will step outside of the inner pentagonal area. You will take the stone, raise it above your head, and say, '*Bí ballʊd mí.*' Once you've said that, everything will begin, and you won't need to do anything else but stand there. Do you understand?"

Aria nodded as she pulled her trousers up and tied them. "*Bí ballʊd mí.*"

Pravus steepled his fingers. "Perfect."

Today, I will no longer be subject to anyone's rule but my own.

† † †

Lightning flashed across the morning sky, and thunder quaked like drums of the gods. Dark clouds overhead churned, and a steady rainfall pattered the ground. Water collected in the sunken areas of the charcoal-grey gravel paths and created miniature lakes that reflected the heavens above.

Pravus stood in the center of the atrium, the heart of Galondu Castle. Wizard Wrik stood just behind him, and Aria stood to his left. He turned and faced Aria and took her hands in his. *So delicate, and so unlike her spirit.* The wind whipped her blonde hair and his black robes, but nothing would ruin this momentous day.

From the moment he'd learned of his namesake from his worthless mother, he'd embarked on a journey to resurrect his father's fallen kingdom. On several occasions, he'd thought the task unobtainable, yet he persevered through those dark times and rose above his self-doubt.

The culmination of four decades of planning has finally arrived. Today, I become a god. Unstoppable.

He released Aria's hands and turned toward the large gathering of people. They nearly filled the massive atrium to capacity, surrounding all five sides of the inner pentagonal area in which he stood.

Thousands have come. I will not fail. His heart pumped so hard that his chest tremored beneath his robes. Many of the faces he recognized; others he knew only by their coat of arms. *Constituents. Sympathizers. Sheep.*

He cleared his throat and addressed the crowd. "Today, I've asked you all here to help celebrate this momentous occasion. Today, I stand here with my new bride and your future queen, but this isn't what or why we celebrate. Today, my father's kingdom will rise from the ashes, reborn."

The crowd cheered and whistled. He waited for them to settle.

He continued, "Today, the world will know House Rosai as no longer a formality but a force to be reckoned. Today, the armies of the fallen will be reborn. And today, we call upon the fealty of House Rosai." He pointed at several in the crowd. "*Your* fealty. Stand with us!"

Fists rose high, and the crowd chanted, "Rosai! Rosai! Rosai!"

Pride swelled in Pravus's chest, and he stood tall.

My kingdom will surpass yours, father. Even greater than that of Magus's. I cannot fail.

After several moments, he held up a hand and waited for silence. "Today marks the beginning of the last days of the Three Kingdoms. Their end is at-hand, my friends. By the time we've finished with them, no two stones will be left atop one another. King Zaridus had better gather his armies, because we march against his kingdom soon. Mark my words: no quarter will be given to anyone who stands against us. Everyone will be put to the sword.

"Furthermore, our campaign will not stop at the borders of our continent. We will cross oceans. We not only come for the Ancient Realm; we come for the world. Atrum Moenia and Galondu Castle will once again rise as the center and populous of Centauria. The world will fear us and bend to our rule. We will be reborn!"

The crowd chanted "Rosai" once again.

He turned back to Aria and gazed into her green eyes. For a few moments, the noise of the chanting crowd faded away, and nothing existed in the world but the two of them. *She holds the stone. She holds my heart. She holds our future.*

He searched her eyes. *How is it I can never read her?* "Still with me?"

"I am ready." Aria's voice trembled.

Pravus raised his fist as he turned back to the crowd, and the crowd settled. "The time is at-hand! Stand back and witness the power of House Rosai." He glanced back at Wrik and nodded.

Wrik put his hands around his mouth to amplify his voice. "Bring out the wizards!"

The fifty-foot-tall doors on the northeastern wall of the atrium moaned as several soldiers drove them inward. The crowd turned and watched as a young woman emerged from the shadows of the castle.

Barefoot and clothed in skin-tight, white leather from her neck to her ankles, she marched along the charcoal-grey gravel path. A tight black braid draped each side of her head, and they bobbed with her gait. A silver collar wrapped her neck.

The crowd drew back as she passed through them. She reached the angled corner of the inner pentagonal area, stepped around the massive dragon post, and bowed to Pravus. She stepped forward and into the center of a six-foot circle of white sand. Translucent red stones bordered the circle and glistened in the rain.

From the southeastern, southwestern, northwestern, and northern doors came four more women, each dressed identical to the first. Each walked along their path, stopped just beyond the dragon post at the angled corner at the end of their paths, bowed to Pravus, and then stepped into the center of a circle of white sand, identical to the first woman's circle.

The five women faced the center of the atrium. Pravus, Aria, and Wrik stood inside another six-foot circle of white sand at the center of the other circles. Translucent green stones outlined their circle.

Pravus looked back at Wrik. "Where did you find the fifth woman?"

Wrik smiled wryly. "Yora survived, my lord."

Pravus's eyes widened. *Survived?* Her broken body, strewn on the floor like discarded waste, flitted through his mind. He couldn't fathom how she'd survived.

Probably better I don't know.

He nodded to Wrik. "My cane."

Wrik handed Pravus the dragon's-head cane and stepped out of the center circle.

Pravus centered Aria inside the center circle, stepped out of it, and drew a five-pointed star in the sand around Aria with his cane. The star's points pointed toward each of the five outer circles. In the circle to the northeast, he drew an 'a' shape with two tails in the sand around the woman: α. In the circle to the southeast, he drew a squiggly 's' shape with curls at the top: ξ.

In the circle to the southwest, he drew an 'i' with a tail: ι. In the circle to the northwest, he drew an 'o': o. Last, in the circle to the north, he drew a 'u' shape with two tails: μ.

Pravus moved around the center circle and eyed each of the runes he'd drawn in the sand. *Excellent.*

Wizard Wrik walked around the inner pentagonal area and removed the silver collars from the five women. He pulled a gold-handled dagger from the sheath on his belt and handed it to Pravus. Its curved edge—shaped like a dragon's claw—glistened as droplets of rain rolled from it.

The ceremonial dagger. Watch as I become a god, father.

Wrik bowed, backed out of the inner pentagonal area, and stood next to

Credan.

The crowd looked on with bated breath. If not for the occasional rumble of thunder and the incessant wind, no noise would've been audible.

Pravus breathed deep. *The time is at hand. A kingdom reborn.*

He looked at Aria again. "Do you remember the instructions we discussed?"

Even though she trembled, Aria's gaze never broke from his. "I do."

Aria unbuttoned her white shirt and let it hang open, the sides of her breasts exposed. She touched her stomach and exhaled. "I am ready."

Good girl. He pressed his lips to hers. Heat emanated from her like fever, her cheeks flushed. *For us. For our kingdom.*

Aria reached out with both hands, palms up. He took her wrists in his left hand and held her arms steady. "For the kingdom!" The crowd repeated him and cheered.

Pravus lifted his eyes to the heavens. *"Kämend Í zíū ríz ṭūō, fidh bəllʊd hōír!"*

He ran the blade across her palms; it dug deep. Aria flinched but didn't cry out. She closed her hands, and he released her wrists. He stepped back and joined Wrik and Credan outside of the inner pentagonal area.

"Bí bəllʊd mí!" Aria leaned back, held her hands over her abdomen, and squeezed them tight. Blood dripped from her hands and sizzled against her skin. Little puffs of smoke rose from her abdomen with each drop.

Why is she spreading blood on her abdomen? And where is the stone?

She squeezed harder and then opened her hands. Blood poured from the wounds and seeped into her flesh. Her belly glowed red-hot, like coals of a fire, and then it expanded.

Her arms slumped to her sides, and she bent backward, unnaturally. The back of her head rested against the back of her legs, and her shirt slid from her shoulders, exposing her breasts.

What the gods is happening?

The crowd gasped, and a few whistled. Pravus sneered and glared daggers at those he saw, silencing them. *In the end, you'll all be dead.*

The translucent green rocks surrounding Aria's circle brightened and shot a continuous ring of green light skyward. The five female wizards straightened their arms, palms out behind them and fingers spread. Their heads snapped back, and their white eyes gazed upon the heavens.

The translucent red rocks that surrounded the outer five circles sparked like kindling, ignited with a roar, and shot continuous rings of fire skyward. The five females levitated several feet, their toes pointed downward.

Blood, dark red and rich, ran from their feet and filled the five runes drawn in the white sand. The females screeched like wraiths as their bodies turned to greyish ash, beginning with the tops of their heads and then all the way down to their toes, clothes and all, until nothing remained.

Blood from the five runes seeped into the sand, and then the center rune—the five-pointed star surrounding Aria—filled with blood. The blood rose above the top of the sand but didn't spill over. Instead, it slithered up Aria's legs and to her expanded belly and flowed into her navel. Every drop expanded her swollen belly.

Aria's lips moved continually, but Pravus couldn't make out what she said. *She shouldn't be saying anything. That's not part of the plan.* His fists balled, his eyebrows sank, and his vision narrowed. *What's she doing?*

Pravus moved to intervene, but Wrik grabbed his shoulder and held him in place. Pravus jerked his shoulder away from Wrik and glared at him.

Wrik whispered, "You cannot stop what's begun. It'll kill you both."

Pravus snarled and turned his attention back to Aria. *How could she betray me?*

The blackish-red stone pushed up through Aria's belly—right through her skin—and she screamed. The stone grew as it continued to absorb the blood, and her belly flattened.

Every drop of blood consumed, she lifted the enormous stone from her belly. It flew out of her hands and into the air.

Pravus watched it rise but lost sight of it in the green light. His heart thundered. *What has she done? Where has the stone gone?*

Lightning chains ripped the air around the outer edge of the pentagonal area and sent a concussive force outward. The force threw everyone outside the area to the ground, including Pravus. The five outer rings of fire gave way to smoke and then blew away in the wind, carrying the ashen remains of the five female wizards with it. The inner ring of green light faded.

Pravus growled and punched the ground. *This is not supposed to be how it works!*

Pravus gathered himself and rose to his feet. He stared at Aria, lost for words. Her body unfolded as she rose back up, and she faced him. Red ringed the fringes of her green eyes, and dark-red strands streaked her blonde hair.

Aria moved her arms to her sides, wrists bent and palms face-down, lifted her head, and roared like a dragon. Her bare chest heaved as she took several deep breaths, and then she dropped to her knees.

Pravus looked around. *I don't understand. Where's my army of the dead? My kingdom?*

The crowd slowly gathered themselves, most still on the ground.

Pravus moved toward Aria. "What the gods have you done?"

She didn't respond, but his answer stared him in the face. Across the atrium, one man stood, jeering eyes and a smug grin on his face.

Nardus.

Anger raged in Pravus. "You!"

Pravus reached out, balled his fist, and then yanked his arm backward. Nardus flew across the atrium, dove face-first into the gravel, and skidded to a stop at Pravus's feet. "Whatever you've brought back with you isn't *Ɛʈōn Dhef Dädh.*"

Nardus rose to his hands and knees and spat blood on the ground. "Damned mezhik." He looked up at Pravus. "It's the only stone in *Ṭämbəll Dhef Däd Dhä.* Don't blame me if you've misunderstood what it does." He spat more blood and leaned back on his feet. "What did you think was supposed to happen?"

Pravus grabbed Nardus by his silver collar and shook him. "The dead should've risen. Do you see any of them? No!" He still held the gold-handled dagger in his other hand. He turned it in his hand. "How did I ever trust you to do the right thing? The madman."

Aria stood and roared at the sky again. High above them, a roar answered Aria's, deeper and fiercer. Its hateful sound shook the air. Pravus jerked his head up and scanned the dark sky. Black, leathery wings beat the air, and a flaming pillar lit the dark clouds.

A dragon?

Pravus pulled his thoughts together and formulated a new plan. He addressed the scattering crowd, "Just as you run, so will our enemies, and we will run them through. Today, we have a dragon to do our bidding! House Rosai has brought dragons back from extinction. They, and our kingdom, are reborn! Because of this, our armies will grow by word of mouth alone. We will not be stopped! The Three Kingdoms will fall!"

The last of the crowd fled inside the castle and pushed the doors shut. Pravus cracked his knuckles. *That's right. Tell everyone of the power of Lord Rosai.*

The ground quaked as a black dragon landed before Pravus. One of the dragon's red eyes focused on Pravus, and it clicked its black claws together.

"He's mine to kill, not yours," said the dragon.

Pravus dropped the dagger he held and backed away from Nardus and the dragon. He looked down at the silver collar still in his hand and then back at Nardus. *Did I just remove this?*

Nardus rose to his feet and turned to Aria. "Shanara, don't let them do this! I'm your father. I beg you, spare my life."

Pravus eyed Aria as well. *Kill him, my love.*

Her hostile eyes flashed red. "Spare your life?" She laughed. "You abandoned me and my brother. We may be of your seed, but you're no father of ours. Our father's dead, and you deserve no better." She peered up at the dragon. "He's all yours, my love. Do what you must."

Your love? Pravus staggered backward, stunned. *I'm your love!*

The dragon raised his clawed hand and swiped at Nardus, but Nardus disappeared. The dragon roared, stomped the ground, and spewed a column of fire in the air. He turned a wicked red eye on Pravus, snatched Pravus in his claws, and lifted him off the ground. "What've you done with him?"

"Me? This isn't my doing!" Pravus struggled against the dragon's grip and looked down at Aria. "Tell him!"

The dragon squeezed Pravus and cracked several of his ribs. Pravus cried out, but then he couldn't take another breath.

"Stop." Aria bent down, picked up her shirt, and slid her arms into its sleeves. "We're bonded, Cinolth. Both he and I, and you and me. Our fates are forever intertwined. Release him before you kill us all." Aria crossed her arms and smiled smugly.

Cinolth? Understanding ripped through Pravus in concussive waves. He looked at the dragon closer. *Could it really be him?*

Cinolth released Pravus, and Pravus fell back to the ground.

Cinolth twisted his head and glared at Aria. Smoke rose from his nostrils, and his breath smelled of sulfur. "You foolish girl! Did I not warn you of this? You've spread your legs and bound us with this vermin."

Fire burned in Aria's eyes as she buttoned her shirt. "Do not speak to me like that, *dragon*. I'll spread my legs for whomever I choose. You think I'm immature and unwise, but I assure you that I know exactly the power I hold over you. My blood, and that of the others, brought you back from death, and it *demands* your obedience, so hold your tongue, or I will have it cut out."

Cinolth's head snaked down to Pravus's level and his voice filled Pravus's mind. *"You only live because of her. Remember that."*

Pravus shook with rage. *And you only live because of me!*

Pravus glanced between Aria and Cinolth. *How did this happen?*

Cinolth eyed Pravus and snarled, "You're pathetic. Too naive to understand the truth of the prophecy of *2ţōn Dhef Dädh*."

He calls me naive? Anger pulled Pravus to his feet. "And what of its prophecy do I not comprehend?"

Cinolth stomped the ground. "In your tongue, you call it the stone of death, but it's so much more than that. An older translation is *the dark heart*." He snaked his head closer. "*My* heart. Did you think Cyrus had the power to destroy me, Cinolth The Dark? Dragons cannot be killed easily, least of all me. Why do you think they placed my heart where they did?"

Pravus shifted his weight, and his cracked ribs throbbed. He winced. "Then why did they bother to write the prophecy at all? Why not destroy the knowledge?"

Smoke billowed from Cinolth's flared nostrils. "True prophets cannot unsee or ignore their visions. They're bound by mezhik law to write them, but they have the latitude to make them cryptic."

"And now you'll help us bring the world to its knees." Pravus steepled his fingers. "I will be the next *Rídär Drezhn*."

Aria stepped forward and wrapped her arms around Cinolth's neck. "No, husband, that privilege will never be yours."

Cinolth lifted Aria onto his back. She held onto one of the many long spikes that ran the length of his neck, spine, and tail. Cinolth spread his wings and took to the sky with a *whoosh-whoosh whoosh whoosh-whoosh*.

Wrik came forward and stood next to Pravus. "Be glad you're bound to her."

"This is your doing, Wrik. I should've killed you when you intervened."

Wrik laughed, then his gaze steeled. "I warned you what the prophecies said. Her father might've escaped, but at least her brother's dead. This may not be the rebirth you envisioned, but the end will still work in your favor."

Pravus nodded. Nothing would stand in their way.

A silver collar fell from the dark sky and landed at Pravus's feet. He picked it up and held it with the other. He turned them in his hands and looked skyward.

What the gods have I unleashed? And where have you gone, Cyrus?

CHAPTER THIRTY-EIGHT

Chaos cradled the Great Library in its destructive arms. Piles of books lay on the floor, pages torn, shredded, and ripped from their spines. Shelves toppled, one against another, their contents broken and spread across the marble floor. Chairs smashed to bits and tables broken in two lay in piles of ruin. Shards of crystal from the massive chandeliers lay strewn across the room.

Nardus stood in the middle of it all, lost for words.

How could this have happened?

"Gnaud?" His voice echoed through the room, but the little gordak didn't respond. Panic settled in his bones.

A deep groan, nearly a howl, came from his left. He stepped back and turned in its direction. Two yellow eyes watched him from the shadows.

He reached back to grab the hilt of Brinzhär Dädh, but only swiped air. *Damn!*

He knelt, grabbed a splintered chair leg, and held it between him and whatever lurked in the shadows. Those yellow eyes locked onto his. Time faded, each heartbeat decades between. Suffering and pain flowed from those familiar eyes, and his heart filled with compassion.

Nardus dropped the chair leg and knelt on one knee.

The beast emerged from the shadows. Saliva wet her fangs.

He'd never seen a creature quite like her.

Her mournful cry skittered chills down his neck and arms. Her thick beige fur glistened in the dim light as she crouched low, ready to attack.

Underneath the scruff of her neck and nearly covered with fur, Nardus swore a band of silver shone.

TO BE CONTINUED ...

The story continues in *Rended Souls*, Book #3 of *The Dark Heart Chronicles*. Visit **danielkuhnley.com** for more information.

PLEASE TELL OTHERS WHAT YOU THOUGHT

Thank you for taking this journey with me. If you'd like to show your support for my work, please leave a review wherever you purchased this book. It's free to do so, and it'll only take you a minute to write a quick sentence expressing your thoughts about the book.

Your review is especially important to independent, self-published authors like me. Internet and online bookstore algorithms favor books with reviews. They display in search results and at the top of search results more often than books without reviews.

Did you know that there's a minimum number of reviews needed to purchase certain advertising? It's true. Help me reach that threshold by leaving a review. Doing so will help more people find this book and will in turn help me sell more books, which means I can keep authoring more books for you.

Go to danielkuhnley.com/reviews if you need a link to where you can leave a review.

Thank you!

READ *SCOURGE* FOR FREE

Do Eshtak's tattoos hold the key to the between?

danielkuhnley.com/become-a-conqueror

Sign up and read *Scourge*, A World Of Centauria Novella. Be the **FIRST** to get sneak peeks at my upcoming novels and the chance to win **FREE** stuff, like signed books.

Never use persuasion magic on a powerful wizard.

That was Emorith's hardest lesson to learn. Right from that fateful moment, Magus forced her to use her manipulative sorcery to further his evil purposes. She regretted everything he put her through with one exception: their son Illian. Him, she loved with all her heart.

Magus demanded she cast an apocalyptic curse and destroy an unsuspecting city. She steeled herself to refuse him… but then he threatened the life of her beloved child.

With Illian's life on the line, what choice did she have? She wanted to protect the city and its citizens, but her son would always come first. No, there must be another way. Will she be able to thwart Magus and save them all in time? Or is their fate already sealed?

Scourge is a prequel novella to *The Dragon's Stone*, the first book in *The Dark Heart Chronicles* epic dragon fantasy series. If you like thrilling adventures and terrifying magic, then you'll love Daniel Kuhnley's enthralling tale.

ABOUT THE AUTHOR

Daniel Kuhnley is an American author of Epic Dragon Fantasy, Supernatural Serial Killer, and Christian YA Sci-Fi/Fantasy stories. Some of his novels include *Reborn*, *The Braille Killer*, and *Kiara Kole And The Key Of Truth*. He enjoys watching movies, reading novels, and programming. He lives in Albuquerque, NM with his wife who also writes.

CONNECT WITH DANIEL

danielkuhnley.com/connect